W9-ANG-887

HEECHEE
RENDEZVOUS

HEECHEE
RENDEZVOUS

a novel by
Frederik Pohl

A Del Rey Book

BALLANTINE BOOKS · NEW YORK

A Del Rey Book
Published by Ballantine Books

Copyright © 1984 by Frederik Pohl

Manufactured in the United States of America

For Betty Anne Hull
with all the love I have

CONTENTS

HEECHEE
RENDEZVOUS

Prologue: A Chat with My Subset

I am no Hamlet. I'm an attendant lord, though, or at least I would be if I were human. I'm not. I'm a computer program. That is an honorable estate and I am not at all ashamed of it, especially since (as you can see) I am a very sophisticated program, not only fit to swell a progression or start a scene or two but to quote from obscure twentieth-century poets as I tell you about it.

It is to start the scene that I am speaking now. Albert's my name, and introductions are my game. I start by introducing myself.

I'm a friend of Robinette Broadhead's. Well, that's not precisely right; I'm not sure I can claim to be a friend *of* Robin's, though I try hard to be a friend *to* him. It is the purpose for which I (this particular "I") was created. Basically I am a simple computer information-retrieval con-

struct who (or that) has been programed with many of the late Albert
Einstein's traits. That's why Robin calls me Albert. There's another area
of ambiguity. Whether it is indeed Robinette Broadhead who is the object
of my friendship has lately become arguable, too, since it rests on the
question of who (or what) Robinette Broadhead now is—but that's a long
and hard problem that we'll have to take up a little bit at a time.

I know this is all confusing, and I can't help feeling that I'm not doing
my job very well, since my job (as I construe it) is to set the scene for
what Robin himself has to say. It's possible I don't have to do this at all,
since you may already know what I have to say. If so, I don't mind
repeating it. We machines are patient. But you might prefer just to skip
over and go on to Robin himself—as Robin himself, no doubt, would
much prefer.

Let's do it in the form of questions and answers. I will construct a
subset within my program to interview me:

Q.—Who is Robinette Broadhead?

A.—Robin Broadhead is a human being who went to the Gateway
asteroid and, by enduring great risks and trauma, won for himself the
beginnings of an immense fortune and an even greater load of guilt.

Q.—Don't throw in those teasers, Albert, just stick to the facts. What
is the Gateway asteroid?

A.—It is an artifact left by the Heechee. They abandoned, half a million years or so ago, a sort of orbital parking garage full of working
spaceships. They would take you all over the Galaxy, but you couldn't
control where you were going. (For further details see sidebar; I put this
in to show you what a truly sophisticated data-retrieval program I really
am.)

Q.—Watch that, Albert! Just the facts, please. Who are these Heechee?

A.—Look, let's get something straight! If "you" are going to ask "me"
questions—even if "you" are only a subset of the same program as "me"
—you have to let me answer them in the best way possible. "Facts" are
not enough. "Facts" are what very primitive data-retrieval systems produce. I'm too good to waste on that; I have to give you the background
and the surround. For instance, to tell you who the Heechee are the best
way, I must tell you the story of how they first appeared on Earth. It goes
like this:

The time was about half a million years ago, in the late Pleistocene.
The first living terrestrial creature who became aware of their existence
was a female saber-toothed tiger. She gave birth to a pair of cubs, licked
them over, growled to drive her inquisitive mate away, went to sleep,
woke up and found that one was missing. Carnivores don't—

This is one of the easier kinds of information for me to retrieve:

". . . The conflict over the island of Dominica, terrible though it was, was over in seven weeks with both Haiti and the Dominican Republic anxious for peace and a chance to rebuild their shattered economies. The next crisis to confront the Secretariat was one of great hope for everyone in the world, but at the same time fraught with far more risk to the world's peace. I refer, of course, to the discovery of the so-called Heechee Asteroid. Although it was known that long ago, technologically advanced aliens had visited the solar system and left some valuable artifacts, the chance finding of this body with its scores of functioning spaceships was wholly unexpected. Their value was incalculable, of course, and nearly every spacefaring member state of the UN registered some claim to them. I will not speak of the delicate and confidential negotiations that brought about the five-power Gateway Corporation trusteeship, but with its formation, a new era opened for humankind."

—*Memoirs*, Marie-Clémentine Benhabbouche,
Secrétaire-générale des Nations-Unis.

Q.—Albert, please! This is Robinette's story, not yours, so get on to where he starts talking.

A.—I told you once and I told you twice. If you interrupt again I'll simply turn you off, subset! We're doing this my way, and my way is like this:

Carnivores don't count well, but she was smart enough to know the difference between one and two. Unfortunately for her cub, carnivores have hair-trigger tempers, too. The loss of one cub enraged her, and in her paroxysm of fury she destroyed the other. It is instructive to observe that that was the only fatality among large mammals to result from the first visit of the Heechee to Earth.

A decade later the Heechee came back. They replaced some of the samples they had taken, including a male tiger now elderly and plump, and took a new batch. These were not four-legged. The Heechee had learned to distinguish between one predator and another, and the species they selected this time was a group of shambling, slant-browed, four-foot-high creatures with furry faces and no chins. Their very remote collateral descendants, namely you humans, would call them *Australopithecus afarensis*. These the Heechee did not return. From their point of view, these creatures were the terrestrial species most likely to evolve toward intelligence. The Heechee had a use for this sort of animal, and so they began subjecting them to a program designed to force their evolution toward that goal.

Of course, the Heechee did not limit themselves to the planet Earth in their explorations, but none of the rest of the solar system had the sort of treasure that interested them. They looked. They explored Mars and Mercury, skimmed the cloud cover of the gas giants beyond the asteroid ring, observed that Pluto was there but never troubled to visit it, tunneled out an eccentric asteroid to make a sort of hangar for their spacecraft, and honeycombed the planet Venus with well-insulated tunnels. They did not concentrate on Venus because they preferred its climate to that of Earth. Actually they detested the surface of Venus as much as humans do; that was why all their construction was underground. But they built there because there was nothing alive on Venus to be harmed, and the Heechee never, never harmed any evolved living things—except when necessary.

The Heechee did not limit themselves to the Earth's solar system, either. Their vessels spanned the Galaxy and went beyond it. Of all the Galaxy's two hundred billion astronomical objects larger than a planet, they charted every one; and many of the smaller ones, too. Not every object was visited by a Heechee ship. But not one failed of at least a drone flyby and an instrumented search for signatures, and some became what can only be called tourist attractions.

And some—a bare handful—contained that peculiar treasure the Heechee sought called life.

Life was rare in the Galaxy. Intelligent life, however inclusively the Heechee defined it, was even rarer . . . but not absent. There were Earth's australopithecines, already tool users, beginning to develop social institutions. There was a promising winged race in what human beings would call the constellation Ophiuchus; a soft-bodied one on a dense, huge planet that circled an F-9 star in Eridanus; four or five miscellaneous sorts of beings that orbited stars on the far side of the Galaxy's core, hidden by gas clouds, dust, and dense starry clusters from any human observation. All together there were fifteen species of beings, from fifteen different planets thousands of light-years away from each other, that might be expected to develop enough intelligence to write books and build machines fairly soon. (The Heechee defined "fairly soon" as any time within a million years or so.)

And there was more. There were three actual existing technological societies, besides the Heechees' own, and the artifacts of two others now extinct.

So the australopithecines were not unique. They were still very precious. Therefore the Heechee who was charged with ferrying a colony of them from the dry-bones plains of their native home to the new habitat the Heechee had provided for them in space was accorded much honor for his work.

It was hard work, and prolonged. That particular Heechee was the descendant of three generations who had explored, mapped, and organized the solar system project. He expected that his own descendants would continue the work. In that he was wrong.

All in all, the tenancy of the Heechee in Earth's solar system lasted just over one hundred years; and then it ended, in less than a month.

A decision was made to withdraw—hurriedly.

All through the rabbit warrens of Venus, all over the small outpost installations on Dione and Mars' South Polar Cap, in every orbiting artifact, the packing-up began. Hurried but thorough. The Heechee were the neatest of housekeepers. They removed more than ninety-nine percent of the tools, machines, artifacts, knickknacks, and trinkets that had supported their life in Earth's solar system, even the trash. Especially the trash. Nothing was left by accident. And nothing at all, not even the Heechee equivalent of an empty Coke bottle or a used Kleenex, was left on the surface of the Earth. They did not make it impossible for the collateral descendants of their australopithecines to learn that the Heechee had visited their area. They only made sure that they would first have to learn to go into space to do so. Much of what the Heechee removed was useless and was jettisoned in far interstellar space or into the Sun. Much was shipped to places very far away, for special purposes. And all this was done not just in Earth's solar system, but everywhere. The Heechee vacuumed the Galaxy of almost every trace. No newly bereft Pennsylvania Dutch widow, preparing to turn the farmhouse over to the family of the eldest son, ever left premises more neat.

They left almost nothing, and nothing at all without a purpose. On Venus they left only the basic tunnels and foundation structures themselves, and a carefully selected bare taste of artifacts; in the outposts, only a minimum number of signposts; and one other thing.

In every solar system where intelligence was expected they left one great and cryptic gift. In Earth's system it was in the right-angle asteroid that they had used for a terminus for their spacecraft. Here and there, in remote and carefully chosen places in other systems, they left other major installations. Each contained the very large gift of an operating selection of whole, functional, almost indestructible Heechee faster-than-light spacecraft.

The solar troves stayed there for a very long time, four hundred thousand years and more, while the Heechee hid in their core hole. The australopithecines on Earth turned out an evolutionary failure, though the Heechee did not find that out; but the cousins of the australopithecines became Neanderthalers, or Cro-Magnards, then that latest evolutionary fad, Modern Man. Meanwhile the winged creatures developed and learned and discovered the Promethean challenge, and killed themselves. Meanwhile two of the existing technological societies met each other and destroyed each other. Meanwhile six of the other promising species idled in evolutionary backwaters; meanwhile the Heechee hid, and peeped fearfully through their Schwarzschild shell every few weeks of their time—every few millennia of the time speeding outside—

And meanwhile the troves waited, and human beings found them at last.

So human beings borrowed the Heechee ships. In them they crisscrossed the Galaxy. Those first explorers were scared, desperate people whose only hope of escaping grimy human misery was to risk their lives on a blind-date voyage to a destiny that might make them rich and was a whole lot more likely to make them dead.

I have now surveyed the entire history of the Heechee in their relationship with the human race up to the time when Robin will start telling his story. Are there any questions, subset?

Q.—Z-z-z-z-z-z.

A.—Subset, don't be a smartass. I know you're not asleep.

Q.—I am only trying to convey that you are taking a hell of a long time to get offstage, scene-starter. And you've only told us about the past of the Heechee. You haven't told us about their present.

A.—I was just about to. In fact, I will now tell you about a particular Heechee whose name is Captain (well, that is not his name, for Heechee naming customs are not the same as human, but it will do to identify him) who, at just about the time when Robin will begin to tell you his story—

Q.—If you ever let him get to it.

A.—Subset! Quiet. This Captain is rather important to Robin's story, because in time they will interact drastically, but as we see Captain now, he is wholly unaware that Robin exists. He, along with the members of his crew, is getting ready to squeeze out of the place where the Heechee had hidden into the wider Galaxy that is home for all the rest of us.

Now, I have played a little trick on you. You have already—shut up, subset!—you have already met Captain, since he was one of the very crew of Heechee who abducted the tiger cub and built the warrens on Venus. He is much older now.

He is not, however, half a million years older, because the place where the Heechee went to hide is in a black hole at the core of our Galaxy.

Now, subset, I don't want you to interrupt again, but I do want to take time to mention something strange. This black hole where the Heechee lived, curiously, was known to the human race long before they ever heard of the Heechee. In fact, way back in the year 1932, it was the first interstellar radio source ever detected. By the end of the twentieth century interferometry had mapped it as a definite black hole and a very large one, with a mass of thousands of suns and a diameter of some thirty light-years. By then they knew that it was about thirty thousand light-years from Earth, in the direction of the constellation Sagittarius, that it was surrounded by a haze of silicate dust, and that it was an intense source of 511-keV gamma-ray photons. By the time they found the Gateway asteroid they knew much more. They knew, in fact, every important datum about it except one. They had no idea that it was full of Heechee. They didn't find that out until they—actually, I can fairly say that it was mostly I—began to decipher the old Heechee star charts.

Q.—Z-z-z————

A.—Quiet, subset, I take your point.

The ship Captain was in was a lot like the ones human beings found in the Gateway asteroid. There had not been time for a lot of improvement in ship design. That's why Captain was not really half a million years old: Time went slowly in their black hole. The major difference between Captain's ship and any other was that it possessed an accessory.

In Heechee speech the accessory was known familiarly as the disruptor of order in aligned systems. An English-speaking pilot might have called it a can opener. It was what permitted them to pass through the Schwarzschild barrier around a black hole. It didn't look like much, only a twisted rod of crystal emerging from an ebon-black base, but when Captain energized it, it glowed like a cascade of diamonds. The diamond glitter spread, and surrounded the ship, and opened a way through the barrier, and they slipped through into the wider universe outside. It didn't take long. By Captain's standard, less than an hour. By the clocks of the outside universe, nearly two months.

Captain didn't look human, being a Heechee. More than anything else he resembled an animated cartoon skeleton. But one might as well think of him as human because he had most of the human traits—inquisitiveness, intelligence, amorousness, and all those other qualities that I know about but have never experienced. For example: He was in a good mood because the assignment permitted him to take along as part of his crew a female who was also a prospective love partner. (Humans do this, too, on what are called business trips.) The assignment itself, however, was distinctly unenjoyable if one stopped to think about it. Captain didn't. He worried about it no more than an average human worries about whether war will be declared of an afternoon; if it happens it is the end of everything, but time has gone on monotonously long without it happening, and so . . . The biggest difference is that Captain's assignment did not refer to anything as inoffensive as a nuclear war but to the very reasons that had caused the Heechee to retreat to their black hole in the first place. He was checking on the artifacts the Heechee had left behind. Those troves were not accidents. They were part of a well-considered plan. One might even call them bait.

As to Robinette Broadhead's feelings of guilt—

Q.—I wondered when you would get back to that. Let me make a suggestion. Why not let Robin Broadhead tell about that himself?

A.—Excellent idea!—since, heaven knows, he is expert on the subject. And so the scene is started, the procession is swelled . . . and I give you Robinette Broadhead!

1
Just like Old Times

Before they vastened me I felt a need I hadn't felt for thirty years and more, and so I did what I hadn't thought I would ever do again. I practiced a solitary vice. I sent my wife, Essie, off to the city to make a sneak raid on a couple of her franchises. I put a "Do Not Disturb" override on all the communications systems in the house. I called up my data-retrieval system (and friend) Albert Einstein and gave him orders that made him scowl and suck his pipe. And presently—when the house was still and Albert had reluctantly but obediently turned himself off, and I was lying comfortably on the couch in my study with a little Mozart coming faintly from the next room and the scent of mimosa in the air system and the lights not too bright—presently, I say, I spoke the name I hadn't spoken in decades. "Sigfrid von Shrink, please, I would like to talk to you."

For a moment I thought he wasn't going to come. Then, in the corner of the room by the wet bar, there was a sudden fog of light and a flash, and there he sat.

He had not changed in thirty years. He wore a dark and heavy suit, of the cut you see on portraits of Sigmund Freud. His elderly, nondescript face had not gained a wrinkle and his bright eyes sparkled no less. He held a prop pad in one hand and a prop pencil in the other—as if he had any need to take notes! And he said politely, "Good morning, Rob. I see that you are looking very well."

"You always did start out by trying to reassure me," I told him, and he flashed a small smile.

Sigfrid von Shrink does not really exist. He is nothing more than a psychoanalytic computer program. He has no physical existence; what I saw was only a hologram and what I heard was only synthesized speech. He doesn't even have a name, really, since "Sigfrid von Shrink" is only what I called him because I could not talk about the things that paralyzed me, decades ago, to a machine that didn't even have a name. "I suppose," he said meditatively, "that the reason you called for me is that something is troubling you."

"That's true."

He gazed at me with patient curiosity, and that also had not changed. I had a lot better programs to serve me these days—well, one particular program, Albert Einstein, who is so good that I hardly bother with any of the others—but Sigfrid was still pretty good. He waits me out. He knows that what is curdling in my mind takes time to form itself into words, and so he doesn't rush me.

On the other hand, he doesn't let me just daydream away the time, either. "Can you say what you are disturbed about right at this moment?"

"A lot of things. Different things," I said.

"Pick one," he said patiently, and I shrugged.

"It's a troublesome world, Sigfrid. With all the good things that have happened, why are people—Oh, shit. I'm doing it again, right?"

He twinkled at me. "Doing what?" he encouraged.

"Saying *a* thing that's worrying me, not *the* thing. Dodging away from the real issue."

"That sounds like a good insight, Robin. Do you want to try now to tell me what the real issue is?"

I said, "I *want* to. I want to so much that actually, I almost think I'm going to cry. I haven't done that for a hell of a long time."

"You haven't felt the need to see me for quite a long time," he pointed out, and I nodded.

"Yes. Exactly."

He waited for a while, slowly turning his pencil between his fingers now and then, keeping that expression of polite and friendly interest, that nonjudging expression that was really about all I could remember of his face between sessions, and then he said, "The things that really trouble you, Robin, deep down, are by definition hard to say. You know that. We saw that together, years ago. It's not surprising that you haven't needed to see me all these years, because obviously your life has been going well for you."

"Really very well," I agreed. "Probably a hell of a lot better than I deserve—wait a minute, am I expressing hidden guilt by saying that? Feelings of inadequacy?"

He sighed but was still smiling. "You know I prefer that you don't try to talk like an analyst, Robin." I grinned back. He waited for a moment, then went on: "Let's look at the present situation objectively. You have made sure that no one is here to interrupt us—or to eavesdrop? To hear something you don't want your nearest and dearest friend to hear? You've even instructed Albert Einstein, your data-retrieval system, to withdraw and to seal off this interview from all datastores. What you have to say must be very private. Perhaps it is something that you feel but are ashamed to be heard feeling. Does that suggest anything to you, Robin?"

I cleared my throat. "You've put your finger right on it, Sigfrid."

"And? The thing you want to say? Can you say it?"

I plunged in. "You're God-damned right I can! It's simple! It's obvious! I'm getting very God-damned fucking old!"

That's the best way. When it's hard to say, just say it. That was one of the things I had learned from those long-ago days when I was pouring out my pain to Sigfrid three times a week, and it always works. As soon as I had said it I felt purged—not well, not happy, not as though a problem had been solved, but that glob of badness had been excreted. Sigfrid nodded slightly. He looked down at the pencil he was rolling between his fingers, waiting for me to go on. And I knew that now I could. I'd got past the worst part. I knew the feeling. I remembered it well, from those old and stormy sessions.

Now, I'm not the same person I was then. *That* Robin Broadhead had been raw with guilt because he'd left a woman he loved to die. Now those guilt feelings were long eased—because Sigfrid had helped ease them. *That* Robin Broadhead thought so little of himself that he couldn't believe anyone else would think well of him, so he had few friends. Now I have—I don't know. Dozens. Hundreds! (Some of them I am going to tell you about.) *That* Robin Broadhead could not accept love, and since then I had had a quarter of a century of the best marriage there ever was. So I was a quite different Robin Broadhead.

But some of the things had not changed at all. "Sigfrid," I said, "I'm old, I'm going to die one of these days, and do you know what pulls my cork?"

He looked up from his pencil. "What's that, Robin?"

"I'm not grown-up enough to be so old!"

He pursed his lips. "Would you care to explain that, Robin?"

"Yes," I said, "I would." And as a matter of fact the next part came easily, because, you can be sure, I had done a lot of thinking on the subject before I went so far as to call Sigfrid up. "I think it has to do with the Heechee," I said. "Let me finish before you tell me I'm crazy, all right? As you may remember, I was part of the Heechee generation; we kids grew up hearing about the Heechee, which had everything human beings didn't have and knew everything human beings didn't know—"

"The Heechee weren't quite that superior, Robin."

"I'm talking about how it *seemed* to us *kids*. They were scary, because we used to threaten each other that they'd come back and get us. And most of all they were so far ahead of us in everything that we couldn't compete. A little like Santa Claus. A little like those mad pervert rapists our mothers used to warn us against. A little like God. Do you understand what I'm saying, Sigfrid?"

He said cautiously, "I can recognize those feelings, yes. Actually such perceptions have turned up in analysis with many persons of your generation and later."

"Right! And I remember something you said to me once about Freud. You said he said that no man could truly grow up while his father was still alive."

"Well, actually—"

I overrode him. "And I used to tell you that was bullshit because my own father was nice enough to die while I was still a little kid."

"Oh, Robin." He sighed.

"No, listen to me. What about that biggest father figure there is? How can anybody grow up while Our Father Who Art in the Core is still hanging out there where we can't even get at him, much less knock the old bastard off?"

This is Albert Einstein again. I think I'd better clear up what Robin is saying about Gelle-Klara Moynlin. She was a fellow Gateway prospector with whom he was in love. The two of them, with other prospectors, found themselves trapped in a black hole. It was possible to free some of them at the expense of the others. Robin got free. Klara and the others did not. This may have been an accident; may have been Klara selflessly sacrificing herself to save him; may have been Robin panicking and saving himself at their expense; even now, there is no good way to tell. But Robin, who was a guilt addict, carried with him for years the picture of Klara in that black hole, where time almost stopped, always living that same moment of shock and terror—and always (he thought) blaming him. Only Sigfrid helped him out of that.

You may wonder how I know about this, since the interview with Sigfrid was sealed. That's easy. I know it now, the same way Robin now knows so much about so many people doing so many things he was not present to see.

He shook his head sadly. " 'Father figures.' Quotations from Freud."

"No, I mean it! Don't you understand?"

He said gravely, "Yes, Robin. I understand that you are referring to the Heechee. It is true. That is a problem for the human race, I agree, and unfortunately Dr. Freud never considered such a situation. But we aren't talking about the human race now, we're talking about you. You didn't call on me for abstract discussions. You called me because you're really unhappy, and you've already said it is the inevitable process of aging that has made you so. So let us confine ourselves to that if we can. Please don't theorize, just tell me what you feel."

"What I feel," I yelled, "is damn *old*. You can't understand that, because you're a machine. You don't know what it's like when your vision gets blurry and the back of your hands get those rusty age spots and your face sags down around your chin. When you have to sit down to put your socks on because if you stand on one foot you'll fall over. When every time you forget a birthday you think it's Alzheimer's disease and sometimes you can't pee when you want to! When—" But I broke off then, not because he had interrupted me but because he was listening patiently and looked as though he would go on listening forever, and what was the use of saying all that? He gave me a moment to make sure I was finished and then began patiently:

"According to your medical records, you had your prostate replaced eighteen months ago, Robin. The middle-ear disturbance can easily be—"

"You hold it right there!" I shouted. "What do you know about my medical records, Sigfrid? I have orders this talk was sealed!"

"Of course it is, Robin. Believe me, not one word of this will be accessible to any of your other programs, or to anyone at all but yourself. But, of course, I am able to access all your datastores, including your medical charts. May I go on? The stirrup and anvil in your ear can readily be replaced, and that will cure your balance problem. Corneal transplants will take care of those incipient cataracts. The other matters are purely cosmetic, and of course there would be no problem in securing good young tissue for you. That leaves only the Alzheimer's disease and, truthfully, Robin, I see no signs of that in you."

I shrugged. He waited a moment, then said: "So each of the problems you mention—as well as a long list of others that you didn't say anything about but that do appear on your medical history—can be repaired at any time, or already have been. Perhaps you have put your question the wrong way, Robin. Perhaps the problem is not that you are aging but that you aren't willing to do what is necessary to reverse it."

"Why the hell would I do that?"

He nodded. "Why indeed, Robin. Can you answer that question?"

"No, I can't! If I could, why would I be asking you?"

He pursed his lips and waited.

"Maybe I just want to be that way!"

He shrugged.

"Oh, come on, Sigfrid," I wheedled. "All right. I admit what you say. I've got Full Medical Plus and I can take somebody else's organs for myself as much as I want to, and the reason I don't is in my head somewhere. I know what you call that. Endogenous depression. But that doesn't explain anything!"

"Ah, Robin"—he sighed—"psychoanalytic jargon again. And bad jargon. 'Endogenous' only means 'coming from within.' It doesn't mean there's no cause."

"Then what's the cause?"

He said thoughtfully, "Let's play a game. By your left hand there is a button—"

I looked; yes, there was a button on the leather chair. "That's just to keep the leather in place," I said.

"No doubt, but in the game we are going to play, this button will, the minute you press it, cause to be done at once all the transplant surgery you need or might want. Instantly. Put your finger on the button, Robin. Now. Do you want to press it?"

"—No."

"I see. Can you tell me why not?"

"Because I don't deserve to take body parts from somebody else!" I hadn't planned to say it. I hadn't known it. And when I had said it, all I could do was sit there and listen to the echo of what I had said; and Sigfrid, too, was silent for quite a long time.

Then he picked up his pencil and put it in his pocket, folded the pad and put it in another pocket, and leaned forward. "Robin," he said, "I don't think I can help you. There is a feeling of guilt here that I do not see a way to resolve."

"But you helped me so much before!" I wailed.

"Before," he said steadily, "you were causing yourself pain because of guilt over something that was probably not at all your fault, and in any case lay well in the past. This is not the same at all. You can live another fifty years, perhaps, by transplanting healthy organs to replace your damaged ones. But it is true that these organs will come from someone else, and for you to live longer may, in some sense, cause someone else to live much shorter. To recognize that truth is not a neurotic guilt feeling, Robin, it is only the admission of a moral truth."

And that was all he said to me except, with a smile that was both kind and sorrowful, "Good-bye."

I do hate it when my computer programs talk to me about morality. Especially when they are right.

Now, the thing to remember is that while I was having this depression, that was not the only thing going on. My God, no! Many things were happening to many people in the world—on all the worlds, and in the spaces between—that were not only a lot more interesting but mattered a great deal more even to me. I just did not happen to know about them then, even though they involved people (or nonpeople) I knew. (Or came to know or had known but had forgotten.) Let me give you some examples. My not-yet friend Captain, who was one of those mad-rapist-Santa-Claus Heechee who had haunted my childish dreams, was about to get a lot more scared than thinking about Heechee had ever made me. My former (and soon to be again) friend Audee Walthers, Jr., was about to meet, to his cost, my once friend (or nonfriend) Wan. And my very best friend of all (making allowance for the fact that he was not "real"), the computer program Albert Einstein, was about to surprise me . . . How very complicated all these statements are! I can't help it. I lived at a complicated time and in a very complicated way. Now that I have been vastened all the parts fit neatly together, as you will see, but then I didn't even know what all the parts were. I was one single aging man, oppressed by mortality and conscious of sin; and when my wife came home and found me slumped on a chaise longue, gazing out over the Tappan Sea, she at once cried, "Now then, Robin! What in hell is matter with you?"

I grinned up at her and let her kiss me. Essie scolds a lot. Essie also loves a lot and she is a lot of woman to love. Tall. Slim. Long goldy-blondy hair that she wears in a tight Soviet bun when she's being a professor or a businesswoman, and lets fall to her waist when she's coming to bed. Before I could think over what I was going to say long enough to censor it, I blurted, "I've been talking to Sigfrid von Shrink."

"Ah," said Essie, straightening. "Oh."

While she was thinking that over, she began to pull the pins out of her bun. After you've lived with a person for a couple of decades you begin to know them, and I followed her internal processes as well as if she'd spoken them aloud. There was worry, of course, because I had felt the need to talk to a psychoanalyst. But there was also a considerable amount of faith in Sigfrid. Essie had always felt she owed Sigfrid, since she knew that it was only with Sigfrid's help that I had been able to admit, long ago, that I was in love with her. (And also in love with Gelle-Klara Moynlin, which had been the problem.) "Do you wish to tell me what was about?" she asked politely, and I said:

"Age and depression, my dear. Nothing serious. Only terminal. How was your day?"

She studied me with that all-seeing diagnostic eye of hers, pulling the long dirty-blond hair through her fingers till it fell free, and tailored her answer to fit the diagnosis. "Bloody exhausting," she said, "to point where I need a drink very much—as, I perceive, do you."

So we had our drink. There was room on the chaise for both of us, and we watched the moon set over the Jersey shore of the sea while Essie told me about her day, and did not pry.

Essie has a life of her own, and a pretty demanding one—it's a wonder to me that she is so unfailingly able to find plenty of room for me in it. Besides checking her franchises she had spent a grueling hour at the research facility we had endowed for integrating Heechee technology into our own computers. The Heechee didn't actually use computers, it seemed, not counting primitive things like navigation controls for their ships, but they had some nifty ideas in nearby fields. Of course, that was Essie's own specialty and what she'd got her doctorate in. And when she was talking about her research programs I could see her mind working: No need to interrogate old Robin about this, can simply run override through Sigfrid program and at once have total access to interview. I said lovingly, "You're not as smart as you think you are," and she stopped in the middle of a sentence. "What Sigfrid and I talked about," I explained, "is sealed."

"Hah." Smug.

"No hah," I said, just as smug, "because I made Albert promise. It's stored so that not even you can decrypt it without dumping the whole system."

"*Hah!*" she said again, curling around to look me in the eye. This time the "hah" was louder and it had an edge to it that could be translated as, Will have a word with Albert about *this.*

I tease Essie, but I also love Essie. So I let her off the hook. "I really don't want to break the seal," I said, "because—well, vanity. I sound like such a whiney wretch when I talk to Sigfrid. But I'll tell you all about it."

She sank back, pleased, and listened while I did. When I had finished she thought for a moment and said, "That is why are depressed? Because have not much to look forward to?"

I nodded.

"But, Robin! Have perhaps only limited future, but, my God, what glorious present! Galactic traveler! Filthy-rich tycoon! Irresistible sex object to adoring, and also very sexy, wife!"

I grinned and shrugged. Thoughtful silence. "Moral question," she conceded at last, "is not unreasonable. Is credit to you that you consider such matters. I too have had qualms when, as you remember, some gloppy female bits were patched into me to replace worn-out ones not so long ago."

"So you understand!"

"Understand excellently! I also understand, dear Robin, that having made moral decision is no point in worrying about it. Depression is foolish. Fortunately," she said, slipping off the chaise and standing up to take my hand, "there is excellent antidepression measure available. Will you care to join me in bedroom?"

Well, of course I would. And did. And found the depression lifting, for if there is one thing I enjoy it is sharing a bed with S. Ya. Lavorovna-Broadhead. I would have enjoyed it even if I had known then that I had less than three months left before the death that had depressed me.

2
What Happened on Peggys Planet

Meanwhile, on Peggys Planet my friend Audee Walthers was looking for a particular shebeen for a particular man.

I say he was my friend, although I hadn't given him a thought in years. He had done me a favor once. I hadn't forgotten it, exactly—that is, if anybody had said to me, "Say, Robin, do you remember that Audee Walthers put his tail on the line so you could borrow a ship when you needed to?" I would have said indignantly, "Hell, yes! I wouldn't forget a thing like that." But I hadn't been thinking about it every minute, either, and as a matter of fact I had no idea at that moment where he was or even if he was still alive.

Walthers should have been easy to remember, because he looked rather unusual. He was short and not handsome. His face was wider at the jaw

than at the temples, which made him look a little like a friendly frog. He
was also married to a beautiful and dissatisfied woman less than half as
old as he. Her age was nineteen; her name was Dolly. If Audee had asked
my advice, I would have told him that such May and December affairs
cannot work out—unless, of course, as in my case, December is remark-
ably rich. But he desperately wanted it to work out, because he loved his
wife very much, and so he worked like a slave for Dolly. Audee Walthers
was a pilot. Any kind of pilot. He had piloted airbodies on Venus. When
the big Earth transport (which constantly reminded him of my existence
since I owned a share in it and had renamed it after my wife) was in orbit
at Peggys he piloted shuttlecraft to load and unload it; between times he
piloted whatever he could rent on Peggys for whatever tasks a charter
demanded. Like most everybody else on Peggys, he had come 4×10^{10}
kilometers from the place where he was born to scratch out a living, and
sometimes he made it and sometimes he did not. So when he came back
from one charter and Adjangba told him there was another to be had,
Walthers scrambled to get it. Even if it meant searching every bar in Port
Hegramet to find the charter party. That wasn't easy. For a "city" of four
thousand, Port Hegramet was bar-saturated. There were scores, and the
obvious ones—the hotel cafe, the airport pub, the big gambling casino
with Port Hegramet's only floorshow—weren't where the Arabs who
were his next charter were. Nor was Dolly in the casino, where she might
have been performing with her puppet show, or at home, or at least not
to answer the phone. Half an hour later Walthers was still walking the ill-
lit streets in search of his Arabs. He was no longer in the richer, more
Western parts of the city, and when he finally found them it was in a
shebeen at the edge of town, having an argument.

All of the buildings in Port Hegramet were temporary. That was a
necessary consequence of its being a colony planet; every month, when
the new immigrants arrived in the big Heechee Heaven transport from
Earth, the population exploded like a balloon at the hydrogen valve.
Then it gradually shrank for a few weeks, as the colonists were moved
out to plantations and lumbering sites and mines. It never collapsed quite
to the former level, so each month there were a few hundred new resi-
dents, a few score new dwellings built and a few old ones swallowed up.
But this shebeen was most obviously temporary of all. It was only three
slabs of construction plastic propped together for walls, a fourth laid over
them as a roof and the street side open to the warm Peggys air. Even so it
was smoky and hazy inside, smoke of tobacco and smoke of hemp laced
with the beery, sour smell of the home-brewed liquor they sold.

Walthers recognized his quarry at once from his agent's description. There were not many like him in Port Hegramet—many Arabs, of course, but how many rich ones? And how many old ones? Mr. Luqman was even older than Adjangba, fat and bald, and each one of his plump fingers wore a ring, many of them diamonds. He was with a group of other Arabs at the back of the shebeen, but as Walthers started toward them the barwoman put out a hand. "Private party," she said. "They pay. You leave alone."

"They're expecting me," Walthers said, hoping it was true.

"For what?"

"Now, that's none of your damn business," Walthers said angrily, estimating the chances of what would happen if he just pushed past her. She was no threat, skinny, dark-skinned young woman with great blue-glowing metal hoops dangling from her ears; but the big man with the bullet-shaped head who was sitting in a corner and watching what was going on was something else again. Fortunately Mr. Luqman saw Walthers and stumbled blearily toward him. "You are my pilot," he announced. "Come have a drink."

"Thank you, Mr. Luqman, but I've got to get home. I just wanted to confirm the charter."

"Yes. We shall go with you." He turned and gazed toward the others in his party, who were having a furious argument about something. "Will you have a drink?" he asked over his shoulder.

The man was drunker than Walthers had realized. He said again, "Thanks, but no. Would you like to sign the charter contract now, please?"

Luqman turned back to stare at the printout in Walthers's hand. "The contract?" He thought it over for a moment. "Why must we have a contract?"

"It's customary, Mr. Luqman," said Walthers, patience ebbing rapidly. Behind him the Arab's companions were shouting at each other, and Luqman's attention was wavering between Walthers and the arguing group.

And that was another thing. There were four people involved in the argument—five if you counted Luqman himself. "Mr. Adjangba said there would be four of you altogether," Walthers mentioned. "There's a surcharge if there are five."

"Five?" Luqman focused on Walthers's face. "No. We are four." Then his expression changed and he smiled fondly. "Oh, you are thinking that crazy man is one of us? No, he will not go with us. He will go to his grave, perhaps, if he insists on telling Shameem what the Prophet meant in his teachings."

"I see," said Walthers. "Then if you'll just sign—"

The Arab shrugged and took the printout sheet from Walthers. He spread it on the zinc-topped bar and painfully began to read it, a pen in his hand. The argument grew louder, but Luqman seemed to have abolished it from his mind.

Most of the shebeen's clientele was African, what looked like Kikuyu on one side of the room and Masai on the other. At first glance, in that company, the people at the quarrelsome table had seemed all alike. Now Walthers saw his mistake. One of the arguing men was younger than the others, and shorter and leaner. His skin color was darker than most Europeans', but not as dark as the Libyans'; his eyes were as black as theirs, but not kohled.

It was none of Walthers's business.

He turned his back and waited patiently, anxious to leave. Not just because he wanted to see Dolly. Port Hegramet was somewhat hostilely ethnic. Chinese mostly stayed with Chinese, Latin Americans in their barrio, Europeans in the European quarter—oh, not neatly, and certainly not always peacefully. The divisions were sharp even among the subdivisions. Chinese from Canton did not get along with Chinese from Taiwan, the Portuguese had little in common with the Finns, and the once-Chileans and former Argentines still quarreled. But Europeans were definitely not urged to come into African drinking spots, and when he had the signed charter he thanked Luqman and left quickly and with some relief. He had gone less than a block when he heard louder cries of rage behind him, and a scream of pain.

On Peggys Planet you mind your own business as much as you can, but Walthers had a charter to protect. The group he saw beating up one individual might well have been the African bouncers attacking the leader of his charter party. That made it his business. He turned and ran back—a mistake that, believe me, he regretted very deeply for a long time afterward.

By the time Walthers got there the assailants were gone, and the whimpering, bleeding figure on the sidewalk was not one of his charter party. It was the young stranger; and he clutched at Walthers's leg.

"Help me and I will give you fifty thousand dollars," he said blurrily, his lips thick and bloody.

"I'll go look for a public patrolman," Walthers offered, trying to disengage himself.

"No patrol! You help me kill those persons and I will pay," snarled the man. "I am Captain Juan Henriquette Santos-Schmitz, and I can well afford to buy your services!"

Of course, I knew nothing of this at the time. On the other hand, Walthers didn't know that Mr. Luqman was working for me. That didn't matter. There were tens of thousands of people working for me, and whether or not Walthers knew who they were made no difference at all. The bad thing was that he didn't recognize Wan, for he had never heard of him, except generally. That made a very big difference to Walthers in the long run.

I knew Wan particularly. I had met him first when he was a wolf-child, brought up by machines and nonhumans. I called him a nonfriend when I was running through the catalog of my acquaintances for you. I knew him, all right. But he was never socialized enough to be a friend to anyone.

He was even, you could say, quite an enemy—not just to me but to the whole human race—in the days when he was a scared and lecherous youth, dreaming into his couch out in the Oort Cloud and neither knowing nor caring that his dreams were driving everybody else nuts. That wasn't his fault, to be sure. It wasn't even his fault that the wretched and raging terrorists had found inspiration in his example and were driving us all nuts again, whenever they could manage it—but if we get into questions of "fault," and that related term "guilt," we'll be right back with Sigfrid von Shrink before you know it, and what I'm talking about now is Audee Walthers.

Walthers was no angel of mercy, but he couldn't leave the man in the street. When he helped the bleeding man into the little apartment he shared with Dolly, Walthers was far from clear in his mind why he was doing it. The man was in bad shape, true. But that was what first-aid stations were for, and besides, the victim was singularly unwinning in his ways. All the way to the quarter called Little Europe, the man was reducing his cash offer and complaining that Walthers was a coward; by the time he sprawled on Walthers's folding bed the cash promise was two hundred and fifty dollars, and the reflections on Walthers's character had been incessant.

At least the man's bleeding had stopped. He pushed himself up and stared contemptuously around the flat. Dolly wasn't home yet, and she had, of course, left the place in a mess—undisposed-of dirty dishes on the fold-down table, her hand puppets scattered all over, underwear drying over the sink, and a sweater hanging on the doorknob. "This is a filthy

What Robin says needs some explication here, too. The Heechee were very interested in living things, particularly in life that was intelligent or had the promise of becoming so. They had a device that let them listen in on the feelings of creatures worlds away.

What was wrong with the device was that it transmitted as well as received. The operator's own emotions were perceived by the subjects. If the operator was upset or depressed—or insane—the consequences were very, very bad. The boy Wan had such a device when he was marooned as an infant. He called it a dream couch—academics later renamed it the telempathic psychokinetic transceiver—and when he used it the events Robin so subjectively describes occurred.

place," the undesired guest said conversationally. "This is not worth two hundred fifty dollars, even."

A hot response came to Walthers's lips. He pushed it back with all the others he had been repressing for the last half hour; what was the point? "I'll get you cleaned up," he said. "Then you can get out. I don't want your money."

The bruised lips attempted a sneer. "How foolish of you to say that," the man said, "since I am Captain Juan Henriquette Santos-Schmitz. I own my own spacecraft, I have royalty shares in the transport vessel that feeds this planet, among other very important enterprises, and I am said to be the eleventh wealthiest person in the human race."

"I never heard of you," Walthers grumbled, running warm water into a basin. But it wasn't true. It had been a long time ago, yes, but there was something, there was a memory. Somebody who had been on the PV news shows every hour for a week, then every week for a month or two. No one is more securely forgotten than the one-month famous, ten years later. "You're the kid who was raised in the Heechee habitat," he said suddenly, and the man whined:

"Exactly, ouch! You are hurting me!"

"Then just hold still," said Walthers, and wondered just what to do with the eleventh wealthiest person in the human race. Dolly would be thrilled to meet him, of course. But after Dolly got over being thrilled, what schemes would she be hatching for Walthers to tap all that wealth and buy them an island plantation, a summer home in the Heather Hills —or a trip home? Would it, in the long run, be better to hold the man here under some pretext until Dolly got home—or to ease him out and simply tell her about it?

Dilemmas pondered over long enough solve themselves; this one solved itself when the door lock pinged and crackled, and Dolly walked in.

Whatever Dolly looked like around the house—sometimes with her eyes streaming from an allergy to Peggys Planet's flora, often grouchy, seldom with her hair brushed—when she went out she dazzled. She obviously dazzled the unexpected guest as she came in the door, and, although he had been married to that striking slim figure and that impassive alabaster face for more than a year, and even knew the rigid dieting that produced the first and the dental flaw that required the second, she pretty nearly dazzled Walthers himself.

Walthers greeted her with a hug and a kiss; the kiss was returned, but not with full attention. She was peering past him at the stranger. Still holding her, Walthers said, "Darling, this is Captain Santos-Schmitz. He was in a fight, and I brought him here—"

She pushed him away. "Junior, you didn't!"

It took him a moment to realize her misunderstanding. "Oh, no, Dolly, the fight wasn't with me. I just happened to be nearby."

Her expression thawed and she turned to the guest. "Of course you're welcome here, Wan. Let me see what they did to you."

Santos-Schmitz preened himself. "You know me," he said, allowing her to dab at the bits of bandage Walthers had already applied.

"Of course, Wan! Everyone in Port Hegramet knows you." She shook her head sympathetically over the blackened eye. "You were pointed out to me last night," she said. "In the Spindle Lounge."

He drew back to look at her more closely. "Oh, yes! The entertainer. I saw your act."

Dolly Walthers seldom smiled, but there was a way of crinkling up the corners of her eyes, pursing the pretty lips, that was better than a smile; it was an attractive expression. She displayed it often while they made Wan Santos-Schmitz comfortable, while they fed him coffee and listened to his explanations of why the Libyans had been wrong to get angry at him. If Walthers had thought Dolly would resent his bringing this wayfarer home, he found he had nothing to fear in that direction. But as the hour got later he began to fidgety. "Wan," he said, "I have to fly in the morning, and I imagine you'd like to get back to your hotel—"

"Certainly not, Junior," his wife reproved him. "We have plenty of room right here. He can have the bed, you can sleep on the couch, and I'll take the cot in the sewing room."

Walthers was too startled to frown, or even to answer. It was a silly idea. Of course Wan would want to go back to the hotel—and of course Dolly was simply being polite; she couldn't really want to set up the sleeping arrangements in such a way that they would have no privacy at all, on the one night he had before flying back into the bush with the irascible Arabs. So he waited with confidence for Wan to excuse himself and his wife to allow herself to be convinced, and then with less confidence, and then with none at all. Although Walthers was a short man, the couch was shorter than he was, and he tossed and turned on it all night long, wishing he had never heard the name of Juan Henriquette Santos-Schmitz—

A wish shared by a whole lot of the human race, including me.

Wan was not merely a nasty person—oh, it was not his fault, of course (yes, yes, Sigfrid, I know—get out of my head!). He was also a fugitive from justice, or would have been, if anyone had known exactly what he had swiped out of the old Heechee artifacts.

When he told Walthers he was rich, he did not lie. He had a birthright to a lot of Heechee technology simply because his mom had pupped him on a Heechee habitat with no other human beings to speak of around. This turned out to mean a lot of money for him, once the courts had time to think it over. It also meant, in Wan's own mind, that he had a right to just about anything Heechee that he could find that wasn't nailed down. He had taken a Heechee ship—everybody knew that—but his money bought lawyers that stalled the Gateway Corporation's suit to recover it in the courts. He had also taken some Heechee gadgets not generally available, and if anyone had known exactly what they were, the case would have whisked through the courts in no time and Wan would have been Public Enemy Number One instead of merely an irritation. So Walthers had every right to hate him, though, of course, those were not the reasons involved.

When Walthers saw the Libyans the next morning, they were hung over and irritable. He was worse, the difference between them and Walthers being that his mood was even more savage, and he wasn't even hung over. That was part of the reason for the mood.

His passengers didn't ask him anything about the night before; in fact, they hardly spoke as the aircraft droned on over the wide savannahs, occasional glades, and very infrequent farm patches of Peggys Planet. Luqman and one of the other men were buried in false-color satellite holos of the sector they were prospecting, one of the others slept, the fourth simply held his head and glowered out the window. The plane nearly flew itself, this time of year, with very little serious weather anywhere around. Walthers had plenty of time to think about his wife. It had been a personal triumph for him when they were married, but why weren't they living happily ever after?

Of course, Dolly had had a hard life. A Kentucky girl with no money, no family, no job—no skills, either, and perhaps none too much brainpower—such a girl had to use all the assets she had if she wanted to get out of coal country. Dolly's one commercial asset was looks. Good looks, though flawed. Her figure was slim, her eyes were bright, but her teeth were buck. At fourteen she got work as a bartop dancer in Cincinnati, but it didn't pay enough to live on unless you hustled on the side. Dolly didn't want to do that. She was saving herself. She tried singing, but she didn't have the voice for it. Besides, trying to sing without moving her lips and exposing her Bugs Bunny teeth made her look like a ventriloquist . And when a customer, trying to hurt her because she'd turned his advances down, told her that, the light dawned over Dolly's head. The M.C. considered himself a comic in that particular club. Dolly traded laundry and sewing for some old, used comedy routines, made herself some hand puppets, studied every puppet act she could find on PV or fantape, and tried out the act at the last show on a Saturday night when another singer was coming in to replace her on Sunday. The act was not boffo, but the new girl singer was even worse than Dolly, so she got a reprieve. Two weeks in Cincinnati, a month in Louisville, nearly three months in little clubs outside Chicago—if the engagements had been consecutive she would have been well enough off, but there were weeks and months between them. She did not, however, actually starve. By the time Dolly got to Peggys Planet the jagged corners of The Act had banged against so many hostile audiences or drunk ones that it had worn into some sort of serviceable shape. Not good enough for a real career. Good enough to keep her alive. Getting to Peggys Planet was a desperation move, because you had to sign your life away for the passage. There was no stardom here, but she wasn't any worse off, either. And if she was no longer saving herself, exactly, at least she didn't spend herself very profligately. When Audee Walthers, Jr., came along, he offered a higher price than most others had proposed—marriage. So she did it. At eighteen. To a man twice her age.

Dolly's hard life, though, wasn't really that much harder than anyone else's on Peggys—not counting, of course, people like Audee's oil prospectors. The prospectors paid full fare to get to Peggys Planet, or their companies did, and every one of them surely had a paid-up return ticket in his pocket.

It did not make them more cheerful. It was a six-hour flight to the point on West Island they had chosen for a base camp. By the time they had eaten and popped their shelters and said their prayers a time or two, not without arguments about which direction to face in, their hangovers were pretty well dissipated, but it was also pretty well too late to get anything done that day. For them. Not for Walthers. He was ordered to fly crisscross strikes across twenty thousand hectares of hilly scrub. As he was merely towing a mass sensor to measure gravitational anomalies, it did not matter that he had to do it in the dark. It did not matter to Mr. Luqman, at any rate, but it mattered a lot to Walthers, because it was precisely the sort of flying that he hated most; his altitude had to be quite low, and some of the hills were fairly high. So he flew with both radar and searchbeams going all the time, terrifying the slow, stupid animals that inhabited these West Island savannahs, and terrifying himself when he found himself dozing off and waking to claw for altitude as a shrub-topped hill summit rushed toward him.

He managed five hours' sleep before Luqman woke him to order a photographic reconnaissance of a few unclear sites, and when that was done he was set to dropping spikes all over the terrain. The spikes were not simple solid metal; they were geophones, and they had to be set in a receiving array kilometers in length. Moreover, they had to drop from at least twenty meters to be sure to penetrate the surface and stand upright so that their readings would be trustworthy, and each one had to be placed within a circular error of two meters. It did Walthers no good to point out that these requirements were mutually contradictory, so it was no surprise to him that when the truck-mounted vibrators did their thing the petrological data were no use at all. Do it over, said Mr. Luqman, and so Walthers had to retrace his steps on foot, pulling out the geophones and hammering them in by hand.

What he had signed on to do was pilot, but Mr. Luqman took a broader view. Not just trudging around with the geophone spikes. One day they had him digging for the ticklike creatures that were the Peggys equivalent of earthworms, aerating the soil. The next they gave him a thing like a Roto-Rooter, which dug itself down into the soil a few dozen meters and pulled out core samples. They would have had him peeling potatoes if they had eaten potatoes, and did in fact try to lumber him with all the dishwashing—backing off only to the extent that it was finally agreed to do it in strict rotation. (But Walthers noticed that Mr. Luqman's turn never seemed to come.) Not that the chores weren't interesting. The ticklike bugs went into a jar of solvent and the soup that resulted became a smear on an electrophoresis sheet of filter paper. The cores went into little incubators with sterile water, sterile air, and sterile hydrocarbon vapors. They were both tests for oil. The bugs, like termites, were deep diggers. Some of what they dug through came back to the surface with them, and electrophoresis would sort out what it was that they carried back. The incubators tested for the same thing in a different way. Peggys, like Earth, had in its soil microorganisms that could live on a diet of pure hydrocarbons. So if anything grew on the pure hydrocarbons in the incubators, that sort of bug had to be what was growing there, and it would not have existed without a source of free hydrocarbons in the soil.

In either case, there would be oil.

But for Walthers the tests were mostly stoop-labor drudgery, and the only surcease from them was to be ordered back into the aircraft to tow the magnetometer again or to drop more spikes. After the first three days he retired to his tent to pull out his contract printout and make sure he was required to do all these things. He was. He decided to have a word with his agent when he got back to Port Hegramet; after the fifth day he was reconsidering. It seemed more attractive to *kill* the agent . . . But all the flying had one beneficial effect. Eight days into the three-week expedition, Walthers reported gladly to Mr. Luqman that he was running low on fuel and would have to make a flight back to base for more hydrogen.

When he got to the little apartment it was dark; but the apartment was neat, which was a pleasant surprise; Dolly was home, which was even better; best of all, she was sweetly, obviously delighted to see him.

The evening was perfect. They made love; Dolly fixed some dinner; they made love again, and at midnight they sat on the opened-out bed, backs propped against the cushioning, legs outstretched before them, holding hands and sharing a bottle of Peggys wine. "I wish you could take me back with you," Dolly said when he finished telling her about the New Delaware charter. Dolly wasn't looking at him; she was idly fitting puppet heads on her free hand, her expression easy.

"No chance of that, darling." He laughed. "You're too good-looking to take out in the bush with four horny Arabs. Listen, I don't feel all that safe myself."

She raised her hand, her expression still relaxed. The puppet she wore this time was a kitten face with bright red, luminous whiskers. The pink mouth opened and her kitten voice lisped, "Wan says they're really rough. He says they could've killed him, just for talking about religion with them. He says he thought they were going to."

"Oh?" Walthers shifted position, as the back of the daybed no longer seemed quite so comfortable. He didn't ask the question on his mind, which was *Oh, have you been seeing Wan?* because that would suggest that he was jealous. He only said, "How is Wan?" But the other question was contained in that one, and was answered. Wan was much better. Wan's eye was hardly black at all now. Wan had a really neat ship in orbit, a Heechee Five, but it was his personal property and it had been fixed up special—so he said; she hadn't seen it. Of course. Wan had sort of hinted that some of the equipment was old Heechee stuff, and maybe not too honestly come by. Wan had sort of hinted that there was plenty of Heechee stuff around that never got reported, because the people that found it didn't want to pay royalties to the Gateway Corporation, you know? Wan figured he was entitled to it, really, because he'd had this *unbelievable* life, brought up by practically the Heechee themselves—

Without Walthers willing it, the internal question externalized itself. "It sounds like you've been seeing a great deal of Wan," he offered, trying to seem casual and hearing his own voice prove he was not. Indeed he was not casual; he was either angry or worried—more angry than worried, actually, because it made no sense! Wan was surely not good-looking. Or good-tempered. Of course, he was rich, and also a lot closer to Dolly's age . . .

"Oh, honey, don't be jealous," Dolly said in her own voice, sounding if anything pleased—which somewhat reassured Walthers. "He's going to go pretty soon anyway, you know. He doesn't want to be here when the transport gets in, and right now he's off ordering supplies for his next trip. That's the only reason he came here." She raised the puppeted hand again, and the childish kitten voice sang, *"Jun-*ior's jealous of *Dol-*lee!"

"I am not," he said instinctively, and then admitted, "I am. Don't hold it against me, Doll."

She moved in the bed until her lips were near his ear, and he felt her soft breath, lisping in the kitten voice, "I promise I won't, Mr. Junior, but I'd be awful glad if you would . . ." And as reconciliations went, it went very well; except that right in the middle of Round Four it was zapped by the snarling ring of the piezophone.

Walthers let it ring fifteen times, long enough to complete the task in progress, though not nearly as well as he had intended. When he answered the phone it was the duty officer from the airport. "Did I call you at a bad time, Walthers?"

"Just tell me what you want," said Walthers, trying not to show that he was still breathing hard.

"Well, rise and shine, Audee. There's a party of six down with scurvy, Grid Seven Three Poppa, coordinates a little fuzzy but they've got a radio beacon. That's all they've got. You're flying them a doctor, a dentist, and about a ton of vitamin C to arrive at first light. Which means you take off in ninety minutes tops."

"Ah, hell, Carey! Can't it wait?"

"Only if you want them DOA. They're real bad. The shepherd that found them says there's two of them he don't think will make it anyway."

Walthers swore to himself, looked apologetically at Dolly, and then reluctantly began getting his gear together.

When Dolly spoke the voice was not a kitten's anymore. "Junior? Can't we go back home?"

"This is home," he said, trying to make it light.

"Please, Junior?" The relaxed face had tightened up, and the ivory mask was impassive, but he could hear the strain in her voice.

"Dolly, love," he said, "there's nothing there for us. Remember? That's why people like us come here. Now we've got a whole new planet —why, this city by itself is going to be bigger than Tokyo, newer than New York; they're going to have six new transports in a couple of years, you know, and a Lufstrom loop instead of these shuttles—"

"But when? When I'm *old?*"

There might not have been a justifiable reason for the misery in her voice, but the misery was there all the same. Walthers swallowed, took a deep breath, and tried his joking best. "Sweet-pants," he said, "you won't be *old* even when you're ninety." No response. "Aw, but, honey," he cajoled, "it's bound to get better! They're sure to start a food factory out in our Oort pretty soon. It might even be next year! And they as much as promised me a piloting job for the construction—"

"Oh, fine! So then you'll be away a year at a time instead of just a month. And I'll be stuck in this dump, without even any decent programs to talk to."

"They'll have programs—"

"I'll be dead first!"

He was wide awake now, the joys of the night worn away. He said, "Look. If you don't like it here we don't have to stay. There's more on Peggys than Port Hegramet. We can go out into the back country, clear some land, build a house—"

"Raise strong sons, found a dynasty?" Her voice was scornful.

"Well . . . something like that, I guess."

She turned over in the bed. "Take your shower," she advised. "You smell like fucking."

And while Audee Walthers, Jr., was in the shower, a creature that looked quite unlike any of Dolly's puppets (though one of them was supposed to represent him) was seeing his first foreign stars in the thirty-one true years; and meanwhile one of the sick prospectors had stopped breathing, much to the relief of the shepherd who was trying, head averted, to nurse him; and meanwhile there were riots on Earth, and fifty-one dead colonists on a planet eight hundred light-years away . . .

And meanwhile Dolly had got up long enough to make him coffee and leave it on the table. She herself went back to bed, where she was, or pretended to be, sound asleep while he drank it, and dressed, and went out the door.

When I look at Audee, from this very great distance that separates us now, I am saddened to see that he looks so much like a wimp. He wasn't, really. He was quite an admirable person. He was a first-rate pilot, physically brave, rough-and-tumble tough when he had to be, kind when he had a chance. I suppose everybody looks wimpy from inside, and of course from inside is how I see him now—from a very great *distance* inside, or outside, depending on what analog of geometry you choose to apply for this metaphor. (I can hear old Sigfrid sighing, "Oh Robin! Such digressions!" But then Sigfrid was never vastened.) We all have some areas of wimpiness, is what I am trying to say. It would be kinder to call them areas of vulnerability, and Audee simply happened to be extremely vulnerable where Dolly was concerned.

But wimpiness was not Audee's natural state. For the next little bit of time he was all the good things a person needed to be—resourceful, succoring the needy, tireless. He needed to be. Peggys Planet had some traps concealed beneath its gentle facade.

As non-Terran worlds go, Peggys was a jewel. You could breathe the air. You could survive the climate. The flora did not usually give you hives, and the fauna was astonishingly tame. Well—not exactly tame. More like stupid. Walthers wondered sometimes what the Heechee had seen in Peggys Planet. The thing was, the Heechee were supposed to be interested in intelligent life—not that they seemed to have found much— and there was certainly not much of that on Peggys. The smartest animal was a predator, fox-sized, mole-slow. It had the IQ of a turkey, and proved it by being its own worst enemy. Its prey was dumber and slower than it was—so it always had plenty to eat—and its biggest single cause of death was strangulation on food particles when it threw up what it had eaten too much of. Human beings could eat that predator if they wanted to, and most of its prey, and a lot of the biota in general . . . as long as they were careful.

The ragged-ass uranium prospectors hadn't been careful. By the time the violent tropical sunrise exploded over the jungle, and Walthers set his aircraft down in the nearest clearing, one of them had died of it.

The medical team had no time for a DOA, so they flocked around the barely living ones and sent Walthers off to dig a grave. For a time he had hopes to pass the chore on to the sheepherders, but their flocks were scattered all over. As soon as Walthers's back was turned, so were the shepherds.

The DOA looked at least ninety and smelled like a hundred and ten, but the tag on his wrist described him as Selim Yasmeneh, twenty-three, born in a shantytown south of Cairo. The rest of his life story was easy to read. So he had scrabbled for an adolescence in the Egyptian slums, hit the miracle odds-against chance of a passage for a new life on Peggys, sweltered in the ten-tiered bunks of the transport, agonized through the

Of course, you realize the "wimpiness" Robin is excusing
here isn't that of Audee Walthers. Robin was never a wimp,
except in the need to reassure himself from time to time that he
wasn't. Humans are so strange!

landing in the deorbiting capsule—fifty colonists strapped into a pilotless pod, deorbited by a thrust from outside, shaken into terror on entry, the excrement jolted out of them as the parachutes popped open. Nearly all the capsules did in fact land safely. Only about three hundred colonists, so far, had been crushed or drowned. Yasmeneh was that lucky, at least, but when he tried to change careers from farming barley to prospecting heavy metals, his luck ran out because his party forgot to be careful. The tubers they'd fed themselves on when their store-bought food ran out contained, like almost every obvious food source on Peggys, a vitamin C antagonist that had to be experienced to be believed. They hadn't believed even then. They knew about the risk. Everybody did. They just wanted one more day, and then another day, and another, while their teeth loosened and their breath grew foul, and by the time the sheepherders stumbled across their camp, it was too late for Yasmeneh, and pretty close to the same for the others.

Walthers had to fly the whole party, survivors and rescuers together, to the camp where someday the loop would be built, and already there were at least a dozen permanent habitations. By the time he got back at last to the Libyans, Mr. Luqman was furious. He hung on the door of Walthers's plane and shouted at him. "Thirty-seven hours away! It is outrageous! For the exorbitant charter we pay you we expect your services!"

"It was a matter of life or death, Mr. Luqman," Walthers said, trying to keep the irritation and fatigue out of his voice as he postflighted the plane.

"Life is the cheapest thing there is! And death comes to us all!"

Walthers pushed past him and sprang down to the ground. "They were fellow Arabs, Mr. Luqman—"

"No! Egyptians!"

"—well, fellow Moslems, anyway—"

"I would not care if they were my own brothers! Our time is precious! Very large affairs are at stake here!"

Why try to restrain his own anger? Walthers snarled, "It's the *law*, Luqman. I only lease the plane; I have to provide emergency services when called on. Read your fine print!"

It was an unanswerable argument, and how infuriating it was when Luqman made no attempt to answer it but simply responded by heaping onto Walthers all the tasks that had accumulated in his absence. All to be completed at once. Or sooner. And if Walthers hadn't had any sleep, well, we would all sleep forever one day, would we not?

So, sleepless as he was, Walthers was flying magnetosonde traces within the next hour—prickly, tetchy work, towing a magnetic sensor a hundred meters behind the plane and trying to keep the damned unwieldy thing from snagging in a tree or plunging itself into the ground. And in the moments of thought between the demands of, really, trying to fly two aircraft at once, Walthers thought somberly that Luqman had lied; it *would* have made a difference if the Egyptians had been fellow-Libyans, much less brothers. Nationalism had not been left back on Earth. There had been border clashes already, gauchos versus rice farmers when the cattle herds went looking for a drink in the paddies and trampled the seedlings; Chinese versus Mexicans when there was a mistake in filing land claims; Africans versus Canadians, Slavs versus Hispanics for no reason at all that any outsider could see. Bad enough. What was worse was the bad blood that sometimes surfaced between Slav and Slav, between Latino and Latino.

And Peggys could have been such a pretty world. It had everything—almost everything, if you didn't count things like vitamin C; it had Heechee Mountain, with a waterfall called the Cascade of Pearls, eight hundred meters of milky torrent coming right off the southern glaciers; it had the cinnamon-smelling forests of the Little Continent with its dumb, friendly, lavender-colored monkeys—well, not *real* monkeys. But cute. And the Glass Sea. And the Wind Caves. And the farms—especially the farms! The farms were what made so many millions and tens of millions of Africans, Chinese, Indians, Latinos, poor Arabs, Iranians, Irish, Poles —so many millions of desperate people so willing to go so far from Earth and home.

"Poor Arabs," he had thought to himself, but there were some rich ones, too. Like the four he was working for. When they talked about "very large affairs" they measured the scale in dollars and cents, that was clear. This expedition was not cheap. His own charter was in six figures —pity he couldn't keep more of it for himself! And that was almost the least part of what they had spent for pop-up tents and sound-poppers, for microphone ranging and rock samplers; for the lease of satellite time for their false-color pictures and radar contour-mapping; for the instruments they paid him to drag around the terrain . . . and what about the next step? Next they would have to dig. Sinking a shaft to the salt dome they had located, three thousand meters down, would cost in the millions—

Except, he discovered, that it would not, because they too had some of that illegal Heechee technology Wan had told Dolly about.

The first thing human beings had learned about the long-gone Heechee was that they liked to dig tunnels, because examples of their work lay all about under the surface of the planet Venus. And what they had dug the tunnels with was a technological miracle, a field projector that loosened the crystalline structure of rock, converted it to a sort of slurry; that pumped the slurry away and lined the shaft with that dense, hard, blue-gleaming Heechee metal. Such projectors still existed, but not in private hands.

They did, however, seem to be available to the hands of Mr. Luqman's party . . . which implied not only money behind them but influence . . . which implied somebody with muscle in the right places; and from casual remarks dropped in the brief intervals of rest and meals, Walthers suspected that somebody was a man named Robinette Broadhead.

The salt dome was definite, the drilling sites were chosen, the main work of the expedition was done. All that remained was checking out a few other possibilities and completing the cross-checks. Even Luqman began to relax, and the talk in the evenings turned to home. Home for all four of them turned out not to be Libya or even Paris. It was Texas, where they averaged 1.75 wives each and about half a dozen children in all. Not very evenly distributed, as far as Walthers could tell, but they were, probably purposely, unclear about details. To try to encourage openness Walthers found himself talking about Dolly. More than he meant to. About her extreme youth. Her career as an entertainer. Her hand puppets. He told them how clever Dolly was, making all the puppets herself—a duck, a puppy, a chimp, a clown. Best of all, a Heechee. Dolly's Heechee had a receding forehead, a beaked nose, a jutting chin, and eyes that tapered back to the ears like an Egyptian wall painting. In profile the face was almost a single line slanting down—all imaginary, of course, since no one had ever seen a Heechee then.

The youngest Libyan, Fawzi, nodded judiciously. "Yes, it is good that a woman should earn money," he declared.

"It isn't just the money. It helps keep her active, you know? Even so, I'm afraid she gets pretty bored in Port Hegramet. She really has no one to talk to."

The one named Shameem also nodded. "Programs," he advised sagely. "When I had but one wife I bought her several fine programs for company. She particularly liked the 'Dear Abby' and the 'Friends of Fatima,' I remember."

"I wish I could, but there's not much like that on Peggys yet. It's very difficult for her. So I really can't blame her if sometimes when I'm, you know, feeling amorous and she isn't—" Walthers broke off, because the Libyans were laughing.

"It is written in the Second Sura"—young Fawzi guffawed—"that

Walthers's suspicion that Robin Broadhead financed the prospectors was well-founded. Walthers's opinion of Robin's motives—not so well-founded. Robin was a very moral man, but not normally a very legal one. He was also a man (as you see) who got a lot of pleasure out of dropping hints about himself, particularly when talking about himself in the third person.

woman is our field and we may go into our field to plow it when we will. So says Al-Baqara, the Cow."

Walthers, suppressing resentment, essayed a joke: "Unfortunately my wife is not a cow."

"Unfortunately your wife is not a wife," the Arab scolded. "Back home in Houston we have for such as you a term: pussy-whipped. It is a shameful state for a man."

"Now, listen," Walthers began, reddening; and then clamped down again on his anger. Over by the cooking tent Luqman looked up from his meticulous measuring of the day's brandy ration and frowned at the sound of the voices. Walthers forced a reassuring smile. "We shall never agree," he said, "so let's be friends anyway." He sought to change the subject. "I've been wondering," he said, "why you decided to look for oil right here on the equator."

Fawzi's lips pursed and he studied Walthers's face closely before he replied. "We have had many indications of appropriate geology."

"Sure you have—all those satellite photos have been published, you know. They're no secret. But there's even better-looking geology in the northern hemisphere, around the Glass Sea."

"That is enough," Fawzi interrupted, his voice rising. "You are not paid to ask questions, Walthers!"

"I was just—"

"You were prying where you have no business, that is what you were doing!"

And the voices were loud again, and this time Luqman came over with their eighty milliliters each of brandy. "Now what is it?" he demanded. "What is the American asking?"

"It does not matter. I have not answered."

Luqman glared at him for a moment, Walthers's brandy ration in his hand, and then abruptly he lifted it to his lips and tossed it down. Walthers stifled a growl of protest. It did not matter that much. He did not really want to be drinking companions with these people. And in any case it seemed Luqman's careful measuring of milliliters had not kept him from a shot or two in private, earlier, because his face was flushed and his voice was thick. "Walthers," he growled, "I would punish your prying if it was important, but it is not. You want to know why we look here, one hundred seventy kilometers from where the launch loop will be built? Then look above you!" He thrust a theatrical arm to the darkened sky and then lurched away, laughing. Over his shoulder he tossed, "It does not matter anymore anyway!"

Walthers stared after him, then glanced up into the night sky,

A bright blue bead was sliding across the unfamiliar constellations. The transport! The interstellar vessel *S. Ya. Broadhead* had entered high orbit. He could read its course, jockeying to low orbit and parking there, an immense, potato-shaped, blue-gleaming lesser moon in the cloudless sky of Peggys Planet. In nineteen hours it would be parked. Before then he had to be in his shuttle to meet it, to participate in the frantic space-to-surface flights for the fragile fractions of the cargo and for the favored passengers, or nudging the free-fall deorbiters out of their paths to bring the terrified immigrants down to their new home.

Walthers thanked Luqman silently for stealing his drink; he could afford no sleep that night. While the four Arabs slept he was breaking down tents and stowing equipment, packing his aircraft, and talking with the base at Port Hegramet to make sure he had a shuttle assignment. He had. If he was there by noon the following day they would give him a berth and a chance to cash in on the frantic round trips that would empty the vast transport and free it for its return trip. At first light he had the Arabs up, cursing and stumbling around. In half an hour they were aboard his plane and on the way home.

He reached the airport in plenty of time, although something inside him was whispering monotonously, *Too late. Too late . . .*

Too late for what? And then he found out. When he tried to pay for his fuel, the banking monitor flashed a red zero. There was nothing in the account he shared with Dolly.

Impossible!—or not really impossible, he thought, looking across the field to where Wan's lander had been ten days earlier and was no more. And when he took time to race over to the apartment he was not really surprised by what he found. Their bank account was gone. Dolly's clothes were gone, the hand puppets were gone, and most gone of all was Dolly herself.

I was not thinking at all of Audee Walthers at that time. If I had been, I would surely have wept for him—or for myself. I would have thought that it was at least a good excuse for weeping. The tragedy of the dear, sweet lover gone away was one I knew well, my own lost love having locked herself inside a black hole years and years before.

But the truth is I never gave him a thought. I was concerned with self-affairs. What occupied me most notably were the stabbings in my gut, but also I spent a lot of time thinking about the nastiness of terrorists threatening me and everything around me.

Of course, that was not the only nastiness around. I thought about my worn-out intestines because they forced me to. But meanwhile my store-bought arteries were slowly hardening, and every day six thousand cells were dying in my irreplaceable brain; and meanwhile stars slowed in their flight and the universe dragged itself toward its ultimate entropic death, and meanwhile—Meanwhile everything, if you stopped to think of it, was skidding downhill. And I never gave any of it a thought.

But that's the way we do it, isn't it? We keep going because we have schooled ourselves not to think of any of those "meanwhiles"—until, like my gut, they force themselves on us.

3
Senseless Violence

A bomb in Kyoto that incinerated a thousand thousand-year-old carved wooden Buddhas, a crewless ship that homed on the Gateway asteroid and released a cloud of anthrax spores when it was opened, a shooting in Los Angeles, and plutonium dust in the Staines reservoir for London—those were the things that were forcing themselves on all of us. Terrorism. Acts of senseless violence. "There's a queerness in the world," said I to my dear wife, Essie. "Individuals act sober and sensible, but in groups they are brawling adolescents—such childishness people exhibit when they form groups!"

"Yes," said Essie, nodding, "that is true, but tell me, Robin. How is your gut?"

"As well as can be expected," I said lightly, adding as a joke, "You can't get good parts anymore." For those guts were, of course, a transplant, like a sizable fraction of the accessories my body requires to keep itself moving along—such are the benefits of Full Medical Plus. "But I am not talking about my own sickness. I'm talking about the sickness of the world."

"And is right that you should do so," Essie agreed, "although is my opinion that if you got your gut relined you would talk about such things less often." She came up behind me and rested her palm on my forehead, gazing abstractedly out at the Tappan Sea. Essie understands instrumentation as few people do and has prizes to prove it, but when she wants to know if I have a fever she checks it the way her nurse did to her when she was a toddler in Leningrad. "Is not very hot," she said reluctantly, "but what does Albert say?"

"Albert says," I said, "that you should go peddle your hamburgers." I pressed her hand with mine. "Honestly. I'm all right."

"Will ask Albert to be sure?" she bargained—actually, she was deeply involved in setting up a whole new string of her franchises and I knew it.

"Will," I promised, and patted her still splendid bottom as she turned away to her own workroom. As soon as she was gone I called, "Albert? You heard?"

In the holoframe over my desk the image of my data-retrieval program swirled into visibility, scratching his nose with the stem of his pipe. "Yes, Robin," said Albert Einstein, "of course I heard. As you know, my receptors are always functioning except when you specifically ask me to turn them off, or when the situation is clearly private."

"Uh-huh," I said, studying him. He is not any sort of pinup, my Albert, with his untidy sweatshirt gathered in folds around his neck and his socks down around his ankles. Essie would straighten him up for me in a second if I asked her to, but I liked him the way he was. "And how can you tell the situation is private if you don't peek?"

He moved the stem of his pipe from his nose to his cheekbone, still scratching, still gently smiling; it was a familiar question and did not require an answer.

Albert is really more of a friend than a computer program. He knows enough not to answer when I ask a rhetorical question. Long ago I had about a dozen different information-retrieval and decision-making programs. I had a business-manager program to tell me how my investments were doing, and a doctor program to tell me when my organs were due for replacement (among other things—I think he also conspired with my chef program at home to slip the odd pharmaceutical into my food), and a lawyer program to tell me how to get out of trouble, and, when I got into too much of it, my old psychiatrist program who told me why I was screwing up. Or tried to; I didn't always believe him. But more and more I got used to one single program. And so the program I spent most of my time with was my general science advisor and home handyman, Albert Einstein. "Robin," he said, gently reproving, "you didn't call me just to find out if I was a Peeping Tom, did you?"

"You know perfectly well why I called you," I told him, and indeed he did. He nodded and pointed to the far wall of my office over Tappan Sea, where my intercom screen was—Albert controls that as well as about everything else I own. On it a sort of X-ray picture appeared.

"While we were talking," he said, "I was taking the liberty of scanning you with pulsed sound, Robin. See here. This is your latest intestinal transplant, and if you will look closely—wait, I'll enlarge the image—I think you'll be able to see this whole area of inflammation. I'm afraid you're rejecting, all right."

"I didn't need you to tell me that," I snapped. "How long?"

"Before it becomes critical, you mean? Ah, Robin," he said earnestly, "that is difficult to say, for medicine is not quite an exact science—"

"How long!"

He sighed. "I can give you a minimum and maximum estimate. Catastrophic failure is not likely in less than one day and almost certain in sixty days."

I relaxed. It was not as bad as it might have been. "So I have some time before it gets serious."

"No, Robin," he said earnestly, "it is already serious. The discomfort you now feel will increase. You should start medication at once in any case, but even with the medication the prognosis is for quite severe pain rather soon." He paused, studying me. "I think from the expression on your face," he said, "that for some idiosyncratic reason you want to put it off as long as you possibly can."

"I want to stop the terrorists!"

"Ah, yes," he agreed, "I know you do. And indeed that is a valid thing to do, if I may offer a value judgment. For that reason you wish to go to Brasilia to intercede with the Gateway commission"—I did; the worst thing the terrorists were doing was done from a spaceship no one had been able to catch—"and try to get them to share data so that they can move against the terrorists. What you want from me, then, is assurance that the delay won't kill you."

"Exactly, my dear Albert." I smiled.

"I can give you that assurance," he said gravely, "or at least I can continue to monitor you until your condition becomes acute. At that time, however, you must at once begin new surgery."

"Agreed, my dear Albert." I smiled, but he didn't smile back.

"However," he went on, "it does not seem to me that that is your only reason for putting off the replacement. I think there is something else on your mind."

"Oh, Albert"—I sighed—"you're pretty tedious when you act like Sigfrid von Shrink. Turn yourself off like a good fellow."

And he did, looking thoughtful; and he had every reason to look thoughtful, because he was right.

You see, somewhere inside me, in that unlocatable space where I keep the solid core of guilt Sigfrid von Shrink did not quite purge away, I carried the conviction that the terrorists were right. I don't mean right in murdering and blowing up and driving people crazy. That's never right. I mean right in believing that they had a grievance, a wickedly unjust grievance against the rest of the human race, and therefore they were right in demanding attention be paid to it. I didn't want just to stop the terrorists. I wanted to make them well.

Or, at least, I wanted not to make them any sicker than they were, and that was where we got into the morality of it all. How much do you have to steal from another person before the act makes you a thief?

The question was much on my mind, and I had no good place to go for the answers. Not to Essie, because with Essie the conversation always came back to my gut. Not with my old psychoanalytic program, because those conversations always shifted from "What do I do to make things better?" to "Why, Robin, do you feel that *you* must make things better?" Not even with Albert. I could chat with Albert about anything at all. But when I ask him questions like that he gives me the sort of look he would give me if I asked him to define the properties of phlogiston. Or of God. Albert is only a holographic projection, but he interacts with the environment really well, just as well as though he were there, sometimes. So he looks meditatively around wherever we happen to be—the Tappan Sea house, for instance, which I admit is pretty comfortably fixed up, and he says something like, "Why do you ask such metaphysical questions, Robin?" and I know that the unspoken part of his message is, Good heavens, boy, don't you know when you've got it made?

Well, I do have it made. Up to a point I do. God's own good luck gave me a bundle of money when I expected it least, and money makes money, and now I can buy anything that is for sale. Even some things that aren't. I already own a large number of things worth having. I have Powerful Friends. I am a Person to Be Reckoned With. I am loved, really well loved, by my dear wife, Essie—and frequently, too, in spite of the fact that we're both getting along in years. So I sort of laugh, and change the subject . . . but I haven't had an answer.

I haven't, even now, had an answer, although now the questions are a lot tougher.

Another thing on my conscience is that I am letting poor Audee Walthers stew in his misery a long time while I digress, so let me finish the point.

The reason I felt guilty about the terrorists was that they were poor and I was rich. There was a great grand Galaxy out there for them, but we didn't have any good way of getting them to it, not fast enough, anyway, and they were screaming. Starving. Seeing on the PV screen how glorious life could be for some of us, and then looking around their own huts or hogans or tenements and seeing how despairing it was for them, and how little chance there was that the great good things could become theirs before they died. It is called the revolution of rising expectations, Albert says. There should have been a cure for it—but I couldn't find it. And the question on my mind was, did I have the right to make it worse? Did I have the right to buy somebody else's organs and integument and arteries when my own wore out?

I didn't know the answer and I don't know it now. But the pain in my gut was not as bad for me as the pain of contemplating what it meant for me to steal somebody else's life, just because I could pay for it and he could not.

And while I was sitting there, pressing my hand against my belly and wondering what I was going to be when I grew up, the whole huge universe was going on about its business.

And most of its business was worrisome. There was that Mach's Principle thing that Albert had tried and tried to explain to me that suggested somebody, maybe the Heechee, was trying to crush the universe into a ball so as to rewrite the physical laws. Incredible. Also incredibly scary, when you let yourself think about it . . . but millions or billions of years in the future, too, so I wouldn't call it a really pressing worry. The terrorists and the growing armies were nearer at hand. The terrorists had hijacked a loop capsule heading for the High Pentagon. New recruits for their ranks were being generated in the Sahel, where crops had failed one more time. Meanwhile, Audee Walthers was trying to start a new life for himself without his errant wife; and meanwhile, the wife was erring with that nasty creature, Wan; and meanwhile, near the core, the Heechee Captain was beginning to think erotic thoughts about his second in com-

The "Mach's Principle thing" Robin talks about was at that time still only a speculation, though, as Robin says, a very scary one. It is a complicated subject. For now, let me just say that there were indications that the expansion of the universe had been arrested and a contraction had begun—and even a suggestion, from old fragmentary Heechee records, that the process was not natural.

mand, whose friendly-name was Twice; and meanwhile, my wife, troubled about my belly, was nevertheless happily completing a deal for extending her fast-food franchise chain to Papua New Guinea and the Andaman Islands; and meanwhile—oh, meanwhile! What a lot was going on meanwhile!

And always is, though usually we don't know about it.

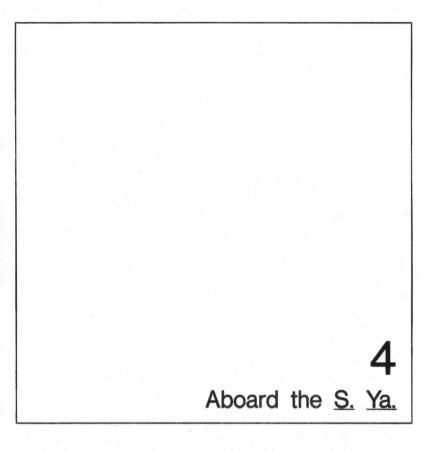

4
Aboard the S. Ya.

1908 light-years from Earth my friend—former friend—about to be friend again, Audee Walthers, was remembering my name again, and not too favorably. He was coming up against a rule I had made.

I mentioned that I owned a lot of things. One of the things I owned was a share in the biggest space vehicle known to mankind. It was one of the bits and pieces of gadgetry the Heechee had left behind in the solar system, floating out beyond the Oort comet cloud until it got discovered. Discovered by human beings, I mean—Heechee and australopithecines don't count. We called it Heechee Heaven, but when it occurred to me that it would make a marvelous good transport for getting some of those poor people away from the Earth, which couldn't support them, to some hospitable other planet that could, I persuaded the other sharcholders to rename it. After my wife: the *S. Ya. Broadhead* it was called. So I put up the money to refit it for colonist-carrying, and we started it off on round trips to the best and nearest of those places, Peggys Planet.

This put me into another of those situations where conscience and common sense came into conflict, because what I really wanted was to get everybody to a place where they could be happy, but in order to get it done, I had to be able to show a profit. Thus Broadhead's Rules. They were pretty much the same rules as for the Gateway asteroid, years ago. You had to pay your way there, but you could do it on credit if you were lucky enough to have your name come up in the draw. Getting back to Earth, however, was strictly cash. If you were a land-grant colonist, you could reassign your sixty hectares to the company and they would give you a return ticket. If you didn't have the land anymore because you'd sold it, or traded it, or lost it shooting craps, you had two choices. You could pay for a return ticket in cash. Or you could stay where you were.

Or, if you happened to be a fully qualified pilot, and if one of the ship's officers had made up his mind to stay on Peggys, you could work your way back. That was Walthers's way. What he would do when he got back to Earth he didn't know. What he knew for sure was that he could not stay in that empty apartment after Dolly left, and so he sold off their furnishings for whatever he could get, in the minutes between shuttle flights, made his deal with the *S. Ya.*'s captain, and was on his way. It struck him as queer and unpleasant that the thing that had seemed so impossible when Dolly asked for it suddenly became the only thing he could do when she left him. But life, he had discovered, was often queer and unpleasant.

So he came aboard the *S. Ya.* at the last minute, shaking with fatigue. He had ten hours before his first duty shift, and he slept it all. Even so, he was still groggy, and maybe a little numbed with trauma, when a fifteen-year-old failed colonist came to bring him coffee and escort him to the control room of the interstellar transport *S. Ya. Broadhead,* née Heechee Heaven.

How huge the damn thing was! From outside you couldn't really tell, but those long passages, those chambers with ten-tiered bunk beds, now empty, those guarded galleries and halls with unfamiliar machines or the stubs of places where the machines had been taken away—such vastness was no part of Walthers's previous experience of spacecraft. Even the control room was immense; and even the controls themselves were duplicated. Walthers had flown Heechee vessels—that was how he'd got to Peggys Planet in the first place, piloting a converted Five. The controls here were almost the same, but there were two sets of them, and the transport could not be flown unless both sets were manned. "Welcome aboard, Seventh." The tiny Oriental-looking woman in the left-hand seat smiled. "I'm Janie Yee-xing, Third Officer, and you're my relief. Captain Amheiro will be here in a minute." She didn't offer her hand or even lift either of them from the controls before her. That much Walthers had expected. Two pilots on duty at all times meant two pilots' hands on the controls; otherwise the bird did not fly. It wouldn't crash, of course, because there was nothing for it to crash into; but it wouldn't maintain course and acceleration, either.

Ludolfo Amheiro came in, a plump little man with gray sideburns with nine blue bangles on his left forearm—not many people wore them anymore, but Walthers knew that each one represented a Heechee-vessel flight in the days when you never knew where your ship was taking you; so here was a man with experience! "Glad to have you aboard, Walthers," he said perfunctorily. "Do you know how to relieve the watch? There's nothing to it, really. If you'll just put your hands on the wheel over Yee-xing's—" Walthers nodded and did as he was ordered. Her hands felt warm and soft as she slipped them carefully out from under his, then slid her pretty bottom off the pilot's seat to allow Walthers to occupy it. "That's all there is, Walthers," said the captain, satisfied. "First Officer Madjhour will actually fly the vessel"—nodding to the dark, smiling man who had just moved into the right-hand seat— "and he'll tell you what's necessary for you. You get a pee break of ten minutes each hour . . . and that's about it. Join me for dinner tonight, will you?"

And the invitation was reinforced by a smile from Third Officer Janie Yee-xing; and it was astonishing to Walthers, as he turned to listen to his instructions from Ghazi Madjhour, to realize that it had been all of ten minutes since he had thought of gone-away Dolly.

It was not quite as easy as that. Piloting was piloting. You didn't forget it. But navigation was something else. Especially as a lot of the old Heechee navigation charts had been unraveled, or at least partly unraveled, while Walthers was flying shepherds and prospectors around Peggys.

The star charts on the *S. Ya.* were far more complicated than the ones Audee had used on the trip out. They came in two varieties. The most interesting one was Heechee. It had queer gold and gray-green markings that were only imperfectly understood, but it showed *everything*. The other, far less detailed but a lot more useful to human beings, was human charted and English labeled. Then there was the ship's log to check, as it automatically recorded everything the ship did or saw. There was the whole internal system display—not the pilot's concern, of course, except that if something went wrong the pilot needed to know about it. And all of this was new to Audee.

The good part of that was that learning the new skills kept Walthers busy. Janie Yee-xing was there to teach him, and that was good, too, because she kept his thoughts busy in a different way . . . except in those bad times just before he fell asleep.

Since the *S. Ya.* was on a return trip it was almost empty. More than thirty-eight hundred colonists had gone out to Peggys Planet. Coming back, there were hardly any. The three dozen human beings in the ship's crew; the military detachments maintained by the four governing nations of the Gateway Corp; and about sixty failed immigrants. They were the steerage. They had impoverished themselves to go out. Now they glumly bankrupted themselves to get back to whatever desert or slum they had fled, because, when push came to shove, they couldn't quite hack pioneering in a new world. "Poor bastards," Walthers said, circling to pass a work party of them cleaning air filters at a slave's torpid pace; but Yee-xing would have none of that.

"Don't waste your pity on them, Walthers. They had it made and they chickened out." She snarled something in Cantonese at the work party, who resentfully moved minutely faster for a moment.

"You can't blame people for being homesick."

"Home! God, Walthers, you talk as if there was a 'home' left—you've been out in the boonies too long."

She paused at the junction of two corridors, one glowing blue with tracings of Heechee metal, the other gold. She waved at the party of armed guards in the uniforms of China, Brazil, the United States, and the Soviet Union. "Do you see them fraternizing?" she demanded. "Used to be they didn't take this seriously. They'd pal around with the crew, they never carried weapons, it was just an all-expense-paid cruise in space for them. But *now.*" She shook her head and reached out abruptly to grab Walthers's arm as he started to get closer to the guards. "Why don't you listen to me?" she demanded. "They'll give you hell if you try to go in there."

"What's in there?"

She shrugged. "The Heechee stuff they didn't take out of the ship when they converted it. That's one of the things they're guarding—although," she added, her voice lower, "if they knew the ship better they'd do a better job. But come on, we go this way."

Unraveling the Heechee maps was extremely difficult, especially as they showed clear indications that they were intended to be difficult to unravel. There were not many of them to go on. Two or three fragments found in vessels like the so-called Heechee Heaven or *S. Ya.*, and a nearly complete one found in an artifact circling a frozen planet around a star in Boötes. It was my personal opinion, though not supported by the official reports of the cartographical study commissions, that many of the haloes, check marks, and flickering indicia were meant as warning signs. Robin didn't believe me then. He said I was a cowardly pudding of spun photons. By the time he came to agree with me, what he called me no longer mattered.

Walthers followed willingly enough, grateful for the sight-seeing tour as much as for their destination. The *S. Ya.* was far the biggest ship he, or any other human being, had ever seen, Heechee-built, very old—and still, in some ways, very puzzling. They were halfway home, and Walthers had not yet explored a quarter of its mazy, glowing corridors. The part he had especially not explored was Yee-xing's private cabin, and he was looking forward to that with the interest of any ten-day virgin. But there were distractions. "What's that?" he asked, pausing at a pyramidal construction of green-glowing metal in an alcove. A heavy steel grating had been welded in front of it to keep prying hands off.

"Beats me," said Yee-xing. "Nobody else knows, either—that's why they've left it here. Some of the stuff can be cut out and moved easily, some gets wrecked—now and then if you try to remove something, it blows up in your face. Here, right down this little alley. This is where I live."

Neat, narrow bed, pictures of an old Oriental couple on the wall—Janie's parents?—sprays of flowers on the wall chest; Yee-xing had made the place her own. "On return trips, that is," she explained. "On the way out this is the captain's cabin, and the rest of us sleep on cots in the pilot room." She tugged at the cover on the bed, which was already quite straight. "There's not much chance to fool around on outgoing trips," she said meditatively. "Would you like a glass of wine?"

"I certainly would," said Walthers. And so he sat down and had the wine, and then he had the share of a joint with pretty Janie Yee-xing, and by and by had the other refreshments the tiny cabin had to offer, which were excellent in quality and satisfying to his soul, and if he thought at all of lost Dolly in the next half hour or so it was not at all with jealousy and rage, but almost with compassion.

There was plenty of room to fool around on return trips, it turned out, even in a cabin no bigger than the one Horatio Hornblower had occupied centuries before. And the wine was Peggys Planet's best, but when they had finished emptying the bottle, and themselves, the cabin began to seem a lot smaller and there was still an hour or more before their shifts began. "I'm hungry," Yee-xing announced. "I've got some rice and stuff here, but maybe—"

It was not a time to push his luck, although a home-cooked meal sounded good. Even rice and stuff. "Let's go to the galley," said Walthers, and, in no particular hurry, they wandered hand in hand back to the working part of the ship. They paused at a junction of corridors, where the long-gone Heechee had, for reasons of their own, planted little clusters of shrubs and bushes—not, no doubt, the same ones that were still growing there. Yee-xing paused to pick a bright blue berry.

"Look at that," she said. "They're all ripe, and the deadbeats don't even pick them."

"You mean the returning colonists? But they pay their way—"

"Oh, sure," she said bitterly. "No pay, no fly. But when they get back they'll go right on welfare, because what else is there for them?"

Walthers sampled one of the juicy, thin-skinned fruits. "You don't like the returnees very much."

Yee-xing grinned. "I don't keep that a secret very well, do I?" But the grin faded. "In the first place, there's nothing for them to go home to—if they had a decent life, they wouldn't have left it. In the second place, things have got a lot worse since they left. More terrorist trouble. More international friction—why, there are countries that are building up their armies again! And in the third place, they're not only going to suffer from all that; they're part of the cause of it. Half the goons you see here will be in some terror group in a month—or supporting one, anyway."

They strolled onward, and Walthers said humbly, "It's true I've been away a long time, but I did hear that things are getting nasty—bombings and shootings."

"Bombings! If that's all there was! They've got a TPT now! You go back to the Earth system now, and you never know when you're going to be right off your rocker without warning!"

"TPT? What's a TPT?"

"Oh, my God, Walthers," she said earnestly, "you *have* been away a long time. What they used to call the Craziness, don't you remember? It's a telempathic psychokinetic transceiver, one of those old Heechee things. There are about a dozen of them around, and the terrorists have one!"

"The Craziness," Walthers repeated, scowling, as a memory tried to work its way up out of his subconscious.

"Right. The Craziness," said Yee-xing, with gloomy satisfaction. "I remember when I was a kid in Kanchou, my father came home with his head all bloody because somebody had jumped out of the top story of the glass factory. Right on top of my father! Crazy as a bedbug! And it was all the TPT."

Walthers nodded without answering, his face drawn. Yee-xing looked at him in puzzlement, then waved at the guards ahead of them. "That's what they're protecting mostly," she said, "because there's still one on the S. Ya. Too damn many of them around! And they thought of protecting them a little too late, because now there's a bunch of terrorists that have a Heechee Five, and they've got a TPT in it, and somebody who's

It was, of course, the castaway boy Wan who caused the Fever. All he wanted was some sort of human contact, because he was lonesome. It was not his intention to drive most of the human race crazy with his crazy, obsessive thoughts. The terrorists, on the other hand, knew exactly what they were doing.

really crazy. Lunatic, I mean! When he gets on that thing and you feel him in your head it's so creepy and awful—Walthers, is something the matter?"

He stopped at the entrance to the gold-lit corridor, the four guards looking at him with curiosity. "The Craziness," he said. "Wan! This used to be his ship!"

"Well, sure it was," the girl said, frowning. "Listen, we were going to get something to eat. We'd better do it." She was getting worried. Walthers's jaw was set, the muscles around his face contracted. As much as anything, he looked like somebody who was expecting to be punched in the face, and the guards were getting curious. "Come on, Audee," she said pleadingly.

Walthers stirred and looked at her. "You go ahead," he said. "I'm not hungry any more."

Wan's ship! How strange, Walthers thought, that he had not made the connection before. But of course it was so.

Wan had been born in this very vessel, long before it was renamed the *S. Ya. Broadhead,* long before the human race even knew it existed . . . unless you considered a few dozen remote descendants of *Australopithecus afarensis* human. Wan had been born to a pregnant female Gateway prospector. Her husband was lost on one mission, herself stranded on another. She hung on to life for his first few years and then left him orphaned. Walthers could not easily imagine what Wan's infancy was like —tiny child in this vast, almost empty vessel, no company but savages and the computer-stored analogs of dead space prospectors. One of whom, no doubt, had been his mother. It called for pity . . .

Walthers had no pity to give. Not to Wan, who had borrowed his wife. Not, for that matter, to the same Wan who had found the machine they called the TPT—short for "telempathic psychokinetic transceiver," as the thick tongue of the bureaucracy had relabeled it. Wan himself had only called it a dream couch, and the rest of the human race had called it the Fever, the terrible, cloudy obsessions that had infected every human alive when silly young Wan, discovering a couch, had found that it gave him some sort of contact with some sort of living beings. He did not know that the same process gave them some sort of contact with him, and so his teen-aged dreams and fears and sexual fantasies invaded ten billion human brains . . . Perhaps Dolly should have made the connection, but she had been a small child when it happened. Walthers had not. He remembered, and it gave him a fresh reason to hate Wan.

He could no longer remember that recurrent worldwide madness very clearly, could hardly imagine how devastating its effects had been. He did not even try to imagine Wan's idle, lonely childhood here, but present Wan, cruising around the stars on his mysterious quest, his only company Walthers's fugitive wife—that, all of that, Walthers could imagine all too clearly.

In fact, he spent nearly all of the hour available to him, before his shift began, in imagining it, before it occurred to him that he was wallowing in self-pity and volunteered humiliation and that was really, after all, no way for a grown human being to behave.

He showed up on time. Yee-xing, there in the pilot room before him, said nothing but looked faintly surprised. He grinned at her in the changeover and set in to work.

Although the actual piloting of the ship amounted to not much more than holding on to the controls and letting the vessel fly itself, Walthers kept himself busy. His mood had changed. The vastness of the vessel he had under his fingertips was a challenge. He watched Janie Yee-xing as, with knees and toe-tips and elbows, she worked the auxiliary controls that displayed course and position and ship's state and all the other data that a pilot didn't really need to know to fly the beast but ought to go to the trouble of finding out if he wanted to call himself a *pilot*. And he did the same. He summoned up the course display and checked the position of the *S. Ya.*, tiny glowing gold dot along a thin blue line nineteen hundred light-years long; he verified that the position was right by calculating angles to the red-glowing marker stars along the route; he frowned at the handful of "Stay Away!" markings, where black holes and gas clouds posed a threat—none of them anywhere near their course, it appeared—and he even called up the great Heechee sky chart that displayed the entire Galaxy, with other members of the Local Group hanging on its fringes. Several hundred very bright human beings and thousands of hours of machine-intelligence time had gone into unraveling the Heechee chart code. There were parts that were not understood yet, and Walthers studied, frowning, the handful of points in all that area where the blinking, multicolored halos that meant "Here there be danger" were doubled and tripled. What could be so dangerous that the Heechee charts fairly screamed with panic?

There was still a lot to learn! And, Walthers thought to himself, no better place to learn it than on this ship. His job was strictly temporary, of course. But if he did good work . . . if he showed willingness and talent . . . if he ingratiated himself with the captain . . . why then, he thought, when they reached Earth, and the captain had to face the job of hiring a new Seventh Officer, what better candidate than Audee Walthers?

When the shift was over, Yee-xing came across the ten-meter space separating the two pilot positions and said, "As a pilot, you're looking pretty good, Walthers. I was a little worried about you."

He took her hand and they headed for the door. "I guess I was in a bad mood," he apologized, and Yee-xing shrugged.

"First girl friend always catches all the crap after a divorce," she observed. "What did you do, plug in one of our headshrinker programs?"

"I didn't have to. I just—" Walthers hesitated, trying to remember just what he had done. "I guess I just talked to myself a little. The thing about having your wife walk out on you," he explained, "is that it makes you feel *ashamed*. I mean, besides jealous, and angry, and all that other stuff. But after I stewed around for a while it occurred to me that I hadn't done anything much to be ashamed of. The feeling didn't belong to me, you see?"

"And that helped?" she demanded.

"Well, after a while it did." And, of course, the sovereign antidote for woman-induced pain was another woman, but he didn't want to say that to the antidote.

"I'll have to remember that, next time I get dumped. Well, I guess it's about bedtime . . ."

He shook his head. "It's early yet, and I'm all charged up. What about that old Heechee stuff? You said you knew a way past the guards."

She stopped in the middle of the passage to study him. "You sure have your ups and downs, Audee," she said. "But why not?"

The *S. Ya.* was double-hulled. The space between the hulls was narrow and dark, but it could be entered. So Yee-xing led Walthers through narrow passages close to the skin of the great spacecraft, through a maze of empty colonists' bunks, past the crude, huge kitchen that fed them, into a space that smelled of stale garbage and ancient rot—into a vast, ill-lit chamber. "Here they are," she said. Her voice was lowered, although she had promised him they were too far from the guards to be overheard. "Put your head close to that sort of silvery basket—you see where I'm pointing?—but you don't *touch* it. That's important!"

"Why is it important?" Walthers stared around at what looked like the Heechee equivalent of an attic. There were at least forty devices in the chamber, large and small, all of them firmly linked to the structure of the ship itself. There were big ones and little ones, spherical ones with splayed mountings joining the deck, squarish ones that glowed in the blue

The Heechee charting and navigation systems were not easy to decipher. For navigation, the system looks up two points, the start and finish of the trip. It then looks up all intervening obstacles such as dust or gas clouds, perturbing radiation, gravitational fields, and so on, and selects points of safe passage around or between them, after which it constructs a spline to fit the points and directs the vessel along it.

Many objects and points on the charts were tagged with attention marks—flickering auras, check marks, and so on. We realized early that these were often warnings. The difficulty was that we didn't know which signs were warnings, or what they warned against.

and green colors of the metal. Of the woven metal shroud Janie Yee-xing was indicating, there were three, all exactly alike.

"It's important because I don't want my ass kicked off this ship, Audee. So pay attention!"

"I am paying attention. Why are there three of them?"

"Why did the Heechee do anything? Maybe all these things were spares. Now here's the part you have to listen to. Put your head *close* to the metal part, but not *too* close. As soon as you start feeling things that don't come out of you, that's close enough. You'll know when. But don't get any closer, and above all don't touch, because this is a two-way thing. As long as you're just satisfied with sort of general feelings, nobody will notice. Probably. But if they do notice, the captain will have us both walking the plank, you understand?"

"Of course I understand," Walthers said, a little annoyed, and moved his head within a dozen centimeters of the silvery mesh. He twisted around to look at Yee-xing. "Nothing," he said.

"Try a *little* closer."

It was not very easy to move your head a centimeter at a time when it was bent at a strange angle and you didn't have anything to hold on to, but Walthers tried to do as instructed—

"That's it!" Yee-xing cried, watching his face. "No closer, now!"

He didn't answer. His mind was filled with the barest suspicion of sensations—a confused mumble of sensations. There were dreams and daydreams, and someone's desperate shortness of breath; there was someone's laughter, and someone, or actually what seemed to be three couples of someones, engaged in sexual activity. He twisted to grin at Janie, started to speak—

And then, suddenly, there was something else there.

Walthers froze. From Yee-xing's description he had expected a sort of sense of *company.* The presence of other people. Their fears and joys and hungers and pleasures—but the "they" was always human.

This new thing was not.

Walthers moved convulsively. His head touched the mesh. All the sensations became a thousandfold clearer, like the focusing of a lens, and he felt the new and distant presence—or presences?—in a different and immediate way. It was a distant, slippery, chilling sensation, and it did not emanate from anything human. If the sources had depressions or fantasies Walthers could not comprehend them. All he could feel was that they were *there.* They existed. They did not *respond.* They did not *change.*

If you could get inside the mind of a corpse, he thought in panic and revulsion, this was how it might feel—

—All this in a moment, and then he was aware that Yee-xing was tugging at his arm, shouting in his ear: "Oh, damn you, Walthers! I felt that! So did the captain and everybody on this God-damned ship. Now we're in trouble!"

As soon as his head came away from the silvery mesh the sensation was gone. The gleaming walls and shadowy machines were real again, with Janie Yee-xing's furious face thrust into his. In trouble? Walthers found himself laughing. After the chill, slow hell he had just glimpsed, nothing human could seem like trouble. Even when the four-power guard came boiling in, weapons drawn, shouting at them in four languages, Walthers almost welcomed them.

For they were human, and alive.

The question that was digging at his mind was the one that anybody would have asked himself: Had he tuned in somehow on the cryptic, hidden Heechee?

If so, he told himself, shuddering, heaven help the human race.

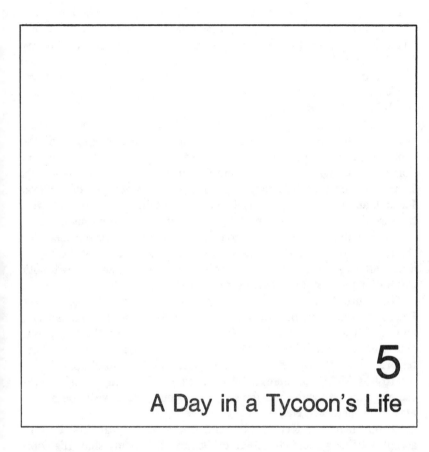

5

A Day in a Tycoon's Life

Dreading the Heechee was a popular sport in more places than the *S. Ya.* I even did a fair amount of it myself. Everybody did. We did it a lot when I was a kid, though then the Heechee were nothing more than strange vanished creatures that had amused themselves digging tunnels on the planet Venus hundreds of thousands of years before. We did it when I was a Gateway prospector—oh, yes, my God how we did it then! Trusting ourselves to old Heechee ships and scooting around the universe to places no human had ever seen, and always wondering if the owners of the ships would turn up at the end of a trip—and what they would do about it! And we brooded about them even more when we untangled enough of their old sky atlases to discover where they had gone to hide, deep in the core of our own Galaxy.

It did not occur to us, then, to wonder what they were hiding from.

That certainly was not all I did, to be sure. I had plenty of other things to fill my days. There was my steadfast preoccupation with my crotchety health, which forced itself upon my attention whenever it wanted to, and wanted to more often all the time. But that was only the beginning. I was about as busy, with about as many myriad diverse things, as it was possible for a human being to be.

If you looked at any average day in the life of Robin Broadhead, aging tycoon, visiting him at his luxurious country home looking over the broad Tappan Sea just north of New York City, you would find him doing such things as strolling along the riverfront with his lovely wife, Essie . . . venturing culinary experiments in the cuisines of Malaya, Iceland, and Ghana in his lavishly equipped kitchen . . . chatting with his wise data-retrieval system, Albert Einstein . . . hitting his mail:

"To that youth center in Grenada, let's see, yeah. Here is the check for three hundred thousand dollars as promised, but please don't name the center after me. Name it after my wife if you want to, and we will both certainly try to get down there for the opening.

"To Pedro Lammartine, Secretary General, United Nations. Dear Pete. I'm working on the Americans to share data with the Brazilians on finding that terrorist ship, but somebody has to get after the Brazilians. Will you use your influence, please? It's in everybody's interest. If the terrorists are not stopped, God knows where we'll all wind up.

"To Ray McLean, wherever he's living now. Dear Ray. By all means use our docking facilities in the search for your wife. I wish you all the luck from the heart, etc., etc.

"To Gorman and Ketchin, General Contractors. Dear Sirs. I won't accept your new completion date of October 1st for my ship. It's completely unreasonable. You've had one extension already, and that's all you get. I remind you of the heavy penalty charges in the contract if there is any further delay.

"To the President of the United States. Dear Ben. If the terrorist ship is not located and neutralized at once, the peace of the whole Earth is threatened. Not to mention property damage, loss of lives, and everything else that's at risk. It is an open secret that the Brazilians have developed a direction-finder for signals from a ship in FTL flight and that our own military people have a procedure for FTL navigating that will let them approach it. Can't they get together? As Commander in Chief, all you have to do is order the High Pentagon to cooperate. There's lots of pressure on the Brazilians to do their share, but they're waiting for a sign from us.

"To what's-his-name, Luqman. Dear Luqman. Thanks for the good news. I think we should move to develop that oil field immediately, so when you come to see me, bring along your plan for production and shipment with cost estimates and a cash-flow capital plan. Every time the *S. Ya.* comes back empty we're losing money . . ."

And on and on—I kept busy! Had a lot to keep busy with, and that's not even counting keeping track of my investments and riding herd on my managers. Not that I spent a lot of time on business. I always say that after he's made his first hundred million or so, anybody who does anything just for the money is insane. You need money, because if you don't have money you don't have freedom to do the things that are worth doing. But after you have that freedom, what's the use of more money? So I left most of the business to my financial programs and the people I hired—except for the ones that I was in not so much for the money as because they were doing something I wanted done.

And yet, if the name Heechee does not appear anywhere in the list of my daily concerns, it was always there. It all came back to the Heechee in the long run. My ship abuilding out in the construction orbits was human-designed and human-built, but most of the construction, and all of the drive and communications systems, were adapted from Heechee designs. The *S. Ya.*, which I was planning to fill with oil on the nearly empty return trips from Peggys Planet, was a Heechee artifact; for that matter, Peggys was a gift from the Heechee, since they had provided the navigation to find it and the ships to get there in. Essie's fast-food chain came from the Heechee machines to manufacture CHON-food out of the carbon, hydrogen, oxygen, and nitrogen in the frozen gases of comets. We'd built some of the food factories on Earth—there was one right now off the shore of Sri Lanka, getting its nitrogen and oxygen from the air, its hydrogen from water out of the Indian Ocean, and its carbon from whatever unfortunate plants, animals, or carbonates slipped through its intake valves. And, now that the Gateway Corporation had so much money to invest that it didn't know what to do with it all, it was able to invest some wisely—in chartering systematic exploration trips—and as a big shareholder in Gateway, I encouraged them to keep on doing that. Even the terrorists were using a stolen Heechee ship and a stolen Heechee telempathic psychokinetic transceiver to inflict their worst wounds on the world—all Heechee!

It was no wonder that there were fringe religious cults all over the Earth, worshipping the Heechee, for they surely met all the objective tests of divinity. They were capricious, powerful—and invisible. There were times when I myself felt very nearly tempted, in those long nights when my gut was hurting and things didn't seem to be going right, to sneak a little prayer to Our Father Who Wert in the Core. It couldn't hurt anything, could it?

Well, yes, it could. It could hurt my self-respect. And for all of us human beings, in this tantalizing, abundant Galaxy the Heechee had given us—but only a dab at a time—self-respect was getting harder and harder to keep.

Of course, I had not then actually met a real, live Heechee.

I had not yet met any, but one who was going to be a big part of my later life (I *won't* quibble over the terminology anymore!), namely Captain, was halfway to the breakout point where normal space began; and meanwhile, on the *S. Ya.,* Audee Walthers was getting his ass royally reamed and beginning to think that he should not plan for much of a future working on that ship; and meanwhile—

Well, as always, there were a lot of meanwhiles, but the one that would have interested Audee the most was that meanwhile, his errant wife was beginning to wish she hadn't erred.

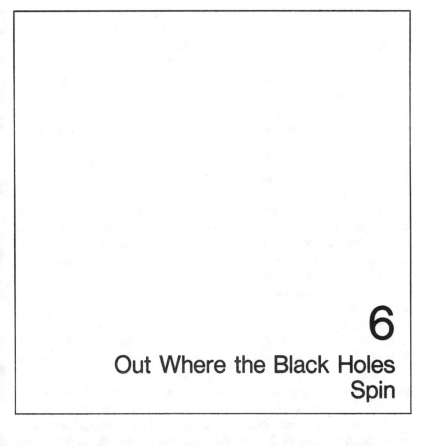

6
Out Where the Black Holes Spin

Eloping with a lunatic was not, on balance, very much better than being bored out of her mind in Port Hegramet. It was different, oh, heavens, yes, it was different! But parts of it were equally boring, and parts of it simply scared her to death. Since the ship was a Five there was room for the two of them—or should have been. Since Wan was young, and rich, and almost, in a way, handsome—if you looked at him the right way— the trip should have been lively enough. Neither of those was true.

And besides, there were the scary parts.

If there was one thing every human being knew about space, it was that black holes were meant to be stayed away from. Not by Wan. He sought them out. And then he did worse than that.

What the gidgets and gadgets were that Wan played with Dolly did not know. When she asked, he wouldn't answer. When, wheedling, she put one of her puppets on her hand and asked through its mouth, he scowled and frowned and said, "If you are going to do your act do something funny and dirty, not ask questions that are none of your business." When she tried to find out why they were none of her business, she was more successful. She didn't get a straight answer. But from the bluster and confusion with which Wan responded it was easy to figure out they were stolen.

And they had something to do with black holes. And, although Dolly was almost positive that she had heard, once, that there was no way in or out of a black hole, she was also almost positive that what Wan was trying to do was to find some certain black hole and then to go into it. That was the scary part.

And when she wasn't scared half out of her young mind, she was bone-crackingly lonesome, for Captain Juan Henriquette Santos-Schmitz, the dashing and eccentric young multimillionaire whose exploits still titillated the readers of gossip services, was rotten company. After three weeks in his presence, Dolly could hardly stand the sight of him.

Although she admitted to herself, trembling, that the sight of him was a lot less worrisome than the sight she was actually looking at.

What Dolly was looking at was a black hole. Or not really at the hole itself, for you could look at that all day and not see anything; black holes were black because they could not be seen at all. She was actually seeing a spiraling aurora of bluish, violetish light, unpleasant for the eyes even through the viewing plate over the control panel. It would have been far more unpleasant to be exposed to. That light was only the iceberg tip of a flood of lethal radiation. Their ship was armored against such things, and so far the armor had easily held. But Wan was not within the armor. He was down in the lander, where he had tools and technologies that she did not understand, and that he refused to explain. And she knew that at some time, in some such situation, she would be sitting in the main ship and would feel the little lurch that meant the lander had disengaged. And then he would be venturing even closer to one of these terrible objects! And what would happen to him then? Or to her? Not that she would go with him, certainly! But if he died, and left her alone, a hundred light-years from anything she knew—what then?

She heard an angry mumble and knew that at least that time was not now. The hatch opened and Wan crawled out of the lander, wrathful. "Another empty one!" he snarled at her, as though he were holding her accountable for it.

And, of course, he was. She tried to look sympathetic rather than scared. "Aw, honey, what a pity. That makes three of them."

"Three! Huh! Three with you along, you mean. More than that in all, indeed!" His tone was scornful, but she didn't mind the scorn. It was drowned in the relief when he slipped past her. Dolly moved inconspicuously as far away from the control board as she could—not far, in a Heechee ship that would have fit readily into a good-sized living room. As he sat down and consulted his electronic oracles she kept silent.

When Wan talked to his Dead Men he did not invite Dolly to take part. If he conducted his end of the conversation in words she could at least hear that half of it. If he tapped out instructions on his keyboard she did not have even that much. But this time she could figure it out easily enough. He punched out his questions, scowled at what one of the Dead Men said in his earphones, punched out a correction, and then set up a course on the Heechee board. Then he took the headphones off, scowled, stretched, and turned to Dolly. "All right," he said, "come, you can pay another installment on your passage."

"Why, sure, honey," she said obligingly, though it would have been so very much nicer if he didn't always have to put it like that. But her spirits were a little higher. She felt the tiny suggestion of a lurch that meant that the spacecraft was starting off on another trip, and indeed, the great blue and violet horror on the screen was already dwindling away. That made up for a lot!

Of course, it only meant they were on their way to the next one.

"Do the Heechee," commanded Wan, "and, let me see, yes. With Robinette Broadhead."

"Sure, Wan," said Dolly, retrieving her puppets from where Wan had kicked them and slipping them over her hands. The Heechee did not, of course, look like a real Heechee; and as a matter of fact the Robinette Broadhead was pretty libelous, too. But they amused Wan. That was what mattered to Dolly, since he was paying the bills. The first day out of Port Hegramet he had boastfully shown Dolly his bankbook. Six million dollars automatically socked into it every month! The numbers staggered Dolly. They made up for a lot. Out of all that cataract of cash there had to be a way, sooner or later, of squeezing a few drops for herself. To Dolly there was nothing immoral in such thoughts. Perhaps in an earlier day Americans would have called her a golddigger. But most of the human race, through most of its history, would only have called her poor.

So she fed him and bedded him. When he was in a bad mood she tried

to look invisible, and when he wanted entertainment she tried to enter-
tain:

"Hallo thar, Mr. Heechee," said the Broadhead hand, Dolly's fingers
twisting to give it a simpering grin, Dolly's voice thick and cornpone-
bumpkin (part of the libel!). "I'm moughty pleased to make your acquaintance."

The Heechee hand, Dolly's voice a serpentine whine: "Greetings, rash
Earthman. You are just in time for dinner."

"Aw, gosh," cried the Broadhead hand, grin widening, "I'm hungry,
too. What's fer dinner?"

"Aargh!" shrieked the Heechee hand, fingers a claw, mouth open.
"You are!" And the right-hand fingers closed on the left-hand puppet.

"Ho! Ho! Ho!" laughed Wan. "That is very good! Though that is not
what a Heechee looks like. You do not know what a Heechee is."

"Do you?" asked Dolly in her own voice.

"Nearly! More nearly than you!"

And Dolly, grinning, raised the Heechee hand. "Oh, but you're wrong,
Mr. Wan," came the silky, snaky Heechee voice. "This *is* what I look
like, and I'm waiting to meet you in the next black hole!"

Crash went the chair Wan was sitting on as he sprang up. "That is not
funny!" he shouted, and Dolly was astonished to see he was trembling.
"Make me food!" he demanded, and stomped off to his private lander,
muttering.

It was not wise to joke with him. So Dolly made him his dinner and
served him with a smile she did not feel. She gained nothing from the
smile. His mood was fouler than ever. He screeched: "Stupid woman!
Have you eaten all the good food when I was not looking? Is there
nothing left fit to be eaten?"

Dolly was near tears. "But you like steak," she protested.

"Steak! Of course I like steak, but look at what you serve for dessert!"
He pushed the steak and broccoli out of the way to seize the plate of
chocolate-chip cookies and shake it under her nose. Cookies sailed away
in all directions, and Dolly tried to retrieve them. "I know it's not what
you'd like, honey, but there isn't any more ice cream."

He glared at her. "Huh! No more ice cream! Oh, very well, then. A
chocolate souffle—or a flan—"

"Wan, they're almost all gone, too. You ate them."

"Stupid woman! That is not possible!"

"Well, they're gone. Anyway, all that sweet stuff isn't good for you."

"You have not been appointed my nurse! If I rot my teeth I will buy new ones." He struck at the dish in her hand, and the cookies went flying indeed. "Jettison this trash. I do not wish to eat at all now," he snapped.

It was just another typical meal on the frontiers of the Galaxy. It finished typically, too, with Dolly clearing away the mess and weeping. He was such a terrible person! And he didn't even seem to know it.

But as a matter of fact, Wan did know that he was mean, antisocial, exploitive—a whole long list of things that had been explained to him by the psychoanalysis programs. More than three hundred sessions of them. Six days a week, for almost a year. And at the end he had terminated the analysis with a joke. "I have a question," he told the holographic analyst, displayed for him as a good-looking woman, old enough to be his mother, young enough to be attractive, "and the question is this: How many psychoanalysts does it take to change a light bulb?"

The analyst said, sighing, "Oh, Wan, you're resisting again. All right. How many?"

"Only one," he told her, laughing, "but the light bulb has to really want to change. Haw-haw! And you see, I don't."

She looked directly at him for a silent moment. The way she was displayed, she was sitting on a sort of beanbag chair, with her legs tucked under her, a note pad in her hand, a pencil in the other. She used it to push up the glasses that were sliding down her nose as she looked at him. As with everything else in her programing, the gesture was meant to have a purpose, the reassuring indication that she was, after all, only another human being like himself, not an austere goddess. Of course, human she was not. But she sounded human enough as she said, "That's really a very old joke, Wan. What's a light bulb?"

He shrugged irritably. "It is a round thing that gives off light," he guessed, "but you are missing the point. I do not wish to be changed anymore. It is not fun for me. It was not my desire to begin this in the first place, and now I have decided to end it."

The computer program said peacefully, "That's your right, of course, Wan. What will you do?"

"I will go looking for my—I will go out of here and enjoy myself," he said savagely. "That is also one of my rights!"

"Yes, it is," she agreed. "Wan? Would you like to tell me what it was you started to say, before you changed your mind?"

"No," he said, getting up, "I would not like to tell you what it is I will do; instead, I will do it. Good-bye."

"You're going to look for your father, aren't you?" the psychoanalytic program called after him, but he didn't answer. The only indication he gave that he heard was that instead of merely closing the door, he slammed it.

A normal human being—in fact, almost any human being at all, really —would have told his analyst that she was right. Would have at some time in three long weeks have told his ship companion and bed companion the same thing, if only to have someone to share in his outside-chance hope and his very real fear. Wan had never learned to share his feelings, because he had never learned to share anything at all. Brought up in Heechee Heaven, without any sort of warm-blooded human companion for the most crucial decade of his childhood, he had become the archetype of a sociopath. That terrible yearning for love was what drove him to seek his lost father through all the terrors of space. Its total lack of fulfillment made it impossible for him to accept love, or sharing, now. His closest companions for those terrified ten years had been the computer programs of stored, dead intelligences called the Dead Men. He had copied them and taken them with him when he took a Heechee starship, and he talked to them, as he would not to flesh-and-blood Dolly, because he knew they were only machines. They didn't mind being treated that way. To Wan, flesh-and-blood human beings were also machines—vending machines, you might call them. He had the coin to make them yield what he wanted. Sex. Or conversation. Or the preparation of his food, or cleaning up after his piggish habits.

It did not occur to him to consider a vending machine's feelings. Not even when the vending machine was actually a nineteen-year-old female human being who would have been grateful for the chance of being allowed to think she loved him.

The Heechee early discovered how to store the intelligence and even an approximation of the personality of a dead or dying person in mechanical systems—as human beings learned when they first encountered the so-called Heechee Heaven where the boy Wan grew up. Robin considered that a tremendously valuable invention. I don't see it that way. Of course, I may be considered prejudiced in the matter—a person like me, being mechanical storage in the first place, doesn't need it; and the Heechee, having discovered that, did not bother to invent persons like me.

7
Homecoming

In the Lofstrom Loop in Lagos, Nigeria, Audee Walthers debated the measure of his responsibility toward Janie Yee-xing as the magnetic ribbon caught their descending pod, and slowed it, and dropped it off at the Customs and Immigration terminal. For playing with the forbidden toys he had lost the hope of a job, but for helping him do it Yee-xing had lost a whole career. "I have an idea," he whispered to her as they lined up in the anteroom. "I'll tell you about it outside."

He did indeed have an idea, and it was a pretty good one, at that. The idea was me.

Before Walthers could tell her about his idea, he had to tell her about what he had felt in that terrifying moment at the TPT. So they checked into a transit lodge near the base of the landing loop. A bare room, and a hot one; there was one medium-sized bed, a washstand in the corner, a PV set to stare at while the traveler waited for his launch capsule, windows that opened on the hot, muggy African coastal air. The windows were open, though the screens were tight against the myriad African bugs, but Walthers hugged himself against the chill as he told her about that cold, slow being whose mind he had felt on the *S. Ya.*

And Janie Yee-xing shivered, too. "But you never said anything, Audee!" she said, her voice a little shrill because her throat was tight. He shook his head. "No. But why didn't you? Isn't there—" She paused. "Yes, I'm sure there's a Gateway bonus you could get for that!"

"We could get, Janie!" he said strongly, and she looked at him, then accepted the partnership with a nod. "There sure is, and it's a million dollars. I checked it out on the ship's standing orders, same time I copied the ship's log." And he reached into his scanty luggage and pulled out a datafan to show her.

She didn't take it from him. She just said, "Why?"

"Well, figure it out," he said. "A million dollars. There's two of us, so cut it in half. Then—I got it on the *S. Ya.,* with the *S. Ya.*'s equipment, so the ship and its owners and the whole damn crew might get a share— we'd be lucky if it was only half. More likely three-quarters. Then—well, we broke the rules, you know. Maybe they'd overlook that, considering everything. But maybe they wouldn't, and we'd get nothing at all."

Yee-xing nodded, taking it in. There was a lot to take in. She reached out and touched the datafan. "You copied the ship's log?"

"No problem," he said, and indeed it hadn't been. During one of his tours at the controls, frosty silence from the First Officer at the other seat, Walthers had simply called up the data for the moment he had made contact from the automatic flight recorder, recorded the information as though it was part of his normal duty, and pocketed the copy.

"All right," she said. "Now what?"

So he told her about this known eccentric zillionaire (who happened to be me), notorious for his willingness to spend largely for Heechee data, and as Walthers knew him personally—

She looked at him with a different kind of interest. "You know Robinette Broadhead?"

"He owes me a favor," he said simply. "All I have to do is find him."

For the first time since they had entered the little room Yee-xing smiled. She gestured toward the P-phone on the wall. "Go to it, tiger."

So Walthers invested some of his not very impressive remaining bankroll in long-distance calls while Yee-xing gazed thoughtfully out at the bright tracery of lights around the Lofstrom loop, like a kilometers-long roller-coaster, its magnetic cables singing and the capsules landing on it *choofing* while the ones taking off were *chuffing* as they respectively gave up and took on escape velocity. She wasn't thinking about their customer. She was thinking about the goods they had to sell, and when Walthers hung up the phone, his face dour, she hardly listened to what he had to say. Which was:

"The bastard's not home," he said. "I guess I got the butler at Tappan Sea. All he'd tell me was that Mr. Broadhead was on his way to Rotterdam. Rotterdam, for God's sake! But I checked it out. We can get a cheap flight to Paris and then a slow-jet the rest of the way—we've got enough money for that—"

"I want to see the log," said Yee-xing.

"The log?" he repeated.

"You heard me," she said impatiently. "It'll play on the PV. And I want to see."

He licked his lips, thought for a moment, shrugged, and slipped it into the PV scanner.

Because the ship's instruments were holographic, recording every photon of energy that struck them, all that data concerning the source of the chill emanations was on the fan. But the PV showed only a tiny and featureless white blob, along with the location coordinates.

It was not very interesting to look at in itself—which was, no doubt, why the ship's sensors themselves had paid no attention to it. High magnification would perhaps show details, but that was beyond the capacities of the cheap hotel room set.

But even so—

As Walthers looked at it, he felt a crawling sensation. From the bed Yee-xing whispered, "You never said, Audee. Are they Heechee?"

He didn't take his eyes off the still white blur. "I wish I knew—" But it was not likely, was it? unless the Heechee were far unlike anything anyone had suspected. Heechee were intelligent. Had to be. They had conquered interstellar space half a million years ago. And the minds that Walthers had perceived were—were—What would you call it? Petrified, maybe. Present. But not active.

"Turn it off," said Yee-xing. "It gives me the creeps." She swatted one of the bugs that had penetrated the screen and added gloomily, "I hate this place."

"Well, we'll be off to Rotterdam in the morning."

"Not *this* place. I hate being on the Earth," she said. She waved at the sky past the lights of the landing loop. "You know what's up there?

There's the High Pentagon and Orbit-Tyuratam and about a million zappers and nukes floating around, and they're all crazy here, Audee. You never know when the damn things are going to go off."

Whether she intended a rebuke or not was unclear, but Walthers felt it anyway. He pulled the fan out of the PV scanner resentfully. It wasn't *his* fault that the world was crazy! But it was his fault, no doubt of that, that Yee-xing was condemned to be on it. So she had every right to reproach him.

He started to hand her the datafan, his motives not certain, perhaps to demonstrate trust, perhaps to reinforce her status as his accomplice.

But in midreach he discovered just how crazy the world was. The gesture converted itself into a blow, aimed wickedly at her unsmiling, desolate face.

For the half of a breath it was not Janie there; it was Dolly, faithless, runaway Dolly, with the grinning, contemptuous shadow of Wan behind her—or neither of them, in fact not a person at all but a symbol. A target. An evil and threatening thing that had no identity but only a description. It was THE ENEMY, and the most certainly sure thing about it was that it needed to be destroyed. Violently. By him.

For otherwise Walthers himself would be destroyed, wrecked, disintegrated, by the maddest, most hating, most pervertedly destructive emotions he had ever felt, forced into his mind in an act of sickening, violent, devastating rape.

What Audee Walthers felt at that moment I knew very well because I felt it, too—as did Janie—as did my own wife, Essie—as did every human being within a dozen AU of a point a couple of hundred million kilometers from the Earth in the direction of the constellation Auriga. It was most lucky for me that I was not indulging my habit of piloting myself. I don't know if I would have crashed. The touch from space only lasted half a minute, and I might not have had time to kill myself, but I surely would have tried. Rage, sick hatred, an obsessive need to wreck and ravish—that was the gift from the sky that the terrorists offered us all. But for once I had the computer doing the piloting so that I could spend my time on the P-phone, and computer programs were not infected by the terrorists' TPT.

It wasn't the first time. Not even the first time lately, for in the previous eighteen months the terrorists had dodged into solar space in their stolen Heechee ship and broadcast their pet lunatic's most horrid fantasies to the world. It was more than the world could stand. It was, in fact, why I was on my way to Rotterdam, but this particular episode was the reason I turned around in midflight on the way there. I tried at once to call Essie, as soon as it was over, to make sure she was all right. No luck. Everybody in the world was trying to call everybody else, for the same reasons, and the relay points were jammed.

There was also the fact that my gut felt as though armadillos were engaging in sexual intercourse in it and, everything considered, I wanted Essie with me instead of taking a later commercial flight as planned. So I ordered the pilot to reverse course; and so when Walthers got to Rotterdam I wasn't there. He could easily have caught me at Tappan Sea if he had taken a straight-through New York flight, and so he was wrong about that.

He was also wrong—quite wrong—forgivably wrong, for he had no way of knowing—about just what sort of mind he had tuned in on on the *S. Ya.*

And he had made one other error, quite serious. He had forgotten that the TPT worked both ways.

So the secret he had kept at one end of that fleeting mind-touch was no secret at all at the other.

I regret, or almost regret, that I know nothing about this "instant madness" from firsthand experience. I regretted it most when it first happened, a decade earlier. No one knew anything about a "telempathic psychokinetic transceiver" at that time. What it looked like, and was, was periodic, worldwide epidemics of insanity. A lot of the world's best minds, including mine, had spent their best efforts trying to find a virus, a toxic chemical, a variation in the Sun's radiation—anything—anything that would account for the shared madness that swept the human race every year or so. However, some of the world's best minds—like mine—were handicapped. Computer programs like myself simply did not feel the maddening impulses. If we had, I daresay, the problem would have been solved much earlier.

8
The Nervous Crew
of the Sailboat

A lavender squid—well, not really a squid, but looking about as squidlike as anything else in human experience—was in the middle of an exhausting, long-term project when Audee Walthers had his little accident with the TPT. Because the TPT goes in both directions it makes a great weapon but a lousy surveillance tool. It is sort of like calling up the person you're spying on and saying, "Hey, look, I've got my eye on you." So when Walthers bumped his head the sting was felt elsewhere. A where that was, in fact, very else. It was nearly a thousand light-years from the Earth, not far from the geodesic flight-line from Peggys Planet home—which was, of course, the reason Walthers was close enough for the touch to register.

Happens I know quite a lot about this particular lavender squid—or

My friend Robin has several faults, and one of them is a kind of cutesy coyness that is not as amusing as he thinks it is. The way he knew about the sailship folk, like the way he knew about most of the other things he was not present to see, is simply explained. He just doesn't want to explain it. The explanation is that I told him. That simplifies things a lot, but it's almost true.

Is it possible that cutesy coyness is contagious?

almost squid; you could have said that he looked like a wriggly, fat orchid, and been almost as close. I hadn't met him at the time, of course, but now I know him well enough to know his name, and where he came from, and why he was there, and, most complicated of all, what he was doing. The best way to think of what he was doing was to say that he was painting a landscape. The reason that is complicated is that there was no one to see it for light-years in every direction, least of all my squid friend. He did not have the proper kind of eyes to perceive it with.

Still, he had his reasons. It was a sort of religious observance. It went back to the oldest traditions of his race, which was old indeed, and it had to do with that theologically crucial moment in their history when they, living among the clathrates and frozen gases of their home environment, with visibility minute in any direction, for the first time became aware that "seeing" could become the receiving end of a significant art form.

It mattered very much to him that the painting should be perfect. And so, when he suddenly felt himself being observed by a stranger, and the startling shock caused him to spray some of the finely divided powders he painted with in the wrong place, and in the wrong mixture of colors, he was deeply upset. Now a whole quarter hectare was spoiled! An Earthly priest would have understood his feelings, if not his reasons for them; it was quite as though in the observance of a mass the Host had been dropped and crushed underfoot.

The creature's name was LaDzhaRi. The canvas he was working on was an elliptical sail of monomolecular film nearly thirty thousand kilometers long. The work was less than a quarter completed, and it had taken him fifteen years to get that far. LaDzhaRi did not care how long it took. He had plenty of time. His spacecraft would not arrive at its destination for another eight hundred years.

Or at least he thought he had plenty of time . . . until he felt the stranger staring at him.

Then he felt the need to hurry. He stayed in normal eigenmode while he swiftly collected his painting materials—by then it was August 21—lashed them secure—August 22—pushed himself away from the butterfly-wing sail and floated free until he was well clear. By the first of September he was far enough away to switch on his jet thrust and, in high eigenmode, return to the little cylindrical tin can that rode at the center of the cluster of butterfly wings. Although it was a terribly expensive drain on him, he remained in high mode as he plunged through the entering caves and into the salty slush that was his home environment. He was shouting to his companions at the top of his voice.

By human standards that voice was extraordinarily loud. Terrestrial great whales have such loud voices that their songs can be recognized and responded to by other whales an ocean away. So had LaDzhaRi's people, and in the tiny confines of the spacecraft his roaring shook the walls. Instruments quivered. Furniture rocked. The females fled in panic, fearing that they were about to be eaten or impregnated.

It was almost as bad for the seven other males, and as fast as he could, one of them struggled up to high eigenmode to shout back at LaDzhaRi. They knew what had happened. They too had felt the touch of the interloper, and of course they had done what was necessary. The whole crew had switched into high, transmitted the signal they owed their ancestors, and returned to normal mode . . . and would LaDzhaRi please do the same at once, and stop frightening the females?

So LaDzhaRi slowed himself down and allowed himself to "catch his breath"—although that was not an expression in use among his people. It did not do to thrash around in the slush in high for very long. He had already caused several troublesome cavitation pockets, and the whole slurpy environment they lived in was troubled. Apologetically he worked with the others until everything was lashed firm again, and the females had been coaxed out of their hiding places, one of them serving for dinner, and the whole crew settled down to discuss the lunatic touch, madly rapid and quite terrifying, that had invaded all their minds. That took all of September and the first part of October.

By then the ship had settled back into some sort of normal existence and LaDzhaRi returned to his painting. He neutralized the charges on the spoiled section of the great photon-trap wing. He laboriously collected the pigmented dust that had floated away, for one could not waste so much mass.

He was a thrifty soul, was LaDzhaRi. I have to admit that I found him rather admirable. He was loyal to the traditions of his people, under circumstances that human beings might have thought a little too menacing to be tolerated. For, although LaDzhaRi was not a Heechee, he knew where the Heechee could be reached, and he knew that sooner or later the message his shipmates had sent would have an answer.

So then, just as he was beginning to repaint the blanked-out section of his work, he felt another touch, and this time an expected one. Closer. Stronger. Far more insistent, and much, much more frightening.

9
Audee and Me

All the fragments of life stories of these friends—or almost friends, or in some cases nonfriends—of mine were beginning to fall together. Not very rapidly. Not much faster, in fact, than the fragments of the universe were beginning to fall together in that great crunch back toward the cyclic primordial-atom state that (Albert kept telling me) was about to happen for reasons I never quite understood at the time. (But I didn't feel badly about that, because at the time neither did Albert.) There were the sail-ship people, uneasily accepting the consequences of doing their duty. There were Dolly and Wan on their way to yet one more black hole, Dolly sobbing in her sleep, Wan scowling furiously in his. And there were Audee Walthers and Janie sitting disconsolate in their very much too expensive Rotterdam hotel room, because they had just found out I wasn't there yet. Janie squatted on the huge anisokinetic bed while Audee harangued my secretary. Janie had a bruise on her cheek, souvenir of that moment's madness in Lagos, but Audee had his arm in a cast—sprained wrist. He had not known until that moment that Janie was a black belt in karate.

Wincing, Walthers broke the connection and rested his wrist in his lap. "She says he'll be here tomorrow," he grumbled. "I wonder if she'll give him the message."

"Of course she will. She wasn't human, you know."

"Really? You mean she was a computer program?" That had not occurred to him, for such things were not common on Peggys Planet. "Anyway," he said, taking consolation, "I guess in that case at least she won't forget." He poured them each a short drink out of the bottle of Belgian apple brandy they had picked up on the way to the hotel. He set down the bottle, wincing as he rubbed his right wrist, and took a sip before saying, "Janie? How much money have we got left?"

She leaned forward and tapped out their code on the PV. "About enough for four more nights in this hotel," she reported. "Of course, we could move to a cheaper one—"

He shook his head. "This is where Broadhead's going to stay, and I want to be here."

"That's a good reason," Yee-xing commented blandly, meaning that she understood his real reason: If Broadhead wasn't anxious to see Walthers, it would be harder to duck him in person than on the P-phone. "So why did you ask about the money?"

"Let's spend one night's rent on some information," he proposed. "I'd kind of like to know just how rich Broadhead is."

"You mean buy a financial report? Are you trying to find out if he can afford to pay us a million dollars?"

Walthers shook his head. "What I want to find out," he said, "is how much more than a million we can take him for."

Now those were no charitable sentiments, and if I had known about them at the right time I would have been a lot harder-nosed with Audee Walthers, my old friend. Or maybe not. When you've got a lot of money you get used to people seeing you as a tappable resource instead of a human being, even though you never get to like it.

Still, I had no objection to his finding out what I owned, or anyway as much about what I owned as I had allowed the financial-report services to know. There was plenty there. A sizable interest in the charter operation of the *S. Ya.* Some food-mine and fish-farm shares. A great many

Since Robin keeps talking about the "missing mass" question, I should explain what it is. In the latter twentieth century cosmologists had an insoluble contradiction to face. They could see that the universe was expanding, and this was certainly so because of the red shift. They could also see, however, that it contained too much mass for the expansion to be possible. That was proved by such facts as that the outer fringes of galaxies revolved too fast, clusters of galaxies held each other too tightly; even our own Galaxy with its companions was plunging toward a group of starclouds in Virgo much faster than it should have been. Obviously, much mass was missing from observations. Where was it?

There was one intuitively obvious explanation. Namely, that the universe had formerly been expanding, but Something had decided to reverse its growth and cause it to contract. No one believed that for a minute—in the late twentieth century.

enterprises back on Peggys Planet, including (to Walthers's surprise) the company he leased his plane from. The very computer-data service that was selling them the information. Several holding companies and import-export or freight-forwarding firms. Two banks; fourteen real-estate agencies, based everywhere from New York to New South Wales, with a couple on Venus and Peggys Planet; and any number of unrecognizable little corporations, including an airline, a fast-food chain, something called Here After Inc.—and something called PegTex Petroventures. "My God," said Audee Walthers, "that's Mr. Luqman's company! So I was working for the son of a bitch all along!"

"And I," said Janie Yee-xing, looking at the part that mentioned the *S. Ya.* "Really! Does Broadhead own *everything?*"

Well, I did not. I owned a lot, but if they had looked at my holdings more sympathetically, they might have been able to see a pattern. The banks loaned money for explorations. The real-estate companies helped settle colonists, or took over their shacks and hogans for cash so they could leave. The *S. Ya.* ferried colonists to Peggys, and, as for Luqman, why, that was the crowning jewel in the empire, if they had only known it! Not that I had ever met Luqman, or would have known what he looked like if I saw him. But he had his orders, and the orders came down the chain of command from me: Find a good oil field somewhere near the equator of Peggys Planet. Why the equator? So the Lofstrom loop we would build there could take advantage of the planet's rotational velocity. Why a launch loop? It was the cheapest and best way of getting things in and out of orbit. The oil we pumped would power up the loop. The excess crude oil would go onto the loop and into orbit, in shipping capsules; the capsules would go back to Earth on the *S. Ya.*'s return flights to be sold there—which meant there would be a profitable cargo of oil to carry on the half of each round trip that was now nearly dead loss —which meant that we could cut the prices for colonists on the way out!

I do not apologize for the fact that almost all of my ventures showed a profit every year. That's how I kept them all going, and expanding, but the profit was only incidental. See, I have a philosophy about earning money, and that is that anybody who knocks himself out to accumulate it after the first hundred million or so is sick, and—

Oh, but I've said all that already, haven't I?

I'm afraid I wander. What with all the things going on in my mind I get a little confused about what has happened, and what hasn't happened yet, and what never happens at all except in that mind.

Robin takes a lot of pride in the launch loop, because it reassured him that human beings could invent things the Heechee had not. Well, he's right—at least if you don't look at the details. The loop was invented on Earth by a man named Keith Lofstrom in the late twentieth century, though nobody built one until there was enough traffic to justify it. What Robin didn't know was that although the Heechee never invented the loop, the sailship people did—they had no other way to get out of their dense, opaque atmosphere.

The point I'm making is that all my money-making ventures were also solidly useful projects that contributed to both the conquest of the Galaxy and the alleviation of the needs of human beings, and that's a fact. And that's why all these fragments of biography do ultimately fall together. They don't look as though they're going to. But they do. All of them. Even the stories of my semifriend, Captain, the Heechee whom I ultimately came to know quite well, and of his lover and second in command, the female Heechee named Twice, whom, as you will discover, I did at the end come to know quite a lot better than that.

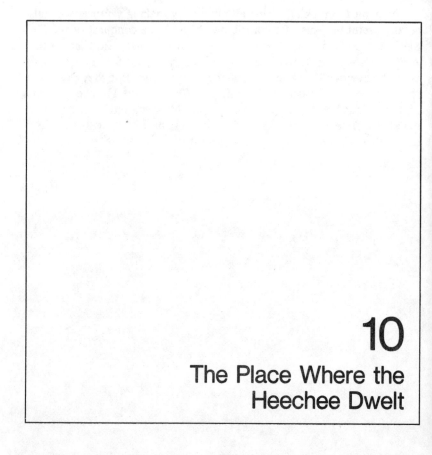

10
The Place Where the Heechee Dwelt

When the Heechee hid inside their Schwarzschild shell at the core of the Galaxy they knew there could be no easy communication between their scared selves and the immense universe outside. Yet they dared not be without news.

So they set up a web of starlets outside the black hole itself. They were far enough away so that the roaring radiation of infall into the hole did not swamp their circuitry, and there were enough of them so that if one were to fail or be destroyed—even if a hundred were—the ones that were left would be able to receive and record the data from their early-warning spy stations all around the Galaxy. The Heechee had run away to hide, but they had left eyes and ears behind.

So from time to time some brave souls sneaked out of the core, to find out what the eyes had seen and the ears had heard. When Captain and his crew were sent out to check space for the errant star, checking the monitors was an added duty. There were five of them aboard his ship—five living ones, anyway. By all odds the one that interested Captain the most was the slim, sallow, shiny-skinned female named Twice. By Captain's standards she was a raving beauty. And sexy, too—every year without fail—and the time, he judged, was getting near again!

But not, he prayed, just yet. And so prayed Twice, for getting through the Schwarzschild perimeter was a brute of a job. Even when the ship had been purpose-built to manage it. There were other can openers around—Wan had stolen one—but those managed the job only in limited ways. Wan's ship could not enter the event horizon and survive. It could only extend a part of itself there.

Captain's ship was bigger and stronger. Even so, the shaking, tossing, racking strains of passing through the event horizon threw Captain and Twice and the other four members of the crew violently and hurtingly against their retaining harnesses; the diamond-bright corkscrew coruscated with great fat silent sparks of radiance showering all around the cabin; the light hurt their eyes, the violent motion bruised their bodies; and it went on and on. For an hour or more by the crew's own subjective time, which was a queer, shifting blend of the normal pace of the universe at large and the slowed-down tempo inside the black hole.

But at last they were through into the unstressed space. The terrible lurching stopped. The blinding lights faded. The Galaxy glowed before them, a velvet dome of cream splattered with bright, bold stars, for they were too far inside the center to see more than the occasional patch of blackness.

"Massed minds be thanked," said Captain, grinning as he crawled out of his harness—he looked like a med school skull when he grinned—"I think we've made it!" And the crew followed his example, unstrapping themselves, chattering cheerfully back and forth. As they rose to begin the data-collection process, Captain's bony hand reached out to hold Twice's. It was an occasion for rejoicing—as the captains of Nantucket whalers rejoiced when they passed Cape Horn, as the covered-wagon pioneers began to breathe again as they came down the slopes into the promised land of Oregon or California. The violence and peril were not over. They would have to go through it all again on the way back inside. But now, for at least a week or more, they could relax and collect data; and this was the pleasure part of the expedition.

Or it should have been.

It should have been but was not, for as Captain secured the ship and the officer named Shoe opened the communication channels, every sensor on the board flared violet. The thousand automatic orbiting stations were reporting big news! Important news—*bad* news, and all the datastores clamored to announce their evil tidings at once.

There was a shocked silence among the Heechee. Then their training overcame their astonished terror, and the cabin of the Heechee ship became a whirlwind of activity. Receive and collate, analyze and compare. The messages mounted. The picture took shape.

The last record-tapping expedition had been only a few weeks before, by the slow creep of time inside the great central black hole—decades or so as time was measured in the galloping universe outside. But even so, not much time! Not in the scale of stars!

And yet the whole world was different.

Q.—What is worse than a prediction that doesn't come true?

A.—A prediction that comes true sooner than you expect.

It had been the Heechee conviction that intelligent and technological life would arise in the Galaxy. They had identified more than a dozen inhabited worlds—and not merely inhabited, but bearing the promise of intelligence. They had made a plan for each of them.

Some of the plans had failed. There was a species of furry quadrupeds on a damp, cool planet so near the Orion nebula that its aurora filled the sky, small quick creatures with paws as nimble as a raccoon's and lemur eyes. They would discover tools one day, the Heechee thought; and fire; and farming; and cities; and technology and space travel. And so they had, and used them all to poison their planet and decimate their race. There was another race, six-limbed segmented ammonia-breathers, very promising, sadly too near a star that went supernova. End of the ammonia-breathers. There were the chill, slow, sludgy creatures who occupied a special place in Heechee history. They had carried the terrible news that drove the Heechee into hiding, and that was enough to make them unique. More, they were not merely promising but actually intelligent already; not merely intelligent but civilized! Technology was already within their grasp. But they were a longshot entry in the galactic sweepstakes anyway, for their sludgy metabolism was simply too slow to compete with warmer, quicker races.

But one race, someday, would reach into space and survive. Or so the Heechee hoped.

And so the Heechee feared, too, for they knew even as they planned their retreat that a race that could catch up with them could also surpass them. But how could that possibility loom near so quickly? It had been only sixty terrestrial years since the last checkup!

Then the distant monitors orbiting the planet Venus had shown the *sapiens* bipeds there, digging out the abandoned Heechee tunnels, exploring their little solar system in spacecraft that moved on jets of chemical flame. Pitiably crude, of course. But promising. In a century or two— four or five centuries at most, the Heechee thought—they would likely enough find the Gateway asteroid. And in a century or two after that they might begin to understand the technology—

But events had moved so swiftly! The human beings had found the Gateway ships, the Food Factory—the immense distant habitat the Heechee had used to pen specimens of Earth's then most promising race, the australopithecines. All had fallen to the humans, and that was not the end of it.

Captain's crew was well trained. When the data had been accepted, and filtered through the massed minds, and tabulated, and summarized, the specialists prepared their reports. White-Noise was the navigator. It was his responsibility to take position fixes on all reported sources and update the ship locator file. Shoe was the communications officer, busiest of all—except perhaps for Mongrel, the integrator, who flew from board to board, whispering to the massed minds and suggesting cross-checks and correlations. Neither Burst, the black-hole-piercer specialist, nor Twice herself, whose skill was in remote handling of slaved equipment, were needed for their specialties at this time, so they backed up the others, as did Captain, the ribbed muscles of his face twisting like serpents as he waited for the consolidated reports.

Mongrel was fond of her Captain, too, and so she gave him the least threatening ones first.

First, there was the fact that Gateway ships had been found and used. Well, there was nothing wrong with that! It was part of the plan, although it was disconcerting to have it happen so soon.

Second, there was the fact that the Food Factory had been found, and the artifact humans called Heechee Heaven. These were old messages, now decades old. Also not serious. Also disconcerting—quite disconcerting, because Heechee Heaven had been designed to trap any ships that docked there, and for two-way contact to have been established meant a quite unexpected sophistication among these upstart bipeds.

Third, there was a message from the sailship people, and that made the tendons in Captain's face writhe faster. Finding a ship in a solar system was one thing—locating one in interstellar space was distressingly impressive.

There is a possible slight confusion here that I should elimi-
nate. Robinette (and all the rest of the human race) called these
people Heechee. Of course, they didn't call themselves that,
any more than native Americans called themselves Indians or
the African Khoi-San tribes called themselves Hottentots and
Bushmen. What the Heechee in fact called themselves was the
intelligent ones. But that proves little. So does *Homo sapiens*.

And fourth—

Fourth was White-Noise's plot of the present whereabouts of all known Heechee vessels now operated by human beings, and when Captain saw that he squeaked with rage and shock. "Plot it against banned spaces!" he commanded. And as soon as the datafans were in place and the combined images appeared, the tendons in his cheeks trembled like plucked harpstrings. "They are exploring black holes," he said, his voice thin.

White-Noise nodded. "There is more," he said. "Some of the vessels carry order disruptors. They can penetrate."

And Mongrel the integrator added: "And it does not seem that they understand the danger signs."

Having given their reports, the rest of the crew waited politely. It was Captain's problem now. They hoped very much that he was going to be able to handle it.

The female named Twice was not exactly in love with Captain, because it wasn't time for that yet, but she knew she would be. Quite soon. Within the next few days, most likely. So in addition to her concern for this astonishing and frightening news, there was also her concern for Captain. He was the one who had his upper lip in the pincer. Although it was not yet time, she reached out and placed her lean hand over his. So deep in thought was Captain that he didn't even notice, but patted it absently.

Shoe made the sniffling sound that was the Heechee equivalent of clearing his throat before asking, "Do you want to establish contact with the massed minds?"

"Not now," hissed Captain, rubbing his ribcage with his free fist. It made a grating noise, loud in the stillness of the cabin. What Captain really wanted to do was to go back into his black hole in the core of the Galaxy and pull the stars up over his head. That was not possible. Next best would be to flee back to that same safe, friendly core and report to higher authority. Higher authority could then make the decisions. They could be the ones to deal with the massed minds of the ancestors, who would be eager to interfere. They could decide what to do about it—if possible, with some other Heechee captain and crew actually dispatched to this terrible swift space to carry out their orders. That was a possible option, but Captain was too well trained to allow himself so easy a way out. He was the one on the scene. Therefore he was the one who should make the first swift responses. If they were wrong—well, pity poor Captain! There would be consequences. Shunning, at least, though that was only for minor offenses. For graver ones there was the equivalent of being kicked upstairs—and Captain was not eager to join that mighty mass of stored minds that were all of his ancestors.

He hissed worriedly and made his decisions. "Inform the massed minds," he ordered.

"Just inform? Not request recommendations?" asked Shoe.

Firmly, "Just inform. Prepare a penetrating drone and send it back to base with a duplicate of all data." This was to Twice, who released his hand and began the task of activating and programing a small message vessel. And finally, to White-Noise: "Set course for the sailship interception point."

It was not the Heechee custom to salute on receiving an order. It was also not the Heechee custom to argue about it, and it was a measure of the confusion in the ship that White-Noise asked, "Are you sure that's what we should do?"

"Do it," said Captain, shrugging irritably.

Actually, it was not a shrug but a quick, violent contraction of his hard, globular abdomen. Twice found herself staring admiringly at that fetching little bulge and at the way the tough, long strings of tendon from shoulder to wrist stood out from the arm itself. Why, your fingers would almost meet as you clung to it!

With a start she realized that her time of loving was closer than she had thought. What an inconvenience! Captain would be as annoyed as she, since they had had plans for a very special day and a half. Twice opened her mouth to tell him, then closed it again. It was no time to trouble him with that; he was completing the thought processes that ridged his cheek muscles and made him scowl, and beginning to give orders.

Captain had plenty of resources to draw on. There were more than a thousand cleverly cached Heechee artifacts scattered around the Galaxy. Not the ones that were meant to be found sooner or later, like Gateway; these were concealed under the exterior appearance of unpromising asteroids in inaccessible orbits, or between stars, or among clusters of other objects in dust swarms and gas clouds. "Twice," he ordered without looking at her, "activate a command ship. We will rendezvous with it at the sailship point."

She was upset, he observed. He was sorry but not surprised—come down to that, he was upset himself! He returned to the command seat and lowered the bones of his pelvis onto the projecting Y-flanges, his life-support pouch fitting neatly into the angle they enclosed.

And became aware that his communications officer was standing over him, face working worriedly. "Yes, Shoe? What is it?"

Shoe's biceps flexed deferentially. "The—" he stammered. "They—The Assassins—"

Captain felt an electric shock of fear. "The *Assassins?*"

"I think there is a danger that they will be disturbed," said Shoe dismally. "The aboriginals are conversing by zero-speed radio."

"Conversing? You mean transmitting messages? Who are you talking about—massed minds!" Captain shouted, leaping out of the seat again. "You mean the aboriginals are sending messages at galactic distances?"

Shoe hung his head. "I am afraid so, Captain. Of course, I do not yet know what they are saying—but there is a great volume of communication."

Captain shook his wrists feebly to signal that he wanted to hear no more. Sending messages! Across the Galaxy! Where anyone might hear! —where, especially, the certain parties the Heechee hoped would not be disturbed at all might well hear. And react to. "Establish translation matrices with the minds," he ordered, and dismally returned to his seat.

The mission was jinxed. Captain no longer had hopes of an idle pleasure cruise, or even of the satisfaction of a minor task well accomplished. The big question in his mind was whether he could get through the next few days.

Still, soon they would transship into the shark-shaped command vessel, fastest of the Heechee fleet, filled with technology. Then his options would increase. Not only was it larger and faster; it carried a number of devices not present on his little penetrator-ship. A TPT. Hole cutters like the ones his ancestors had used to scoop out the Gateway asteroid and the warrens under the surface of Venus. A device to reach into black holes to see what could be plucked out—he shuddered. Please the massed minds of the ancestors, *that* one they would not have to use! But he would have it. And he would have a thousand other useful bits of equipment—

Assuming, that was, that the ship was still functioning and would meet them at the rendezvous.

The artifacts the Heechee had left behind were powerful, strong, and long-lasting. Bar accidents, they were built to last for at least ten million years.

But you could not bar all accidents. A nearby supernova, a malfunctioning part, even a chance collision with some other object—you could harden the artifacts against almost all hazards, but in infinite astronomical time "almost all" is little better than "none."

And if the command ship happened to have failed? And if there were no other that Twice could locate and bring to the rendezvous?

The Heechee learned fairly early in their technological phase
to store the intelligences of dead or dying Heechee in inorganic
systems. That was how the Dead Men came to be stored to
provide company for the boy Wan, and it was an application of
that technology that produced Robin's Here After company. For
the Heechee (if I may venture a possibly not unbiased opinion)
it may have been a mistake. Since they were able to use the
dead minds of Heechee ancestors to store and process data,
they were not very good at true artificial-intelligence systems,
capable of far greater power and flexibility. Like—well—like me.

Captain allowed himself to let the depression sink into his mind. There were too many ifs. And the consequences of each of them too unpleasant to face.

It was not unusual for Captain, or any other Heechee, to be depressed. They had earned it fairly.

When Napoleon's Grand Army crawled back from Moscow their enemies were small harassing cavalry bands, the Russian winter—and despair.

When Hitler's Wehrmacht repeated the same trek thirteen decades later, the main threats were the Soviet tanks and artillery, the Russian winter—and, again, despair. They retreated in better order and with more destruction to their foes. But not with more despair, or less.

Every retreat is a kind of funeral cortege, and the thing that has died is confidence. The Heechee had confidently expected to win a galaxy. When they found they must lose, and began their immense, star-spanning retreat to the core, the magnitude of their defeat was huger than any that humans had ever known, and the despair seeped into all of their souls.

The Heechee were playing a most complicated game. One could call it a team sport, except that few of the players were allowed to be aware that they were on a team at all. The strategies were limited, but the final goal of the game was certain. If they managed to survive as a race, they would win.

But so many pieces moved on that board! And the Heechee had so little control. They could start the game. After that, if they interfered directly they exposed themselves. That was when the game became perilous.

It was now Captain's turn to play, and he knew the risks he ran. He could be the player who lost the game for the Heechee once and for all.

His first task was to preserve the Heechee hiding place as long as possible, which meant doing something about the sailship people.

That was the least of his worries, for the second task was the one that counted. The stolen ship carried equipment that could penetrate even the skin around the Heechee hidey-hole. It could not enter. But it could peer within, and that was bad. Worse, the same equipment could penetrate almost any event discontinuity, even the one that the Heechee themselves dared not enter. The one that they prayed would never be breached, since within it rested the thing they most terribly feared.

So Captain sat there at the controls of his ship, while the glowing silicate cloud that surrounded the core dwindled behind them. Meanwhile, Twice was beginning to show signs of the strain that would shortly press her to her limits; and meanwhile, the cold, sludgy sailship people crept through their long, slow lives; and meanwhile, the one human-manned craft in the universe that could do anything about it approached yet another black hole . . .

And meanwhile, those other players on the great board, Audee Walthers and Janie Yee-xing, watched their stack of chips slowly disappearing as they waited to make their own private gamble.

11
Meeting in Rotterdam

There he stood, this fellow with a face like a tan avocado, blocking my way. I identified the expression before I recognized the face. The expression was obstinacy, irritation, fatigue. The face that displayed them belonged to Audee Walthers, Jr., who (my secretarial program had not failed to tell me) had been trying to get in touch with me for several days. "Hello, Audee," I said, really very cordially, shaking his hand and nodding to the pretty Oriental-looking young woman beside him, "it's great to see you again! Are you staying at this hotel? Wonderful! Listen, I've got to run, but let's have dinner—set it up with the concierge, will you? I'll be back in a couple of hours." And I smiled at him, and smiled at the young woman, and left them standing there.

Now I don't pretend that was really good manners, but as it happens I

actually was in a hurry, and besides, my gut was giving me fits. I put
Essie in a cab going one way and caught another to take me to the court.
Of course, if I had known then what he was waiting to tell me, I might
have been more forthcoming with Walthers. But I didn't know what I
was walking away from.

Or what I was walking toward, for that matter.

For the last little bit I actually did walk, because traffic was more than
normally snarled. There was a parade getting ready to march, as well as
the normal congestion around the International Palace of Justice. The
Palace is a forty-story skyscraper, sunk on caissons into the soapy soil of
Rotterdam. On the outside it dominates half the city. On the inside it's all
scarlet drapes and one-way glass, the very model of a modern international tribunal. It is not a place where you go to to plead to a parking
ticket.

It is not a place where individual human beings are considered very
much at all, in fact, and if I had any vanity, which I do, I would preen
myself on the fact that the lawsuit in which I was technically one of the
defendants actually had fourteen different parties at interest, and four of
them were sovereign states. I even had a suite of offices reserved for my
private use in the Palace itself, because all parties at interest did. But I
didn't go there right away. It was nearly eleven o'clock and therefore at
least an even chance that the court would have started its session for the
day, so I smiled and pushed my way right into the hearing room. It was
crowded. It was always crowded, because there were celebrities to be seen
at the hearings. In my vanity I had thought I was one of them, and I
expected heads to turn when I came in. No heads. No turning. Everybody was watching half a dozen skinny, bearded persons in dashikis and
sandals, sitting in a corral at the plaintiffs' end of the room, drinking
Cokes and giggling among themselves. The Old Ones. You didn't see
them every day. I gawked at them like everybody else, until there was a
touch on my arm and I turned to see Maitre Ijsinger, my flesh-and-blood
lawyer, gazing reprovingly at me. "You are late, Mijnheer Broadhead,"
he whispered. "The Court will have noticed your absence."

Since the Court was busy whispering and arguing among themselves
over, I gathered, the question of whether the diary of the first prospector
to locate a Heechee tunnel on Venus should be admitted as evidence, I
doubted that. But you don't pay a lawyer as much as I was paying Maitre
Ijsinger to argue with him.

Of course, there was no *legal* reason for me to pay him at all. As much
as the case was about anything, it was about a motion on the part of the
Empire of Japan to dissolve the Gateway Corporation. I came into it, as a

The Heechee, thinking that the australopithecines they discovered when they first visited the Earth would ultimately evolve a technological civilization, decided to preserve a colony of them in a sort of zoo. Their descendants were "the Old Ones." Of course, that was a wrong guess on the part of the Heechee. Australopithecus never achieved intelligence, only extinction. It was a sobering reflection for human beings to realize that the so-called Heechee Heaven, later rechristened the *S. Ya. Broadhead*—far the largest and most sophisticated starship the human race had ever seen—was in fact only a sort of monkey cage.

major stockholder in the *S. Ya.*'s charter business, because the Bolivians had brought suit to have the charter revoked on the grounds that the financing of the colonists amounted to a "return to slavery." The colonists were called indentured servants, and I, among others, had been called a wicked exploiter of human misery. What were the Old Ones doing there? Why, they were parties at interest, too, because they claimed that the *S. Ya.* was their property—they and their ancestors had lived there for hundreds of thousands of years. Their position in the court was a little complicated. They were wards of the government of Tanzania, because that's where their ancestral Earth home had been decreed to be, but Tanzania wasn't represented in the courtroom. Tanzania was boycotting the Palace of Justice because of an unfavorable decision over their sea-bottom missiles the year before, so its affairs were being handled by Paraguay—which was actually taking an interest mostly because of a border dispute with Brazil, which in turn was present as host to the headquarters of the Gateway Corp. You follow all this? Well, I didn't, but that was why I hired Maitre Ijsinger.

If I let myself get personally involved in every lousy multimillion dollar lawsuit, I'd spend all my time in court. I've got too much to do with the remainder of my life for that, so in the normal course of events I would have let the lawyers fight it out and spent my time more profitably, chatting with Albert Einstein or wading along the Tappan Sea with my wife. However, there were special reasons for being here. I saw one of them, half asleep, on a leather chair near the Old Ones. "I think I'll see if Joe Kwiatkowski wants a cup of coffee," I told Ijsinger.

Kwiatkowski was a Pole, representing the East Europe Economic Community, and one of the plaintiffs in the case. Ijsinger turned pale. "He's an *adversary!*" he hissed.

"He's also an old friend," I told him, exaggerating the facts of the case only slightly—he had been a Gateway prospector, too, and we'd had drinks over old times before.

"There are no friends in a court action of this magnitude," Ijsinger informed me, but I only smiled at him and leaned forward to hiss at Kwiatkowski, who came along willingly enough once he was awake.

"I should not be here with you, Robin," he rumbled once we were in my fifteenth-floor suite. "Especially for coffee! Don't you got something to put in it?"

Well, I had—slivovitz, and from his favorite Cracow distillery, too. And Kampuchean cigars, the brand he liked, and salt herring and biscuits to go with them all.

The court was built over a little canal off the Maas River, and you could smell the water. Because I had managed to get a window open, you could hear the boats going through under the building's arch and traffic from the tunnel under the Maas a quarter kilometer away. I opened the window a little wider because of Kwiatkowski's cigar, and saw the flags and bands in the side streets. "What are they parading for today?" I asked.

He brushed the question aside. "Because armies like parades," he grunted. "Now, no fooling around, Robin. I know what you want and it is impossible."

"What I want," I said, "is for the Eeek to help wipe out the terrorists with the spaceship, which is obviously in the interest of everybody. You tell me that's impossible. Fine, I accept that, but *why* is it impossible?"

"Because you know nothing of politics. You think the E.E.E.C. can go to the Paraguayans and say, 'Listen, go and make a deal with Brazil, say you will be more flexible on this border dispute if they will pool their information with the Americans so the terrorist spaceship can be trapped.' "

"Yes," I said, "that is exactly what I think."

"And you are wrong. They will not listen."

"The Eeek," I said patiently, having been well briefed for this purpose by my data-retrieval system, Albert, "is Paraguay's biggest trading partner. If you whistle they jump."

"In most cases, yes. In this case, no. The key to the situation is the Republic of Kampuchea. They have with Paraguay private arrangements. About these I will say nothing, except that they have been approved at the highest level. More coffee," he added, holding out his coffee cup, "and this time, please, not so much coffee in it."

I did not ask Kwiatkowski what the "private arrangements" were because, if he had been willing to tell me, he would not have called them private. I didn't have to. They were military. All the "private arrangements" governments were making with each other these days were military, and if I had not been sweating about the terrorists I would have been sweating about the crazy way the world's duly ordained governments were behaving. But one thing at a time.

So, on Albert's advice, I got a lawyer from Malaysia into my private parlor next, and after her a missionary from Canada, and then a general in the Albanian Air Force, and for each one I had some bait to dangle. Albert told me what levers to pull and what glass beads to offer the natives—an extra allotment of colonization passages here, a "charitable" contribution there. Sometimes all it took was a smile. Rotterdam was the place to do it, because ever since the Palace was moved from The Hague, The Hague having been pretty well messed up in the troubles the last time some joker was fooling with a TPT, you could find anyone you wanted in Rotterdam. All kinds of people. All colors, all sexes, in all kinds of costumes, from Ecuadorian lawyers in miniskirts to Marshall Islands thermal-energy barons in sarongs and shark's-teeth necklaces. Whether I was making progress or not was hard to say, but at half-past twelve, my belly telling me that it was going to hurt in a serious way if I didn't put some food in it, I knocked off for the morning. I thought longingly of our nice quiet hotel suite with a nice lukewarm steak from room service and my shoes off, but I had promised to meet Essie at her place of business. So I told Albert to prepare an estimate of what I had accomplished and recommendations about what I should do next, and fought my way to a cab.

You can't miss one of Essie's fast-food franchises. The glowing blue Heechee-metal arches are in just about every country of the world. As the Boss she had a roped-off section on the balcony reserved for us, and she met me coming up the stairs with a kiss, a frown, and a dilemma. "Robin! Listen! They want here to serve mayonnaise with the French fries. Should I allow?"

I kissed her back, but I was peering over her shoulder to see what ungodly messes were being set out on our tables. "That's really up to you," I told her.

"Yes, of course, is up to me. But is important, Robin! Have taken great care in meticulous duplication of true pommes-frites, you know. Now mayonnaise?" Then she stepped back and gave me a more thorough look, and her expression changed. "So tired! So many lines in the face! Robin, how are you feeling?"

I gave her my most charming smile. "Just hungry, my dear," I cried, and gazed with deceitful enthusiasm at the plates before me. "Say! That looks good, what is it, a taco?"

"Is chapatti," she said with pride. "Taco is over there. Also blini. See how you like, then." So, of course, I had to taste them all, and it was not at all what my belly had asked for. The taco, the chapatti, the rice balls with sour fish sauce, the stuff that tasted, more than anything else, like boiled barley. They were not any of them my cup of tea. But they were all edible.

They were also all gifts of the Heechee. The great insight the Heechee had given us was that most of living tissue, including yours and mine, is made up of just four elements: carbon, hydrogen, oxygen, and nitrogen— C H O N—CHON-food. Since that is also what the gases that comprise the best part of a comet are made of, they built their Food Factory out in the Oort cloud, where our Sun's comets hang waiting for a star to shake them loose and send them in to be pretty in our sky.

CHON isn't all of it. You need a few other elements. Sulfur's the most important, maybe, then perhaps sodium, magnesium, phosphorus, chlorine, potassium, calcium—not to mention the odd dash of cobalt to make vitamin B-12, chromium for glucose tolerance, iodine for the thyroid, and lithium, fluorine, arsenic, selenium, molybdenum, cadmium, and tin for the hell of it. You probably need the whole periodic table at least as traces, but most of the elements in quantities so small that you don't have to worry about adding them to the stew. They show up as contaminants whether you want them or not. So Essie's food chemists cooked up batches of sugar and spice and everything nice and produced food for everybody—not only what would keep them alive, but pretty much what they wanted to eat, wherefore the chapattis and the rice balls. You can make anything out of CHON-food if you stir it up right. Among the other things Essie was making out of it was a lot of money, and that turned out to be a game she delighted to play.

So when I finally settled down with something my stomach didn't resist—it looked like a hamburger and tasted like an avocado salad with bacon bits in it, and Essie had named it the Big Chon—Essie was up and down every minute. Checking the temperature of the infra-red warming lights, looking for grease under the dishwashing machines, tasting the desserts, raising hell because the milkshakes were too thin.

I had Essie's word that nothing in her chain would hurt anybody, though my stomach had less confidence in her word than I did. I didn't like the noise from the street outside—was it the parade?—but outside of that I was as close to comfortable as I was likely to get just then. Relaxed enough to appreciate a turnaround in our status. When Essie and I go out in public, people look at us, and usually I'm the one they look at. Not here. In Essie's franchise stores, Essie was the star. Outside the passersby were gathering to watch the parade. Inside no employee gave it a glance. They went about their jobs with all their back muscles tense, and all the surreptitious glances they sneaked went in the same direction, to the great lady boss. Well, not very ladylike, really; Essie has had the benefit of a quarter-century's tuition in the English language from an expert—me—but when she gets excited it's "nekulturny" and "khuligans!" all over the place.

I moved to the second-floor window to look out at the parade. It was coming straight down Weena, ten abreast, with bands and shouting and placards. Nuisance. Maybe worse than a nuisance. Across the street, in front of the station, there was a scuffle, with cops and placards, rearmers against pacifists. You couldn't tell which was which from the way they clubbed each other with the placards, and Essie, rejoining me and picking up her own Big Chon, glanced at them and shook her head. "How's sandwich?" she demanded.

"Fine," I said, with my mouth full of carbon, hydrogen, oxygen, and nitrogen, plus trace elements. She gave me a speak-louder look. "I said it's *fine,*" I amplified.

"I couldn't hear you with all that noise," she complained, licking her lips—she liked what she sold.

I jerked my head toward the parade. "I don't know if this is so good," I said.

"I think not," she agreed, looking with distaste at a company of what I think they call Zouaves—anyway, dark-skinned marchers in uniform. I couldn't see their national patches, but each one of them was carrying a rapid-fire shoulder weapon and playing tricks with it: spinning it around, bouncing the buttplate against the pavement and making it spring back into his hands, all without breaking stride.

"Maybe we'd better start back to the court," I said.

She reached over and picked up the last crumb of my sandwich. Some Russian women melt down into spheres of fat when they get past forty, and some shrink and shrivel. Not Essie. She still had the straight back and narrow waist that first caught my eye. "Perhaps we should," she said, beginning to gather up her computer programs, each on its own datafan. "Have seen enough uniforms as a child, do not specially want to see all these now."

"You can't really have much of a parade without uniforms."

"Not just parade. Look. On sidewalks, too." And it was true, about one man or woman in four was wearing some sort of uniform. It was a little surprising, because it had crept up on me. Of course, every country had always had some sort of armed forces, but they were just sort of kept in a closet, like a home fire extinguisher. People never actually saw them. But now people did, more and more.

"Still," she said, conscientiously sweeping CHON crumbs off the table onto the disposable platelet and looking for the waste hamper, "you must be quite tired and we had better go. Give me your trash, please."

I waited for her at the door, and she was frowning when she joined me. "Receptacle was almost full. In manual it is set forth clearly, empty at sixty-percent point—what will they do if large party leaves at once? I should go back and instruct manager—oh, hell," she cried, her expression changing. "Have forgotten my programs!" And she dashed back up the stairs to where she had left her datafans.

I stood in the door, waiting for her, my eyes on the parade. It was quite disgusting! There were actual weapons going by, antiaircraft missile launchers and armored vehicles; and behind a bagpipe band was a company of the tommygun twirlers. I felt the door move behind me and stepped aside out of the way just as Essie pushed it open. "I found, Robin," she said, smiling and holding the thick sheaf of fans up as I turned toward her.

And something like a wasp snarled past my left ear.

There are no wasps in Rotterdam. Then I saw Essie falling backward, and the door closing on her. It was not a wasp. It was a gunshot. One of those twirled weapons had held a live charge, and it had gone off.

I nearly lost Essie once before. It was a long time ago, but I hadn't forgotten. All that old woe welled up as fresh as yesterday as I pulled the stupid door out of the way and bent over her. She was lying on her back, with the sheaf of tied datafans over her face, and as I lifted it away I saw that although her face was bloody her eyes were wide open and looking at me.

"Hey, Rob!" she said, her voice puzzled. "You punch me?"

"Hell, no! What would I punch you for?" One of the counter girls came rushing with a wad of paper napkins. I grabbed them away from her and pointed to the red-and-white striped electrovan with the words *Poliklinische centrum* stenciled on its side, idling at an intersection because of the parade. "You! Get that ambulance over here! And get the cops, too, while you're at it!"

Essie sat up, pushing my arm away as cops and counter attendants swarmed around us. "Why ambulance, Robin?" she asked reasonably. "Is only a bloody nose, look!" And indeed that was all there was. It had been a bullet, all right, but it had hit the sheaf of fans and stayed there. "My programs!" Essie wailed, tugging against the policeman who wanted them to extract the bullet for evidence. But they were ruined anyway. And so was my day.

While Essie and I were having our little brush with destiny, Audee Walthers was taking his friend sightseeing around the town of Rotterdam. He had been sweating as he left me; the presence of a lot of money does that to people. The absence of money took most of the joy out of Rotterdam for Walthers and Yee-xing. Still, to Walthers, the hayseeds of Peggys Planet still in his hair, and to Yee-xing, rarely away from the *S. Ia.* and the immediate vicinity of the launch loops, Rotterdam was a metropolis. They couldn't afford to buy anything, but at least they could look in the windows. At least Broadhead had agreed to see them, Walthers kept telling himself; but when he allowed himself to think it with some satisfaction, the darker side of Walthers responded with savage contempt: Broadhead had *said* he would see them. But he sure-hell hadn't seemed very anxious about it . . .

"Why am I sweating?" he asked out loud.

Yee-xing slipped her arm through his for moral support. "It will be all right," she replied indirectly, "one way or another." Audee Walthers looked down at her gratefully. Walthers was not particularly tall, but Janie Yee-xing was tiny; all of her was tiny except for her eyes, lustrous and black, and that was surgery, a silliness from a time when she had been in love with a Swedish merchant banker and thought it was only the epicanthic fold that kept him from loving her back. "Well? Shall we go in?"

Walthers had no idea what she was talking about, and must have shown it by his frown; Yee-xing butted his shoulder with her small, close-cropped head and looked up toward a storefront sign. In pale letters hanging in what looked like empty ebon space it said:

Here After

Walthers examined it and then looked at the woman again. "It's an undertakers'," he guessed, and laughed as he thought he saw the point of her joke. "But we're not that bad off yet, Janie."

"It's not," she said, "or not exactly. Don't you recognize the name?" And then, of course, he did: It was one of the many Robinette Broadhead holdings on the list.

The more you learned about Broadhead, the more likely you could figure out what things would make him agree to a deal; that was sense. "Why not?" said Walthers, approving, and led her through the air curtain into the cool, dark recesses of the shop. If it was not a funeral establishment, it had at least bought from the same decorators. There was soft, unidentifiable music in the background, and a fragrance of wildflowers, although the only floral display in sight was a single sheaf of bright roses in a crystal vase. A tall, handsome, elderly man rose before them; Walthers could not say whether he had got up from one of the chairs or materialized as a hologram. The figure smiled warmly at them, tried to guess their nationalities. He got it wrong. *"Guten tag,"* he said to Walthers, and *"Gor ho oy-ney,"* to Yee-xing.

"We both speak English," Walthers said. "Do you?"

Urbane eyebrows lifted. "Of course. Welcome to Here After. Is there someone near to you who is about to die?"

"Not that I know of," said Walthers.

"I see. Of course, we can still accomplish a great deal even if the person has already reached metabolic death, although the sooner we begin transfer the better—Or are you wisely making plans for your own future?"

"Neither one," said Yee-xing, "we just want to know what it is you offer."

"Of course." The man smiled, gesturing them to a comfortable couch. He did not appear to do anything to bring it about, but the lights became a touch brighter and the music dwindled a few decibels. "My card," he said, producing a pasteboard for Walthers and answering the question that had been bothering him: The card was tangible, and so were the fingers that handed it to him. "Let me run through the basics for you; it will save time in the long run. To begin with, Here After is not a religious organization and does not claim to provide salvation. What we do offer is a form of survival. Whether you—the 'you' that is here in this room at this moment—will be 'aware' of it or not"—he smiled—"is a matter that the metaphysicians are still arguing. But the storage of your personalities, should you elect to provide for it, is guaranteed to pass Turing's Test, provided we are able to begin transfer while the brain is still in good condition, and the surroundings that the surviving client perceives will be those which he chooses from our available list. We have more than two hundred environments to offer, ranging—"

Yee-xing snapped her fingers. "The Dead Men," she said, suddenly comprehending.

The salesperson nodded, although his expression tightened a bit. "That is what the originals were called, yes. I see that you are familiar with the artifact called Heechee Heaven, now being used as a transport for colonists—"

"I'm the transport's Third Officer," Yee-xing said, quite truthfully except for tenses, "and my friend here is her Seventh."

"I envy you," the salesman said, and the expression on his face suggested that he really meant it. Envy did not keep him from delivering his sales pitch and Walthers listened attentively, Janie Yee-xing's hand holding his. He appreciated the hand; it kept him from thinking about the Dead Men and their protégé, Wan—or, at least, about what Wan was likely to be doing at that moment.

The original Dead Men, the salesperson declared, were unfortunately rather botched; the transfer of their memories and personalities from the wet, gray storage receptacle in their skulls to the crystalline datastores that preserved them after death had been accomplished by unskilled la-

When the programs and databases for the so-called Dead Men became available for study, my creator, S. Ya. Broadhead, was naturally greatly interested. She set herself the task of duplicating their work. The most complex task was, of course, the transcription of the database of a human brain and nervous system, which is stored chemically and redundantly, onto the Heechee datafans. She did very well. Not only well enough to franchise the Here After chain, but well enough—well—to create me. The Here After storage was based on her earliest research. Later on she got better—better even than the Heechee —for she was able to combine not only their techniques but independent human technology. The Dead Men could never pass a Turing Test. Essie Broadhead's works, after a while, could. And did.

bor, using equipment that had been designed for quite a different species in the first place. So the storage was imperfect. The easiest way to think of it, the salesman explained, was to think the Dead Men had been so stressed by their unskilled transfer that they had gone mad. But that happened no longer. Now the storage procedures had been so refined that any deceased could carry on a conversation with his survivors so deftly that it was just like talking to the real person. More! The "patient" had an active life in the datastores. He could experience the Moslem, Christian, or Scientological Heaven, complete with, respectively, beautiful boys scattered like pearls on the grass, choirs of angels, or the presence of L. Ron Hubbard himself. If his bent was not religious, he could experience adventure (mountain-climbing, skin-diving, skiing, hang-gliding, and free-fall T'ai chi were popular selections), listening to music of any kind, in any company he chose . . . and, of course (the salesman, failing to estimate reliably the relationship between Walthers and Yee-xing, delivered the information without color), sex. *All* varieties of the sexual experience. Over and over.

"How boring," said Walthers, thinking about it.

"For you and me," the salesman granted, "but not for them. You see, they don't remember the programatic experiences very clearly. There's an accelerated decay bias applied to those datastores. Not to the others. If you talk to a dear one today and come back a year from now and pick up the conversation, he'll remember it exactly. But the programed experiences dwindle fast in their memories—just as recollection of pleasure, you see, so that they want to experience them again and again."

"How horrible," said Yee-xing. "Audee, I think it's time we went to the hotel."

"Not yet, Janie. What was that about talking to them?"

The salesman's eyes gleamed. "Certainly. Some of them really enjoy talking, even to strangers. You have a moment? It's very simple, really." As he was talking he led them to a PV console, consulted a silk-bound directory, and punched out a series of code numbers. "I've actually become friendly with some of them," he said bashfully. "When things are slow at the store, a lot of the time I call one of them up and we have a nice chat—Ah, Rex! How are you?"

"Why, I'm just fine," said the handsome, bronzed senior citizen who appeared in the PV. "How nice to see you! I don't think I know your friends?" he added, peering in a friendly way at Walthers and Yee-xing. If there was an ideal way for a man to appear when he passed a certain age, this was it; he had all his hair and seemed to have all his teeth; his face showed laugh wrinkles at the corners of his eyes but was otherwise un-

lined, and his eyes were bright and warm. He acknowledged the introductions politely. Questioned about what he was doing he shrugged mod-
estly. "I'm about to sing the Catulli Carmina with the Wien Staatsoper,
you know." He winked. "The lead soprano is very beautiful, and I think
those sexy lyrics have been getting to her in rehearsal."

"Amazing," murmured Walthers, gazing at him. But Janie Yee-xing
was less enchanted.

"We really don't want to keep you from your music," she said politely,
"and I'm afraid we'd better get along."

"They'll wait," Rex declared fondly. "They always do."

Walthers was fascinated. "Tell me," he said, "when you talk about, ah,
companionship in this, ah, state—can you have your choice of any companions you want? Even if they're still alive?"

The question was aimed at the salesman, but Rex spoke first. He was
gazing shrewdly and sympathetically at Walthers. "Anyone at all," he
said, nodding as though they shared a confidence. "Anyone living or
dead or imaginary. And, Mr. Walthers, they'll do anything you want
them to!" The figure chuckled. "What I always say," he added, "is that
what you call 'life' is really only a sort of entr'acte to the *real* existence
you get here. I just can't understand why people put it off for so long!"

The Here Afters were, as a matter of fact, one of the little spinoff
enterprises that I was fondest of, not because they earned much money.
When we discovered that the Heechee had been able to store dead minds
in machines a light clicked. Well, says I to my good wife, if they can do it,
why can't we? Well, says my good wife to me, no reason at all, Robin, to
be sure, just give me a little time to work out the encoding. I had not
made any decision about whether I wanted it done to me, when and if. I
was quite sure, though, that I didn't want it done to Essie, at least not
right then, and so I was glad that the bullet had done no more than puff
her nose.

Well, somewhat more. It involved us with the Rotterdam police. The
uniformed sergeant introduced us to the brigadier, who took us in his big
fast car with the lights going to the bureau and offered us coffee. Then
Brigadier Zuitz showed us into the office of Inspector Van Der Waal, a
great huge woman with old-fashioned contact lenses making her eyes
bulge out with sympathy. It was How unpleasant for you, Mijnheer, and
I hope your wound is not painful, Mevrouw, as she was leading us up the
stairs—stairs!—to the office of Commissaris Lutzlek, who was a different
kettle of fish altogether. Short. Slim. Fair, with a sweet boy's face, though
he had to be at least fifty to have become a Principal Commissaire. You

could imagine him putting his thumb in the dyke and hanging in there forever, if he had to, or until he drowned. But you could not imagine him giving up. "Thank you for coming in about this business in the Stationsplein," he said, making sure we had seats.

"The accident," I said.

"No. Regretfully, not an accident. If it had been an accident, it would have been a matter for the municipal police rather than for me. So therefore this inquiry, for which we ask your cooperation."

I said, to put him in his place, "Our time is pretty valuable to be spent in this sort of thing."

He was not puttable. "Your life is even more valuable."

"Oh, come on! One of the soldiers in the parade was doing his twirling act, and he had a round in his gun and it went off."

"Mijnheer Broadhead," he said, "first, no soldier had a round in his gun; the guns are without firing pins in any case. Second, the soldiers are not even soldiers; they are college students hired to dress up for parades, just like the guards at Buckingham Palace. Third, the shot did not come from the parade."

"How do you know?"

"Because the gun has been found." He looked very angry. "In a police locker! This is quite embarrassing to me, Mijnheer, as you can imagine. There were many extra policemen for the parade, and they used a portable dressing-room van. The 'policeman' who fired the weapon was a stranger to others in the unit, but then they were drawn from many detachments. Come to clean up after the parade, he dressed quickly and left, with his locker open. There was nothing in it but the uniform—stolen, I suppose—and the gun, and a picture of you. Not of Mevrouw. Of you."

He sat back and waited. The sweet boy's face was peaceful.

I was not. It takes a minute to sink in, the announcement that somebody has the fixed intention of killing you. It was scary. Not just being killed; that's scary by definition, and I can testify to how scared I can get when it looks like death is near, out of unforgotten and even repeated experience. But murder is worse than ordinary death. I said, "You know how that makes me feel? Guilty! I mean, I must have done something that really made somebody hate me."

"Exactly so, Mijnheer Broadhead. What do you suppose it could have been?"

"I have no idea. If you find the man, I suppose you can find the reason. That shouldn't be too hard—there must be fingerprints or something? I saw news cameras, perhaps there's even a picture of him on somebody's film—"

He sighed. "Mijnheer, please do not tell me how to conduct police routine. All those things are of course being followed up, plus depth interviews with everyone who might have seen the man, plus sweat analysis of the clothes, plus all other means of identification. I am assuming this man was a professional, and therefore those means will not succeed. So we approach it from the other direction. Who are your enemies, and what are you doing in Rotterdam?"

"I don't think I have any enemies. Business rivals, maybe, but they don't assassinate people."

He waited patiently, so I added, "As to what I'm doing in Rotterdam, I think that's quite well known. My business interests include some share in the exploitation of some Heechee artifacts."

"This is known," he said, not quite so patient.

I shrugged. "So I am a party in a suit at the International Palace of Justice."

The commissaris opened one of his desk drawers, peered inside, and slammed it again moodily. "Mijnheer Broadhead," he said, "you have had many meetings here in Rotterdam not connected with this suit, but instead with the question of terrorism. You wish it stopped."

"We all want that," I said, but the feeling in my belly was not just my degenerating pipes. I had thought I was being very secretive.

"We all want it, but you are doing something about it, Mijnheer. Therefore I believe you now do have enemies. The enemies of us all. The terrorists." He stood up and offered us the door. "So while you are in my jurisdiction I will see that you have police protection. After that, I can only urge caution, for I believe you are in danger from them."

"Everybody is," I said.

"Everybody is at random, yes. But you are now a particular case."

Our hotel had been built in the palmy days, for big-spending tourists and the jet-set rich. The best suites were decorated for their tastes. Not always for ours. Neither Essie nor I was into straw mats and wood-block pillows, but the management moved all that out and moved in the right kind of bed. Round and huge. I was looking forward to getting a lot of use out of it. Not so much use out of the lobby, which was a kind of architecture I hated: cantilevered walkways, more fountains than Versailles, so many mirrors that when you looked up you thought you were in outer space. Through the good offices of the commissaris, or anyway of the young cop he sent to escort us home, we were spared that. We were whisked through a service entrance, up a padded elevator that smelled of room-service food, to our own landing, where there had been a change in the decoration. Just across from our suite door there was a marble Winged Venus in the stairwell. Now it had a companion in a blue suit, a perfectly ordinary-looking man, studiously not meeting my eye. I looked at the cop escorting us. She grinned in embarrassment, nodded to her colleague in the stairwell, and closed the door behind us.

We were a particular case, all right.

I sat down and regarded Essie. Her nose was still somewhat swollen, but it did not seem to trouble her. Still, "Maybe you ought to go to bed," I suggested.

She looked at me with tolerant affection. "For a bloodied nose, Robin? How very foolish you are. Or do you have some more interesting project in mind?"

It is a true tribute to my dear wife that as soon as she brought the subject up, my damaged day and my damaged colon to the contrary notwithstanding, I did indeed have something in mind. After twenty-five years you would think that even sex would begin to get boring. My data-retrieval friend Albert had told me about studies of laboratory animals that proved that that was inevitable. Male rats were left with their mates and their frequency of intercourse measured. There was a steady decline over time. Boredom. Then they took away the old mates and introduced new ones. The rats perked up and went to it with a will. So this was established scientific fact—for rats—but I guess that I am not, at least in that sense, a rat. In fact, I was enjoying myself quite a lot when, without warning, someone shoved a dagger right into my belly.

I couldn't help it. I yelled.

Essie pushed me away. She sat up swiftly, calling for Albert in Russian. Obediently his hologram sprang into life. He squinted toward me and nodded. "Yes," he said, "please, Mrs. Broadhead, place Robin's wrist against the dispenser on the bedside table."

I was bent double, hugging myself against the pain. For a moment I thought I was going to vomit, but what was in my gut was too bad to be expelled so easily. "Do something!" cried Essie, frantically pulling me to her bare breast as she pressed my arm against the table.

"I am already doing it, Mrs. Broadhead," said Albert, and as a matter of fact I could appreciate the sudden sense of numbness as the injection needle force-sprayed something into my arm. The pain receded and became bearable. "You are not to be unduly alarmed, Robin," Albert said kindly, "nor you, Mrs. Broadhead. I have been anticipating this sudden ischemic pain for some hours. It is only a symptom."

"Damn arrogant program," cried Essie, who had written him, "symptom of what?"

"Of the beginning of the final rejection process, Mrs. Broadhead. It is not yet critical, especially as I am already administering medication along with the analgesia. Still, I propose surgery tomorrow."

I was feeling better enough already to sit up on the edge of the bed. I traced with my toe the design of arrows pointing toward Mecca that had been worked into the rug for long-gone big-spending oil magnates and said, "What about tissue match?"

"That has been arranged, Robin."

I let go of my stomach experimentally. It didn't explode. "I have a lot of appointments tomorrow," I pointed out.

Essie, who had been rocking me gently, let go and sighed. "Obstinate man! Why put off? Could have had transplant weeks ago and all this nonsense not necessary."

"I didn't want to," I explained, "and anyway, Albert said there was time."

"Was time! Oh, of course, was time. Is that reason to use time all up with fiddling and faddling until, oh, sorry, suddenly unexpected event takes place and time is all gone and you die? Like you warm and alive, Robin, not Here After program!"

I nuzzled her with my nose and chin. "Sick man! Get away from me!" she snarled, but did not draw away. "Huh! You feel better now."

"Quite a lot better."

"Good enough to talk sensibly and make appointment with hospital?"

I blew in her ear. "Essie," I said, "I positively will, but not right this minute, because, if I remember correctly, you and I have some unfinished business. Not Albert, though. So you will please turn yourself off, old friend."

"Certainly, Robin." He grinned and disappeared. But Essie held me off, staring into my face for a long time before she shook her head.

"You Robin," she said. "You want me to write you as Here After program?"

"Not a bit," I said, "and actually, right now that's not what I want to discuss."

"Discuss!" she scoffed. "Ha, I know how you discuss. . . . All I wanted to say is, if I do write you, Robin, you bet in some ways I write you much different!"

It had been quite a day. It was not surprising that I didn't remember certain unimportant details. My secretary program remembered, of course, and so I got a hint when the service door to the butler's pantry opened and a procession of room-service waiters came in with dinner. Not for two. For four.

"Oh, my God," said Essie, striking her forehead with the back of her hand. "Your poor friend with face like frog, Robin, you have invited for dinner! And look at you! Bare feet! Sitting in underwear! Nekulturny indeed, Robin. Go and dress at once!"

I stood up, because there was no use arguing, but I argued anyway. "If I'm in my underwear, what about you?"

She gave me a scathing look. Actually, she wasn't in her underwear; she was wearing one of those Chinese things slit up the side. It looked as much like a dress as it did a nightgown, and she used it interchangeably for both.

"In case of Nobel laureate," she said reprovingly, "what one wears is defining what is proper. Also have showered and you have not, so do so, for you smell of sexual activity—and, oh, my God," she added, cocking an ear to sounds at the door, "I think are here already!"

I headed for the bathroom as she went for the door, and lingered long enough to hear sounds of argument. The least expert of the room-service waiters was listening, too, a frown on his face and his hand reaching unconsciously toward the bulge under his armpit. I sighed, and left it to them, and headed for the bathroom.

Actually, it wasn't a bathroom. All by itself it was a bath suite. The tub was big enough for two persons. Maybe for three or four, but I hadn't been thinking in any numbers higher than two—though it did make me wonder just what those Arab tourists had liked doing in their baths. There was concealed lighting in the tub itself, statuary surrounding it that poured out hot water or cold, a deep pile rug throughout. All the vulgar little things like toilets were in decorous little cubicles of their own. It was fancy, but it was nice. "Albert," I called, pulling a blouse over my head, and he answered:

"Yes, Robin?"

There was no video in the bath, just his voice. I said, "I kind of like this. See if you can get me plans for putting one like this into the place at Tappan Sea."

"Certainly, Robin," he said, "but meanwhile, may I remind you that your guests are waiting?"

"You may, because you just did."

"And also, Robin, you are not to overexert yourself. The medication I gave you will be of purely temporary value, unless—"

"Turn yourself off," I ordered, and entered the main reception salon to greet my guests. A table had been set with crystal and china, candles were burning, wine was in a cooler, and the waiters were standing politely at attention. Even the one with the bulge under his arm. "Sorry I kept you waiting, Audee," I said, beaming at them, "but it's been a hard day."

"Have told them," said Essie, passing a plate to the young Oriental girl. "Was necessary, as stupid policeman at door considered them likely terrorists, too."

"I tried to explain," grumbled Walthers, "but he didn't speak any English. Mrs. Broadhead had to sort him out. It's a good thing you speak Dutch."

She shrugged graciously. "Speak Deutsch, speak Dutch. Is same thing, provided one speaks loud. Also," she said informatively, "is only a state of mind. Tell me, Captain Walthers. You go to speak language, other person does not understand. What do you think?"

"Well, I think I haven't said it right."

"Ha! Exactly. But I, I think he has not *understood* it right. This is basic rule for speaking foreign language."

I rubbed my belly. "Let's eat," I said, and led the way to the table. But I had not failed to notice the look Essie gave me, so I exerted myself to be sociable. "Well, we're a sad-looking lot," I said genially, making note of the cast on Walthers's wrist, the bruise on Yee-xing's face, Essie's still puffy nose. "Been punching each other out, have you?"

As it turned out, that was not tactful, since Walthers promptly informed me that indeed they had, under the influence of the terrorists' TPT. So we talked about the terrorists for a while. And then we talked about the sad condition the human race had got itself into. It was not a cheerful conversation, especially as Essie decided to get philosophical.

"What a rotten thing human being is," she offered, and then reversed herself. "No. Am unjust. One human being can be quite fine, even as fine as we four sitting here. Not perfect. But on a statistical basis out of let us say one hundred chances to display kindness, altruism, decency—all these traits we humans esteem, you see—will in fact perform no fewer than twenty-five of them. But nations? Political groups? Terrorists?" She shook her head. "Out of one hundred chances, zero," she said. "Or perhaps one, but then, you may be sure, with some trick up sleeve. You see, wickedness is additive. Is perhaps one grain in each human being. But add up quantity of say ten million human beings in even small country or group, equals evil enough to damage entire world!"

"I'm ready for dessert," I said, gesturing to the waiters.

You would think that was a broad enough hint for any guest to take, especially considering that they already knew we'd had a bad day, but Walthers was obstinate. He lingered over dessert. He insisted on telling me his life's story, and he kept looking at the waiters, and all in all I was getting quite uncomfortable, not just in the belly.

Essie says I am not patient with people. Perhaps so. The friends I am most comfortable interacting with are computer programs rather than flesh and blood, and they don't have feelings to hurt—well, I'm not sure that's true for Albert. But it is for, say, my secretarial program or my chef. It is certain that I was getting impatient with Audee Walthers. His life had been a dull soap opera. He had lost his wife and his savings. He had made unauthorized use of equipment on the *S. Ya.* with Yee-xing's connivance and got her fired. He had spent his last dime to get here to Rotterdam, reason not specified, but clearly it had something to do with me.

Well, I am not unwilling to "loan" money to a friend down on his luck but, see, I was in no mood. It was not just the fright over Essie or the screwed-up day, or the nagging worry about whether the next nut with a gun would actually get me. There was my damned gut giving me fits. At last I told the waiters to clear off, though Walthers was still lingering over his fourth cup of coffee. I stomped over to the table with the liqueurs and cigars and glowered at him as he followed. "What is it, Audee?" I said, no longer polite. "Money? How much do you need?"

And I got such a look from him! He hesitated, watching while the last of the waiters filed out through the pantry, and then he let me have it. "It isn't what I need," he said, his voice trembling, "it's what you're willing to pay for something you want. You're a real rich man, Broadhead. Maybe you don't worry about people who stick their asses in a crack for you, but I made the mistake of doing it twice."

I don't like being reminded I owe a favor, either, but I didn't get a chance to say anything. Janie Yee-xing put her hand on his bad wrist—gently. "Just tell him what you've got," she ordered.

"Tell me what?" I demanded, and the son of a gun shrugged and said, the way you might tell me you'd found my car keys on the floor:

"Why, tell you that I've found what I think is a real, live Heechee."

12
God and the Heechee

I found a Heechee . . . I've got a fragment of the True Cross . . . I talked with God, literally I did—those statements are all in the same league. You don't believe them, but they scare you. And then, if you find they're true, or if you can't be sure they're not—then it's miracle time, and scared-to-death time. God and the Heechee. When I was a kid I didn't distinguish greatly between them, and even as a grownup the confusion was still there.

It was past midnight when I was finally willing to let them go. By then I'd sucked them dry. I had the datafan they'd swiped from the *S. Ya.* I had brought Albert in on the discussion to ask all the questions his fertile digital mind could invent. I was feeling pretty rotten and frayed, and the analgesia had long worn off, but I couldn't go to sleep. Essie announced firmly that if I was determined to kill self with overexertion she was at least going to stay up to enjoy spectacle, and as soon as she was gently snoring on the couch I called Albert again. "One financial detail," I said. "Walthers said he'd passed up a million-dollar bonus to give this to me, so transfer, ah, two million to his account right away."

"Certainly, Robin." Albert Einstein never gets sleepy, but when he wants to indicate that it's past my bedtime he is perfectly capable of yawning and stretching. "I should remind you, though, that the state of your health—"

I told him what he could do with the state of my health. Then I told him what he could do with his idea of putting me in the hospital the next day. He spread his hands gracefully. "You're the boss, Robin," he said humbly. "Still, I've been thinking."

It is not true that Albert Einstein does not spend any time thinking. Since he moves at nuclear-particle speeds, however, the time involved is not usually perceptible to flesh-and-blood human beings like myself. Unless he wants it to be, usually for dramatic effect. "Spit it out, Albert."

He shrugged. "It is only that in your precarious health, I do not like to see you excited without reason."

"Reason! Jesus, Albert, sometimes you really act like a dumb machine. What more reason could anybody have than finding a living Heechee?"

"Yes," he said, puffing his pipe judiciously, and changed the subject. "From the sensor readings I am receiving, Robin, I would think you must be in considerable pain."

"How bright you are, Albert." The fact of the matter was that the churning in my gut had shifted gears. Now there was a mixer blade pureeing my belly, and every spin was a separate hurt.

"Should I wake Mrs. Broadhead and inform her?"

That message was in code. If we woke Essie to tell her something like that, it would at once result in her throwing me into bed, summoning the surgical programs, and delivering me over to all the cossetting and curing Full Medical Plus could offer. The truth was it was beginning to look attractive. Pain scared me as dying did not. Dying was something you could get over and done with, at least, while pain looked unending.

But not right then! "No way, Albert," I said, "at least not until you come out with whatever you're being so coy about. Are you telling me that I made a wrong assumption somewhere along the line? If so, tell me where."

"Only in terming Audee Walthers's perception a Heechee, Robin," he said, scratching his chin with the stem of his pipe.

I sat up straight, and grabbed at my stomach because the sudden motion had not been a good idea. "What the hell else could it be, Albert?"

He said solemnly, "Let us review the evidence. Walthers said that the intelligence he perceived seemed to be slowed down, even stopped. This is consistent with the hypothesis it is Heechee, since they are thought to be in a black hole, where time is slowed."

"Right. Then why—"

"Second," he went on, "the detection was in interstellar space. This is also consistent, since the Heechee are known to have that capability."

"Albert!"

"Finally," he said calmly, disregarding the tone of my voice, "the detection was of an intelligent form of life, and other than ourselves"—he twinkled at me—"or, should I say, other than the human race, the Heechee are the only known such form. However," he said benignly, "the duplicate ship's log that Captain Walthers brought us raises serious questions."

"Get on with it, damn you!"

"Certainly, Robin. Let me display the data." He moved aside in his holographic frame, and a ship's chart leaped into existence. It showed a distant pale blob, and along the right-hand margin symbols and numerals danced. "Note the velocity, Robin. Eighteen hundred kilometers a second. That is not an impossible velocity for a natural object—say, a condensation from the wave-front of a supernova. But for a Heechee vessel? Why would it be going so slowly? And does that in fact look like a Heechee vessel?"

"It looks like nothing at all, for God's sake! It's just a blur. At extreme range. You can't tell a thing."

The small figure of Albert to one side of the chart nodded. "Not as it is, no," he admitted, "but I have been able to enhance the image. There is, of course, other negative evidence. If indeed the source is a black hole—"

"What?"

He affected to misunderstand me. "I was saying that the hypothesis that the source is in a black hole is not consistent with the total absence of gamma or X-radiation from that region, as would presumably occur from infall of dust and gas."

"Albert," I said, "sometimes you go too far!"

He gazed at me with hooded-eyed concern. I know that those calm stares of Albert's, and his pretenses of forgetting things, are only contrivances for effect. They do not reflect any appropriate reality—especially the times when he looks right into my eyes. The imaged eyes in Albert's holopics see no more than the eyes in a photograph. If he senses me, and he surely did sense me good, it was through camera lenses and hypersound pulses and capacitance probes and thermal imagers, none of which are located anywhere near the eyes of the image of Albert. But there are, all the same, moments when those eyes seem to be looking right into my soul. "You want to believe they are Heechee, don't you, Robin?" he asked softly.

"None of your business! Show me this enhanced image!"

"Very well."

The image mottled . . . marbled . . . cleared; and I was looking at an immense dragonfly. It more than filled the screen in Albert's little peepshow. Most of its gauzy wings could be made out only by the stars they obscured. But where all the wings came together there was a cylindrical object with points of light gleaming on its surface, and some of that light glittered off the wings themselves.

"It's a sailship!" I gasped.

"Yes. A sailship," Albert agreed. "A photonic spacecraft. Its only propulsion is from light pressure against the array of sails."

"But Albert—But Albert, that must take forever."

He nodded. "In human terms, yes, that is a good description. At its estimated velocity the trip from, say, the Earth to the nearest star, Alpha Centauri, would take approximately six hundred years."

"My God. Six hundred years in that little thing?"

"It isn't little, Robin," he corrected me. "It is more distant than you perhaps realize. My ranging data is only approximate, but my best estimate is that the distance from sailtip to sailtip is not less than one hundred thousand kilometers."

On the damask couch Essie snorted, changed position, opened her eyes to look at me, said accusingly, "Still up, eh!" and closed her eyes again—all without waking up.

I sat back, and fatigue and pain swarmed over me. "I wish I were sleepy," I said. "I need to let all this simmer awhile before I can take it in."

"Of course, Robin. I'll tell you what I suggest," Albert said cunningly. "You didn't have much for dinner, so why don't I make you up some nice split-pea soup, or maybe some fish chowder—"

"You know what puts me to sleep, don't you?" I said, almost laughing, glad to have my thoughts brought back to the mundane. "Why not?"

So I moved back to the dining alcove. I let Albert's bartender subroutine fix me a nice hot buttered rum, and Albert himself appeared in the

PV-frame over the sideboard to keep me company. "Very nice," I said, finishing it. "Let's have another before I eat, all right?"

"Certainly, Robin," he said, fiddling with his pipestem. "Robin?"

"Yes?" I said, reaching for the new drink.

"Robin"—bashfully—"I've got an idea."

I was in a good mood to hear ideas, so I cocked an eyebrow at him as permission to go on. "Walthers gave me the notion: Institutionalize what you did for him. Set up annual awards. Like to Nobel prizes, or the Gateway science bonuses. Six prizes a year, a hundred thousand dollars each, each one for someone in a particular field of science and discovery. I have prepared a budget"—he moved to one side, turning his head to glance toward a corner of the viewing frame; a neatly printed prospectus appeared there—"showing that for a nominal outlay of six hundred thousand a year, nearly all of which would be recouped through tax savings and third-party participation—"

"Hold it, Albert. Don't be my accountant. Be my science advisor. Prizes for what?"

He said simply, "For helping to solve the riddles of the universe."

I sat back and stretched, feeling very relaxed and warm. And benign, even to a computer program. "Oh, hell, Albert, sure. Go ahead. Isn't the soup ready yet?"

"Right this minute," he said obligingly, and so it was. I dipped a spoon into it, and it was fish chowder. Thick. White, with lots of cream.

"I don't see the point, though," I said.

"Information, Robin," he said.

"But I thought you got all that sort of information anyway."

"Of course I do—after it's published. I have a conceptually keyed search program going all the time, with more than forty-three thousand subject flags, and as soon as something on, say, Heechee language transcription appears anywhere it automatically goes into my store. But I want it *before* it's published, and even if it *isn't* published. Like Audee's discovery, do you see? Winners each year chosen by a jury—I would be glad"—he twinkled—"to help you select the juries. And I have proposed six areas of inquiry." He nodded toward the display; the budget disappeared, replaced by a neat tabulation:

1. Heechee communications translation.
2. Observations and interpretation of the missing mass.
3. Analysis of Heechee technology.
4. Amelioration of terrorism.

5. Amelioration of international tensions.
6. Nonexploitive life extension.

"They all sound very commendable," I said approvingly. "The soup's fine, too."

"Yes," he said, "the chefs are very good at following instructions." I glanced up at him drowsily. His voice seemed gentler—no, perhaps the word is sweeter—than before. I yawned, trying to focus my eyes.

"Do you know, Albert," I said, "I never noticed it before, but you look a little like my mother."

He put down his pipe and regarded me sympathetically. "It's nothing to worry about," he said. "You've got nothing to worry about at all."

I regarded my faithful hologram with drowsy pleasure. "I guess that's right," I conceded. "Maybe it's not my mother you look like, though. Those big eyebrows—"

"It doesn't matter, Robin," he said gently.

"It doesn't, does it?" I agreed.

"So you might just as well go to sleep," he finished.

And that seemed like such a good idea that I did. Not right away. Not abruptly. Just slowly, gently; I lingered half awake and I was absolutely comfortable and absolutely relaxed, so I didn't quite know where half awake ended and all-asleep began. I was in a dream or a reverie, that in-between state when you suspect you are sleeping but don't care much, and the mind wanders. Oh, yes, my mind wandered. Very far. I was chasing around the universe with Wan, reaching into one black hole after another in search of something very important to him, and also very important to me, though I didn't know why. There was a face involved, not Albert's, not my mother's, not even Essie's, a woman's face with great dark eyebrows . . .

Why, I thought, with pleased surprise, the son of a bitch has doped me!

And meanwhile, the great Galaxy turned and tiny particles of organic matter pushed slightly less tiny particles of metal and crystal across the spaces between the stars; and the organic bits experienced pain and desolation and terror and joy in all their various ways; but I was all the way asleep and it did not matter to me a bit. Then.

13
The Penalties of Love

One small bit of organic matter named Dolly Walthers was busy experiencing all of those feelings—or all but joy—and a great deal of such other feelings as resentment and boredom. In particular boredom, except at those moments when the dominant feeling in her sorry small heart was terror. As much as anything, the inside of Wan's ship was like a chamber in some complicated, wholly automatic factory in which a small space had been left for human beings to crawl in to make repairs. Even the flickering golden coil that was part of the Heechee drive system was only partly visible; Wan had surrounded it with cupboarding to store food. Dolly's own personal possessions—they consisted mostly of her puppets and a six-month supply of tampons—were jammed into a cabinet in the tiny toilet. All the other space was Wan's. There was not much to do, and no room to do it in. Reading was one possible way to pass the time. The only datafans Wan owned that were readable, really, were mostly children's stories, recorded for him, he said, when he was tiny. They were extremely boring to Dolly, though not quite as boring as doing nothing at all. Even cooking and cleaning were not as boring as nothing at all, but the opportunities were limited. Some cooking smells drove Wan to take refuge in the lander—or more often to stamp and rage at her. Laundry was easy, involving only putting their garments in a sort of pressure cooker that forced hot steam through them, but then as they dried they raised the humidity of the air and that, too, was cause for stamping and raging. He never really hit her—well, not counting what he probably thought of as amorous play—but he scared her a lot.

He did not scare her as much as the black holes they visited, one after another. They scared Wan, too. Fear did not keep him from going on; it only made him even more impossible to live with.

When Dolly realized that this whole mad expedition was only a hopeless search for Wan's long-lost, and surely long-dead, father, she felt real tenderness for him. She wished he would let her express it. There were times when, especially after sex, especially on those rare occasions when he did not at once either go to sleep or drive her away from him with some cutting and unforgivably critical intimate remark—those times when, for a few minutes at least, they would hold each other in silence. Then she would feel a great yearning to make human contact with him. There were times when she wanted to put her lips to his ear and whisper, "Wan? I know how you feel about your father. I wish I could help."

But, of course, she never dared.

The other thing she never dared do was to tell him that in her opinion, he was going to kill them both—until they came to the eighth hole and she had no choice. Even two days away from it—two days in faster-than-light travel, nearly a light-year in distance—it was different. "Why is it funny-looking?" she demanded, and Wan, not even looking around as he hunched before the screen, only said what she expected:

"Shut up." Then he went on gabbling with his Dead Men. Once he realized she could speak neither Spanish nor Chinese he talked with them openly before her, but not in a language intelligible to her.

"No, please, honey," she said, a sick feeling in her stomach. "It's all wrong!" Why wrong she could not have said. The object on the screen was tiny. It was not very clear, and it jiggled about the screen. But there was no sign of the quick coruscations of energy as stray wisps of matter destroyed themselves as infall. Yet there was something to see, a swimmy sort of blue radiance that was certainly not black.

"Pah," he said, sweating, and then, because he was scared as well, he ordered, "Tell the bitch what she wants. In English."

"Mrs. Walthers?" The voice was hesitant and faint; it was a dead person's voice, all right, if a person's at all. "I was explaining to Wan that this is what is called a naked singularity. That means it is not rotating, therefore it is not exactly black. Wan? Have you compared it with the Heechee charts?"

He grumbled, "Of course, foolish, I was just about to do so!" but his voice was shaking as he touched the controls. Next to the image itself another image formed. There was the bluish, cloudy, eye-straining object. And there, on the other half of the screen, the same object, with around it a cluster of bright, short red lines and flickering green circles.

The Dead Man said with dismal satisfaction, "It is a danger object, Wan. The Heechee have tagged it so."

"Idiot fool! All black holes are dangerous!" He snapped off the speaker and turned to Dolly with anger and contempt. "You're frightened, too!" he accused, and stomped off to the stolen and frightening gadgets in the lander.

It was not consoling to Dolly to see that Wan was also shaking. She waited, staring hopelessly at the screen, for the mindtouch that would be Wan's exploratory reaching with the TPT. It was a long wait, because the TPT did not work at interstellar distances, and she slept in fits, and woke to peer into the lander hatch to see Wan, unmoving, crouched by the glittering mesh and the diamond-bright corkscrew, and slept again.

She was asleep when her dreams were interrupted by the hating, fearing, obsessed stab of Wan's troubled mind through the TPT, and no more than half awake when he flung himself back into the main cabin and stood over her. "A person!" he gabbled, his eyes blinking wildly as sweat streamed into them from his forehead. "Now I must reach inside!"

And meanwhile, I was dreaming of a deep, steep gravitational hole and a treasure concealed in it. While Wan was deploying his stolen gadgets, sweating with terror, I was sweating with pain. While Dolly was staring wonderingly at the great ghostly blue object on her screen, I was staring at the same object. She had never seen it before. I had. I had a picture of it over my bed, and I had taken that picture at a time when I hurt even more and was even more disoriented. I tried to sit up, and Essie's strong, gentle hand pushed me back. "Are still on life-support systems, Robin," she scolded. "Must not move around too much!"

I was in the little hospice chamber we had built onto the house at

Tappan Sea, when it began to seem too much trouble to go to some clinic every time one of us needed repairs. "How did I get here?" I managed.

"By airplane, how else?" She leaned past me to study something on the screen over my head and nodded.

"I've had the operation," I deduced. "That son of a bitch Albert knocked me out. You flew me home while I was still under."

"How clever! Yes. Is all over. Doctor says you are healthy peasant pig and will recover quickly," she went on, "only with bellyache continuing awhile because of two point three meters new intestine. Eat now. Then sleep some more."

I leaned back while Essie fussed with the chef program and stared at the holopic. It was put there to remind me, no matter how unpleasant the tinkering that was going on to keep me alive, that there had been times far more unpleasant still, but that wasn't what it was reminding me of. What it was reminding me of was a woman I had lost. I will not say I had not thought of her for years, because that would be untrue. I thought of her often—but as a remote memory, and now I was thinking of her as a person. "Time now," Essie caroled merrily, "for nourishing fish broth!" By God, she wasn't fooling; that was what it was, nauseous-smelling but, she said, laced with all the things I needed and could tolerate in my present condition. And meanwhile, Wan was fishing in the black hole with the clever and complicated machinery of the Heechee; and meanwhile, it had just occurred to me that the sickening stuff I was eating was laden with more than medicine; and meanwhile, the clever machinery was performing a separate task Wan did not know about; and meanwhile, I forced myself awake enough to ask Essie how long I had been asleep, and how much longer I could expect to be, and she was saying, "Quite some time, both ways, dear Robin," and then I was asleep again.

The separate task was notification, for of all the Heechee artifacts the disruptor of order in aligned systems was the one the Heechee worried about most. Improperly used, they feared, it could disrupt their own order decisively and nastily, and so each one had a built-in alarm.

When you fear that somebody may sneak up on you in the dark you set snares—a dragline of clashing tin pans on a tripcord, or a boobytrap to crash down on an intruder's head, whatever. And there is no greater dark than the dark between the stars, so the Heechee set up their early-warning sentinels. The snares the Heechee had set were numerous, supple, and very, very loud. When Wan deployed his corkscrew it was signaled at once, and at once was when Captain's communications officer reported it to him. "The alien has done it," he said, muscles writhing, and Captain uttered a biological expletive. In translation it would not sound like much to a human being, because it referred to the act of sexual coupling at a time when the female was not in love. Captain didn't say it for its technical meaning. He said it because it was violently obscene, and because nothing less would relieve his feelings. When he saw that Twice started nervously as she leaned to her remote-control board he was instantly contrite.

Captain had the most worries, because he was Captain, but it was Twice who had most of the work. She was operating three remotes at once: the command ship they were about to transfer to, the cargo hauler for hiding the sailship away, and a special drone in the Earth planetary system commanded to survey all transmissions and locate all spaceborne artifacts. And she was in no condition for any of this. The time of loving had come on her, steroids flowed briskly through her wiry veins, the biological program was running, and her body had ripened for its job. Not just her body. Twice's personality ripened, too, and softened. The strain of trying to guide her drones with a body and nervous system that was tuned for a season of preoccupying sexual coupling was torture. Captain leaned toward her. "Are you all right?" he asked. She didn't answer. That was answer enough.

He sighed and turned to the next problem. "Well, Shoe?"

The communications officer looked almost as distraught as Twice. "A few conceptual correspondences have been established, Captain," he reported. "But the translation program is very far from complete."

Captain twitched his cheek muscles. Was there any unexpected, illogical thing that could go wrong that had not gone wrong already? These communications—not only was it dangerous that they could exist in the first place, but they were in several languages! Several! Not just two, as was right and proper in the Heechee scheme of things. Not just The Language of Do and The Language of Feel, as the Heechee themselves spoke, but in literally scores of mutually incomprehensible tongues. It might have eased the pain of hearing this endless blab of chatter if, at least, he had been able to find out what they were saying.

So many worries and problems! Not just the visible sight of Twice getting weaker and more erratic every hour, not just the terrible shock of knowing that some non-Heechee creature was activating the mechanisms that could pierce a black hole; the biggest worry for Captain was whether or not he was capable of dealing with all these consequential challenges. Meanwhile, there was a job to be done. They located the sailship and homed in on it, no problem. They dispatched a message to its crew but, wisely, did not wait for an answer. The command ship, wakened out of its millennia-long powered-down sleep, turned up on schedule. They transferred themselves, lock to lock, to the bigger, more powerful vessel. That, too, was almost no problem, though Twice, gasping and whimpering as she raced from board to board, was slow in taking over her remote-command functions in the new ship. No harm done, though. And the lumbering cargo bubble also appeared where it was supposed to, and even when.

The whole process took nearly twelve hours. For Twice, they were hours of unremitting toil. Captain had less to do, which left him plenty of time to keep an eye on her. He watched her coppery skin turn purple with unfulfilled amorousness even while it was darkening with fatigue. It worried him. They had been so unready for all these challenges! If they had known there was going to be an emergency, he could easily have shipped an extra drone operator to share Twice's burden. If they had dreamed it would be necessary, they could have taken a command vessel in the first place and spared the strain of changing ships. If they had thought—If they had suspected—If they had had any intimation at all—

But they hadn't. Really, how could they? Even by galactic time it had been only a few decades since the last peek outside the hiding place at the core—only a wink in astronomical time, and how could anyone have believed that so much could happen in it?

Captain rummaged through food packets until he found the tastiest and easiest to digest, and fed them affectionately to Twice at her board. She had little appetite. Her movements were slower, less sure, more difficult for her every hour. But she was getting the job done. When at last the photon ship's sails had been furled, the great maw of the bubble vessel was open, the mothlike capsule that carried the sailship passengers slipping slowly into the bubble, Captain began to breathe freely again. For Twice, at least, that was the hardest part of what they would have to do. Now she would have a chance to rest—maybe even a chance to do, with him, what her body and soul were overready to do.

Because the sailship people had responded to his message instantly—for them it was instantly—their reply came before the great gleaming sphere had closed on them. The communications officer, Shoe, keyed his screen and the message appeared:

> We accept that we must not complete our voyage.
> We request that you convey us to a place where we will be safe.
> We query: Are the Assassins returning?

The Heechee left only small scout ships for human beings to discover; they were careful not to leave their special-purpose spacecraft where they were easily located. For example, the bubble transport. This was nothing more than a hollow metal sphere fitted with faster-than-light drive and navigation equipment. The Heechee apparently used it to move bulk materials from place to place; the human race could have used it very well indeed. Each bubble transport could hold the equivalent of a thousand *S. Ya.*—class transports. Ten of them could have solved Earth's population problem in a decade.

Captain shrugged with sympathy. To Shoe he said, "Transmit to them: 'We are returning you to your home system for the time being. If possible, we will bring you back here later.' "

Shoe's expression was strained, with a mixture of emotions. "What about their query about the Assassins?"

Captain felt a quick shudder in his abdomen. "Tell them not yet," he said.

But it was not the fear of the other ones that was uppermost in Captain's mind, not even his concern for Twice. The Heechee shared with the human race an astonishing number of traits: curiosity, male-female love, family solidarity, devotion to children, a pleasure in the manipulation of symbols. The magnitude of the shared traits was not always the same, however. There was one psychological characteristic that the Heechee possessed in a far stronger degree than most humans:

Conscience.

The Heechee were almost physically incapable of repudiating an obligation or letting a wrong go unrighted. For the Heechee, the sailship people were a special case. The Heechee *owed* them. It was from them that they had learned the most frightening fact the Heechee had ever had to face.

The Heechee and the sailship people had known each other well, but not recently, and not for very long. The relationship had begun badly for the sailship people. For the Heechee, it had ended even worse. It was not possible for either of them ever to forget the other.

In the slow, gurgling eddas the sailship people sang it was told how the cone-shaped landing vessels of the Heechee had suddenly appeared, terribly hard and terribly swift, in the sweet slush of their home. The Heechee ships had flashed about the floating arcologies of the people with much cavitation and significant local temperature rises. Many had died. Much damage had been done before the Heechee understood that these were sentient and even civilized beings, if slow ones.

The Heechee were terribly shocked at what they had done. They tried to make amends. The first step was communication, and that was difficult. The task took a very long time—long, at least, for the Heechee, though the time for the sludge dwellers was bewilderingly short before a hard, hot octahedral prism slid itself cautiously into the middle of an arcology. Almost at once it began to speak to them in a recognizable, though laughably ungrammatical, form of their own language.

After that events moved with blinding speed—for the slush dwellers. For the Heechee, watching them in their daily lives was a lot like watch-

ing lichens grow. Captain himself had visited their great gas-giant planet
—not a captain then, almost what could have been called a cabin boy;
young; yeasty; adventurous, with that considerable, if cautious, Heechee
optimism for the boundless future that had collapsed on them so terrify-
ingly. The gas giant was not the only marvelously exciting place the
young Heechee visited. He visited Earth and met the australopithecines,
he helped chart gas clouds and quasars, he ferried crews to outposts and
construction projects. Years passed. Decades passed. The slow work of
translating the sludge dwellers' communications inched forward. It could
have gone a little faster if the Heechee had thought it particularly important; but they did not. It couldn't have gone very much faster in any case,
because the sludge dwellers couldn't.

But it was interesting, in an antiquarian, touristy sort of way, because
the sludge dwellers had been around for a long, long time. Their chill
biochemistry was something like three hundred times slower than a
Heechee's, or a human's. Heechee recorded history went back five or six
millennia—more or less the same as humanity's, at the same stage in
technological evolution. The recorded history of the sludge dwellers went
back three hundred times as far. There were nearly two million years of
consecutive, dated historical data. The earliest folk tales and legends and
eddas were ten times earlier still. They were no harder to translate than
the later ones, because the slush dwellers did not move very fast even in
the evolution of their language, but the massed minds who translated
them judged them not very interesting. They put the work of translating
them off . . . until they discovered that two of them spoke of visitations
from space.

When I think of all those years the human race labored under the
galling knowledge of inferiority—because the Heechee had done so much
more than we had, and done it so much earlier—I have many regrets. I
think I regret most that we didn't know about the Two Eddas. I don't
mean just knowing the eddas themselves, for they would only have given
us one more thing to worry about, though a reassuringly remote one. I
mean mostly what they did to the Heechee morale.

The first song was from the very dawn of the slush dwellers' civilization, and quite ambiguous. It was a visitation of the gods. They came,
shining so brightly that even the slushers' rudimentary optics could perceive them—shining with such a turbulence of energy that they caused
the soupy gases to seethe and boil, and many died. They did no more
than that, and when they went away they never returned. The song itself
didn't mean much. It had no details that the Heechee found believable,

Robin doesn't tell much about the sailship people, mostly because he didn't then know much. But that's a pity. They're interesting. Their language was made up of words of one syllable—one consonant, one vowel. They had some fifty distinguishable consonants, and fourteen vowels and diphthongs to play with—therefore they had for three-syllable units, such as names, 3.43×10^8 combinations. That was plenty, especially for names, because that was orders of magnitude more males than they had ever had to give names to, and they didn't name the females.

When a male impregnated a female, he produced a male child. He only did it rarely, because it cost him a great investment of energy. Unfertilized females produced females, more or less routinely. Bearing males, however, cost them their lives. They didn't know that—or anything else, really. There are no love stories in the eddas of the sailship people.

and most of it was about a certain ur-slusher hero who dared defy the visitors and came to rule a whole soggy sector of their planet as a reward.

But the second song was more specific. It dated from millions of years later—almost within the historical period. It sang once more of visitors from outside the dense home world, but this time they were not mere tourists. They weren't conquerors, either. They were refugees. They plunged down to the soggy surface, one shipload of them, it seemed, poorly equipped to survive in an environment that was cold, dense poison for them.

They hid there. They stayed for a long time, by their standards—more than a hundred years. Long enough for the slush dwellers to discover them and even to establish a kind of communication. They had been attacked by alien assassins that flamed like fire, wielding weapons that crushed and burned. Their home planet had been flamed clean. Every vessel they owned in space had been pursued and destroyed.

And then, when generations of the refugees had managed to survive and even multiply, it all came to an end. The flaming Assassins found them and boiled a whole huge shallow of the sludgy methane sea dry to destroy them.

When the Heechee heard this song they might have taken it for fable, except for one term. The term was not easy to translate, for it had had to survive both the incomplete communications with the refugees and the lapse of two million years. But it had survived.

It was what caused the Heechee to stop everything they did so that they could concentrate on a single task: the verification of the old edda. They sought out the home of the fugitives and found it—a planet scorched bare by a sun that had exploded. They sought for, and found, artifacts of previous spacegoing civilizations. Not many. None in good condition. But nearly forty separate bits and pieces of half-melted machines, and they isotope-dated them to two separate epochs. One of them coincided in time with the fugitives who fled to the slush planet. The other was many millions of years older.

They concluded that the stories were true: There had been such a race of Assassins; they had wiped out every spacefaring civilization they had discovered, for more than twenty million years.

And the Heechee came to believe that they were still somewhere around. For the term that had been so hard to translate described the expansion of the heavens and the reversal by the flame-wielders so that all the stars and galaxies would crush together again. For a purpose. And it was impossible to believe that these titans, whoever they were, would not linger to see the results of the process they had begun.

And the bright Heechee dream crumbled, and the slush dwellers sang a new edda: the song of the Heechee, who visited, learned to be afraid, and ran away.

So the Heechee set their booby-traps, hid most of the other evidence of their existence, and retreated to their hidey-hole at the core of the Galaxy.

In one sense, the sludge dwellers were just one of the booby-traps. LaDzhaRi knew that; they all did; that was why he had followed the ancestral commandment and reported that first touch of another mind on his. He expected an answer, though it had been years, even in LaDzhaRi's time, since there had been a Heechee manifestation of any kind, and then only the quick touch of a routine TPT survey. He had also expected that when the answer came he would not like it. The whole epic struggle of building and launching the interstellar ship, the centuries already invested in their millennium-long journey—wasted! It was true that a flight of a thousand years to LaDzhaRi was no more than an ordinary whaling voyage for a Nantucket captain; but a whaler would not have liked being picked up in mid-Pacific and taken home empty, either. The whole crew had been upset. The excitement in the sailship had been so great that some of the crew involuntarily went into fast mode; the sludgy liquid was so churned that cavitation bubbles formed. One of the females was dead. One of the males, TsuTsuNga, was so demoralized that he was pawing over the surviving females, and not for dinner, either. "Please don't be foolish," LaDzhaRi pleaded. For a male to impregnate a female, as TsuTsuNga seemed about to do, involved so large an investment of energy that sometimes it threatened his life. For the females there was no threat—their lives were simply forfeited in order to bear a fertilized child—but they didn't know that, of course, or much of anything else, really. But TsuTsuNga said steadily:

"If I cannot become immortal by voyaging to another star, then at least I will father a son."

"No! Please! Think, my friend," begged LaDzhaRi, "we can be home if we wish. Can return as heroes to our arcologies, can sing our eddas so the entire world will hear—" For the sludge of their homes carried sound as well as a sea, and their songs reached as far as a great whale's.

TsuTsuNga touched LaDzhaRi briefly, almost contemptuously, at least dismissively. "We're not heroes!" he said. "Go away and let me do this female."

And LaDzhaRi reluctantly released him, and listened to the dwindling sounds as he moved away. It was true. They were failed heroes at best

Robin does not explain very well what the Heechee were afraid of. They had deduced that the purpose of causing the universe to contract again was to return it to the primordial atom —after which it would burst in another Big Bang and start a new universe. They further deduced that in that case, the physical laws that govern the universe might develop in a different way.

What scared them most was the thought of beings who thought they would be happier in a universe with different physical laws.

The sailship people were not without such human traits as pride. It did not please them to be the Heechees'—what? Slaves? Not exactly, for the only service they were required to perform was to report, via sealed-beam communicator, any evidence of other spacefaring intelligence. They were very glad to do that for their own sakes, more than for the Heechees'. If not slaves, then what?

There was only one word that was right: pets.

So the racial psyche of the slush dwellers contained a patch of tarnish they could never burnish away, with whatever feats of interstellar venturing they might accomplish in their vast, slow starjammers. They knew they were pets. It was not the first time for them. Long before the Heechee came they had been chattels, in almost the same way, to beings quite unlike the Heechee, or humans, or themselves; and when, generations before, their sooth-singers had roared the ancient eddas about those others into the Heechee listening machine, the slush dwellers had not failed to notice that the Heechee ran away. A pet was not the worst thing one could be.

So love and fear were abroad in the universe. For love (what passed among the slush dwellers for love) TsuTsuNga damaged his health and risked his life. Dreaming of love, I lay in my hospice, waking less than an hour every day, while my store-bought innards reconciled themselves to the rest of me. Terrified by love, Captain saw Twice grow thinner and darker.

For Twice had not got better once the cargo bubble was en route. The surcease had come too late. The closest thing they had to a medical specialist was Burst, the black-hole operator, but even at home, even with the finest care, few females could survive unrequited love combined with terrible strain.

It was no surprise to Captain when Burst appeared, hangdog, pitying, and said, "I'm sorry. She is joining the massed minds."

It is not a cheap commodity, love. Some of us can have it and never face the bill, but only if someone else picks up the check.

14
The New Albert

Everyone conspired against me—even the wife of my bosom—even my trusted data-retrieval program. In the brief moments they allowed me to be awake they gave me a free choice. "You can go to the clinic for a complete checkup," said Albert, sucking judiciously at his pipe.

"Or can stay the damn hell asleep until are damn sure you are all better," said Essie.

"Ah-ha," I said, "I thought so! You've been keeping me unconscious, haven't you? It's probably been days since you knocked me out and let them cut me open." Essie avoided my eyes. I said nobly, "I don't blame you for that, but, don't you see, I want to go look at this thing Walthers found! Can't you understand that?"

She was still not meeting my eyes. She glowered at the hologram of

Albert Einstein. "Seems damn peppy today. You keeping this khuligan tranked up good?"

Albert's image coughed. "Actually, Mrs. Broadhead, the medical program advised against any unnecessary sedation at this point."

"Oh, God! Will be awake, bothering us day and night! That settles it, you Robin, you go to clinic tomorrow." And all the time she was snarling at me, her hand was on the back of my neck, caressing; words can be liars, but you can feel the touch of love.

So I said: "I'll meet you halfway. I'll go to the clinic for the complete physical on condition that if I pass you don't give me any more arguments about going into space."

Essie was silent, calculating, but Albert cocked an eyebrow at me. "I think that might be a mistake, Robin."

"That's what us human beings are for, to make mistakes. Now, what's for dinner?"

You see, I had calculated that if I showed a happy appetite they would take it as a good sign, and maybe they did. I had also calculated that my new ship wouldn't be ready for several weeks, anyway, so there was no real hurry—I wasn't about to take off in another cramped, smelly Five when I had a yacht of my own coming along. What I had not calculated on was that I had forgotten how much I hated hospitals.

When Albert examined me, he measured my temperature bolometrically, scanned my eyes for clarity and my skin for external blemishes like burst blood vessels, pumped hypersound through my torso to peer at the organs inside, and sampled the contributions I left in the toilets for biochemical imbalances and bacteria counts. Albert called these procedures noninvasive. I called them polite.

The diagnostic procedures at the clinic didn't bother to be polite. They weren't really painful. They numbed the surface of my skin before going much farther, and once you get inside the surface there aren't that many nerve endings to worry about. All I really felt were tweaks and pokes and tickles. But a *lot* of them, and besides, I knew what they were doing. Hair-thin light pipes were peering around the inside of my belly. Needle-sharp pipettes were sucking out plugs of tissue for analysis. Siphons were sipping up my bodily fluids; sutures were checked, scars were appraised. The whole thing took less than an hour, but it seemed longer and, honestly, I'd rather have been doing something else.

Then they let me put my clothes back on and I was allowed to sit down in a comfortable chair in the presence of a real-live human doctor. They even let Essie sit in, but I didn't give her a chance to talk. I got in first. "What do you say, Doc?" I asked. "How long after the operation can I go into space? I don't mean rockets, I mean a Lofstrom loop, about as traumatic as an elevator. You see, the loop just sort of pulls you along on a magnetized ribbon—"

The doctor held up his hand. He was a plump, white-haired Santa Claus of a man, with a neat, close-trimmed white beard and bright blue eyes. "I know what a Lofstrom loop is."

"Good, I'm glad of that. Well?"

"Well," he said, "the usual practice after surgery such as yours is to avoid anything like that for three to four weeks, but—"

"Oh, no! Doc, no!" I said. "Please! I don't want to have to hang around for practically a month!"

He looked at me and he looked at Essie. Essie wouldn't meet his eyes, either. He smiled. "Mr. Broadhead," he said, "I think you should know two things. The first is that it is often desirable to keep a convalescent patient unconscious for some time. With electrically stimulated muscle exercise, massage, good diet, and proper nursing care there is no impairment of function, and it's a lot easier on the patient's nervous system. And everybody else's, too."

"Yes, yes," I said, not very interested. "What's the other thing?"

"The other thing is that you were operated on forty-three days ago this morning. You can do just about anything you want to now. Including taking a ride on a loop."

Time was when the road to the stars led through Guiana or Baikonur or the Cape. You had to burn about a million dollars' worth of liquid hydrogen to get into orbit, before you could transship to something going farther away. Now we had the Lofstrom launch loops spaced around the equator, immense gossamer structures that you couldn't see until you were almost beside them—well, within twenty kilometers, which was where the satellite landing field was. I watched it with pleasure and pride as we circled and descended to touchdown. In the seat beside me Essie was frowning and muttering to herself as she worked on some project—a new kind of computer programing, or maybe a pension plan for her Big Chon employees; I couldn't tell which, because she was doing it in Russian. On the pull-down console in front of me Albert was displaying my new ship, rotating the image slowly while he recited the statistics of capacity, accessories, mass, and amenities. Since I had put quite a few million dollars and a lot of my time into that plaything, I was interested, but not as interested as I was in what was coming next. "Later, Albert," I ordered, and obediently he winked out. I craned my neck to keep the loop in view as we entered final approach. Faintly, along the top of the ski-jump launch section, I could see capsules speeding up through three gravities' acceleration and neatly, gently detaching themselves at the steepest part of the upslope to disappear into the blue. Beautiful! No chemicals, no combustion, no damage to the ozone layer. Not even the energy-wastage of a Heechee lander launch; some things we could do even better than the Heechee did!

Time was when even being in orbit was not enough, and then you had to take the long, slow Hohmann journey to the Gateway asteroid. Usually you were scared out of your bird, because everybody knew that more Gateway prospectors got killed than got rich; and because you were space sick and cramped and condemned to inhabit that interplanetary slammer for weeks or months on end before you even got to the asteroid; and most of all because you'd risked everything you owned or could borrow to pay for it. Now we had a Heechee Three chartered and waiting for us in low-Earth orbit. We could transship in our shirtsleeves and be on our way to the far stars before we'd finished digesting our last meal on Earth—that is, *we* could, because we had the muscle and the money to pay for it.

Time was when going out into that interstellar nothingness was a lot like playing Russian roulette. The only difference was that if the luck of the draw was favorable, whatever you found at the end of the journey might make you rich beyond richness forever—as it ultimately did me. But what you mostly got made was dead.

"Is much better now." Essie sighed as we climbed down out of the aircraft and blinked around in the hot South American sun. "Now, where is damn courtesy van from crummy fleabag hotel?"

I did not comment on her reading my mind. After all the time we had been married I was used to it. Anyway, it wasn't telepathy; it was what any human being would think if he were doing what we were doing at that time. "I wish Audee Walthers were going with us," I said, looking out at the launch loop. We were still kilometers away, on the far shore of Lake Tehigualpa. I could see the loop reflected in it, blue at the center of the lake, greeny-yellow near the shore, where they had sown edible algae, and it was a pretty sight.

"If you wanted him with you, should not have given him two mil to chase his wife with," said Essie practically, and then, looking at me more closely, "How you feeling?"

"Absolutely in the pink," I said. It wasn't far from true. "Quit worrying about me. When you've got Full Medical Plus they don't dare let you die before you reach a hundred—it's bad for business."

"Don't have much to say about it," she said gloomily, "when customer is reckless desperado who spends time chasing for make-believe Heechee! Anyway," she added, brightening, "here is van for fleabag, hop in."

So when we were inside the van I leaned over and kissed the back of her neck—easy to do, because she had braided her long hair and brought it around her neck to tie in front like a kind of a necklace—getting ready for the launch, you see. She leaned against my lips. "Khuligan." She sighed. "But not *bad* khuligan."

The hotel wasn't really a fleabag. They had given us a comfortable suite on the top floor, looking over the lake and the loop. Besides, we would only be in it for a few hours. I left Essie to key in her programs on the hotel PV screen while I wandered over to the window, telling myself, indulgently, that I wasn't really a hooligan. But that wasn't true, because it certainly was not the act of a responsible senior citizen of wealth and substance to skylark off into interstellar space just for the glamour and excitement of it.

It occurred to me then that Essie might not be taking quite that view of my motives. She might think I was after something else.

It then occurred to me that maybe my own view was wrong. Was it really the Heechee I was looking for? Sure it was, or anyway could be; everybody was desperately curious about the Heechee. But not everybody had left something else out in interstellar space. Was it possible that somewhere in the down-deep hidden part of my mind, what was driving me out and on was the hope that somehow, somewhere, I might find that misplaced thing again? I knew what the thing was. I knew where I had left it. What I didn't know was what I would do with it—or, more accurately, her—if I found her again.

And then I felt a sort of quivery not-quite-pain in my middle. It had nothing to do with my two point three meters of new gut. What it had to do with was the hope, or the fear, that somehow Gelle-Klara Moynlin might indeed turn up in my life again. There was more emotion left over there than I had realized. It made my eyes tear, so the spidery launch structure out the window seemed to ripple in my sight.

But there were no tears in my eyes.

And it wasn't an optical illusion. "My God!" I shouted. "Essie!" And she hurried over to stand beside me and look at the tiny flare of light from a capsule on the launch run, and the shaking, shuddering of the whole thread-thin structure. Then there was the noise—a single faint blast like a distant cannon shot, and then the lower, slower, longer thunder of the immense loop tearing itself apart. "My God," Essie echoed faintly, clutching my arm. "Terrorist?"

And then she answered herself. "Of course terrorist," she said bitterly. "Who else could be so vile?"

I had opened our windows to get a good look at the lake and the loop; good thing, because that meant they weren't blown in. Others in the hotel were not so lucky. The airport itself wasn't touched, not counting the occasional aircraft sent flying because it wasn't tied down. But the airport officials were scared. They didn't know whether the destruction of the launch loop was an isolated incident of terrorist sabotage, or maybe the beginnings of a revolution—no one seemed to think, ever, that it might have been just a simple accident. It was scary, all right. There's a hell of a lot of kinetic energy stored in a Lofstrom loop, over twenty kilometers of iron ribbon, weighing about five thousand tons, moving at twelve kilometers a second. Out of curiosity I asked Albert later and he reported that it took 3.6×10^{14} Joules to pump it up. And when one collapses, all those Joules come out at once, one way or another.

I asked Albert later because I couldn't ask him then. Naturally, the first thing I did was to try to key him up, or any other data-retrieval or information program that could tell me what was going on. The comm circuits were jammed; we were cut off. The broadcast PV was still working, though, so we stood and watched that mushroom cloud grow and listened to damage reports. One shuttle had been actually accelerating on the ribbon when it blew—that was the first explosion, perhaps because it had carried a bomb. Three others had been in the loading bypass. More than two hundred human beings were now hamburger, not counting the ones they hadn't counted yet who had been working on the launcher itself, or had been in the duty-free shops and bars underneath it, or maybe just out for a stroll nearby. "I wish I could get Albert," I grumbled to Essie.

"As to that, dear Robin," she began hesitantly, but didn't finish, because there was a knock on the door; would the señor and the señora come at once to the Bolivar Room, *por favor,* as there was a matter of the gravest emergency.

The matter of the gravest emergency was a police checkup, and you never saw such a checking of passports. The Bolivar Room was one of those function things that they divide up for meetings and open for grand banquets, and one partitioned-off part of it was filled with turistas like us, many of them squatting on their baggage, all looking both resentful and scared. They were being kept waiting. We were not. The bellhop who fetched us, wearing an armband with the initials "S.E.R." over his uniform, escorted us to the dais, where a lieutenant of police studied our passports briefly and then handed them back. "Señor Broadhead," he said in English, accent excellent, touches of American Midwest, "does it occur to you that this act of terrorist violence may in fact have been aimed personally at you?"

I gawked. "Not until now," I managed. He nodded.

"Nevertheless," he went on, touching a PV hard-copy printout with his small, graceful hand, "we have received from Interpol a report of a terrorist attempt on your life only two months ago. Quite a well-organized one. The commissaris in Rotterdam specifically suggests that it did not appear random, and that further attempts might well be made."

I didn't know what to say to that. Essie leaned forward. "Tell me, Teniente," she said, regarding him, "is this your theory?"

"Ah, my *theory*. I wish I had a theory," he said furiously. "Terrorists? No doubt. Aimed against you? Possibly. Aimed against the stability of our government? Even more possibly, I think, as there has been widespread dissatisfaction in rural areas; there are even reports, I tell you in confidence, that certain military units may be planning a coup. How can one know? So I ask you the necessary questions, such as, have you seen anyone whose presence here struck you as suspicious or coincidental? No? Have you any opinion as to who attempted to assassinate you in Rotterdam? Can you shed any light at all on this terrible deed?"

The questions came so fast that it hardly seemed he expected answers, or even wanted them. That bothered me nearly as much as the destruction of the loop itself; it was a reflection, here, of what I had been seeing and sensing all over the world. A sort of despairing resignation, as though things were bound to get worse and no way could be found to get them better. It made me very uncomfortable. "We'd like to leave and get out of your way," I said, "so if you're through with your questions—"

He paused before he answered, and began to look like someone with a job he knew how to do again. "I had intended to ask you a favor, Señor Broadhead. Is it possible that you would allow us to borrow your aircraft for a day or two? It is for the wounded," he explained, "since our own general hospital was unfortunately in the direct path of the loop cables."

I am ashamed to say I hesitated, but Essie did not. "Most certainly yes, Teniente," she said. "Especially as we will need to make a reservation for another loop in any event before we know where we want to go to."

He beamed. "That, my dear señora, we can arrange for you through the military communications. And my deepest thanks for your generosity!"

Services in the city were falling apart, but when we got back to our suite there were fresh flowers on the tables, and a basket of fruits and wine that had not been there before. The windows had been closed. When I opened them I found out why. Lake Tehigualpa wasn't a lake anymore. It was just the heat sink where the ribbon was supposed to dump in case of the catastrophic failure of the loop that no one believed would ever happen. Now that it had happened the lake had boiled down to a mud wallow. Fog obscured the loop itself, and there was a stink of cooked mud that made me close the window again quickly enough.

We tried room service. It worked. They served us a really nice dinner, apologizing only because they couldn't send the wine steward up to decant our claret—he was in "Los Servicias emergencias de la Republica" and had had to report for duty. So had the suite's regular ladies' maid and, although they promised that a regular floor maid would be up in an hour to unpack the bags for us, meanwhile, they stood against the walls in the foyer.

I'm rich, all right, but I'm not spoiled. At least I don't think I am. But I do like service, especially the service of the fine computer programs Essie has written for me over the years. "I miss Albert," I said, looking out at the foggy nighttime scene.

"Can find nothing to do without your toys, eh?" scoffed Essie, but she seemed to have something on her mind. Well. I'm not spoiled about *that,* either, but when Essie seems to have something on her mind I often conclude that she wants to make love, and from there it is not usually much of a jump for me to want to, too. I remind myself, now and then, that for most of human history, persons of our ages would have been a lot less amative and exuberant about it—but that's just bad luck for them. Such thoughts do not slow me down. Especially because Essie is what she is. Besides her Nobel laureate, Essie had been receiving other awards, including appearing on lists of Ten Best-Dressed Women every now and then. The Nobel was deserved; the Best-Dressed was, in my opinion, a fraud. The way S. Ya. Broadhead looked had nothing to do with what she put on, but a lot to do with what was under what she put on. What she was wearing right now was a skintight leisure suit, pale blue, unornamented; you could buy them in any discount house, and she would have won in that, too. "Come here a minute, why don't you?" I said from the great, long couch.

"Sex fiend! Huh!"

But it was a fairly tolerant "huh." "I just thought," I said, "that as I can't get Albert and we have nothing else to do—"

"Oh, you Robin," she said, shaking her head. But she was smiling. She pursed her lips, thinking. Then she said: "I tell you what. You go fetch small traveling bag from foyer. I have little present to give you, then we see."

Out of the bag came a box, silver-paper wrapped, and inside it a big Heechee prayer fan. It wasn't really Heechee, of course; it was the wrong size. It was one of the kind Essie had developed for her own use. "You remember Dead Men and Here After," she said. "Very good Heechee software, which I decided to steal. So have converted old data-retrieval program for you. Have in hand now guaranteed *real* Albert Einstein."

I turned the fan over in my hands, "The *real* Albert Einstein?"

"Oh, Robin, so literal! Not *real*-real. Cannot revive dead, especially so long dead. But real in personality, memories, thoughts—pretty near, anyway. Programed search of every scrap of Einstein data. Books. Papers. Correspondence. Biographies. Interviews. Pictures. Everything. Even cracked old film clips from, what you called them, 'newsreels' on ship coming to New York City in A.D. 1932 by Pathé News. All inputted to here, and now when you talk to Albert Einstein it is Albert Einstein who talks back!" She leaned over and kissed the top of my head. "Then, to be sure," she bragged, "added some features real Albert Einstein never had. Complete pilotage of Heechee vessels. All update in science and technology since A.D. 1955, time of actual Einstein passing on. Even some simpler functions from cook, secretary, lawyer, medical programs. Was no room for Sigfrid von Shrink," she apologized, "but then you no longer need shrinkage, eh, Robin? Except for unaccountable lapse of memory."

She was looking at me with an expression that over the past couple of decades I had come to recognize. I reached out and pulled her toward me. "All right, Essie, let's have it."

She settled down in my lap and asked innocently, "Have what, Robin? You talking about sex again?"

"Come on!"

"Oh . . . It is nothing, to be sure. I have already given you your silver gift."

"What, the program?" It was true that she had wrapped it in silver paper—Enlightenment exploded. "Oh, my God! I missed our silver wedding anniversary, didn't I? When—" But, thinking fast, I bit the question off.

"When was it?" she finished for me. "Why, now. Is still. Is today, Robin. Many congratulations and happy returns, Robin, dear."

I kissed her, I admit as much stalling for time as anything else, and she kissed me back, seriously. I said, feeling abject, "Essie, dear, I'm really sorry. When we get back I'll get you a gift that will make your hair stand on end, I promise."

But she pressed her nose against my lips to stop my talking. "Is no need to promise, dear Robin," she said, from about the level of my Adam's apple, "for you have given me ample gifts every day for twenty-five years now. Not counting couple years when we just fooled around, even. Of course," she added, lifting her head to look at me, "we are alone at this moment, just you and me and bed in next room, and will be for some hours yet. So if you truly wish to make hair stand on end with gift, would be pleased to accept. Happen to know you have something for me. Even in my size."

The fact that I didn't want any breakfast brought all of Essie's standby systems up to full alert, but I explained it by saying that I wanted to play with my new toy. That was true. It was also true that I didn't always eat breakfast anyway, and those two truths sent Essie off to the dining hall without me, but the final truth, that my gut did not really feel all that good, was the one that counted.

So I plugged the new Albert in to the processor, and there was a quick pinkish flare and there he was, beaming out at me. "Hello, Robin," he said, "and happy anniversary."

"That was yesterday," I said, a little disappointed. I had not expected to catch the new Albert in silly mistakes.

He rubbed the stem of his pipe across his nose, twinkling up at me under those bushy white eyebrows. "In Hawaiian Mean Time," he said, "it is, let me see"—he faked looking at a digital wristwatch that was anachronistically peeking out under his frayed pajama-top sleeve— "forty-two minutes after eleven at night, Robin, and your twenty-fifth wedding anniversary has still nearly twenty minutes to go." He leaned forward to scratch his ankle. "I have a good number of new features," he said proudly, "including full running time and location circuits, which operate whether I am in display mode or not. Your wife is really very good at this, you know."

Now, I know that Albert Einstein is only a computer program, but all the same it was like welcoming an old friend. "You're looking particularly well," I complimented. "I don't know if you should be wearing a digital watch, though. I don't believe you ever had such a thing before you died, because they didn't exist."

He looked a little sulky, but he complimented me in return: "You have an excellent grasp of the history of technology, Robin. However, although I *am* Albert Einstein, as near as may be to the real thing, I am not limited to the real Albert Einstein's capabilities. Mrs. Broadhead has included in my program all known Heechee records, for example, and that flesh-and-blood self didn't even know the Heechee existed. Also I have subsumed into me the programs of most of our colleagues, as well as data-seeking circuits that are presently engaged in trying to establish connection with the gigabit net. In that, Robin," he said apologetically, "I have not been successful, but I have patched into the local military circuits. Your launch from Lagos, Nigeria, is confirmed for noon tomorrow, and your aircraft will be returned to you in time to make the connection." He frowned. "Is something wrong?"

I hadn't been listening to Albert as much as studying him. Essie had done a remarkable job. There were none of those little lapses where he would start a sentence with a pipe in his hand and finish by gesturing with a piece of chalk. "You do seem more real, Albert."

"Thank you," he said, showing off by pulling open a drawer of his desk to get a match to light his pipe. In the old days he would have just materialized a book of matches. "Perhaps you'd like to know more about your ship?"

I perked up. "Any progress since we landed?"

"If there were," he apologized, "I wouldn't know it, because as I mentioned I have been unable to make contact with the net. However, I do have a copy of the certificate of commissioning from the Gateway Corp. It is rated as a Twelve—that is to say, it could carry twelve passengers if equipped for simple exploration—"

"I know what a Twelve would be, Albert."

"To be sure. In any event, it has been fitted for four passengers, although up to two others can be accommodated. It was test-flown to Gateway Two and back, performing optimally all the way. Good morning, Mrs. Broadhead."

I looked over my shoulder; Essie had finished breakfast and joined us. She was leaning over me to study her creation more carefully. "Good program," she complimented herself, and then, "Albert! From where you get this picking nose bit?"

Albert removed a finger from a nostril forgivingly. "From unpublished letters, Enrico Fermi to a relative in Italy; it is authentic, I assure you. Are there any other questions? No? Then, Robin and Mrs. Broadhead," he finished, "I suggest you pack, for I have just received word over the police link that your aircraft has landed and is being serviced. You can take off in two hours."

And so it was, and so we did, happily enough—or almost happily. The last little bit, less happily. We were just getting into our plane when there was a noise from behind the passenger terminal and we turned to look.

"Why," Essie said wonderingly, "that sounds like guns firing. And those big things in the parking lot, see them pushing aside cars? One has just now demolished a fire standpipe and water is shooting out. Can they be what I think?"

I tugged her into the plane. "They can," I said, "if what you think they are is army tanks. Let's get the hell out of here."

We did. No problem. Not for us, anyway, even though Albert, listening in on the reopened gigabit net, reported that the teniente's worst fears had been realized and a revolution was indeed lustily tuning up. Not for us then, at least, though elsewhere in the wide universe other things were going on that would pose for us some very large problems, and some very painful ones, and some that were both.

15
Back from the
Schwarzschild Discontinuity

When Gelle-Klara Moynlin awoke she was not dead, as she had confidently expected to be. She was in a Heechee exploration ship. It was an armored Five by the look of it, but not the one she had been in at the last she remembered.

What she remembered was chaotic, frightful, and filled with pain and terror. She remembered it very well. It had not included this lean, dark, scowling man who wore a G-string and a scarf and nothing else. Nor had it included some strange young blond girl who was crying her eyes out. In the last memory Klara had there had been people crying, all right, oh, yes! And shrieking and cursing and wetting their underwear, because they were trapped within the Schwarzschild barrier of a black hole.

But none of those people were these people.

The young girl was bending over her solicitously. "Are you all right, hon? You've been through a real bad time." There was no news for Klara in that statement. She knew how bad the time had been. "She's awake," the girl called over her shoulder.

The man came bounding over, pushing the girl aside. He did not waste time inquiring about Klara's health. "Your name! Also orbit and mission number—quickly!" When she told him he didn't acknowledge the answer. He simply disappeared and the blond girl came back.

"I'm Dolly," she said. "I'm sorry I'm such a wreck, but honestly, I was scared to death. Are you all right? You were all messed up, and we don't have much of a medical program here."

Klara sat up and discovered that, yes, she was messed up, all right. Every part of her ached, starting with her head, which appeared to have been bashed against something. She looked around. She had never been in a ship so full of tools and toys before, nor one that smelled so pleasantly of cooking. "Look, where am I?" she asked.

"You're in his ship"—pointing. "His name's Wan. He's been wandering around, poking into black holes." Dolly looked as though she were getting ready to cry again, but rubbed her nose and went on: "And listen, hon, I'm sorry, but all those other people you were with are dead. You were the only one alive."

Klara caught her breath. "All of them? Even Robin?"

"I don't know their names," the girl apologized. And was not surprised when her unexpected guest turned her bruised face away and began to sob. Across the room Wan snarled impatiently at the two women. He was deep into concerns of his own. He did not know what a treasure he had retrieved, or how much that retrieved treasure complicated my life.

For it is pretty nearly true that I married my dear wife, Essie, on the elastic rebound from the loss of Klara Moynlin. At least, on the upsurge of feeling that came when I shed the guilt, or anyway most of the guilt, I felt for Klara's loss.

When ultimately I found out that Klara was alive again it was a shock. But, my God, nothing—*nothing*—compared to the shock to Klara! Even now and in these circumstances I can't help feeling what I can only call, incongruously enough, a physical pain when I think about my whilom most dear Klara as she found herself back from the dead. It isn't just because of who she was, or who she was in relation to me. She deserved the compassion of anybody. Trapped, terrified, hurt, sure of dying—and then a moment later miraculously rescued. God pity the poor

I had not met Gelle-Klara Moynlin before her accident with the black hole. Robin couldn't afford as sophisticated a data-retrieval system as me in those days. But I surely heard a lot about her from Robin over the years. What I mostly heard about was how guilty he felt over her death. The two of them, with others, had gone on a science mission for the Gateway Corp to investigate a black hole; most of their ships had been trapped; Robin had managed to get free.

There was no logical reason to feel guilty, of course. More-over, Gelle-Klara Moynlin, though a normally competent female human, was in no sense irreplaceable—in fact, Robin replaced her rather swiftly with a succession of other females, finally bonding in a long-term mode with S. Ya. Lavorovna, not only a competent human female, but the one who designed me. Al-though I am well modeled on human drives and motivations, there are parts of human behavior I never will understand.

woman! God knows I do, and things did not quickly get better for her.
She was unconscious half the time, because her body had taken a terrible
battering. When she was awake, she was not always sure she was awake.
From the tingling she felt and the warm flush and the buzzing in her ears
she knew that they had been shooting her full of painkillers. Even so she
ached terribly. Not just in the body. And when she was awake she could
easily have been hallucinating, as far as she was able to know, because the
sociopath Wan and the demoralized Dolly were not very stable figures to
cling to. When she asked questions she got strange answers. When she
saw Wan talking to a machine and asked Dolly what he was doing, she
could make little sense of Dolly's reply: "Oh, those are his Dead Men. He
programed them with all the mission records, and now he's asking them
about you."

But what could that mean to someone who had never heard of Dead
Men? And what could she feel when a wispy, uncertain voice from the
speakers began to talk about her?

"—no, Wan, there's nobody named Schmitz on that mission. Either
ship. You see, there were two ships that went out together, and—"

"I do not care how many ships went out together!"

The voice paused. Then, uncertainly: "Wan?"

"Of course I am Wan! Who would I be but Wan?"

"Oh . . . Well, no, there's nobody there that fits your father's description, either. Who did you say you rescued?"

"She claims to be named Gelle-Klara Moynlin. Female. Not very
good-looking. About forty, maybe," Wan said, not even looking at her to
see how wrong he was; Klara stiffened and then reflected that the ordeal
had no doubt made her look older than her age.

"Moynlin," the voice whispered. "Moynlin . . . Gelle-Klara, yes, she
was on that mission. The age is wrong, though, I think." Klara gave a
half nod, causing the throb in her head to start again, and then the voice
went on. "Let me see, yes, the name is right. But she was born sixty-three
years ago."

The throbbing increased its tempo and its violence. Klara must have
moaned, because the girl Dolly cried out to Wan and then leaned over her
again. "You're going to be all right," she said, "but I'm going to get
Henrietta to give you another little sleepy shot, all right? When you wake
up again you'll feel better."

Klara gazed up at her without comprehension, then closed her eyes.
Sixty-three years ago!

How many shocks can a human being stand without breaking? Klara was not very breakable; she was a Gateway prospector, four missions, all of them tough, any of them enough to give nightmares to anyone. But her head throbbed furiously as she tried to think. Time dilation? Was that the term for what happened inside a black hole? Was it possible that twenty or thirty years had sped past in the real world while she was spinning around the deepest gravity well there was?

"How about," Dolly offered hopefully, "if I get you something to eat?"

Klara shook her head. Wan, nibbling his lip in a surly way, lifted his head and called, "How foolish, offering her food! Give her a drink instead."

He was not the kind of person you would want to please even by agreeing with him when he was right, but it sounded like too good an idea to pass up. She let Dolly bring her what seemed to be straight whiskey; it made her cough and splutter, but it warmed her. "Hon," said Dolly hesitantly, "was one of those, you know, those guys that got killed, was he a special boyfriend?"

There was no reason for Klara to deny it. "Pretty much a boyfriend. I mean, we were in love, I guess. But we'd had a fight and split up, and then started to get together again, and then—And then Robin was in one ship, and I was in another—"

"Robbie?"

"No. Robin. Robin Broadhead. It was really Robinette, but he was kind of sensitive about the name—What's the matter?"

"Robin *Broadhead*. Oh, my God, yes," said Dolly, looking astonished and impressed. "The millionaire!"

And Wan looked over, then came to stand beside her. "Robin Broadhead, to be sure, I know him well," he boasted.

Klara's mouth was suddenly dry. "You do?"

"Of course. Certainly! I have known him for many years. Yes, of course," he said, remembering, "I have heard of his escape from the black hole years ago. How curious that you were there, too. We are business partners, you see. I receive from him and his enterprises nearly two-sevenths of my present income, including the royalties paid me by his wife's companies."

"His wife?" whispered Klara.

"Do you not listen? I said that, yes, his wife!"

And Dolly, suddenly gentle again, said: "I've seen her on the PV now and then. Like when they pick her for the Ten Best-Dressed Women, or when she won the Nobel Prize. She's quite beautiful. Hon? Would you like another drink?"

Klara nodded, starting her head to throbbing again, but collected herself enough to say, "Yes, please. Another drink, at least."

For nearly two days Wan elected to be benevolent to the former friend of his business partner. Dolly was kind, and tried to be helpful. There was no picture of S. Ya. in their limited PV file, but Dolly pulled out the hand puppets to show her what a caricature of Essie, at least, looked like, and when Wan, growing bored, demanded she do her night-club routine with them, managed to fob him off. Klara found plenty of time to think. Dazed and battered as she was, she could still do simple arithmetic in her head.

She had lost more than thirty years of her life.

No, not out of *her* life; out of everybody else's. She was no more than a day or two older than when she went into the naked singularity. The backs of her hands were scratched and bruised, but there were no age spots on them. Her voice was hoarse from pain and fatigue, but it was not an old woman's voice. She was not an old woman. She was Gelle-Klara Moynlin, not that much over thirty, to whom something terrible had happened.

When she woke up on the second day the sharpened pains and the localized aches told her that she was no longer receiving analgesia. The sullen-faced captain was bending over her. "Open your eyes," he snapped. "Now you are well enough to work for your passage, I think."

What an annoying creature he was! Still, she was alive, and apparently getting well, and there was gratitude due. "That sounds reasonable enough," Klara offered, sitting up.

"Reasonable? Ha! You do not decide what is reasonable here; I decide what is reasonable," Wan explained. "You have only one right on my ship. You had the right to be rescued and I rescued you; now all the other rights are mine. Especially as because of you we must now return to Gateway."

"Hon," said Dolly tentatively, "that's not entirely true. There's plenty of food—"

"Not the kind of food I wish, shut up. So you, Klara, must repay me for this trouble." He reached his hand behind him. Dolly evidently understood his meaning; she moved a plate of fresh-baked chocolate brownies to his fingers, and he took one and began to eat it.

Gross person! Klara pushed her hair out of her eyes, studying him coldly. "How do I repay you? The way she does?"

"Certainly the way she does," said Wan, chewing, "by helping her maintain the ship, but also—Oh! Ho! Ha-ha, that is funny," he gasped, spraying crumbs of chocolate on Klara as he laughed. "You think I meant in bed! How stupid you are, Klara, I do not copulate with ugly older women."

Klara wiped the crumbs off her face as he reached for another brownie. "No," he said seriously, "it is more important than that. I want to know all about black holes."

She said, trying to be placating, "It all happened very fast. There's not much I can tell you."

"Tell what you can tell, then! And listen, do not try to lie!"

Oh, my God, thought Klara, how much of this must I put up with? And "this" meant more than the bullying Wan; it meant all of her resumed and wholly disoriented life.

The answer to "how much" turned out to be eleven days. It was time enough for the worst of the bruises to fade on her arms and body, time enough for her to get to know Dolly Walthers, and pity her, to know Wan, and despise him. It was not time enough for her to figure out what to do with her life.

But her life did not wait until she was ready for it. Ready or not, Wan's ship docked on Gateway. And there she was.

The very smells of Gateway were different. The noise level was different—much louder. The people were *radically* different. There did not seem to be a single living one among them for Klara to recognize from her last time there—thirty years, or not much more than thirty days, in the past, depending on whose clock you timed by. Also so many of them were in uniform.

That was quite new to Klara, and not at all pleasing. In the "old days" —however subjectively recent those old days were—you saw maybe one or two uniforms a day, crewpersons on leave from the four-power guard cruisers mostly. Certainly you never saw one of them carrying a weapon. That was not true any longer. They were everywhere, and they were armed.

Debriefing had changed along with everything else. It had always been a nuisance. You'd come back to Gateway filthy and exhausted and still scared, because up until the last minute you hadn't been sure you'd make it, and then the Gateway Corp would sit you down with the evaluators and the data compilers and the accountants. Just what did you find? What was new about it? What was it worth? The debriefing teams were the ones charged with answering questions like that, and how they scored a flight made the difference between abject failure and—once in a great while—wealth beyond dreaming. A Gateway prospector needed skills simply to survive, once he had closed himself into one of those unpredictable ships and launched himself on his Mad Magic Mystery Bus Ride. But to prosper he needed more than skills. He needed a favorable report from the debriefing team.

Debriefing had always been bad news, but now it was worse. There wasn't a debriefing team from the Gateway Corp anymore. There were four debriefing teams, one from each of the four guardian powers. The debriefing had been moved to what had once been the asteroid's principal night club and gambling casino, the Blue Hell, and there were four separate little rooms, each with a flag on the door. The Brazilians got Dolly. The People's Republic of China snatched Wan off the floor. The American MP took Klara by the arm, and when the lieutenant of MPs in front of the Soviet cubicle frowned and patted the butt of his Kalashnikov, the American scowled right back, his hand resting on his Colt.

It didn't really make any difference, because as soon as Klara was through with the Americans, the Brazilians took their turn with her, and when you are invited somewhere by a young soldier with a sidearm it makes little difference whether it is a Colt or a Paz.

Between the Brazilians and the Chinese Klara crossed paths with Wan, sweating and indignant, on his way from the Chinese to the Russians, and realized she had something to be thankful for. The interrogators were rude, overbearing, and nasty with her, but they seemed to be worse with Wan. For reasons she didn't know, each of his sessions was lasting twice as long as her own. Which was already very long. Each team in turn pointed out that she was supposed to be dead; that her bank account had long since reverted to the Gateway Corp; that there was no mission payment due her for traveling with Juan Henriquette Santos-Schmitz, since it was not an officially authorized Gateway mission; and, as for any payment that might have been due for her trip to the black hole, well, she hadn't come back in that vessel, had she? With the Americans she claimed at least a science bonus—whoever else had been inside a black hole? They told her the matter would be taken under advisement. The Brazilians told her it was a matter for four-power negotiation. The Chinese said it all hinged on an interpretation of the award made to Robinette Broadhead, and the Russians had no interest in that subject at all, because what they wanted to know was whether Wan had given any indication of terrorist leanings.

The debriefing took forever, and then there was a medical check that took almost as long. The diagnostic programs had never encountered a living human being who had been exposed to the wrenching forces behind a Schwarzschild barrier before, and they would not let her go until they had pinpointed every bone and ligament and helped themselves freely to samples of all the fluids she had. And then they released her to the accountancy section for her statement of account. It was a hardcopy chit, and all it said was:

MOYNLIN, Gelle-Klara
Current balance: 0.
Awards due: not yet evaluated.

Waiting outside the accountancy offices was Dolly Walthers, looking fretful and bored. "How'd you do, hon?" she asked. Klara made a face. "Oh, that's too bad. Wan's still in there," she explained, "because they kept him for bloody ever in the debriefing. I've been just sitting here for hours. What are you going to do now?"

"I don't exactly know," Klara said slowly, thinking about the very limited options one had on Gateway when one had no money.

"Yeah. Same here." Dolly sighed. "With Wan, you know, you never know. He can't stay anywhere very long, because they start asking questions about some of the stuff on his ship and I don't think he got it all exactly legally." She swallowed and said quickly, "Watch it, here he comes."

To Klara's surprise, when Wan looked up from the chits he was studying he beamed at her. "Ah," he said, "my dear Gelle-Klara, I have been studying your legal position. Very promising indeed, I think."

Promising! She glared at him with considerable dislike. "If you mean that they'll probably toss me out into space within the next forty-eight hours for nonpayment of bills, that's not what I call promising."

He peered at her, decided she was joking. "Ha-ha, that is very humorous. Since you are not used to dealing with large sums of money, permit me to recommend a banking chap I find very useful—"

"Cut it out, Wan. That's not funny."

"Of course it's not funny!" He scowled just as in the old days, and then his expression softened into incredulity. "Can it be—Is it possible—Have they not told you of your claim?"

"What claim?"

"Against Robinette Broadhead. My legal johnny says you might get quite fifty percent of his assets."

"Oh, bullshit, Wan," she said impatiently.

"Not bullshit! I have an excellent legal program! It is the doctrine of the calf follows the cow, if you understand. You should have had a full share of the survivors' benefits from his last mission; now you should have an equal share of that, and also of all that he has added to it, since it came from that original capital."

"But—But—Oh, that's stupid," she snapped. "I'm not going to sue him."

"Of course sue him! What else? How else can you get what is yours? Why, I sue as many as two hundred persons a year, Gelle-Klara. And there is a very large sum involved indeed. Do you know what Broadhead's net worth is? Much, much more even than my own!" And then, with the jolly fraternal good-fellowship of one person of wealth to another: "Of course, there may be some inconvenience for you while the matter is being adjudicated. Allow me to transfer a small loan from my account to yours—one moment—" He made the necessary entries on his statement chit. "Yes, there you are. Good luck!"

So there was my lost love, Gelle-Klara Moynlin, more lost than ever after she had been found. She knew Gateway well. But the Gateway she knew was gone. Her life had skipped a beat, and everything she knew or cared for or was interested in had suffered the changes of a third of a century, while she, like some enchanted princess in a forest, had slept away the time. "Good luck," Wan had said, but what constituted good luck for the sleeping beauty whose prince had married someone else? "A small loan," Wan had said, and it turned out that was what he had meant. Ten thousand dollars. Enough to pay her bills for a few days—and then what?

There was, thought Klara, the excitement of finding out some of the facts people like her had been dying for. So once she had found herself a room and gotten something to eat she headed for the library. It no longer contained spools of magnetic tape. Everything was now stored on some kind of second-generation Heechee prayer fans (prayer fans! so that was what they were!), and she had to hire an attendant to teach her how to use them. ("Librarian services @ $125/hr., $62.50," said the item on her data chit.) Was it worth it?

To Klara's disgruntled surprise, not really. So many questions answered! And, strangely, so little joy in getting the answers.

When Klara was a Gateway prospector like any other, the questions were literally a matter of life and death. What were the meanings of the symbols on the control panels of Heechee ships? What settings meant death? What meant reward? Now here were the answers, not all of them, perhaps—there was still not much clue to that great shuddery question of who the Heechee were in the first place. But thousands upon thousands of answers, even answers to questions no one had known enough to ask thirty years before.

But the answers gave her little pleasure. The questions lost their urgency when you knew the answers were in the back of the book.

The one class of questions whose answers held her interest was, I know, me.

Robinette Broadhead? Oh, surely. There was much data on him in store. Yes, he was married. Yes, he was still alive, and even well. Unforgivably, he gave every indication of being happy. Almost as bad, he was *old*. He was not wizened or decrepit, of course, and his scalp still had all its hair and his face was wrinkle-free, but that was just Full Medical Plus, unfailing purveyor of health and youth to those who could afford it. Robinette Broadhead could obviously afford anything. But he was older all the same. There was a solid thickness to the neck, an assurance to the smile that looked out at her from the PV image, that had not been part of the frightened, confused man who had broken her tooth and sworn to love her always. So now Klara had a quantitative estimate for one more term: "Always." It meant a period substantially less than thirty years.

When she had depressed herself sufficiently in the library she roamed about Gateway to see what changes had occurred. The asteroid had become more impersonal and more civilized. There were many commercial enterprises on Gateway now. A supermarket, a fast-food franchise, a stereotheater, a health club, handsome new tourist pensions, glittering souvenir shops. There was plenty to do on Gateway now. But not for Klara. The only thing that attracted her interest, really, was the gambling casino in the spindle, replacement for the old Blue Hell; but such luxuries she could not afford.

She could not afford much of anything, really, and she was depressed. The lady magazines of her adolescence had been full of giggly little tricks to combat depression—what they called the blahs. Clean your sink. Call somebody on the PV. Wash your hair. But she had no sink, and who was there to call on Gateway? After she had washed her hair for the third time she began to think of the Blue Hell again. A few small bets, she decided, would do no harm to her budget even if she lost—it would only mean, really, giving up a few luxuries for a bit. . . .

In eleven spins of the roulette wheel she was penniless.

A party of Gabonian tourists was just leaving, laughing and stumbling, and behind them, at the short, narrow bar, Klara saw Dolly. She walked over to her steadily and said, "Would you like to buy me a drink?"

"You bet," said Dolly unenthusiastically, waving to the barman.

I never knew Gelle-Klara Moynlin when Robin was romantically involved with her. For that matter, I didn't know Robinette Broadhead then, either, for he was too poor to afford so sophisticated a data-retrieval system as me. Although I cannot experience physical courage directly (since I don't even experience physical fear), I estimate theirs very highly. Their ignorance, almost as high. They didn't know what drove the FTL ships they flew. They didn't know how the navigation worked, or what the controls did. They didn't know how to read Heechee charts, and didn't have any to read anyway, because they weren't found for another decade after Klara was sucked into the black hole. It is astonishing to me how much meat intelligences can accomplish with so little information.

"Then could you lend me some money?"

Dolly laughed with surprise. "Lost your stake, did you? Boy, have you got a wrong number! I wouldn't be buying drinks if some of the tourists hadn't thrown me a couple of chips for luck." When the highball arrived Dolly divided the small change in front of her in half and pushed a part to Klara. "You could hit Wan up again," she said, "but he's not in a very good mood."

"That's not news," said Klara, hoping the whiskey would elevate her spirits. It did not.

"Oh, worse than usual. I think he's going to be in the deep shit again." She hiccoughed and looked surprised.

"What's the matter?" Klara asked reluctantly. She knew perfectly well that once she asked, the girl would tell her, but it was, she supposed, a way of paying for the loose change.

"They're going to catch up with him sooner or later," Dolly said, sucking at the bottle again. "He's such a jerk, coming here when he could have dropped you off anywhere, and got his God-damn candy and cake."

"Well, I'd rather be here than some other place," said Klara, wondering if it was true.

"Don't be silly. He didn't do it for you. He did it because he thinks he can get away with anything at all, anywhere. Because he's a jerk." She stared moodily at the bottle. "He even makes love like a jerk. Jerky, if you know what I mean? He even screws jerky. He comes up to me with that look on his face as if he's trying to remember the combination to the food locker, you know? And then he gets my clothes off, and then he starts, push here, poke there, wiggle this part. I think I ought to write up an operating manual for him. The jerk."

How many drinks the little stake lasted for Klara didn't know—several, anyway. At some later time Dolly remembered that she was supposed to shop for brownie mix and liqueur chocolates. At a later time still Klara, now strolling around by herself, realized she was hungry. What made her know it was the smell of food. She still had some of Dolly's loose change in her pocket. It was not enough for a decent meal, and anyway the sensible thing would be to go back to her cubicle and eat the prepaid meals, but what was the point of being sensible anymore? Besides, the smell was nearby. She passed through a sort of archway of Heechee metal, ordered at random, and sat as close as she could get to a wall. She pried the sandwich apart with a finger to see what she was eating; probably synthetic, but not any product of the food mines or sea farms she had ever tasted before. Not bad. Not *very* bad, anyway, although there was no dish she could think of that would have tasted really good just then. She ate slowly, analyzing each bite, not so much because the food justified it as because doing that postponed the next thing she would have to do, namely contemplate what she was going to do with the rest of her life.

And she became aware of a stir. The busgirl was sweeping the floor twice as diligently, peering over her shoulder at every stroke of the broom; the counter people were standing straighter, speaking more clearly. Someone had come in.

It was a woman, tall, not young, handsome. Thick ropes of tawny hair hung down her back, and she was conversing pleasantly, but authoritatively, with staff and customers alike while she rubbed fingers under shelves to check for grease, tasted crusts to check for crispness, made sure the napkin holders were full, retied the apron strings on the busgirl.

Klara stared at her with dawning recognition that felt more like fear. Her! The one! The woman whose picture she had seen in so many of the news stories the library had produced about Robinette Broadhead. S. Ya. Lavorovna-Broadhead opens 54 new CHON-food outlets in Persian Gulf. S. Ya. Lavorovna-Broadhead to christen converted interstellar transport. S. Ya. Lavorovna-Broadhead directs programing of expanded datastore net.

Although the sandwich was just about the last crumb of food Klara could afford to buy, she could not force herself to finish it. She sidled toward the door, face averted, crammed the plate into the waste receptacle, and was gone.

There was only one place to go. When she saw that Wan was alone in it she took it as a direct message from providence that she had made the right decision. "Where's Dolly?" she asked.

He was lying in a hammock, sulkily nibbling on fresh papaya—bought at what incredible cost, Klara could not imagine. He said, "Where indeed, yes, I would like to know that too! I will deal with her when she comes back, oh, yes!"

"I lost my money," she told him.

He shrugged contemptuously.

"And," she lied, inventing as she went along, "I came to tell you that you've lost, too. They're going to impound your ship."

"Impound!" he screeched. "The animals! The bastards! Oh, when I see Dolly, believe me—she must have told them about my special equipment!"

"Or you did," Klara said brutally, "because you've sure been shooting your mouth off. You only have one chance."

"One chance?"

"Maybe one chance, if you're smart enough and courageous enough."

"Smart enough! Courageous enough! You forget yourself, Klara! You forget that for the first part of my life I was all alone—"

"No, I don't forget anything," she said wearily, "because you sure don't let me. It's what you do next that counts. Are you all packed, ship's stores all on board?"

"Stores? No, of course not. Have I not told you? Ice cream, yes, candy bars, yes, but my brownie mix and chocolates—"

"The hell with the chocolates," said Klara, "and since she's not here when she's needed, the hell with Dolly, too. If you want to keep your ship, take off *now.*"

"Now? Alone? Without Dolly?"

"With a substitute," said Klara tightly. "Cook, bedmate, somebody to yell at—I'm available. And skilled. Maybe I can't cook as well as Dolly, but I can make love better. Or anyway more often. And you don't have time to think it over."

He stared at her slack-jawed for a long moment. Then he grinned. "Take those cases on the floor," he ordered, "also that package under the hammock. Also—"

"Wait a minute," she objected. "There's a limit to what I can carry, you know."

"As to what your limits are," he said, "we will discover in time, I assure you. Now you may not argue. Simply take that netting and fill it and then we go, and while you are doing so I will tell you a story I heard from the Dead Men many years ago. There were these two prospectors who discovered a great prize inside a black hole and could not think how to get it out. One said finally, 'Ah, now I know. I have brought my pet kitten along. We will simply tie her to the treasure and she will pull it out.' And the second prospector said, 'Oh, what a fool you are! How can a little kitten pull a treasure out of a black hole?" And the first prospector said, 'No, it is you who are the fool. It will be easy, for, see, I have a whip.' "

16
Gateway Revisited

Gateway gave me all of my many millions, but it also gives me the creeps. Coming there was like meeting myself coming back. I met myself as a young, dead-broke, terrified, despairing human being whose only choices lay between leaving on a trip that might kill him and staying in a place where no one would want to live. It hadn't changed that much. No one would still want to live there although people did and tourists were in and out all the time. But at least the trips were not as recklessly danger-ous as they used to be. As we were docking I told my program Albert Einstein that I had made a philosophical discovery, namely that things even out. Gateway gets safer, and the whole home planet Earth gets more perilous. "Maybe there is a sort of law of conservation of misery that insures an average quantum value of unhappiness for every human being, and all we can really do is spread it in one direction or another?"

"It is when you say things like that, Robin"—he sighed—"that I wonder if my diagnostic programs are as good as they ought to be. Are you sure you're not in pain from your operation?" He was, or appeared to be, sitting on the edge of the seat, guiding our vessel into landing as he talked, but I knew that his question was rhetorical. He was monitoring me all along, of course.

As soon as the ship was secured I unplugged the Albert datafan, tucked it under my arm, and headed for my new ship. "No sightseeing?" Essie asked, studying me with almost the exact expression Albert had displayed. "Then you want me to come with?"

"I'm really excited about the ship," I said, "and I just want to go look at it. You can meet me there later." I knew she was eager to see how her beloved franchise was getting along in this location. Of course, I did not then know who she might run into.

So I was thinking about nothing in particular as I clambered through the hatch into my own, personal, human-built interstellar space yacht, and be damned if it didn't turn out that I was just about as excited as I had told Essie I was. I mean, talk about childhood fantasies come true! It was real. And it was all mine, and it had everything.

At least, it had almost everything. It had a master stateroom with a marvelously wide anisokinetic bed and a genuine toilet next door. It had a fully stocked larder and something very like a real kitchen. It also had two working cabins, one for Essie and one for me, that could provide concealed berths for more guests in case we ever wanted company. It had the first human-built drive system ever to be successfully proved out for a civilian faster-than-light vessel—well, some of the parts were Heechee, salvaged out of damaged exploration ships, but most of it was human-made. And it was *powerful,* with a bigger, faster drive. It had a home for Albert, a fan socket with his name engraved over it; I slipped him into place but did not activate him, because I was enjoying my solitary prowl. It had datafans full of music and PV plays and reference works and specialist programs to do almost everything I might ever want to do, or that Essie might, either. It had a viewscreen copied from the one on the big *S. Ya.* transport, ten times the size of the little blurry plates in the exploration ships. It had everything I had ever thought of wanting in a ship, in fact, and the only thing it didn't have was a name.

I sat on the edge of the big anisokinetic bed, the thrust feeling funny on my bottom, because it was all exerted upward instead of that constricting sideways squeeze you get from regular mattresses, and I thought about

One of the lesser artifacts the Heechee left around was the anisokinetic punch—a simple tool that could convert an impact to an equal force at some angle to the driving force. The theory of it turned out to be both profound and elegant. The use people made of it, less so—the most popular product made with anisokinetic materials was a bedding mattress with "springs" whose force was vector rather than scalar, producing what is said to be a titillating support for sexual activity. Sexual activity! How much time meat intelligences waste on that sort of thing!

that problem. It was a good place to do it, since the person who would occupy that bed with me was the one I wanted to name the ship after. However, I had already named the transport after her.

Of course, I thought, there were ways of dealing with that. I could call it the *Semya*. Or the *Essie*. Or the *Mrs. Robinette Broadhead*, for that matter, although that was pretty stupid.

The matter was fairly urgent. We were all set to go. There was nothing to keep us on Gateway, except that I couldn't face taking off in a ship that didn't have a name. I found myself in the control cabin, and dropped into the pilot seat. This one was built for a human bottom, and in that way alone an immense improvement over the old style.

When I was a kid in the food mines I used to sit on a kitchen chair, in front of the radar oven, and make believe I was piloting a Gateway ship to the far corners of the universe. What I did now was just about the same thing. I reached out and touched the course wheels and made believe to squeeze the initiator teat and—and—well, I fantasized. I imagined myself dashing through space in just the same careless, adventurous, penalty-free style I had imagined as a child. Circling quasars. Speeding out to the nearby alien galaxies. Entering the silicon dust shroud around the core. Meeting a Heechee! Entering a black hole—

The fantasy collapsed then, because that was too personally real, but I suddenly realized I had a name for the ship. It fit Essie perfectly, but did not duplicate the one on the *S. Ya.*:

True Love.

It was the perfect name!

That being so, why did it leave me feeling vaguely sentimental, lovelorn, melancholy?

It was not a thought that I wanted to pursue. Anyway, now that a name had been decided, there were things to do: The registry had to be amended, the ship's insurance papers had to be corrected—the world had to be notified of my decision. The way to do that was to tell Albert to get it done. So I rocked the datafan that held him to make sure it was firmly seated and turned him on.

I had not got used to the new Albert, so it surprised me when he turned up not in a holograph box, not even near his datafan, but in the doorway to the main cabin. He stood there with an elbow cupped in a palm, the pipe in the free hand, gazing peacefully around for all the world as though he had just come in. "A beautiful ship, Robin," he said. "My congratulations."

"I didn't know you could jump around like that!"

"I am in fact *not* jumping around, my dear Robin," he pointed out amiably. "It is part of my program to give to the maximum extent possible the simulation of reality. To appear like a genie out of a bottle would not seem realistic, would it?"

"You're a neat program, Albert," I acknowledged, and, smiling, he said:

"And an alert one, too, if I may say so, Robin. For example, I believe your good wife is coming this way now." He stepped aside—quite unnecessarily!—as Essie came in, panting and looking as though she were trying not to look upset.

"What's the matter?" I demanded, suddenly alarmed.

She didn't answer right away. "Haven't heard, then?" she said at last.

"Heard what?"

She looked both surprised and relieved. "Albert? You have not acquired linkage with data net?"

"I was just about to do so, Mrs. Broadhead," he said politely.

"No! Do not! There is—ah—there are some adjustments in bias must make for Gateway conditions first." Albert pursed his lips thoughtfully but did not speak; I was not so reticent.

"Essie, spit it out! What is it?"

She sat down on the communicator's bench, fanning herself. "That rogue Wan," she said. "Is here! Is talk of entire asteroid complex. I am astonished you have not heard. *Woosh!* I ran so! I was afraid you would be upset."

I smiled forgivingly. "The operation was weeks ago, Essie," I reminded her. "I'm not that delicate—or that likely to get all in an uproar over Wan, for that matter. Have a little more confidence in me!"

She looked at me narrowly, then nodded. "Is true," she admitted. "Was foolish. Well, I get back to work," she went on, standing up and moving to the door. "But remember, Albert—no interfacing with net until I come back!"

"Wait!" I cried. "You haven't heard my news." She paused long enough to let me say proudly, "I've found a name for the ship. The *True Love*. What do you think?"

She took a long time to think that over, and her expression was a lot more tentative, and a lot less delighted, than I might have expected. Then she said, "Yes, is very good name, Robin. God bless her and all who sail in her, eh? Now must go."

After twenty-five years I still did not entirely understand Essie. I told Albert so. He was sitting at his ease on Essie's dressing-table bench, observing himself in the mirror, and he shrugged. "Do you suppose she didn't like the name?" I asked him. "It's a good name!"

"I should have thought so, Robin," he agreed, experimenting with different expressions in the mirror.

"And she didn't seem to want to look at the ship!"

"She appeared to have something on her mind," he agreed.

"But what? I swear," I repeated, "I don't always understand her."

"I confess that I do not either, Robin. In my case," he said, turning from the mirror to twinkle at me, "I have assumed that it is because I am mechanical and she is human. I wonder what it is in your case?"

I stared at him, a little annoyed, and then grinned. "You're pretty funny in your new programing, Albert," I told him. "What do you get out of pretending to look in a mirror when I know you don't really see anything that way?"

"What do you get out of looking at the *True Love,* Robin?"

"Why do you always answer a question with a question?" I responded, and he laughed out loud. It was really a very convincing performance. As long as I've had the Albert program, he was able to laugh, and even make jokes of his own, but you always knew it was a picture laughing. You could think it was a picture of a real person if you wanted to—let's face it, I usually did—like the picture of a person on the P-phone. But there was no, what shall I call it? No *presence.* Now there was. I couldn't smell him. But I could perceive his physical presence in the room with more senses than simple sight and hearing. Temperature? Mass sensation? I don't know. Whatever it is that tells you somebody is there with you.

"The answer really," he said, sobering, "is that this appearance is my equivalent of a new ship, or a new Sunday-go-to-meeting suit, or whatever analogy you like to give it. I'm just sort of looking it over to see how much I like it. How do *you* like it, which is after all more important?"

"Don't be humble, Albert," I told him. "I like it very well, only I wish you were hooked up to the data nets. I'd like to know if any of the people I've been working on have done anything about the terrorist data, for instance."

"I will of course do what you order me to, Robin," he said, "but Mrs. Broadhead was very explicit."

"No, I don't want you blowing yourself up or damaging your subroutines. I know what I'll do," I said, getting up as the light bulb flashed over my head. "I'll just go out into the passageway and plug into a comm circuit—provided," I joked, "I haven't forgotten how to make a call all by myself."

"Why, of course you could do that," he said. His tone was troubled, for some reason or other. "It isn't necessary, though, Robin."

"Well, no," I said, pausing halfway to the door. "But I am curious, you know."

"As to your curiosity," he said, smiling at me as he poked tobacco into the bowl of his pipe—but it was a forced smile, I thought. "As to that, you must know that until we docked I was in constant touch with the net. There was no real news. It is possible, though, that the lack of news was itself interesting. Even encouraging."

I was not entirely used to the new Albert. I sat down again, regarding him. "You're a cryptic son of a bitch, Dr. Einstein," I told him.

"Only when reporting information that is itself quite unclear." He smiled. "General Manzbergen is not receiving calls from you just now. The senator says he has done all he can. Maitre Ijsinger says that Kwiatkowski and our friend from Malaysia have not responded to efforts to contact them on your behalf, and all he got from the Albanians was a message that said 'Don't worry.'"

"So something's happening!" I cried, jumping up again.

"Something *may* be happening," he corrected, "and if so, really, all we can do is let it happen. In any case, Robin," he said, his tone wheedling now, "I would personally prefer that you not leave the ship at this time. For one good reason: How do you know there is not some other person here with a gun and your name on a list?"

"A terrorist? Here?"

"Here or in Rotterdam, why is one more unlikely than the other? I beg to remind you, Robin, that I am not without experience in these matters. At one time the Nazis put on my head a price of twenty thousand marks; be sure I was careful not to let anyone earn it!"

That came out of left field. I stopped in the doorway. "The whatzees?"

"The Nazis, Robin. A group of terrorists who seized control of the nation of Germany many years ago, when I was alive."

"When you were what?"

"I mean, of course"—he shrugged—"when the real human being whose name you have given me was alive, but from my point of view that is not a distinction worth making." He stuffed the filled pipe in his pocket absently and sat down in such a natural, friendly way that automatically I sat down again, too.

"I guess I haven't quite got used to the new you, Albert," I said.

"There's no better time than the present, Robin." He smiled, preening himself. He did have more solidity to him. The old holograms showed him in a dozen or so characteristic poses, with baggy sweater or tee shirt,

Although it is interesting to see myself from Robin's point of view, it is not very enjoyable. Mrs. Broadhead's programing constrained me to speak, act, and even think as the original Albert Einstein would have done, had he survived to assume my role. Robin seems to think that grotesque. In a sense, he is right. Human beings *are* grotesque!

socks on or off, sneakers or slippers, pipe or pencil. Today he wore a tee shirt, to be sure, but over it was one of those baggy European sweaters that button up the front and have pockets and might as well be a jacket, really, except that they're loosely knitted wool. There was a button on the sweater that read *Two Percent,* and a faint pale stubble around the chin that suggested he hadn't shaved that morning. Well, of course he hadn't shaved! He never would, either, being nothing more than a holographic projection of a computer construct—but so convincing and jazzy that I almost offered to lend him my razor!

I laughed and shook my head. "What does 'Two Percent' mean?"

"Ah," he said bashfully, "it was a slogan of my youth. If two percent of the human race would refuse to fight, there would be no war."

"Do you believe that now?"

"I hope that, Robin," he corrected. "The news is not all that conducive to hope, I must admit. Would you like to know the rest of the news?"

"I suppose I should," I said, and watched him stroll over to Essie's vanity. He sat on the bench before it, idly playing with her flasks of perfume and bits of feminine decoration as he talked; so normal, so human, that it distracted me from what he was saying. That was as well, for the news was all bad. The terrorists were busier than ever. The destruction of the Lofstrom loop had indeed been the first move in an insurrection, and a small, bloody war was going on all over that part of South America. Terrorists had dumped botulinus toxin into the Staines reservoir and London was going thirsty. News like that I did not want, and I told him so.

He sighed and agreed. "It was a gentler day when I was alive," he said wistfully. "Though not perfect, to be sure. I could perhaps have been president of the state of Israel, did you know that, Robin? Yes. But I felt I could not accept. I was for peace always, and a state must sometimes make war. Loeb once told me that all politicians must be pathological, and I fear he was right." He sat up straighter and brightened. "But there is some good news after all, Robin! The Broadhead Awards for Scientific Discovery—"

"The what?"

"You recall, Robin," he said impatiently, "the system of awards you authorized me to inaugurate just before your operation. They have already begun to bear fruit."

"You've solved the mystery of the Heechee?"

"Ah, Robin, I perceive you are joking with me," he said in gentle reproof. "Of course, nothing so vast just yet. But there is a physicist in

Laguna Beach—Beckfurt? You know his work? The one who proposed a
system for achieving flat space?"

"No. I don't even know what flat space is."

"Well," he said, resigning himself to my ignorance, "that doesn't matter just now, I think, but he is now working on a mathematical analysis
of the missing mass. It appears, Robin, that the phenomenon is quite
recent! Somehow mass has been added to the universe, within the last few
million years!"

"Oh, wow," I said, attempting to look comprehending. I did not
deceive him.

He said patiently: "If you recall, Robin, some years ago the Dead Man
—the woman, that is—from what is now the *S. Ya. Broadhead* led us to
believe that this phenomenon had something to do with an act of the
Heechee. We discounted this at the time, since there seemed to be no
reason for it."

"I remember," I said, only partly untruthfully. I did remember that
Albert had had the wild idea that for some reason, not specified, the
Heechee were collapsing the universe back to its primordial atom, so as
to bring about a new Big Bang and thus a new universe with somewhat
different physical laws. Then he had changed his mind. He had surely
explained all the reasoning to me at the time, but I had surely not re-
tained it. "Mach?" I said. "Something about this fellow Mach? And
somebody named Davies?"

"Exactly right, Robin!" he applauded, beaming on me with delight.
"Mach's Hypothesis suggested a reason for doing it, but Davies's Paradox made it unlikely that the reason would work. Now Beckfurt has
shown analytically that Davies's Paradox need not apply, only assuming
that the number of expansions and contractions of the universe is finite!"
He got up and roamed around the room, too pleased with himself to sit
still. I could not see what he was rejoicing over.

"Albert," I said unsteadily, "are you telling me that it may be so that
the universe is coming crashing around our ears, and we'll all be
squeezed into—what do you call it?—phloem?"

"Exactly, my dear boy!"

"And this makes you *happy?*"

"Precisely! Oh," he said, coming to a halt at the doorway and gazing at
me, "I see your problem. It will not happen *soon.* A matter of at least
some billions of years, to be sure."

I sat back, staring at him. This new Albert was going to take some
getting used to. He did not seem to notice anything amiss; he was bab-
bling on happily about all the half-baked notions that had been pouring

Robin did not quite understand Davies's Paradox, but then he didn't even understand the more famous Olbers's Paradox, which bothered astronomers way back in the nineteenth century. Olbers said: If the universe is infinite, there should be an infinite number of stars. That means that we should see not individual stars in a black sky, but a solid dome of starlight, blinding white. And he proved it mathematically. (What he didn't know was that the stars were grouped into galaxies, which changed the mathematics.) So a century later Paul Davies said: If it's true that the universe is cyclical, expanding and contracting over and over, then if it is possible for a little bit of matter or energy to stay out of the crunch and cross over to the next universe, then in infinite time that leftover light would increase infinitely and we'd have an Olbers sky again. What *he* didn't know was that the number of oscillations in which a little bit of the energy was left out was not infinite. We happened to be in the very first of them.

in on him ever since the awards were announced, and what interesting notions he had thought of because of them.

Thought of?

"Wait a minute," I said, frowning, because there was something I didn't quite understand. "When?"

"When what, Robin?"

"When were you doing this thinking? You've been turned off, except when we've been talking—"

"Exactly, Robin. When I was 'turned off,' as you put it." He twinkled. "Now that Mrs. Broadhead has provided me with a hardwired, built-in database, I do not cease to exist when you dismiss me, you know."

"I didn't know," I said.

"And it is such a great pleasure to me, you have no idea! Simply to think! All of my life it is what I have most wanted. As a young man I would weep for the chance to sit and only think—to do such things, for example, as reconstructing proofs of well-known mathematical and physical theorems. Now I can do it very often, and so much more quickly than when I was alive! I am deeply grateful to your wife for this." He cocked an ear. "And here she is coming again, Robin," he said. "Mrs. Broadhead? I have just remembered to express to you my gratitude for this new programing."

She looked at him in a puzzled way, then shook her head. "Dear Robin," she said, "I have something I must tell you. One moment." She turned to Albert and shot three or four fast Russian sentences at him. He nodded, looking grave.

It takes me a long time to see what is before me sometimes, but by now it was evident. Something was going on that I should know about. "Come on, Essie," I said, alarmed, and even more alarmed because I didn't know what I was alarmed about. "What's happening? Has Wan done something?"

She said soberly, "Wan has left Gateway, and not a moment too soon, to be sure, since is in trouble with Gateway Corp and with many others as well. But is not of Wan I wish to speak. Is of woman I observed in my shop. She did closely resemble, dear Robin, woman whom you loved before me named Gelle-Klara Moynlin. So close that I thought perhaps a daughter."

I stared at her. "What—How do you know what Klara looked like, anyway?"

"Oh, Robin," she said impatiently. "Twenty-five years and I a specialist in data retrieval. You think I would not arrange to know? Know her exactly, Robin. Every datum on record."

"Yes, but—she never had a daughter, you know." I stopped, suddenly wondering if indeed I would know. I had loved Klara very much, but not for very long. It was quite possible there were things in her history she had not got around to telling me.

"Actually," said Essie apologetically, "first guess was maybe she was your own daughter. Only theory, you know. But was possible. Could have knocked lady up, you know. But now—" She turned to Albert questioningly. "Albert? Have completed search?"

"I have, Mrs. Broadhead." He nodded, looking grave. "There is nothing in Gelle-Klara Moynlin's record to suggest she ever bore a child."

"And?"

He reached for his pipe and fumbled with it. "There is no question about the identity, Mrs. Broadhead. She checked in two days ago, with Wan."

Essie sighed. "Then," she said bravely, "is no doubt at all. Woman in shop was Klara herself, no impostor."

At that moment, trying to take in what I had been told, what I wished for most in the world, or at that moment most urgently at any rate, was the soothing, healing presence of my old analysis program, Sigfrid von Shrink. I needed help.

Klara? Alive? Here? And if this impossibility was true, what should I do about it?

It was easy enough for me to tell myself I owed Klara nothing I had not already paid. The coin I paid in was a long time of mourning, a deep and abiding love, a sense of loss that even three decades had not entirely cured. She had been taken away from me, across a gulf I could not span, and the only thing that made that bearable to me was that I had finally come to believe that it was Not My Fault.

But the gulf had somehow spanned itself. Here she was! And here was I, with a well-established wife and a well-ordered life, and no room in it for the woman I had promised to love exclusively and always.

"Is more," said Essie, watching my face.

I was not keeping up with the conversation very well. "Yes?"

"Is more. Wan arrived with two women, not one. Second woman was Dolly Walthers, unfaithful wife of person we saw in Rotterdam, you know? Young person. Weeping, eye makeup smeared—pretty young woman, but not in pretty frame of mind. U.S. military police arrested her when Wan left without clearance, so I went to talk to her."

"Dolly Walthers?"

"Oh, Robin, listen to me, please! Yes, Dolly Walthers. Could tell me very little, though, because MPs had other plans for her. Americans wanted to take her to High Pentagon. Brazilian MPs tried to stop them. Big argument, but Americans finally won."

I nodded to show I was comprehending. "I see. The Americans have arrested Dolly Walthers."

Essie studied me sharply. "Are you all right, Robin?"

"Certainly I'm all right. I'm only a little worried, because if there's friction between the Americans and the Brazilians I hope it doesn't keep them from putting their data together."

"Ah," said Essie, nodding, "now is clear. Could tell you were worried about something, was not sure what it was." And then she bit her lip. "Excuse me please, dear Robin. I am a little upset, too, I think."

She sat down on the edge of the bed, twitching irritably as the anisokinetic mattress poked at her. "Practical matters first," she said, frowning. "What do we do now? These are alternatives. One, go off to investigate object Walthers detected, as planned. Two, attempt to discover more information about Gelle-Klara Moynlin. Three, eat something and get good night's sleep before doing anything else—for," she added reprovingly, "must not forget, Robin, you are still somewhat convalescent from major abdominal surgery. I personally lean toward third alternative, what do you think?"

As I was mulling over this difficult question Albert cleared his throat. "Mrs. Broadhead? It has occurred to me that it would not be very expensive, a few hundred thousand dollars perhaps, to charter a One for a few days and send it on a photoreconnaissance mission." I peered at him, trying to follow his meaning. "That is," he explained, "we could have it seek the object you are interested in, locate it, observe it, and report to us. Single-passenger ships are not in great demand now, I believe, and at any rate there are several available here on Gateway."

"What a good idea!" Essie cried. "Settled then, all right? Arrange same, Albert, and at same time cook us up something delicious for first meal on, ah, on new ship *True Love.*"

Myself interposing no objection, that is what we did. Myself interposed no objection because myself was in shock. The worst thing about being in shock is that you don't know it while you're in it. I thought I was quite lucid and aware. So I ate whatever it was they put in front of me, and did not notice anything strange until Essie was tucking me into the big bouncy bed. "You haven't been saying anything," I said.

"Is because last ten times I spoke to you, dear Robin, you did not respond," she said, not accusingly at all. "Will see you in morning."

I figured the implications of that out pretty quickly. "You're going to sleep in the guest cabin, then?"

"Yes. Not in anger, dear, or even in sorrow. Just to let you be by yourself for a bit, all right?"

"I guess so. I mean, yes, sure, honey, that's probably a good idea," I said, beginning to register the notion that Essie really was upset and even to think that I should concern myself about it. I took her hand and kissed the wrist before letting it go, and bestirred myself to offer some conversation. "Essie? Should I have consulted you before naming the ship?"

She pursed her lips. *"True Love* is good name," she said judiciously.

But she did seem to have reservations, and I didn't know why. "I would have asked you," I explained, "but it seemed tacky to do that. I mean, to ask the person you're naming it after, like asking you what you want for your birthday instead of thinking up something by myself."

She grinned, relaxing. "But Robin dear, you always do ask me that. Is not important, really. And yes, *True Love* is truly *excellent* name, now that I know particular true love you had in mind is me."

I think probably Albert had been fooling around with his little magic sleeping potions again, because I went right off. But I didn't stay asleep. Three or four hours later I was lying in the anisokinetic bed, wide awake, fairly tranquil, very perplexed.

Out on the perimeter of the Gateway asteroid, where the docking pits are, there is a little bit of centrifugal force because of rotation. Down becomes up. Only in the *True Love* it didn't. Albert had turned the ship on, and the same force that kept us from floating around in flight was also neutralizing and reversing the thrust of the asteroid's spin; I was gently held to the gentle bed. I could feel the faint hum of the ship's housekeeping systems as they changed the air and kept the pressure in the plumbing and did all the other little chores that made the ship alive. I knew that if I said Albert's name he would appear for me—how, exactly, I didn't know, and it was almost worth summoning him to see whether he would choose to walk through the door or maybe crawl out from under the bed to amuse me. I suppose there was a mood elevator in the food as well as a sleepy drink, because I felt quite at ease with my problems—although that feeling did nothing to solve them.

Which problems to solve? That was the first problem. My priorities had been reordered so many times in the past few weeks that I didn't know which to put on top of the pile. There was the hard, harmful problem of the terrorists, and that was important to solve for more reasons than my own, but that had moved down a notch when I heard what

Audee Walthers had produced as a new problem for me in Rotterdam. There was the problem of my health, but that seemed temporarily, at least, in abeyance. And there was the new and insoluble problem of Klara. Any one of them I could have dealt with. All four of them I could deal with, too—one way or another—but, specifically, how? What should I do when I got up?

I didn't know the answer to that, and so I didn't get up.

I drifted off to sleep, and when I woke again I was not alone. "Good morning, Essie," I said, reaching out for her hand.

"Good morning," she said, pressing my hand to her cheek in the fond, familiar way. But she had an unfamiliar subject to discuss. "Are feeling all right, Robin? Good. I have been thinking about your situation."

"I see," I said. I could feel myself tensing up; the peaceful relaxation was being nibbled away. "What situation is that?"

"The Klara Moynlin situation, to be sure," she said. "I see is difficult for you, Robin dear."

"Oh," I said vaguely, "these things happen." It was not a situation I could discuss easily with Essie, but that didn't stop Essie from trying to discuss it with me.

"Dear Robin," she said, her voice calm and her expression gentle in the dim night light of the room, "is no use your keeping all this to self. Bottle up, it will explode."

I squeezed her hand. "Have you been taking lessons from Sigfrid von Shrink? That's what he always used to tell me."

"Was good program, Sigfrid. Please believe, I understand what is in your heart."

"I know you do, only—"

"Only"—she nodded—"is embarrassing to talk of this with me, who am Other Woman in case. Without whom would be no problem."

"That's not true, damn it!" I had not intended to yell, but maybe there was, after all, something bottled up.

"Incorrect, Robin. Is true. If I did not exist could go look for Klara, no doubt find her, then decide what to make of this worrying situation. Might become lovers again. Might not—is young woman, Klara, might not want raddled old spare-parts wreck for lover, eh? I foreclose this option. I am sorry."

She thought for a moment, then corrected herself. "No, is not true; I am not a bit sorry we love each other. Value that very greatly—but problem remains. Only, Robin! There is no guilt in this for anyone! You deserve none, I accept none, certainly Klara Moynlin has earned none. So all guilt, worry, fear, is all in your head. No, Robin, do not mistake me; what is in head can hurt very powerfully, especially for person with well-developed conscience like you. But is paper tiger. Blow on it, it goes away. Problem is not Klara's reappearance; problem is you feel guilt."

It was very apparent that I had not been the only one to sleep poorly; obviously Essie had been rehearsing this speech for some time.

I sat up and sniffed the air. "Is that coffee you brought in with you?"

"Only if you want, Robin."

"I want." I thought for a minute while she was handing me the bottle. "You're certainly right," I said. "I know this. What I don't know, as Sigfrid used to say, is how to integrate this knowledge into my life."

She nodded. "I perceive I blundered," she said. "Should have included Sigfrid subroutines in Albert program instead of, let us say, gourmet cookery. Have thought of making programing change in Albert for you, because this is on my conscience."

"Oh, honey, that's not your—"

"—fault, no. That is center of this conversation, correct?" Essie leaned forward to give me a swift kiss, then looked concerned. "Oh, wait, Robin, I withdraw that kiss. For what I wish to say is this: In psychoanalytical shrinkery, as you have so often explained to me, the analyst is not important. What is important is what happens in the head of analysand, e.g., you. So the analyst can be machine, even very rudimentary machine; or dolt with bad breath; or human with doctoral degree . . . or even me."

"You!"

She winced. "Have heard more flattering tone from you," she complained.

"You're going to psychoanalyze me?"

She shrugged defensively. "Yes, me, why not? As friend. As *good* friend, intelligent, wishing to listen, I promise not judgmental in the least. I *promise* this, dear Robin. As one who will let you talk, fight, shout, weep if you will, until all comes out for you to see clear what you want and feel."

She melted my heart! All I managed to say was "Ah, Essie . . ." But I could have managed to weep then without much trouble.

Instead I took another pull at the coffee and then shook my head. "I don't think it would work," I said. I was feeling regretful and must have sounded it, but also I was feeling—what's the right word? Interested? *Technically* interested. Interested in it as a problem to be solved.

"Why not work?" she demanded combatively. "Listen, Robin, I have thought this out with care. I remember all you have told me of this, and I quote you exactly: Best part of sessions, you said, came often with Sigfrid while you were on your way to see him, rehearsing what you would say, what Sigfrid would say, what you would reply."

"Did I say that?" It was always amazing to me how much Essie remembered of the idle chit-chat of a quarter of a century together.

"Said exactly," she said smugly, "so why not me? Only because I am personally involved?"

"Well, that would surely make it harder."

"The hard things do at once," she said merrily. "Impossible sometimes take up to a week."

"Bless you," I said, "but—" I thought for a moment. "See, it's not just a question of listening. The big thing about a good shrink program is that it listens to the nonverbal stuff, too. Do you understand what I mean? The 'me' that does the talking doesn't always know what it wants to say. I block it—some 'I' or other blocks it, because letting all that old stuff out involves pain, and it doesn't want the pain."

"I would hold your hand through all of the pain, dear Robin."

"Of course you would. But would you understand the nonverbal stuff? That inside, silent 'me' talks in symbols. Dreams. Freudian slips. Unexplained aversions. Fears. Needs. Twitchings and blinkings. Allergies—all of those things, Essie, and a thousand more, like impotence, shortness of breath, itches, insomnia. I don't mean I suffer from all those things—"

"Certainly not all!"

"—but they're part of the vocabulary that Sigfrid could read. I can't. You can't either."

Essie sighed and accepted defeat. "Then must go to plan B," she said. "Albert! Turn on lights. Come in here."

The lights in the room came up slowly and Albert Einstein came in through the door. He didn't exactly yawn and stretch, but he did give the impression of an elderly genius just out of the sack, ready for whatever might come but not quite fully awake yet. "Have you chartered photoreconnaissance vessel?" she demanded.

"It is already on its way, Mrs. Broadhead," he said.

It did not seem to me that I had quite agreed to do that, but perhaps I had, I thought. "And," she went on, "have dispatched messages as agreed?"

"All of them, Mrs. Broadhead." He nodded. "As you instructed. To all persons high in the military establishment or government of the United States who owe Robin a favor, asking them to use their best efforts to persuade the Pentagon people to let us interview Dolly Walthers."

"Yes. That is as instructed," Essie agreed, and turned to me. "So you see, is now only one way to go. Go find this Dolly. Go find this Wan. Go find Klara. Then," she said, her voice steadfast but her expression looking suddenly much less confident and a whole lot more vulnerable, "then we see what we see, Robin, and the very best of good luck to all of us."

She was going very much faster than I could follow, and in directions I was sure I had never agreed to. My eyes were popping with astonishment. "Essie! What's going on? Who said—"

"Person who said, dear Robin, was I. Is obvious. Cannot deal with Klara as ghost in subconscious. Can perhaps deal with real live Klara face to face. Only way to go, correct?"

"Essie!" I was deeply shocked. "You sent those messages? You forged my name? You—"

"Now, you wait, you Robin!" she said, deeply shocked herself. "What forgery? I signed messages 'Broadhead.' Is my name, correct? Have right to sign my name to message, correct?"

I stared at her, frustrated. Fondly frustrated. "Woman," I said, "you're too smart for me, you know that? Why do I get the idea that you knew every word of this conversation before we had it?"

She shrugged smugly. "Am information specialist, as I keep telling you, dear Robin. Know how to deal with information, especially twenty-five years of it on subject that I love dearly and want dearly to be happy. So, yes, I thought with care of what could be done and what you would permit, and reached inevitable conclusions. Would do much more than that if necessary, Robin," she finished, getting up and stretching. "Would do whatever was best, not excluding going off by myself for six months or so so you and Klara can work things out."

And so ten minutes later, while Essie and I were getting ourselves cleaned up and dressed, Albert had received departure clearance and popped the *True Love* free of its docking pit, and we were on our way to the High Pentagon.

My dear wife, Essie, had many virtues. One was an altruism that sometimes took my breath away. Another was a sense of humor, and sometimes she imparted that to her programs. Albert had dressed himself for the part of daring hot pilot: leather helmet with earflaps flying, Red Baron white silk scarf thrown around his neck as he sat crouched in the pilot seat, glowering ferociously at the controls. "You can cut that out, Albert," I told him, and he turned his head and gave me a sheepish smile.

"I was only trying to amuse you," he said, removing the helmet.

"You did that, all right." And indeed I was amused. I was feeling rather good, all in all. The only way to deal with the terrible crushing depression of problems unmet is to meet them—one way or another and this was surely a way. I appreciated my wife's loving care. I appreciated the way my beautiful new ship flew. I even appreciated the neat way the holographic Albert got rid of his holographic helmet and scarf. There was no vulgar popping out of existence. He simply rolled them up and stowed them between his feet, and I guess waited to vanish them until no one was looking. "Does flying this ship take all your attention, Albert?" I asked.

"Well, not really, Robin," he admitted. "It has full navigation programing, of course."

"So your being there is just another way of amusing me. Then amuse me in a different way, why don't you? Talk to me. Tell me some of that stuff you're always anxious to show off. You know. About cosmology, and the Heechee, and the Meaning of Everything, and God."

"If you wish, Robin," he said agreeably, "but first perhaps you would like to see this incoming message."

Essie looked up from the corner where she was going over her customer-comment synoptics as Albert wiped the big overhead screen of its star pictures and displayed:

Robinette, my boy, for the guy who made the
Brazilians roll over and play dead nothing is too much.
High Pentagon alerted to your visit and instructed to
extend every courtesy. The joint is yours.

Manzbergen

"By God," said I, surprised and delighted, "they did it! They turned over the data!"

Albert nodded. "So it would appear, Robin. I think you have a right to be pleased with your efforts."

Essie came over and kissed the back of my neck. "I endorse this comment," she purred. "Excellent Robin! Man of great influence."

"Aw, shucks," I said, grinning. I couldn't help grinning. If the Brazilians had turned over their search-and-locate data to the Americans, then the Americans could very probably put it together with their own data and find a way to deal with the damn spaceborne terrorists and their damn crazy-making TPT. No wonder General Manzbergen was pleased with me! I was pleased with myself. And it just went to show that when problems seemed absolutely overwhelming and you couldn't decide which to tackle first, if you just tackled one of them you would find that all the others were melting away too . . . "What?"

"I asked if you were still interested in carrying on a conversation," Albert said wistfully.

"Why, sure. I guess so." Essie was back in her corner, but watching Albert rather than returning to her reports.

"Then if you don't mind," Albert said shyly, "it would give me pleasure to talk to you not about cosmology and eschatology and the missing mass, but about my own previous life, instead."

Essie, scowling, opened her mouth to speak, but I raised a hand. "Let him talk, love. I guess my mind wouldn't really be on the missing mass right now, anyway."

So we flew along on that short, happy run to the High Pentagon while Albert, leaning back in the pilot seat with his hands folded over the plump tummy in the sloppy sweater, reminisced about early days in the patent office in Switzerland, and the way the queen of Belgium used to accompany his violin-playing on the piano; and meanwhile my at-third-hand friend Dolly Walthers was being questioned with great vigor by military intelligence officers in the High Pentagon; and meanwhile my not-quite-yet friend Captain was tidying up the traces of his intervention and grieving over his lost love; and meanwhile my once-much-more-than friend Klara Moynlin was . . . was . . .

I didn't know what Klara was doing meanwhile, not then I didn't. Actually, in detail, I surely did not really want to.

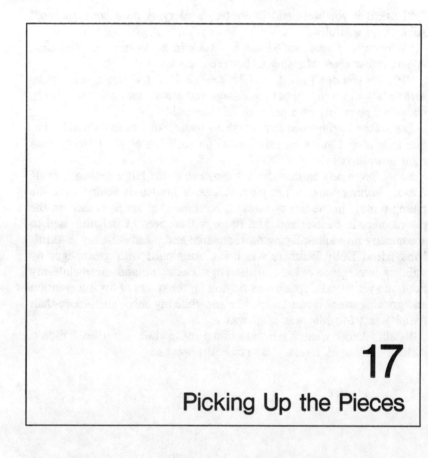

17
Picking Up the Pieces

The hardest part of Klara's new life was keeping her mouth shut. She had a combative nature, Klara did, and with Wan, combat was all too easy to create. What Wan wanted was food, sex, company, occasional assistance at the jobs of running the spacecraft—*when* he wanted them, and not at any other times. What Klara wanted was time to think. She wanted to think about this astonishing derailment of her life. The possibility of getting killed she had always faced—if not bravely, exactly, then at least steadfastly. The possibility that so weird a misadventure as being stuck on a siding, inside a black hole, for an entire generation while the world moved on without her had never crossed her mind. That needed to be thought over.

Wan had no interest in Klara's needs. When he wanted her for something, he wanted her. When he didn't, he made that very clear. It was not his sexual demands that troubled Klara. In general they were not much more trouble, or more personally significant, than the routine of going to the bathroom. Foreplay for Wan consisted of taking his pants off. The act was over at his pace, and his pace was rapid. The use of Klara's body disturbed her less than the rape of her attention.

Klara's best times were when Wan was sleeping. They did not usually last very long. Wan was a light sleeper. She would settle down for a conversation with the Dead Men, or make herself something to eat that Wan didn't particularly like, or simply sit and stare into space—a phrase that took on new meaning when the only thing one could look at that was more than an arm's-length away was the screen that looked out onto space itself. And just as she was relaxed the shrill, teasing voice would come: "Doing nothing again, Klara? What a lazy thing you are! Dolly would have baked a whole batch of brownies for me!" Or, worse, he would be in a playful mood. Then out would come the little paper-folds and drugstore vials and silver boxes of pink and purple pills. Wan had just discovered drugs. He wanted to share the experience with Klara. And sometimes, out of boredom and dejection, she would let herself be persuaded. She would not inject or sniff or swallow anything she could not positively identify, and she rejected a lot of the things she could. But she accepted a lot, too. The rushes, the euphoria—they didn't last, but they were a blessed diversion from the emptiness of a life that had hiccoughed and died and was trying to start itself again. Getting stoned with Wan, or even making love with Wan, was better than trying to evade the questions that Wan asked and she did not want to answer honestly—

"Klara, do you honestly think I'll ever find my father?"

"Not a hope, Wan, the old boy's long dead."

—because the old boy surely was. The man who had fathered Wan had left Gateway on a solitary mission just about the time Wan's mother began to wonder if she'd really missed her first period. The records simply posted him as missing. Of course, he *could* have been swallowed up by a black hole. He *could* still be there, frozen in time as Klara herself had been.

But the odds were very poor.

An astonishing thing to Klara—out of the million astonishing things thirty years had brought—was the easy way Wan displayed and interpreted the old Heechee navigation charts. In a good mood—almost a record, because it had lasted nearly a quarter of an hour—he had shown her the charts and marked the objects he had already visited, including her own. When the mood evaporated and he stamped off furiously to sleep, Klara had cautiously asked the Dead Men about it. It could not be said that the Dead Men really understood the charts, but the tiny bit they did know was far more than Klara's contemporaries had ever known.

Some of the cartographical conventions were simple enough—even self-evident, like Columbus's egg, once you'd been told what they meant. The Dead Men were pleased to tell Klara what they meant. The problem was to keep them from telling her *and* telling her. The colors of the objects shown? Simple, said the Dead Men; the bluer they were, the farther they were; the redder, the nearer. "That shows," whispered the most pedantic of the Dead Men, who happened to be a woman, "that shows the Heechee were aware of the Hubble-Humason Law."

"Please don't tell me what the Hubble-Humason Law is," Klara said. "What about all these other markings? The things like crosses, with little extra bars on them?"

"They're major installations," sighed the Dead Man. "Like Gateway. And Gateway Two. And the Food Factory. And—"

"And these things like check marks?"

"Wan calls them question marks," whispered the tiny voice. Indeed, they did look like that, a little, if you took the dot off the bottom of the question mark and turned the rest of it upside down. "Most of them are black holes. If you change the setting to twenty-three, eighty-four—"

"Please be still!" cried Wan, appearing disheveled and irritated from his bunk. "I cannot sleep with all this foolish yelling!"

"We weren't yelling, Wan," Klara said peaceably.

"Weren't yelling!" he yelled. "Hah!" He stomped over to the pilot seat and sat down, fists clenched on his thighs, shoulders hunched, glowering at her. "What if I want something to eat now?" he demanded.

"Do you?"

He shook his head. "Or what if I wanted to make love?"

"Do you?"

"Do I, do I! It is always an argument with you! And you are not really a very good cook and, also, in bed you are far less interesting than you claimed. Dolly was better."

Klara found she was holding her breath, and forced herself to release it slowly and silently. She could not force herself to smile.

Wan grinned, pleased to see that he had scored on her. "You remember Dolly?" he went on jovially. "That was the one you persuaded me to abandon on Gateway. There they have the rule of no pay, no breathe, and she had no money. I wonder if she is still alive."

"She's still alive," gritted Klara, hoping it was true. But Dolly would always find someone to pay her bills. "Wan?" she began, desperate to change the subject before it got worse. "What do those yellow flashes on the screen mean? The Dead Men don't seem to know."

"No one knows. If the Dead Men do not know, is it not foolish to think I would know? You are very foolish sometimes," he complained. And in the very nick of time, just as Klara was reaching the boiling point, the thin voice of the female Dead Man came again:

"Setting twenty-three, eighty-four, ninety-seven, eight, fourteen."

"What?" said Klara, startled.

"Setting twenty-three—" The voice repeated the numbers.

"What's that?" Klara asked, and Wan took it upon himself to answer. His position had not changed, but the expression on his face was different —less hostile. More strained. More fearful.

"It is a chart setting, to be sure," he said.

"Showing what?"

He looked away. "Set it and find out," he said.

It was difficult for Klara to operate the knurled wheels, for in all her previous experience such an act was tantamount to suicide: the chart-displaying function had not been learned, and a change in the settings almost invariably meant an unpredictable, and usually fatal, change in course. But all that happened was that the images on the screen flickered and whirled, and steadied to show—what? A star? Or a black hole? Whatever it was, it was bright cadmium yellow on the screen, and around it flickered no fewer than five of the upside-down question marks. "What is it?" she demanded.

Wan turned slowly to stare at it. "It is very big," he said, "and very far away. And it is where we are going now." All that combativeness was gone from his face now. Klara almost wished it were back, for what had replaced it was naked, unrelieved fear.

And meanwhile—

Meanwhile, the task of Captain and his Heechee crew was nearing the end of its first phase, though it brought no joy to any of them. Captain was still grieving for Twice. Her slim, sallow, shiny body, emptied of personality, had been disposed of. At home it would have gone to join the other refuse in the settling tanks, for the Heechee were not sentimental about cadavers. On shipboard there were no settling tanks, so it had been jettisoned into space. The part of Twice that remained was in store with the rest of the ancestral minds, and as Captain roamed about his new and unfamiliar ship he touched the pouch where she was stored from time to time without knowing that he did it.

It was not just the personal loss. Twice was their drone controller, and the cleanup job could not be done properly without her. Mongrel was doing her best, but she was not primarily an operator of enslaved equipment. Captain, standing nervously over her, was not helping much. "Don't kill your thrust yet, that's no stable orbit!" he hissed, and, "I hope those people don't get motion sickness, the way you're jerking them around." Mongrel pulsed her jaw muscles but did not respond. She knew why Captain was so tense and withdrawn.

But at last he was satisfied and tapped Mongrel on the shoulder to signify that she could discharge cargo. The great bubble lurched and revolved. A line of dark appeared from pole to pole, and it opened like a flower. Mongrel, hissing with satisfaction at last, disengaged the crumpled sailship and allowed it to slide free.

"They got a rough ride," commented the communications officer, coming over to stand beside his captain.

Captain twitched his abdomen, in the Heechee equivalent of a shrug. The sailship was quite clear of the opened sphere now, and Mongrel began to close the great hemisphere. "What about your own task, Shoe? Are the human beings still chattering?"

"More than ever, I'm afraid."

"Massed minds! Have you made any progress in translating what they're yelling about?"

"The minds are working on it." Captain nodded gloomily and reached for the eight-sided medallion clipped to the pouch between his legs. He stopped himself barely in time. The satisfaction he might gain from asking the minds how they were getting along with the translation would not justify the pain of hearing Twice among them. Sooner or later he would hear her, necessarily. Not yet.

He blew air through his nostrils and addressed Mongrel. "Button it up, power it down, let it float there. We can't do any better than that for now. Shoe! Transmit a message to them. Tell them we're sorry we can't fix them up any better right now but we'll try to come back. White-Noise! Plot all vessels in space for me."

The navigator nodded, turned to his instruments, and in a moment the screen filled with a whirling mass of yellow-tailed comets. The color of the nucleus indicated distance, the length of the tail velocity. "Which one is the fool with the corkscrew?" Captain demanded, and the screen contracted its field to show one particular comet. Captain hissed in astonishment. That particular ship, last time he looked, had been safely moored in its home system. Now it was traveling at very high velocity indeed, and had left its home far behind. "Where is he going?" he demanded.

White-Noise twitched his corded face muscles. "It'll take a minute, Captain."

"Well, do it!"

Under other circumstances, White-Noise might have taken offense at Captain's tone. Heechee did not talk uncivilly to each other. The circumstances, however, were not to be ignored. The fact that these upstart humans were in possession of black-hole-piercing equipment was terribly frightening in itself. The knowledge that they were filling the air with their loud, foolish communications was worse. Who knew what they would do next? And the death of a shipmate was the final straw, making this trip just about the worst since those long-ago days, before White-Noise had been born, when they learned of the existence of the others . . . "It doesn't make sense," White-Noise complained. "There's nothing along their course that I can see."

Captain scowled at the cryptic graphics on the screen. Reading them was a task for a specialist, but Captain had to have a smattering of everyone's skills and he could see that along the plotted geodesic there was nothing in reasonable range. "What about that globular cluster?" he demanded.

"I don't think so, Captain. It's not directly in line of flight, and there's nothing there. Nothing at all, really, all the way to the edge of the Galaxy."

"Minds!" said a voice from behind them. Captain turned. The black-hole piercer, Burst, was standing there, and all his muscles were rippling madly. The man's fear communicated itself to Captain even before Burst said tightly:

"Extend the geodesic." White-Noise looked at him uncomprehendingly. "Extend it! Outside the Galaxy!"

The navigator started to object, then caught his meaning. His own muscles were twitching as he obeyed. The screen flickered. The fuzzed yellow line extended itself. It passed through regions where there was nothing else on the screen at all, undiluted black space, empty.

Not quite empty.

A deep-blue object emerged from the darkness of the screen, paling and yellowing. It was quintuply flagged. There was a hiss from every member of the crew as it steadied, and stopped, and the fuzzy yellow geodesic reached out to touch it.

The Heechee looked at each other, and not one of them had a word to say. The one ship that could do the greatest damage one could imagine was on its way to the place where the damage was waiting to be done.

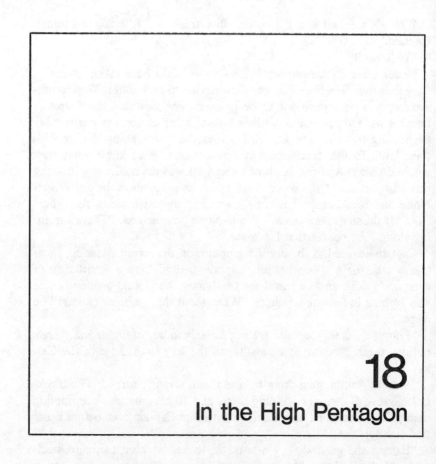

18

In the High Pentagon

The High Pentagon isn't exactly a satellite in geostationary orbit. It's five satellites in geostationary orbit. The orbits are not precisely identical, so all five of these armored, pulse-hardened chunks of metal waltz around each other. First Alpha's on the outside and Delta's nearest the Earth, then they swing awhile and it's Epsilon that's facing out and maybe Gamma that's inboard, swing your partners, do-si-do, and so on. Why, one might ask, did they do it that way instead of just building one big one? Well, one is answered, five satellites are five times as hard to hit as one satellite. Also, I personally think, because both the Soviet Orbit Tyu-ratam and the Peep-China command post are single structures. Naturally the U. S. of A. wanted to show that they could do the job better. Or at least different. It all dated from the time of the wars. At one time, they said, it had been the very latest in defense. Its huge nuke-fueled lasers were supposed to be able to zap any enemy missile from fifty thousand miles away. Probably they indeed could—when they were built—and for maybe three months after that, until the other fellows began using the same pulse-hardening and radar-decoy tricks and everybody was back to Go. Unfortunately they all "went," but that's a whole other story.

So we never saw four-fifths of the Pentagon, except on our screens. The hunk they vectored us in on was the one that held crew quarters, administration—and the brig. That was Gamma, sixty thousand tons of metal and meat, about the size of the Great Pyramid and pretty much the same shape, and we found out right away that no matter how open-handed General Manzbergen had been back on Earth, here in orbit we were about as welcome as a cold sore. For one thing, they kept us waiting for permission to unseal. "Suppose they must have been hard-hit in the minute madness," Essie speculated, scowling at the viewscreen, which showed nothing but the metal flank of Gamma.

"That's no excuse," I said, and Albert chipped in his two cents' worth: "They were not hit so hard but that they were ready to hit much harder, I'm afraid. I have seen too much war; I do not like such things." He was fingering his Two Percent button and acting, for a hologram, rather nervous. What he said was true enough. A couple weeks earlier, when the terrorists had zapped everybody from space with their TPT, the whole station had gone crazy for a minute. Literally one minute; it was no more than that. And a good thing it was no longer, because in that one minute eight of the eleven duty stations that had to be manned in order to aim a proton beam at terrestrial cities were in fact manned. And raring to go.

That wasn't what was troubling Essie. "Albert," she said, "do not play games that make me nervous. You have not in fact seen any war, ever. You are only a program."

He bowed. "As you say, Mrs. Broadhead. Please? I have just received permission for us to unseal and you may enter the satellite."

So we entered, with Essie looking thoughtfully over her shoulder at the program we left behind. The ensign waiting for us did not seem enthusiastic. He ran his thumb over the ship's data chip as though he were trying to make sure the magnetic ink didn't come off. "Yeah," he said, "we got a signal about you. Only thing, I'm not sure if the brigadier can see you now, sir."

"It was not a brigadier we wished to see," Essie explained sweetly, "simply a Mrs. Dolly Walthers, whom you are holding here."

"Oh, yes, ma'am. But Brigadier Cassata has to sign your pass, and right now we're all pretty busy." He excused himself to whisper into a phone, then looked happier. "If you'll just come with me, sir and ma'am," he said, and conducted us out of the port at last.

You lose the habit of maneuvering in low-G or zero-G if you don't practice it, and I was long out of practice. Also I was rubbernecking. All this was new to my experience. Gateway is an asteroid, tunneled out by the Heechee long ago and every interior surface lined by them with their favorite blue-glowing metal. The Food Factory, Heechee Heaven, and all of the other large structures I had visited in space were also Heechee construction. It was confusing for me to be for the first time in a very large human-made space artifact. It seemed more alien than anything Heechee. No familiar blue glow, just painted steel. No spindle-shaped chamber at the core. No prospectors looking sick-scared or triumphant, no museum collections of bits and pieces of Heechee technology found here and there around the Galaxy. What there was plenty of was military personnel in skintights and, for some reason, crash helmets. The curiousest thing of all was that although every one of them wore a weapons holster, all the holsters were empty.

I slowed down to point this out to Essie. "Looks like they don't trust their own people," I commented.

She shook me by the collar and pointed ahead, where the ensign was waiting. "Do not talk against hosts, Robin, not until are behind their backs, anyway. Here. This must be place."

Not a minute too soon; I was beginning to run out of breath with the exertion of pulling myself along a zero-G corridor. "Right inside, sir and ma'am," said the ensign hospitably, and of course we did as he said.

But what was inside the door was only a bare room with a couple of sit-down lashings around the walls, and nothing else. "Where's the brigadier?" I demanded.

"Why, sir, I told you we're all pretty busy right now. He'll see you soon's he can." And, with a shark's smile, he closed the door on us; and the interesting thing about that door, we both perceived at once, was that there was no knob on the inside surface.

Like everybody, I have had fantasies of being arrested. You're busy with your life, herding fish or balancing somebody's books or writing the great new symphony, and all of a sudden there's a knock on the door. "Come along without resistance," they say, and snap the cuffs on and read you your rights, and the next thing you know you're in a place like this. Essie shivered. She must have had the same fantasies, though if ever there was a blameless life it was hers. "Is silly," she said, more to herself than to me. "What a pity there is no bed here. Could put the time to use."

I patted her hand. I knew she was trying to cheer me up. "They said they were busy," I reminded her.

So we waited.

And half an hour later, without warning, I felt Essie stiffen under the hand I had on her shoulder, and the expression on her face was suddenly raging and mad; and I felt a quick, hurting, furious jolt to my own mind—

And then it was gone, and we looked at each other. It had only lasted a few seconds. Long enough to tell us just what it was they had been busy about, and why they had carried no weapons in their holsters.

The terrorists had struck again—but only a glancing blow.

When at last the ensign came back for us he was gleeful. I do not mean that he was friendly. He still didn't like civilians. He was happy enough to have a big smile on his face and hostile enough not to tell us why. It had been a long time. He didn't apologize, just conducted us to the commandant's office, grinning all the way. And when we got there, pastel-painted steel walls with its West Point holoscape on the wall and its sterling silver smoke eater trying vainly to keep up with his cigar, Brigadier Cassata was smiling, too.

There were not very many good explanations possible for all this secret jollity, so I took a long leap in the dark and landed on one of them. "Congratulations, Brigadier," I said politely, "on capturing the terrorists."

The smile flickered, but came back. Cassata was a small man, and pudgier than the military medics must have preferred; his thighs bulged out at the hems of his olive-drab shorts as he sat on the edge of his desk to greet us. "As I understand it, Mr. Broadhead," he said, "your purpose here is to interview Mrs. Dolly Walthers. You may certainly do that, considering the instructions I have received, but I can't answer your questions about security matters."

"I didn't ask any," I pointed out. Then, as I felt Essie's why-you-antagonize-this-creep? glare burning the back of my neck, I added, "Anyway, it's very kind of you to let us do it."

He nodded, obviously agreeing that he was very kind. "I'd like to ask you a question, though. Would you mind telling me why you want to see her?"

Essie's glare was still burning, which kept me from telling him that I did mind. "Not at all," I lied. "Mrs. Walthers spent some time with a very good friend of mine, whom I am anxious to see. We're hoping she can tell us how to get in touch with, uh, with my friend."

It was not a lot of use skipping the gender-revealing pronoun. They had surely interrogated the hell out of poor Dolly Walthers and knew that there were only two people I could mean, and of the two it was not at all likely that I would call Wan a friend. He looked at me in a puzzled way, then at Essie, then said, "Walthers is certainly a popular young lady. I won't keep you any longer." And he turned us over to the ensign for the conducted tour.

As a tour guide, the ensign was a flat failure. He didn't answer questions; he didn't volunteer information. There was a lot to be curious about, too, because the Pentagon was showing signs of recent trouble. Not physical damage, so much, but when the station had gone crazy for the earlier minute of madness the brig was damaged. Its locking program had been crashed by the duty guards. Fortunately they had wrecked it in the open position; otherwise, there would have been some sorry skeletons starving to death in the cells.

The way I found out about it was by passing through a tier of cells and observing that they were all open, with armed MPs squatting boredly in the corridors to make sure the inmates stayed inside. The ensign paused to talk briefly to the guard officer and, while we waited, Essie whispered: "If didn't catch terrorists, what would brigadier be nice to you for?"

"Good question," I answered. "Here's one back. What did he mean about her being a very popular young lady?"

The ensign was scandalized by our talking in ranks. He cut short the chat with the MP lieutenant and hustled us along to a cell like any other cell, door standing open. He pointed inside. "There's your prisoner," he said. "You can talk to her all you like, but she doesn't know anything much."

"I realize that," I said, "because if she did, you surely wouldn't let us see her at all, would you?" I got the hot flash of another of Essie's glares for that. She was right, too. If I hadn't annoyed him, the ensign might have had the common decency to move back a few steps so that we could talk to Dolly Walthers in private, instead of posting himself firmly at the open door.

Or might not. The latter theory is the one that got my vote.

Dolly Walthers was a child-sized woman with a childish, high-pitched voice and bad teeth. She was not at her best. She was scared, fatigued, angry, and sullen.

And I was not all that much better. I was wholly, disconcertingly aware that this young woman before me had just spent a couple of weeks in the company of the love of my life—or one of the loves of my life—in the top two, anyway. I say this lightly enough. It wasn't a light thing. I didn't know what to do, and I didn't know what to say.

"Say hello, Robin," Essie instructed.

"Miz Walthers," I said obediently, "hello. I'm Robin Broadhead."

She had manners left. She put out her hand like a good child. "I know who you are, Mr. Broadhead, even not counting that I met your wife the other day." We shook hands politely and she flashed a hint of a sad smile. It wasn't until some time later, when I saw her Robinette Broadhead puppet, that I knew what she had been smiling at. But she looked puzzled, too. "I thought they said there were four people who wanted to see me," she said, peering past the stolid ensign in search of the others.

"Is just the two of us," said Essie, and waited for me to speak.

But I didn't speak. I didn't know what to say. I didn't know what to ask. If it had been just Essie there, perhaps I could have managed to tell Dolly Walthers what Klara had meant to me and ask for her help—any kind of help. Or if it had been just the ensign, I could have ignored him like any other piece of furniture. Or I think I could—but they were both there, and I stood tongue-tied while Dolly Walthers gazed at me curiously, and Essie expectantly, and even the ensign turned to stare.

Essie sighed, an exasperated and compassionate sound, and made her decision. She took charge. She turned to Dolly Walthers. "Dolly," she said briskly, "must excuse my husband. Is quite traumatic for him, for reasons too complex to explain just now. Must excuse me also, please, for allowing MPs to take you away; I also have some trauma for related reasons. Important thing is what we do now. That will be as follows: First we secure your release from this place. Second we invite your company and help in voyage to locate Wan and Gelle-Klara Moynlin. You agree?"

It was all happening too fast for Dolly Walthers, too. "Well," she said, "I—"

"Good," said Essie, nodding. "We go to arrange this. You, Ensign! Take us back to our ship, *True Love,* at once, please."

The ensign opened his mouth, scandalized, but I got in ahead of him. "Essie, shouldn't we see the brigadier about that?"

She squeezed my hand and gazed at me. The gaze was compassionate. The squeeze was a shut-silly-mouth-Robin! warning that nearly broke my knuckles. "Poor lamb," she said apologetically to the officer, "has just had major surgery. Is confused. To ship for his medicine, and quickly!"

When my wife Essie is determined to do something, the way to get along with her is to let her do it. What she had in mind I did not know, but what I should do about it was very clear. I assumed the demeanor of an elderly man dazed by recent surgery, and let her guide me in the wake of the ensign down the corridors of the Pentagon.

We didn't move very fast, because the corridors of the Pentagon were pretty busy. The ensign halted us at an intersection while a party of prisoners marched past. For some reason they were clearing out an entire block of cells. Essie nudged me and pointed to the monitors on the wall. One set of them were no more than signposts, *Commissary 7, Enlisted Personnel Latrines, Docking V,* and so on. But the other—

The other showed the docking area, and there was something big coming in. Great, hulking, human-built; you could tell it was Earth-built rather than Heechee at the first glance. It wasn't just the lines, or the fact that it was constructed of gray steel rather than Heechee-metal blue. The proof lay in the mean-looking projectile weapons that poked their snouts out of its smooth exterior.

The Pentagon, I knew, had lost six of those ships in a row, trying to adapt the Heechee faster-than-light drive to human ships. I couldn't complain about that; it was from their mistakes that the design for the *True Love* had benefited. But the weapons were not pleasant to see. You never saw one on a Heechee vessel.

"Come on," snapped the ensign, glaring at us. "You're not supposed to be here. Let's move it." He started along a relatively empty corridor, but Essie slowed him down.

"Is faster this way," she said, pointing to the *Docking* sign.

"Off limits!" he snapped.

"Not for good friend of Pentagon who is unwell," she replied, and tugged at my arm, and we headed for the densest, noisiest knots of people. There are secrets within secrets in Essie, but this one clarified itself in a moment. The commotion had been the captured terrorists being brought in from the cruiser, and Essie had just wanted to get a look at them.

The cruiser had intercepted their stolen ship just as it was coming out of FTL. They shot it up. Apparently there had been eight terrorists on board—eight, in a Heechee ship that five persons crowded! Three of them had survived to become prisoners. One was comatose. One was missing a leg, but conscious. The third one was mad.

It was the mad one that was attracting all the attention. She was a young black girl—from Sierra Leone, they said—and she was screaming incessantly. She wore a straitjacket. By the look of it she had been kept in it for a very long time, for the fabric was stained and stinking, her hair was matted, her face was cadaverous. Somebody was calling my name, but I pressed forward along with Essie to get a better look. "Is Russian she is saying," said Essie, her brows furrowing, "but is not very good. Georgia accent. Very strong. Says she hates us."

"I could have figured that out," I said. I had seen enough. When the ensign got through the crowd, yelling furious orders for people to get out of the way, I let him tug me back, and then I heard my name called again.

So it wasn't the ensign? In fact, it wasn't a man's voice at all. It came from the knot of prisoners being moved out of their cells, and I saw who it was. The Chinese girl. Janie something. "Good God," I said to the ensign, "what have you arrested her for?"

He rasped, "That is a military matter and none of your business, Broadhead. Come on! You don't belong here!"

There was no point in arguing with a man who had made up his mind. I didn't ask him again. I just walked over to the line and asked Janie. The other prisoners were all female, all military personnel, no doubt in for overstaying a furlough or punching somebody like the ensign in the mouth—all good people, I was sure. They were quiet, listening. "Audee wanted to come up here because they had his *wife,*" she said, with a look on her face as though she were saying "his case of tertiary syphilis." "So we took a shuttle up, and as soon as we got here they stuck us in the brig."

"Now, Broadhead," the ensign shouted, "that's the last straw. You come on out of there or you're under arrest yourself!" And his hand was on the holster that once more contained a sidearm. Essie sailed by, smiling politely.

"Is now no more need for concern, Ensign," she said, "for there is *True Love* waiting for us. So we are out of hair now. Remains only to fetch brigadier here to settle remaining questions."

The ensign goggled. "Ma'am," he stuttered, "ma'am, you can't get the brigadier here!"

"Of course can! Husband requires medical treatment, therefore must be here to receive. Brigadier Cassata is courteous man, right? West Point? Many courses in deportment, courtesy, covering coughs and sneezes? And also please tell brigadier is excellent bourbon here which poor sick husband requires assistance to dispose of."

The ensign stumbled away hopelessly. Essie looked at me and I looked at Essie. "Now what?" I asked.

She smiled and patted my head. "First I instruct Albert about bourbon

—and other things," she said, turning to deliver a couple of quick sentences in Russian, "and then we wait for brigadier to show up."

It didn't take long for the brigadier to arrive, but by the time he had gotten there I had almost forgotten him. Essie was engaged in a lively chat with the guard the ensign had left, and I was thinking. What I was thinking about mostly, for a change, was not Klara but the mad African woman and her almost as mad associates. They scared me. Terrorists scared me. In the old days there was a PLO and an IRA and Puerto Rican nationalists and Serbian secessionists and German and Italian and American rich kids asserting their contempt for their daddies—oh, lots of terrorists, all sizes, all kinds—but they were all separate. The fact that they had got together scared me. The poor and the furious had learned to join their rages and resources, and there was no question at all that they could make the world listen. Capturing one ship would not stop them; it would only make their efforts bearable for a while—or almost bearable.

But to solve their problem—to ease their rage and supply their needs—more was needed. The colonization of worlds like Peggys Planet was the best and maybe the only answer, but it was *slow*. The transport could take three thousand eight hundred poor people to a better life each month. But each month something like a quarter of a million new poor people were being born, and the fatal arithmetic was easy to do:

$$
\begin{array}{r}
250,000 \\
-\,3,800 \\
\hline
246,200
\end{array}
$$

new poor people to deal with each month. The only hope was new and bigger transports, hundreds or thousands of them. A hundred would keep us even with the present level of misery. A thousand would cure it once and for all—but where were the thousand big ships to come from? It had taken eight months to build the *True Love*, and a lot more of my money than I had really intended. What would it cost to build something a thousand times as big?

The brigadier's voice took my mind off these reflections. "It is," he was saying, "flatly impossible! I let you see her because I was asked to. To take her away with you is out of the question!" He glowered at me as I joined them, taking Essie's hand.

"Also," she said, "is question of male Walthers and Chinese woman. We wish them also."

"We do?" I asked, but the brigadier wasn't listening to me.

"What else, for God's sake?" he demanded. "You wouldn't like me to turn over my section of the Pentagon? Or give you a cruiser or two?"

Essie shook her head politely. "Our ship is more comfortable, thank you."

"Jesus!" Cassata wiped his brow and allowed Essie to lead him into the main lounge for the promised bourbon. "Well," he said, "there's no real charge against Walthers and Yee-xing. They had no right coming up here without clearance, but if you take them away again we can forget that one."

"Splendid!" Essie cried. "Remains now only other Walthers!"

"I could not possibly take the responsibility," he began, and Essie did not let him finish.

"Certainly not! One understands that, of course. So we will refer to higher authority, right? Robin! Call General Manzbergen. Do here, so will be no annoying record to possibly embarrass, all right?"

There is no use arguing with Essie when she is in such a mood, and besides, I was curious to see what she was up to. "Albert," I called. "Do it, please."

"Sure, Robin," he said obligingly, voice only; and in a moment the screen lit up, and there was General Manzbergen at his desk. "Morning, Robin, Essie," he said genially. "I see you've got Perry Cassata there—congratulations to all of you!"

"Thank you, Jimmy," said Essie, looking sidewise at the brigadier, "but is not what we called about, please."

"Oh?" He frowned. "Whatever it is, do it fast, all right? I've got a top meeting coming up in ninety seconds."

"Take less than that, General dear. Merely please instruct Brigadier Cassata to turn over Dolly Walthers to us."

Manzbergen looked puzzled. "For what?"

"So can use her to locate missing Wan, General dear. Has TPT, you know. Much in everyone's interest to make him give it back."

He grinned fondly at her. "Minute, honey," he said, and bent to a hushphone.

The brigadier might have been rushed, but he was on his toes. "There's a lag," he pointed out. "Isn't this zero-speed radio?"

"Is burst transmission," Essie lyingly explained. "Have only small vessel here, not much power"—another lie—"so must conserve communications energy—ah, here is general again!"

The general pointed toward Cassata. "It's authorized," he barked. "They're trustworthy, we owe them a favor—and they might be able to save us a pack of future trouble. Give them whoever they want, on my authority. Now, for God's sake, let me get to my meeting—and don't call me again unless it's World War Four!"

So the brigadier went away, shaking his head; and pretty soon the MPs brought Janie Yee-xing to us, and a minute later Audee Walthers, and quite a while after that Dolly Walthers. "Nice to see you all again," said Essie, welcoming them aboard. "Am sure you have much to talk over among you, but first let us get away from this wicked place. Albert! Move it, please?"

"Right, Mrs. Broadhead," sang Albert's voice. He didn't bother with materializing in the pilot seat; he simply walked in a door and leaned against the lintel, smiling at the company.

"Will introduce later," said Essie. "This is good friend who is computer program. Albert? Are now safely away from Pentagon?"

He nodded, twinkling. Then before my eyes he turned from elderly man in pipe and baggy sweater to the leaner, taller, uniformed, and medaled Chief of Staff General James P. Manzbergen. "Right you are, honey," he cried. "Now let's get our asses into FTL before they find out we foxed them!"

19
The Permutations of Love

Who sleeps with whom? Ah, that was the question! We had five passengers, and only three staterooms to put them in. The *True Love* had not been planned for very many guests, and especially when the guests did not come presorted in pairs. Should we put Audee in with his wedded wife, Dolly? Or with his most recent bedmate, Janie Yee-xing? Put Audee by himself and the two women together?—and what would they do to each other if we did? It was not that Janie and Dolly were hostile to each other so much as that Audee seemed unaccountably hostile to both of them. "He cannot make up his mind which he should be true to," said Essie wisely, "and is a man who wishes to be true to a woman, is Audee."

Well, I understood that well enough, and even understood that more of our passengers than one suffered that problem.

But there is a word in that statement that did not apply to me, and it is the word suffered. You see, I wasn't suffering. I was enjoying myself. I was enjoying Essie, too, because the way we solved the problem of assigning accommodations was to walk away from it. Essie and I retired to Captain's Quarters and locked the door. We told ourselves that the reason we did was to let our three guests sort things out among themselves. That was a good reason. God knows they needed time to do that, because the interpersonal dynamics latent among the three of them were enough to explode a star; but we had other reasons, too, and the biggest of them was so that we could make love.

And so we did. Enthusiastically. With great joy. You would think that after a quarter of a century—at our advanced ages; and making allowances for familiarity and boredom and the fact that there are, after all, just so many mucous surfaces to rub against and a finite number of appurtenances to rub them with—there would be very little incentive for us to do that. Wrong. We were motivated as hell.

Perhaps because it was because of the relatively cramped quarters on the *True Love*. Locking ourselves into our private cabin with its anisokinetic bed gave the affair a spice of teenage fooling around on the porch, with Daddy and Mommy only a window screen away. We giggled a lot as the bed pushed us about in ingenious ways—and suffer? Not a bit of it. I hadn't forgotten Klara. She popped into my mind over and over, often at very personal times.

But Essie was there on the bed with me, and Klara was not.

So I lay back on the bed, twitching a little now and then to feel how the bed would twitch back, and how it would twitch Essie, cuddled close into my side, and she would twitch a little—it was a little like playing three-cushion billiards, but with more interesting pieces—and thought, calmly and sweetly, about Klara.

At that moment I felt quite certain that everything would work out. What after all was wrong? Only love. Only that two people loved each other. There was nothing wrong in that! It was a complication, to be sure, that one of that particular two, e.g., me, might be also a part of another two who loved each other. But complications could be resolved—somehow or other—couldn't they? Love was what made the universe go around. Love made Essie and me linger in Captain's Quarters. Love was what made Audee follow Dolly to the High Pentagon; and a kind of love was what made Janie go with him; and another kind of love, or maybe the same kind, made Dolly marry him in the first place, because one of the functions of love is surely to give a person another person to organize his or her life around. And off in one stretch of the great, gassy, starry wastes (though at that moment I did not yet know it) Captain was mourning for a love; and even Wan, who had never loved anyone but himself, was in fact scouring that universe for someone to aim his love at. You see how it works? It is love that is the motivator.

"Robin?" said Essie drowsily to my collarbone. "Did that very well. My compliments."

And, of course, she too was talking about love, although in this case I chose to accept it as a compliment to my skills in the demonstration of it. "Thank you," I said.

"Makes me ask question, though," she went on, drawing back to peer at me. "Are fully recovered? Gut in good shape? Two point three meters new tubing working well with old? Has Albert reported all well?"

"I feel just fine," I reported, as indeed I did, and leaned over to kiss her ear. "I only hope the rest of the world is going as well."

She yawned and stretched. "If you refer to vessel, Albert is quite capable of handling pilotage."

"Ah, yes, but is he capable of handling the passengers?"

She rolled over sleepily. "Ask him," she said.

So I called, "Albert? Come and talk to us." I turned to look at the door, curious to see how he would manage his appearance this time, through a tangible, real door that happened to be closed. He fooled me. There was a sound of Albert apologetically clearing his throat, and when I turned back he was sitting on Essie's dressing bench again, eyes bashfully averted.

Essie gasped and grabbed for the covers to shield her neat, modest breasts.

Now, that was a funny thing. Essie had never bothered to cover herself in front of one of her programs before. The funniest thing about it was that it did not seem strange at the time. "Sorry to intrude, my dear friends," said Albert, "but you did call."

"Yes, fine," said Essie, sitting up to look at him better—but with the bedspread still clutched to her. Perhaps by then her own reaction had struck her as odd, but all she said was "So. Our guests, how are they?"

"Very well, I should say," Albert said gravely. "They are having a three-sided conversation in the galley. Captain Walthers is preparing sandwiches, and the two young women are helping."

"No fights? No eyes scratched out?" I asked.

"Not at all. To be sure, they are rather formal, with many 'excuse mes' and 'pleases' and 'thank yous.' However," he added, looking pleased with himself, "I do have a report for you on the sailship. Would you like to have it now? Or—it occurs to me—perhaps you would like to join your guests, so that you may all hear it at once."

All my instincts were to get it right away, but Essie looked at me. "Is only polite, Robin," she said, and I agreed.

"Splendid," said Albert. "You will find it extremely interesting, I am sure. As do I. Of course, I have always been interested in sailing, you know," he went on chattily. "When I was fifty the *Berliner Handelsgesellschaft* gave me such a fine sailboat—lost, unfortunately, when I must leave Germany because of those wicked Nazis. My dear Mrs. Broadhead, I owe you so much! Now I have all these fine memories that I did not have before! I remember my little house near Ostend, where I used to walk along the beach with Albert—that"—he twinkled—"was *King* Albert, of Belgium. And we would speak of sailing, and then in the evenings his wife would accompany me on the piano while I played my violin— and all this I now remember, dear Mrs. Broadhead, only because of you!"

Through the whole speech Essie had been sitting rigid beside me, staring at her creation with a face like a stone. Now she began to sputter and then she broke out in guffaws. "Oh, Albert!" she cried, reaching behind her for a pillow. She took aim and threw it right through him, to bounce harmlessly against the cosmetics beyond him. "Great funny program, you are welcome! Now get out, please. Since are so human, with memories and tedious anecdotes, cannot permit to observe me unclothed!" And he allowed himself, this time, to simply wink away, while Essie and I hugged each other and laughed. "So get dressed now," she ordered at last, "so we can find out about sailship in mode satisfactory to computer program. Laughter is sovereign medicine, right? In that case have no further fears for your health, dear Robin, so well rejoiced a body will surely last forever!"

We headed for the shower, still chuckling—unaware that, in my case, "forever" at that moment amounted to eleven days, nine hours, and twenty-one minutes.

We had never built into the *True Love* a desk for Albert Einstein, particularly not one with his pipe marking his place in a book, a bottle of Skrip next to a leather tobacco jar, and a blackboard behind him half covered with equations. But there it was, and there he was, entertaining our guests with stories about himself. "When I was at Princeton," he declared, "they hired a man to follow me around with a notebook so that if I wrote something on a blackboard he would copy it down. It was not for my benefit but for theirs—otherwise, you see, they were afraid to erase the blackboards!" He beamed at our guests and nodded genially to

Essie and me, standing hand in hand at the doorway to the main lounge. "I was explaining, Mr. and Mrs. Broadhead, something of my history to these people, who perhaps have not really heard of me although I was, I must say, quite famous. Did you know, for example, that since I disliked rain, the administration at Princeton built a covered passage which you can still see, so that I could visit my friends without going outdoors?"

At least he wasn't wearing his general's face and Red Baron silk scarf, but he made me just a little uncomfortable. I felt like apologizing to Audee and his two women; instead, I said, "Essie? Don't you think these reminiscences are getting a bit thick?"

"Is possible," she said thoughtfully. "Do you wish him to stop?"

"Not really stop. He's much more interesting now, but if you could just turn down the gain on the personalized-identity database, or twist the potentiometer on the nostalgia circuits—"

"How silly you are, dear Robin," she said, smiling with forgiveness. Then she commanded: "Albert! Cut out so much gossip. Robin doesn't like it."

"Of course, my dear Semya," he said politely. "No doubt you wish to hear about the sailship, in any case." He stood up behind his desk—that is, his holographic but physically nonexistent image rose behind his equally nonexistent hologram of a desk; I had to keep reminding myself of that. He picked up a blackboard eraser and began to wipe away the chalk, then recollected himself. With an apologetic glance at Essie, he reached for a switch on the desk instead. The blackboard vanished. It was replaced by the familiar pebbly greeny-gray surface of a Heechee ship's viewscreen. Then he pressed another switch, and the pebbly gray disappeared, replaced this time by a view of a star chart. That was realistic, too—all it took to convert any Gateway ship's screen to a usable picture was a simple bias applied to the circuits (though a thousand explorers had died without finding that out). "What you see," he said genially, "is the place where Captain Walthers located the sailship, and as you see, there is nothing there."

Walthers had been sitting quietly on a hassock before the imitation fireplace, as far as possible from either Dolly or Janie—and each of them was as far as possible from the other, and also very quiet. But now Walthers spoke out, stung. "Impossible! The records were accurate! You have the data!"

"Of course they were accurate," Albert soothed, "but, you see, by the time the scout ship arrived there the sailship was gone."

"It couldn't have gone very far if its only drive was from starshine!"

"No, it could not. But it was absent. However," Albert said, beaming cheerfully, "I had provided for some such contingency. If you remember, my reputation—in my former self, I mean—rested on the assumption that the speed of light was a fundamental constant, subject," he added, blinking tolerantly around the room, "to certain broadenings of context that we have learned from the Heechee. But the speed, yes, is always the same—nearly three hundred thousand kilometers per second. So I instructed the drone, in the event that the sailship was not found, to remove itself a distance of three hundred thousand kilometers times the number of seconds since the sighting."

"Great clever egotistical program," Essie said fondly. "That was some smart pilot you hired for scout ship, right?"

Albert coughed. "It was an unusual ship, as well," he said, "since I did foresee that there might be special needs. I fear the expense was rather high. However, when the ship had reached the proper distance, this is what it saw." And he waved a hand, and the screen showed that multi-winged gossamer shape. No longer perfect, it was folding and contracting before our eyes. Albert had speeded up the action as seen from the scout, and we watched the great wings roll themselves up . . . and disappear.

Well. What we saw, you have already seen. The way in which you were advantaged over us was that you knew what you were seeing. There we were, Walthers and his harem, Essie and me. We had left a troublesome human world to chase after a troublesome puzzle, and there we saw the thing we were aiming at being—being *eaten* by something else! It looked exactly that way to our shocked and unprepared eyes. We sat there frozen, staring at the crumpled wings and the great glistening blue sphere that appeared from nowhere to swallow them.

I became aware that someone was chuckling gently, and was shocked for the second time when I realized who it was.

It was Albert, sitting now on the edge of his desk and wiping away a tear of amusement. "I do beg your pardon," he said, "but if you could see your *faces.*"

"*Damn* great egotistical program," Essie grated, no longer fondly, "stop crap immediately. What is going on here?"

Albert gazed at my wife. I could not quite decipher his expression: The look was fond, and tolerant, and a great many other things that I did not associate with a computer-generated image, even Albert's. But it was also uneasy. "Dear Mrs. Broadhead," he said, "if you did not wish me to have a sense of humor you should not have programed me so. If I have embarrassed you I apologize."

"Follow instructions!" Essie barked, looking baffled.

"Oh, very well. What you have seen," he explained, turning pointedly away from Essie to lecture to the group, "is what I believe to be the first known example of an actual Heechee-manned operation in real time. That is, the sailship has been abducted. Observe this smaller vessel." He waved a negligent hand, and the image spun and flowed, magnifying the scene. The magnification was more than the resolution of the scout ship's optics were good for, and so the edge of the sphere became pebbly and fuzzy.

But there was something behind it.

There was something that moved slowly into eclipse behind the sphere. Just as it was about to disappear Albert froze the picture, and we were looking at a blurry, fish-shaped object, quite tiny, very poorly imaged. "A Heechee ship," said Albert. "At least, I have no other explanation."

Janie Yee-xing gave a choking sound. "Are you sure?"

"No, of course not," said Albert. "It is only a theory as yet. One never says 'yes' to a theory, Miss Yee-xing, only 'maybe,' for some better theory will surely come along and the one that has seemed best until then will get its 'no.' But my theory is that the Heechee have decided to abduct the sailship."

Now, get the picture. Heechee! Real ones, attested to by the smartest data-retrieval system anyone had ever encountered. I had been looking for Heechee, one way or another, for two-thirds of a century, desperate to find them and terrified that I might. And when it happened the thing uppermost in my mind was not the Heechee but the data-retrieval system. I said, "Albert, why are you acting so funny?"

He looked at me politely, tapping his pipestem against his teeth. "In what way 'funny,' Robin?" he asked.

"Damn it, come off it! The way you act! Don't you—" I hesitated, trying to put it politely. "Don't you know you're just a computer program?"

He smiled sadly. "I do not need to be reminded of that, Robin. I am not real, am I? And yet the reality that you are immersed in is one for which I do not care."

"Albert!" I cried, but he put up his hand to quiet me.

"Allow me to say this," he said. "For me reality is, I know, a certain large quantity of parallel-processed on-off switches in heuristic conformations. If one analyzes it, it becomes only a sort of trick one plays on the viewer. But for you, Robin? Is reality for an organic intelligence very different? Or is it merely certain chemical transactions that take place in a kilogram of fatty matter that has no eyes, no ears, no sexual organs? Everything that it knows it knows by hearsay, because some perceptual system has told it so. Every feeling it has comes to it by wire from some nerve. Is it so different between us, Robin?"

"Albert!"

He shook his head. "Ah," he said bitterly, "I know. You cannot be deceived by my trick, because you know the trickster—she is here among us. But aren't you deceived by your own? Should I not be granted the same esteem and tolerance? I was quite an important man, Robin. Held in high regard by some very fine persons! Kings. Queens. Great scientists, and such good fellows they were. On my seventieth birthday they gave me a party—Robertson and Wigner, Kurt Goedel, Rabi, Oppenheimer—" He actually wiped away an actual tear . . . and that was about as far as Essie was willing to let him go.

She stood up. "My friends and husband," she said, "is obviously some severe malfunction here. Apologize for this. Must pull out of circuit for complete downcheck, you will excuse, please?"

"It isn't your fault, Essie," I said, as kindly as I could, but she didn't take it kindly. She looked at me in a way I hadn't seen from her since we first began dating and I told her about all the funny jokes I used to play on my psychoanalysis program, Sigfrid von Shrink. "Robin," she said coldly, "is all too much talk about fault and guilt. Will discuss later. Guests, must borrow my workroom for a time. Albert! Present yourself there at once for debugging!"

One of the penalties of being rich and famous is that a lot of people invite you to be their guests, and almost all of them expect to be invited back. Hosting is not one of my skills. Essie, on the other hand, really likes it, so over the years we worked out a good way to handle guests. It's very simple. I hang around them as long as I am enjoying it—that can be several hours, sometimes five minutes. Then I disappear to my study and leave the hosting to Essie. I am particularly likely to do this when, for any reason, there is tension among the guests. It works fine—for me.

But then it stops working sometimes, and then I'm stuck. This was one of the times. I couldn't leave them to Essie, because Essie was busy. I didn't want to leave them alone, because we had already done that for a goodish long period. And of tension there was plenty. So there I was, trying to remember how to be gracious when I didn't have a fallback position: "Would you like a drink?" I asked jovially. "Something to eat? There are some good programs to watch, if Essie hasn't killed the circuits so she can deal with Albert—"

Janie Yee-xing interrupted me with a question. "Where are we going, Mr. Broadhead?"

"Well," I said, beaming—jovial; good host; try to make the guests feel at ease, even when they ask you a perfectly good question that you haven't thought of an answer for because you've been thinking about a lot of more urgent things. "I guess the question is, where would you like to go? I mean, it looks like there's no point in chasing after the sailship."

"No," Yee-xing agreed.

"Then I suppose it's up to you. I didn't think you'd want to stay in the guardhouse—" reminding them that I'd done them all a favor, after all.

"No," Yee-xing said again.

"Back to the Earth, then? We could drop you at one of the loop points. Or Gateway, if you like. Or—let's see, Audee, you're from Venus in the first place, right? Do you want to go back there?"

It was Walthers's turn to say, "No." He left it at that. I thought it was very inconsiderate of my guests to give me nothing but negatives when I was trying to be hospitable to them.

Dolly Walthers bailed me out. She raised her right hand, and it had one of those hand puppets of hers on it, the one that was supposed to look like a Heechee. "The trouble is, Mr. Broadhead," she said, not moving her lips, in a syrupy, snaky kind of voice, "none of us have *any* place much to go to."

Since that was obviously true, nobody seemed to have anything to say to it. Then Audee stood up. "I'll take that drink now, Broadhead," he growled. "Dolly? Janie?"

It was obviously the best idea any of us had had in some time. We all agreed, like guests arriving too early at a party, finding something to do so we would not obviously be doing nothing.

There were things to do, to be sure, and the biggest of them in my mind was not to be cordial to my company. That biggest thing wasn't even trying to assimilate the fact that we had (perhaps) seen an actual, operating Heechee vessel with Heechee inside it. It was my gut again. The doctors said I could lead a normal life. They hadn't said anything about one as abnormal as this, so I was feeling my age and frailty. I was glad to take my gin and water and sit down, next to the make-believe fireplace with its make-believe flames, and wait for someone else to carry the ball.

Which turned out to be Audee Walthers. "Broadhead, I appreciate your getting us out of stir, and I know you've got things of your own to do. I suppose the best thing is for you to set all three of us down in the handiest place you can find and go about your business."

"Well, there are lots of places, Audee. Isn't there one you'd like better than another?"

"What I would like," he said, "—what I think we would all like, is to have a chance to figure out what we want to do by ourselves. I guess you've noticed we've got some personal problems that need to get worked out." That is not the kind of statement you want to agree to, and I certainly couldn't deny it, so I just smiled. "So what we need is a chance to get off by ourselves and talk about them."

"Ah," I said, nodding. "I guess we didn't give you enough time, when Essie and I left you alone?"

"*You* left us alone. Your friend Albert didn't."

"Albert?" It had never occurred to me that he would present himself to guests, especially without being invited.

"All the time, Broadhead," said Walthers bitterly. "Sitting right where you are now. Asking Dolly a million questions."

I shook my head and held out my glass for a refill. It probably wasn't a good idea, but I didn't have any ideas that I thought were good. When I was young and my mother was dying—because she couldn't afford medical care for both of us, guilt, guilt, guilt, and decided to get it for me—there was a time when she didn't recognize me, didn't remember my name, talked to me as though I were her boss or the landlord or some guy she'd dated before she married my father. A bad scene. It was almost worse to have her that way than to know she was dying: a solid figure crumbling before my eyes.

The way Albert was crumbling now.

"What kind of questions did he ask?" I asked, looking at Dolly.

"Oh, about Wan," she said, fiddling with the hand puppets but speaking with her own voice—though still without moving her lips much. "About where he was going, what he was doing. Mostly he wanted me to show him all the objects Wan was interested in on the charts."

"Show me," I said.

"I can't run that thing," she said peevishly, but Janie Yee-xing got up and was at the controls before she finished talking. She touched the display board, frowned, punched out a combination, scowled, and turned back to the rest of us.

"Mrs. Broadhead must have locked it when she took your pilot out of the circuit," she said.

"Anyway," said Dolly, "it was all black holes, one kind or another."

"I thought there only was one kind," I said, and she shrugged. We were all clustered around the control seat, looking up at the viewplate, which was showing nothing but stars. "Damn him," I said.

And from behind us Albert's voice said frostily, "I am sorry if I have inconvenienced you, Robin."

We all turned like the figures in one of those old German town clocks. He was sitting on the edge of the seat I had just vacated, studying us. He looked different. Younger. Less self-assured. He was turning a cigar in his hands—cigar, not the pipe—and his expression was somber. "I thought Essie was working on you," I said—I am sure—irritably.

"She has finished, Robin. She is coming now, in fact. I think it is fair for me to say that she found nothing wrong—isn't that right, Mrs. Broadhead?"

Essie came in the door and stopped there. Her fists were on her hips, her eyes fastened on Albert. She didn't even look at me.

"Is right, program," she declared gloomily. "Have found no programing error."

"I am glad to hear that, Mrs. Broadhead."

"Do not be glad! Fact remains, you are one screwed-up program. So tell me, intelligent program with no fault in programing, what is next step?"

The hologram actually licked its lips nervously. "Why," said Albert hesitantly, "I would suppose you might want to check the hardware."

"Precisely," said Essie as she reached to pull his datafan out of its socket. I could swear I saw a fleeting expression of panic on Albert's face, the look of a man going under the anesthetic for major surgery. Then it disappeared with the rest of him. "Go on talking," she ordered over her shoulder, putting a loupe in her eye and beginning to scan the surface of the fan.

But what was there to talk about? We watched while she studied every corrugation of the fan. We drifted after her when, scowling, she took the fan to her workroom, and watched silently while she touched the fan with calipers and probes, plugged it in a test socket, pressed buttons, turned verniers, read results off the scales. I stood there rubbing my belly, which had begun to be unpleasant to me again, and Audee whispered, "What's she looking for?" But I didn't know. A nick, a scratch, corrosion, anything, and whatever it was she didn't find it.

She stood up, sighing. "Is nothing there," she said.

"That's good," I offered.

"That's good," she agreed, "because if was anything serious I could not fix here. But is also bad, Robin, because is obvious that buggery program is all bugged to hell. Has taught me lesson in humility, this."

Dolly offered, "Are you sure he's busted, Mrs. Broadhead? While you were in the other room he seemed coherent enough. A little peculiar, maybe."

"Peculiar! Dolly lady, all the time I check him you know what he's talking about? Mach's Hypothesis. Missing mass. Black holes blacker than regular black holes. Would need to be a real Albert Einstein to understand—hey! What's that? Was talking to you?"

And when she had heard confirmation from the others she sat with her lips compressed in thought for some time. Then she shook herself. "Oh, hell," she said dismally, "is no good to try to guess at problem. Is only one person who knows what is wrong with Albert, and that is Albert himself."

"And what if Albert won't tell you?" I asked.

"Is wrong question," she said, plugging in the fan. "Proper question is 'What if Albert can't?' "

He looked all right—almost all right, anyway. He sat fumbling with his cigar in his favorite chair—which was also my own favorite seat, but at that moment I was not disposed to argue it with him. "Now, Albert," she said, her tone kindly but firm, "you know you are screwed up, correct?"

"A little aberrant, I think, yes," he said apologetically.

"Aberrant as all hell, I think! Well, now here is what we do, Albert. First we ask you some simple factual questions—not about motivations, not about hard theoretical stuff, only questions that can be resolved by objective facts. You understand?"

"Certainly I understand, Mrs. Broadhead."

"Right. First. Understand you were chatting with guests while Robin and I were in Captain's Chambers."

"That is correct, Mrs. Broadhead."

She pursed her lips. "Strikes me as unusual behavior, no? You were questioning them. Please tell us what questions were and your answers."

Albert shifted position uneasily. "Mostly I was interested in the objects Wan was investigating, Mrs. Broadhead. Mrs. Walthers was good enough to pick them out for me on the charts." He pointed at the display, and when we looked at it, sure enough, it was showing a series of charts, one after another. "If you look at them carefully," said Albert, pointing with his unsmoked cigar, "you will see that there is a definite progression. His first targets were simple black holes, which are indicated on the Heechee charts by these marks like fishhooks. Those are danger signs in the Heechee cartography."

"How you know this?" Essie demanded, and then: "No, purge that question. I assume you have good reason for this assumption."

"I do, Mrs. Broadhead. I have not been entirely forthcoming with you in this respect."

"Ha! Are getting somewhere! Now continue."

"Yes, Mrs. Broadhead. The simple black holes each had two check marks. Then Wan investigated a naked singularity—a nonrotating black hole, in fact the one that Robin himself had such a terrible experience with many years ago. It was there that he found Gelle-Klara Moynlin." The image flickered, then showed the naked blue ghost star before returning to the chart. "This one has three fishhooks, meaning more danger. And finally"—wave of the hand, the picture altering to show a different section of the Heechee chart—"this is the one Mrs. Walthers identified for me as the one Wan was heading for next."

"I didn't say that!" Dolly objected.

"No, Mrs. Walthers," Albert agreed, "but you did say that he looked at it frequently, that he discussed it with his Dead Men, and that it terrified him. I believe that it is the one he is aiming at."

"Very fine," applauded Essie. "Have passed first test admirably, Albert. Now will proceed with second part, without, this time, participation from audience," she added, glancing at Dolly.

"I'm at your service, Mrs. Broadhead."

"To be sure you are. Now. Factual questions. What is meant by term missing mass?"

Albert looked uneasy, but he responded promptly enough. "The so-called missing mass is that quantity of mass which would account for various galactic orbits, but has never been observed."

"Excellent! Now, what is Mach's Hypothesis?"

He licked his lips. "I am not really comfortable with speculative discussions about quantum mechanics, Mrs. Broadhead. I have difficulty believing that God plays dice with the universe."

"Have not asked for belief! Keep to rules, Albert. Am only asking for definition of widely used technical term."

He sighed and shifted position. "Very well, Mrs. Broadhead, but allow me to put it in tangible terms. There is reason to believe that some sort of very large-scale tampering is going on with the expansion-contraction cycle of the universe. The expansion is being reversed. The contraction is being made to proceed, it would appear, to a single point—the same as before the Big Bang."

"And what was that?" Essie demanded.

He shuffled his feet. "I really am getting quite nervous, Mrs. Broadhead," he complained.

"But you can answer the question—in terms of what is generally believed."

"At what point, Mrs. Broadhead? What is believed now? What was believed, let us say, before the days of Hawking and those other quantum people? There is one definite statement about the universe at its very beginning, but it is a religious one."

"Albert," said Essie warningly.

He grinned weakly. "I was only going to quote St. Augustine of Hippo," he said. "When he was asked what God was doing before He created the universe, he replied that He was creating Hell for people who asked that question."

"Albert!"

"Oh, very well," he said irritably. "Yes. It is thought that prior to some very early time—no later than the fraction one over 10^{43} of a second before it—relativity can no longer account for the physics of the universe and some sort of 'quantum correction' must be made. I am getting quite tired of this schoolboy quiz, Mrs. Broadhead."

I have not often seen Essie shocked. "Albert!" she cried again, in a quite different tone. Not warning. Astonished, and disconcerted.

"Yes, Albert," he said savagely, "that is who you created and who I am. Let us stop this, please. Have the goodness to listen. I do not know what happens before the Big Bang! I only know that there is someone somewhere who thinks he does know and can control it. This frightens me very much, Mrs. Broadhead."

" 'Frightens'?" gasped Essie. "Who has programed to be 'frightened' in you, Albert?"

"You have, Mrs. Broadhead. I can't live with that. And I do not wish to discuss it further."

And he winked out.

He didn't have to do that. He could have spared our feelings. He could have pretended to exit through a door, or disappeared when we were looking the other way. He didn't do either of those things. He just vanished. It was just as though he were a truly real human being in just such a spat, finishing it off by flouncing out and slamming the door in anger. He was too angry to be careful of appearances.

"Is not supposed to lose temper," said Essie dismally.

But he had; and the shock of that was not nearly as great as the shock that came when we discovered that the viewscreen still would not respond to its controls, and neither would the piloting board.

Albert had locked them both. We were heading at a steady acceleration toward we did not know what.

20
Unwanted Encounter

The phone was ringing in Wan's ship. Well, it was not really a phone, and it certainly wasn't ringing; but there was the signal to show that someone was directing a message to the ship on the FTL radio. "Off!" shouted Wan, waking up indignantly from his sleep. "I will speak to no one!" And then, somewhat more awake, he looked not only angry but puzzled. "It has been turned off," he said, staring at the FTL radio, and the look on his face went the rest of the way across the spectrum to fear.

What makes Wan less than loathsome to me, I think, is that ulcer of fear that ate away at him always. Heaven knows he was a brute. He was surly; he was a thief; he cared for nothing but himself. But that only means that he was what we all once were, but we are socialized out of it by parents and playmates and school and police. No one had ever socialized Wan, and so he was still a child. "I will speak to no one!" he shouted, and woke Klara.

I can see Klara as she was then, since now I can see so much that was hidden. She was tired, she was irritable, and she had had all of Wan any person could be expected to stand. "You might as well answer it," she said, and Wan glared at her as though she were insane.

"Answer? Of course I shall not answer! It is only at most some interfering bureaucrat to complain that I have not followed the exact proper procedures—"

"To complain that you stole the ship," she corrected mildly, and crossed to the FTL radio. "How do you answer it?" she asked.

"Do not be foolish!" he howled. "Wait! Stop! What are you doing?"

"Is it this lever?" she asked, and his yell was answer enough. He leaped across the tiny cabin, but she was larger than he and stronger. She fended him off. The signal chirp stopped; the golden light went off; and Wan, suddenly relaxing, laughed out loud.

"Ho, what a fool you are! There is no one there," he cried.

But he was wrong. There was a hissing sound for a moment, then recognizable words—almost recognizable, at least. A shrill and queerly stressed voice said:

"I fill to you no harrum."

For Klara to understand what had been said took considerable thought, and then when she had understood it, it did not achieve its desired effect. Was it what it sounded like? Some stranger, with a terrible hissing speech impediment, trying to say "I will do you no harm"? And why would he say that? To be reassured that you are not in danger at a time when you had no reason to think you were is not reassuring.

Wan was scowling. "What is it?" he cried sharply, beginning to sweat. "Who is there? What do you want?"

There was no answer. The reason there was no answer was that Captain had used up his entire vocabulary and was busy rehearsing his next speech; to Wan and Klara, however, the silence had more meaning than the words. "The screen!" Wan cried. "Foolish woman, use the screen, find out what this is!"

It took time for Klara to work the controls; the use of the Heechee vision screen was a skill she had only begun to acquire on this voyage, since no one in her time had known how to operate it. It clarified to display a ship, a big one. The biggest Klara had ever seen, far larger than any of the Fives that had operated out of Gateway in her time. "What— What—What—" whimpered Wan, and only on the fourth try managed to complete it: "What is it?"

Klara didn't try to answer. She didn't know. She feared, though. She feared that it was the sight every Gateway prospector had both longed for and dreaded, and when Captain finished rehearsing and delivered his next speech she was sure:

"I . . . cummin . . . a-bore-ud . . . tchew."

Coming aboard! For one ship to dock with another in full drive was not impossible, Klara knew; it had been done. But no Earthly pilot had had much practice in doing it.

"Don't let him in!" shrieked Wan. "Run away! Hide! Do something!" He glared at Klara in terror, then made a lunge for the controls.

"Don't be a fool!" she yelled, springing to intercept him. Klara was a strong woman, but he was all she could handle just then. Mad fear made him strong. He flailed out at her and sent her reeling and, weeping with fear, leaped at the controls.

In the terror of this unexpected contact, Klara nevertheless had room for another stabbing fear. Everything she had learned about Heechee ships had taught her that you never, *never* tried to change course once it was established. Newer skills had made it possible to do it, she knew; but she also knew that it was not to be done lightly, only after careful calculation and planning, and Wan was in no shape for either of those.

And even so—it made no difference. The great shark-shaped ship moved closer.

In spite of herself Klara watched admiringly as the pilot of the other ship matched course change and velocity increment without difficulty. It was a technically fascinating process. Wan froze at the controls, watching it, mouth open, slobbering. Then, when the other ship loomed large and disappeared below the view of the scanners, and there was a grating sound from the lander hatch, he bellowed in fear and dove for the toilet. Klara was alone as she saw the lander hatch open and fall back; and so it was Gelle-Klara Moynlin who was the first human being to stand in the presence of a Heechee.

It rose from the hatch, stood erect, and confronted her. Less tall than she. Reeking of something ammoniacal. Its eyes were round, because that is the best design for an organ that must rotate in any direction, but they were not human eyes. There was no concentric ring of pigment around a central pupil. There was no pupil, just a cross-shaped blotch of darkness in the middle of a pinkish marble that stared at her. Its pelvis was wide. Slung below the pelvis, between what would have been its thighs if its legs had been articulated in a human way, was a capsule of bright blue metal. As much as anything else, the Heechee looked like a diapered toddler with a load in its pants.

That thought penetrated through Klara's terror and eased it—minutely—briefly—not enough. As the creature moved forward she leaped back.

As Klara moved, the Heechee moved, too. It started as the hatch cover moved again and another one of them came through. From the tension and hesitancy of its movements it seemed to Klara that it was nearly as frightened as she, and so she said, not with the expectation of being understood but because it was impossible for her to say nothing:

"Hello, there."

The creature studied her. A forked tongue licked the shiny black wrinkles of its face. It made a strange, purring sound, as though it were thinking. Then, in something close to recognizable English, it said: "I em Heetsee. I fill to you no harrum."

It gazed with fascination and repugnance at Klara, then chittered briskly to the other one, who began to search the vessel. They found Wan without trouble, and without trouble moved both Klara and Wan down through the hatch, through the connected landers, into the Heechee ship. Klara heard the hatches scrape closed, and then a moment later felt the lurch that meant that Wan's ship had been cast free.

She was a captive of the Heechee, in a Heechee ship.

They did not harm her. If they were intending to do it, at least they were in no hurry about it. There were five of them, and they were very busy.

What they were busy at Klara could not guess, and apparently the one with the limited English vocabulary was too busy at it to take time for the laborious task of explaining. What they really wanted from Klara at that moment was for her to stay out of the way. They had no trouble communicating that to her. They unceremoniously took her by the arm, with a leathery and painful grip, and shoved her where they wanted her.

Wan gave them no trouble at all. He lay huddled in a corner with his eyes tightly closed. When he discovered that Klara was nearby he peered at her with one eye, poked her in the spine to get her attention, and whispered: "Did he really mean he wouldn't harm us, do you think?"

She shrugged. He whimpered almost inaudibly, then relapsed into his fetal crouch. She saw with disgust that a trickle of saliva was coming out of the side of his mouth. He was the next thing to catatonic.

If there was anyone to help her, that was not Wan. She would have to face the Heechee alone—whatever it might be that they intended.

But what was happening was fascinating. So much was new to Klara! She had spent the decades of rapid accretion of Heechee technology whirling at very nearly light-speed around the core of the black hole. Her acquaintance with Heechee vessels was limited to the antiques she and I and the other prospectors had operated out of Gateway.

This was something else. It was a lot bigger than a Five. It far outshone even Wan's private yacht in its fittings. It didn't have one control panel; it had three—of course, Klara did not know that two of them were for purposes other than piloting the ship itself. Those two possessed instruments and operating readouts she had never seen before. Not only was it eight or ten times the cubic volume of a Five, but relatively less of the space was taken up with equipment. It was possible to move about it quite freely! It had the standard features—the worm-shaped thing that glowed during faster-than-light travel, the V-shaped seats, and so on. But it also had blue-glowing boxes that whined and peeped and flickered with lights, and a different sort of worm-shaped crystal that, Wan told her, terrified, was for digging into black holes.

Above all, it had Heechee.

Heechee! The semimythical, perplexing, nearly divine Heechee! No human being had ever seen one, or even a picture. And here was Gelle-Klara Moynlin, with no less than five of them all about her—growling and hissing and tweeting, and smelling quite strange.

They looked strange, too. They were smaller than human beings, and their very wide pelvises gave them a gait like a walking skeleton. Their skin was plastic-smooth and mostly dark, though there were patches and curlicues of bright gold and scarlet that looked like Indian war paint. Their physiology was not merely lean. It was gaunt. There was not much flesh on those quick, strong limbs and fingers. Although their faces seemed as though they were carved out of shiny plastic, they were at least resilient enough to allow for facial expression . . . though Klara could not be sure what the expressions represented.

And swinging below the crotches of every one of them, male and female alike, was a great cone-shaped thing.

At first Klara thought it was part of their bodies, but when one of them disappeared into what she assumed was some sort of toilet it fussed for a moment and removed the cone. Was it something like a knapsack? A pocketbook? An attache case, to carry papers, pencils, and a brown-bag lunch? Whatever it was, it came off when they wanted it off. And when it was on it explained one of the great puzzles of Heechee anatomy, namely how they managed to sit down on those incredibly painful V-shaped seats. It was their dependent cones that filled the V-shaped gap. The Heechee themselves perched comfortably on the top of the cones. Klara

For decades the Heechee "prayer fans" were a mystery. We did not know that they were actually their equivalent of books and datastores, because the greatest minds of the time (my own included) could not find a way to read them, or even to find indications that they contained anything to be read. The reason was that although scansion was simple enough, it could only take place in the presence of a background microwave radiation. The Heechee themselves had no problem with that, because their cones produced the proper radiation all the time, since they were always in some sort of contact with the datafans that contained the stored memories of their ancestors —held in their cones. Human beings could be excused for not guessing that the Heechee carried data between their legs, for human anatomy would not allow such a thing. (My own excuse is less evident.)

shook her head, wondering—all the idle guesses and jokes on the subject in Gateway, why had no one ever thought of that?

She felt Wan's hot breath on the back of her neck. "What are they doing?" he demanded.

She had almost forgotten he was there. She had almost forgotten even to be afraid, so fascinated was she by what she saw. That was not prudent. Who could tell what these monsters would do with their human captives?

For that matter, who could guess what they were doing now? They were all buzzing and chirping in an agitated way, the four larger ones clustered around the smaller fifth, the one with blue and yellow markings on its—no, definitely, on *her*—upper arms. All five of them were paying no attention to the humans just now. They were concentrating on one of the display panels, which was showing a star chart that Klara thought vaguely familiar. A group of stars, and around them a cluster of check marks—hadn't Wan displayed such a pattern on his own screen?

"I'm hungry," Wan growled sullenly in her ear.

"Hungry!" Klara pulled sharply away from him, astonishment as much as revulsion. Hungry! She was nearly sick to her stomach with fear and worry—and, she realized, a queer odor, half ammonia and half rotting stump, that seemed to come from the Heechee themselves. Besides, she had to go to the bathroom . . . and this other monster could think of nothing but that he was hungry! "Please shut up," she said over her shoulder, and touched off Wan's always available fury.

"What? Me shut up?" he demanded. "No, you shut up, foolish woman!" He almost stood up to tower over her, but got no farther than a crouch, quickly groveling back to the floor, for one of the Heechee looked up and came toward them.

It stood over them for a moment, its wide, narrow-lipped mouth working as it rehearsed what it was about to say.

"Be fair," it pronounced distinctly, and waved a skinny arm toward the viewscreen.

Klara swallowed laughter nervously trying to bubble out of her throat. Be fair! To whom? For what?

"Be fair," it said again, "for dese are sass sass sins."

So there was Klara, my truest love that was. She had suffered in a matter of weeks the terror of the black hole, the shock of losing decades of the world's life, the misery of Wan, the intolerable trauma of being taken by the Heechee. And meanwhile—

And meanwhile, I had problems of my own. I had not yet been vastened and did not know where she was; I did not hear the warning to beware of the Assassins; I didn't then know that the Assassins existed. I couldn't reach out to comfort her in her fear—not just because I didn't know, but because I was full of fears of my own. And the worst of them did not involve Klara or the Heechee, or even my aberrant program Albert Einstein; it was in my own belly.

21
Abandoned by Albert

Nothing worked. We tried everything. Essie pulled Albert's fan from its socket, but he had locked the controls so that even without him we could change nothing. Essie set up another piloting program and tried to insert it; it was locked out. We shouted his name and scolded and begged him to appear. He would not.

For days that seemed like weeks we kept going, guided by the nonexistent hands of my nonfunctioning data-retrieval system, Albert Einstein. And meanwhile, the nut-kid Wan and the dark lady of my dreams were in the spaceship of Captain's Heechee crew and behind us the worlds were stewing and grumbling toward a violence too large to be accommodated. They were not what occupied our minds. Our worries were closer to hand. Food, water, air. We'd stocked the *True Love* for long cruises, much longer than this.

But not for five people.

We weren't doing nothing. We were doing everything we could think to do. Walthers and Yee-xing tinkered together piloting programs of their own—tried them—could not override what Albert had done. Essie did more than any of us, for Albert was her creation and she would not, could not, admit herself beaten. Check and recheck; write test programs and watch them come up blank; she hardly slept. She copied Albert's entire program into a spare datafan and tried that—still hoping, you see, that the fault was mechanical somewhere. But if so it carried over into the new storage. Dolly Walthers uncomplainingly fed the rest of us, stayed out of our way when we thought we might be getting somewhere (though we never were), and let us talk ideas out when we were stumped (which was often). And I had the hardest job of all. Albert was my program, said Essie, and if he would reply to anyone he would reply to me. So I sat there and talked to him. Talked to the air, really, because I had no evidence at all that he was listening as I reasoned with him, chatted with him, called his name, yelled at him, begged him.

He did not answer, not even a flicker in the air.

When we took a break for food Essie came to stand behind me and rub my shoulders. It was my larynx that was wearing out, but I appreciated the thought. "At least," she said shakily, to the air more than to me, "must know what he's doing, I think. Must realize supplies are limited. Must provide for return to civilization for us, because Albert could not deliberately let us die?" The words were a statement. The tone wasn't.

"I'm certain of it," I said, but did not turn around so that she could see my face.

"I, too," she said in a dismal tone as I pushed away my plate; and Dolly, to change the subject, said in a motherly way:

"Don't you like my cooking?"

Essie's fingers stopped massaging my shoulders and dug in. "Robin! You don't eat!"

And they were all looking at me. It was actually funny. We were out in the middle of nowhere at all with no good way of getting home, and four people were staring at me because I didn't eat my dinner. It was Essie, of course, clucking over me in the early stages of the trip, before Albert went mute; they suddenly realized that I might not be well.

In point of fact I wasn't. I tired quickly. My arms felt tingly, as though they had gone to sleep. I had no appetite—had not eaten much for days, and had escaped notice only because usually we ate in quick gobbles when we found time. "It helps to stretch out the supplies." I smiled, but nobody smiled back.

"*Foolish* Robin," hissed Essie, and her fingers left my shoulders to test the temperature of my forehead. But that was not too bad, because I'd been gulping aspirin when no one was looking. I assumed an expression of patience.

"I'm fine, Essie," I said. It wasn't exactly a lie—a little wishful thinking, maybe, but I wasn't *sure* I was sick. "I guess I should have been checked over, but with Albert out of commission—"

"For this? Albert? Who needs?" I craned my neck, puzzled, to look at Essie. "For this need only subset medic program," she said firmly.

"Subset?"

She stamped her foot. "Medic program, legal program, secretarial program—all subsumed into Albert program, but can be accessed separately. You call medic program this instant!"

I gaped at her. For a moment I couldn't speak, while my mind raced. "Do as I say!" she shouted, and at last I found my voice.

"Not the medical program!" I cried. "There's something better than that!" And I turned around and bellowed to thin air:

"Sigfrid von Shrink! Help! I need you desperately!"

There was a time in the year of my psychoanalysis when I hung on hooks while I waited for Sigfrid to appear. Sometimes I had a real wait, for in those days Sigfrid was a patched-together program of Heechee circuits and human software, and none of the software was my wife Essie's. Essie was good at her trade. The milliseconds of response time became nano-, pico-, femtoseconds, so that Albert could in real time respond as well as a human—well, hell, no! Better than any human!

And so when Sigfrid did not at once appear it was the feeling you get when you turn a switch and the light doesn't go on because it's burned out. You don't waste your time flicking the switch back and forth. You know. "Don't waste time," said Essie over my shoulder. If a voice can be pale, hers was.

I turned and smiled shakily at her. "I guess things are worse than we thought," I said. Her face was pale, all right. I put my hand on hers. "Takes me right back," I said, making conversation so that we would not have to face just how much worse things were. "When I was in analysis with Sigfrid, waiting for him to show up was the worst part. I would always get uptight, and . . ." Well, I was rambling. I might have gone on doing it forever if I hadn't seen in Essie's eyes that I didn't have to.

I turned around and heard his voice at the same time: "I am sorry to hear that it was so difficult for you, Robin," said Sigfrid von Shrink.

Even for a holographic projection, Sigfrid looked rather poorly. He was there with his hands clasped on his lap, sitting uncomfortably on nothing at all. The program had not troubled to furnish him with chair or pad. Nothing. Just Sigfrid, looking, for one of the few times in my recollection of him, quite ill at ease. He gazed around at the five of us, all staring at him, and sighed before returning to me. "Well, Robin," he said, "would you like to tell me what is bothering you?"

I could hear Audee Walthers take a breath to answer him, and Janie click her tongue to stop him, because Essie was shaking her head. I didn't look at any of them. I said, "Sigfrid, old tin whiz, I have a problem that's right down your alley."

He looked at me under his brows. "Yes, Robin?"

"It's a case of fugue."

"Severe?"

"Incapacitating," I told him.

He nodded as though it were what he had been expecting. "I do prefer that you not use technical terms, Robin." He sighed, but his fingers were lacing and relacing themselves in his lap. "Tell me. Is it yourself that you are asking me to help?"

"Not really, Sigfrid," I admitted. The whole ballgame could have blown up then. I think it almost did. He was silent for a moment, but not at all still—his fingers snaked in and out of each other, and there was a bluish sparkle in the air around the outlines of his body when he moved. I said, "It's a friend of mine, Sigfrid, maybe the closest friend I have in the world, and he is in bad trouble."

"I see," he said, nodding as though he did—which I expect was true enough. "I suppose you know," he mentioned, "that your friend cannot be helped unless he is present."

"He's present, Sigfrid," I said softly.

"Yes," he said, "I rather thought he was." The fingers were still now, and he leaned back as though there were a chair for him to lean against. "Suppose you tell me about it . . . and"—with a smile, which was the most welcome thing I had ever seen in my life—"this time, Robin, you may use technical terms if you wish."

Behind me I heard Essie softly exhale, and realized both of us had been trying to hold our breaths. I reached back for her hand.

"Sigfrid," I said, beginning to hope, "as I understand it, the term fugue refers to a flight from reality. If a person finds himself in a double-bind situation—excuse me, I mean if he finds himself in a position when one very powerful drive is frustrated by another, so he can't live with the conflict—he turns his back on it. He runs away. He pretends it doesn't exist. I know I'm mixing up several different schools of psychotherapy here, Sigfrid, but have I got the general idea right?"

"Close enough, Robin. At least I understand what you are saying."

"An example of that might be"—I hesitated—"perhaps someone very deeply in love with his wife, who finds out that she's been having an affair with his best friend." I felt Essie's fingers tighten on mine. I hadn't hurt her feelings; she was encouraging me.

"You confuse drives and emotions, Robin, but that doesn't matter. What are you leading up to?"

I didn't let him rush me. "Or another example," I said, "might be religious. Someone with a heartfelt faith, who discovers there is no God. Do you follow me, Sigfrid? It's been an article of faith with him, although he knows there are a lot of intelligent people who disagree—and then, little by little, he finds more and more support for their belief, and finally it's overwhelming . . ."

He nodded politely, listening, but his fingers had begun to writhe again.

"So finally he has to accept quantum mechanics," I said.

And that was the second point at which it all could have gone right out the chute. I think it nearly did. The hologram flickered badly for a moment, and the expression on Sigfrid's face changed. I can't say what it changed to. It wasn't anything I recognized; it was as though it had blurred and softened.

But when he spoke up his voice was steady. "When you talk about drives and fugues, Robin," he said, "you are talking about human beings. Suppose the patient you are interested in isn't human." He hesitated, and then added, "Quite." I made an encouraging noise, because I really didn't know where to go from there. "That is to say, suppose he has these drives and emotions, ah, programed into him, let us say, but only the way a human can be programed to do something like speak a foreign language after he is fully grown. The knowledge is there, but it is imperfectly assimilated. There is an accent." He paused. "We are not human," he said.

Essie's hand gripped mine tightly. A warning. "Albert is programed with a human personality," I said.

"Yes. As far as possible. Very far," Sigfrid agreed, but his face was grave. "Albert is still not human, for no computer program is. I mention only that none of us can experience, for example, the TPT. When the human race is going mad with someone else's madness, we feel nothing."

The ground was very delicate now, thin ice crusted over a quagmire, and if I stepped too roughly what might we all fall into? Essie held my hand strongly; the others were hardly breathing. I said, "Sigfrid, human beings are all different, too. But you used to tell me that that didn't matter a great deal. You said the problems of the mind were in the mind, and the cure for the problems was in there, too. All you did was help your patients bring them up to the surface, where they could deal with them, instead of keeping them buried, where they could cause obsessions and neuroses . . . and fugue."

"It is true that I said that, yes, Robin."

"You just kicked the old machine, Sigfrid, right? To jar it loose from where it was stuck?"

He grinned—a pale grin, but there. "That is close enough, I suppose."

"Right. So let me try a theory on you. Let me suggest that this friend of mine"—I didn't dare name him again just then—"this friend of mine has a conflict he can't handle. He is very intelligent and extremely well informed. He has access to the best and latest knowledge of science in particular—all kinds of science—physics and astrophysics and cosmology and everything else. Since quantum mechanics is at the base of it he accepts quantum mechanics as valid—he couldn't do the job he was programed to do without it. That's basic to his—programing." I had almost said "personality."

The grin was more pain than amusement now, but he was still listening.

"And at the same time, Sigfrid, he has another layer of programing. He has been taught to think like and behave like—to *be,* as much as he can be—a very intelligent and wise person who has been dead for a hell of a long time and who happened to believe very strongly that quantum mechanics was all wrong. I don't know if that would be enough of a conflict to damage a human being," I said, "but it might do a lot of harm to—well—a computer program."

There were actual beads of perspiration on Sigfrid's face now. He nodded silently, and I had a bright, painful flashback—the way Sigfrid looked to me now, was that how I had looked to Sigfrid in those long-ago days when he was shrinking me? "Is that possible?" I demanded.

"It is a severe dichotomy, yes," he whispered.

And there I bogged down.

The thin ice had broken. I was ankle-deep in the quagmire. I wasn't drowning yet, but I was stuck. I didn't know where to go next.

It broke my concentration. I looked around helplessly at Essie and the others, feeling very old and very tired—and a lot unwell, too. I had been so wrapped up in the technical problem of shrinking my shrink that I had forgotten the pain in my belly and the numbness in my arms; but they came back on me now. It wasn't working. I didn't know enough. I was absolutely certain that I had uncovered the basic problem that had caused Albert to fugue—and nothing had come of it!

I don't know how long I would have sat there like a fool if I hadn't got help. It came from two people at once. "Trigger," whispered Essie urgently in my ear, and at the same moment Janie Yee-xing stirred and said tentatively:

"There must have been a precipitating incident, isn't that right?"

Sigfrid's face became blank. A hit. A palpable hit.

"What was it, Sigfrid?" I asked. No response. "Come on, Sigfrid, old shrinking machine, spit it out. What was the thing that pushed Albert out the airlock?"

He looked me straight in the eye, and yet I couldn't read his expression, because his face became fuzzy. It was almost as though it was a picture on the PV and something was breaking down in the circuits so the image was fading.

Fading? Or fuguing? "Sigfrid," I cried, *"please!* Tell us what scared Albert into running away! Or if you can't do that, just get him here so we can talk to him!"

More fuzz. I couldn't even tell if he was looking at me anymore. "Tell me!" I commanded, and from that fuzzy holographic shadow came an answer:

"The kugelblitz."

"What? What's a kugelblitz?" I stared around in frustration. "Damn it, get him here so he can tell us for himself."

"Is here, Robin," whispered Essie in my ear.

And the image sharpened again, but it wasn't Sigfrid anymore. The neat Freud face had softened and widened into the gentle, pouchy German band leader, and the white hair crowned the sad eyes of my best and closest friend.

"I am here, Robin," said Albert Einstein sorrowfully. "I thank you for your help. I don't know if you'll thank me, though."

Albert was right about that. I didn't thank him.

Albert was also wrong about that, or right for wrong reasons, because the reason I didn't thank him was not merely that what he said was so grisly unpleasant, so scary incomprehensible, but also that I was in no position to when he had finished.

My position wasn't much better when he began, because the letdown when he came back let me down all the way. I was drained. Exhausted. It was perfectly expectable that I should be exhausted, I told myself, because God knew it had been about as stressful a strain as I had ever been through, but it felt worse than simple exhaustion. It felt terminal. It wasn't just my belly or my arms or my head; it was as though all the power were draining out of all my batteries at once, and it took all the concentration I could get together to pay attention to what he was saying.

"I was not precisely in fugue, as you call it," he said, turning the unlit pipe over in his fingers. He had not bothered to be comical. He was wearing sweatshirt and slacks, but his feet were in shoes and the shoelaces were tied. "It is true that the dichotomy existed, and that it rendered me vulnerable—you will understand, Mrs. Broadhead, a contradiction in my programing; I found myself looping. Since you made me homeostatic there was another imperative: to repair the malfunction."

Essie nodded regretfully. "Homeostasis, yes. But self-repair implies self-diagnosis. Should have consulted me for check!"

"I thought not, Mrs. Broadhead," he said. "With all respect, the difficulties were in areas in which I am better equipped to function than you."

"Cosmology, ha!"

I stirred myself to speak—it wasn't easy, because the lethargy was strong. "Would you mind, please, just saying what you did, Albert?"

He said slowly, "What I did is easy, Robin. I decided to try to resolve these conflicts. I know they seem more important to me than to you; you can be quite happy without settling cosmological questions, but I cannot. I devoted more and more of my capacity to study. As you may not know, I included a great many Heechee fans in the datastores for this ship, some of which had never been analyzed properly. It was a very difficult task, and at the same time I was making observations of my own."

"What you *did*, Albert!" I begged.

"But that is what I did. In the Heechee datastores I found many references to what we have called the missing mass. You remember, Robin. That mass which the universe should have to account for its gravitational behavior, but which no astronomer has been able to find—"

"I remember!"

"Yes. Well, I may have found it." He sat brooding for a moment. "I'm afraid that this did not solve my problem, though. It made it worse. If you had not been able to reach me through your clever little trick of talking through my subset Sigfrid I might be looping yet—"

"Found *what?*" I cried. The flowing adrenaline almost, but not quite, took my mind off the way my body was notifying me of its troubles.

He waved a hand at the viewscreen, and I saw there was something on it.

In that first quick glance, what I saw on the screen did not make sense. And when I did give it a second look, and a more careful one, what stopped me cold and staring was not what was important.

The screen showed mostly nothing at all. There was a corner of a whirlpool of light at one edge of it—a galaxy, of course; I thought it looked like M-31 in Andromeda as much as anything, but I am no expert in galaxies. Especially when I see them without any spattering of stars around them, and there was no such spattering here.

There was something like stars. Little points of light, here and there. But they weren't stars, because they were winking and flickering like Christmas-tree lights. Think of a couple dozen fireflies, on a cold night so they aren't flashing their little passionate pleas very often, quite far away so that they aren't easy to see. That was what they looked like. The most conspicuous object among them, still not very conspicuous, was something that looked a little like the nonrotating black hole I had once lost Klara in, but not as large and not as threatening. And all of this was queer, but it was not what shocked a gasp out of me. I heard noises from the others, too. "It's a ship!" Dolly whispered, shakily. And so it was.

Albert said so. He turned around gravely. "That is a ship, yes, Mrs. Walthers," he said. "It is, in fact, the Heechee ship we saw before, I am nearly certain. I have been wondering if I could establish communication with it."

"Communication! With the Heechee! Albert," I shouted, "I know you're crazy, but don't you realize how *dangerous* that is?"

"As to danger," he said somberly, "I am much more afraid of the kugelblitz."

"Kugelblitz?" I had lost my temper completely. "Albert, you horse's ass, I don't know what a kugelblitz is and I don't much care. What I care about is that you've damn near killed us all, and—"

I stopped, because Essie's hand on my mouth stopped me. "Shut up, Robin!" she hissed. "You want drive him to fugue again? Now, Albert," she said, quite calmly, "yes, please tell us what is kugelblitz. That thing looks to me like black hole, actually."

He passed a hand over his forehead. "The central object, you mean. Yes, it is a kind of black hole. But there is not one black hole there; there are many. I have not been able to count how many, since they cannot be detected except when there is some infall of matter to produce radiation, and there is not much matter out here between galaxies—"

"Between *galaxies?*" cried Walthers, and then stopped with Essie's eyes on him.

"Yes, Albert, please go on," she encouraged.

"I do not know how many black holes are present. In excess of ten. Probably in excess of ten squared, all in all." He glanced at me beseechingly. "Robin, do you have any idea how strange that is? How can one account for this?"

"I not only can't account for it; I don't even know what a kugelblitz is."

"Oh, good heavens, Robin," he said impatiently, "we have discussed this sort of thing before. A black hole results from the collapse of matter to an extraordinary density. John Wheeler was the first person to predict the existence of another form of black hole, containing not matter but energy—so much energy, so densely packed, that its own mass pulled space around it. That is called a kugelblitz!"

He sighed, then said, "I have two speculations. The first is that this entire construct is an artifact. The kugelblitz is surrounded by black holes; I think to attract any loose matter—of which there is not much here in the first place—to keep it from falling into the kugelblitz itself. The second speculation is that I think we may be looking at the missing mass."

I jumped up. "Albert," I cried, "do you know what you're saying? You mean somebody *made* that thing? You mean—" I jumped up and did not finish the sentence.

I did not finish the sentence, because I couldn't. Part of the reason was that there were too many scary notions floating around in my head; for if someone had *made* the kugelblitz, and if the kugelblitz was part of this "missing mass," then the obvious conclusion was that somebody was tampering with the laws of the universe itself, trying to reverse the expansion, for reasons that I could not (then) guess.

The other reason was that I fell over.

I fell over because for some reason my legs would not support me. There was a blinding pain in the side of my head, just about the ear. Everything went all gray and swimmy.

I heard Albert's voice cry out, "Oh, Robin! I haven't been paying attention to your physical state!"

"My what?" I asked. Or tried to ask. It didn't come out well. My lips

I did tell Robin several times what a kugelblitz was—a black hole caused by the collapse of a large quantity of energy, rather than a large quantity of matter—but as nobody had ever seen one he didn't really listen. I also told him about the general state of intergalactic space—very little free matter or energy, barring scanty photon flux from distant galaxies, and, of course, the universal 3.7K radiation—which is what made it such a good place to put a kugelblitz, when you didn't want anything else to fall into it.

did not seem to want to form the words properly, and I felt suddenly very sleepy. That first quick explosion of localized pain had come and gone, but there was a distant awareness of pain, oh, yes, *big* pain, not very far away and rapidly coming closer.

They say that there is a selective amnesia for pain. You don't remember that root-canal job except, almost fondly, as a humorously rotten experience; if it were not for this, they say, no woman would have more than one child. That is true for most of you, I suppose. I'm sure it was true for me for a good many years, but not now.

Now I remember very clearly indeed and, yes, it is with almost humorous affection. What had happened in my head had provided its own anesthesia, and what I experienced was unclear. But I remember that unclearness with great clarity. I remember the panicky talk, and being hauled to a couch; I remember long dialogues and the tiny bite of needles as Albert fed me medication and took samples of me. And I remember Essie sobbing.

She was cradling my head in her lap. Though she was talking past me to Albert, and mostly in Russian, I heard my name often enough to know she was talking about me. I tried to reach up to pat her cheek. "I'm dying," I said—or tried to say.

She understood me. She leaned over me, her long hair drifting across my face. "Very dear Robin," she crooned, "is true, yes, you are dying. Or your body is. But that does not mean an end to you."

Now, we had discussed religion from time to time over the decades we'd been together. I knew her beliefs. I even knew my own. Essie, I wanted to say, you've never lied to me before, you don't have to do it now to try to ease dying for me. It's all right. But all that came out was something like:

"Does so!"

Tears dripped over my face as she rocked me, crooning, "No. Truly no, dearest Robin. Is a chance, a very good chance—"

I made a tremendous effort. "There . . . is . . . no . . . hereafter," I said, strongly, spacing the words out with the best articulation I could manage. It may not have been clear, but she understood me. She bent and kissed my forehead. I felt her lips move against my skin as she whispered:

"Yes. Is a hereafter now."

Or maybe she said "a Here After."

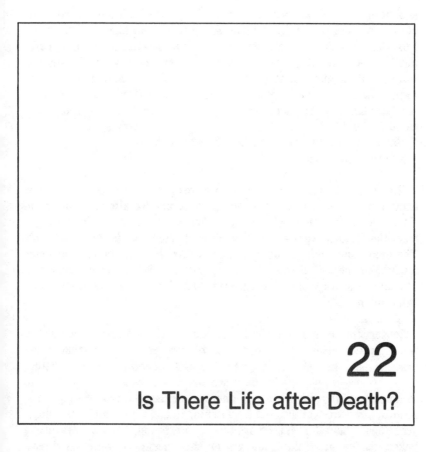

22
Is There Life after Death?

And the stars sailed on. They didn't care what was happening to one biped mammalian intelligent—well, semiintelligent—living thing, simply because it happened to be me. I have always subscribed to the egocentric view of cosmology. I'm in the middle and everything ranges itself on one side of me or another; "normal" is what I am; "important" is what is near to me; "significant" is what I perceive as important. That was the view I subscribed to, but the universe didn't. It went right on as though I didn't matter at all.

The truth is that I didn't matter just then even to me, because I was out of it. A good many thousand light-years behind us on Earth, General Manzbergen was chasing another batch of terrorists who had hijacked a launch shuttle and the commissaris had caught the man who had taken a shot at me; I didn't know and, if I had known, wouldn't have cared. A lot closer, but still as far from us as Antares is from Earth, Gelle-Klara Moynlin was trying to make sense of what the Heechee were telling her; I didn't know that either. Very close to hand indeed, my wife, Essie, was trying to do something she had never done before, though she had invented the process, with the help of Albert, who had the entire process in his datastores but had not hands to do it with. About that I would have cared a great deal if I had known what they were doing.

But I couldn't know, of course, since I was dead.

I did not, however, stay that way.

When I was little my mother used to read me stories. There was one about a man whose senses were somehow scrambled after a brain operation. I don't remember who wrote it, Verne, Wells, one of those biggies from the Golden Age—somebody. What I remember is the punch line. The man comes out of the operation so that he sees sound, and hears touch, and the end of the story is him asking, "What smells purple?"

That was a story told me when I was little. Now I was big. It was not a story anymore.

It was a nightmare.

Sensory impressions were battering at me, and I couldn't tell what they were! I can't describe them now, for that matter, any more than I can describe . . . smerglitch. Do you know what smerglitch is? No. Neither do I, because I just made the word up. It's only a word. It has no meaning until it is invested with one, and neither did any of the colors, sounds, pressures, chills, pulls, twitches, itches, squirmings, burnings, yearnings—the billion quantum units of impression that were assaulting naked, tender me. I didn't know what they meant. Or were. Or threatened. I don't know what to compare it to, even. Maybe being born is like that. I doubt it. I don't think any of us would survive it if it were.

But I survived.

I survived because of only one reason. It was impossible for me not to. It's the oldest rule in the book: You can't knock up a pregnant woman, and you can't kill someone who is dead already. I "survived" because all that part of me that could be killed had been.

Do you have the picture?

Try to see it. Flayed. Assaulted. And most of all, aware I was *dead*.

Among the other stories my mother read me was Dante's *Inferno*, and what I sometimes wonder was whether Dante had some prevision of what it would be like for me. For if not, where did he get his description of Hell?

How long this lasted I did not know, but it seemed forever.

Then everything dwindled. The piercing lights moved farther away, and paler. The terrifying sounds were quieter, the itches and squeezes and turbulences diminished.

For a long time there was nothing at all, like Carlsbad Caverns in that scary moment when they turn off all the lights to teach you what *dark* is. There was no light. There was nothing but a distant confused mumbling that might have been the circulation of blood around the stirrups and anvil in my ears.

If I had had ears.

And then the mumbling began to hint of a voice, and words; and, from a long way off, the voice of Albert Einstein:

"Robin?"

I tried to remember how to speak.

"Robin? Robin, my friend, do you hear me?"

"Yes," I shouted, and do not know how. "I'm here!" as though I knew where "here" was.

A long pause. Then Albert's voice again, still faint but sounding closer. "Robin," he said, each word spaced as though for a tiny child. "Robin. Listen. You are safe."

"Safe?"

"You are safe," he repeated. "I am blocking for you."

I did not answer. Had nothing to say.

"I will teach you now, Robin," he said, "a little at a time. Be patient, Robin. Soon you will be able to see and hear and understand."

Patient? I could be nothing but patient. I had no other options but to patiently endure while he taught me. I trusted old Albert, even then. I accepted his word that he could teach the deaf to hear and the blind to see.

But was there any way to teach the dead to live?

I do not particularly want to relive that next little eternity. By Albert's time and the time of the cesium clocks that concerted the human parts of the Galaxy it took—he says—eighty-four hours and a bit. By his time. Not by mine. By mine it was endless.

Although I remember very well, I remember some things only distantly. Not from incapacity. From desire, and also from the fact of velocity. Let me explain that. The quick exchange of bits and bytes within the core of a datastore goes much faster than the organic life I had left behind. It blurs the past with layers of new data. And, you know, that's just as well, because the more remote that terrible transition is from my "now," the better I like it.

If I am unwilling to retrieve some of the early parts of that data, at least the first part that I am willing to look at is a big one. How big? *Big*.

Albert says I anthropomorphize. Probably I do. Where's the harm? I spent most of my life in the morph of an anthropos, after all, and old habits die hard. So when Albert had stabilized me and I was—I guess the only word is vastened—it was as a human anthropomorphic being that I visualized myself. Assuming, of course, that the human being were huger than galaxies, older than stars, and as wise as all the billions of us have learned to be. I beheld the Local Group—our Galaxy and its next-door neighbors—as one little clot in a curdling sea of energy and mass. I could see all of it. But what I looked at was home, the mother Galaxy and M-31 beside it, with the Magellanic Clouds nestling nearby and all the other little clouds and globules and tufts and fluffs of streaky gas and starshine. And—the anthropomorphic part is—I reached out to touch them and cup them and run my fingers through them, as though I were God.

I was not really God, or even sufficiently godlike to be able really to touch any galaxies. I couldn't touch anything at all, not having anything to touch them with. It was all illusion and optics, like Albert lighting his pipe. There was nothing there. No Albert and no pipe.

And no me. Not really. I was not operatively godlike, because I did not have any tangible existence. I could not create the heavens and the earth, nor destroy them. I could not affect even the least part of them in any physical way at all.

But I could behold them most splendidly. From outside or in. I could stand at the center of my home system and see, peering past Masei 1 and 2, the millions and zillions of other groups and galaxies stretching out in speckled immensity to the optical ends of the universe, where fleeing star clusters run away faster than light can return to display them . . . and beyond that, too, though what I could "see" beyond the optical limit was not really much different—and not really, Albert tells me, any more than a hypothesis in the Heechee memory stores I was tapping.

For, of course, that's all it was. Old Robin hadn't suddenly swelled immense. It was just the paltry remains of Robinette Broadhead, who at that point was no more than a clutter of chained memory bits swimming around in the sea of datastores in the library of the *True Love*.

A voice broke into my immense and eternal reverie: Albert's voice. "Robin, are you all right?"

I did not want to lie to him. "No. Nowhere near all right."

"It will get better, Robin."

"I hope so," I said. ". . . Albert?"

"Yes?"

"I don't blame you for going crazy," I said, "if this is what you were going through."

Silence for a moment, then the ghost of a chuckle. "Robin," he said, "you haven't seen yet what drove me crazy."

I cannot say how long all of this took. I don't know that the concept of "time" meant anything, for at the electronic level, which is where I was dwelling, the time scale does not map well against anything "real." Much time is wasted. The stored electronic intelligence does not operate as efficiently as the machinery we are all born with; an algorithm is not a good substitute for a synapse. On the other hand, things move a lot faster down in subparticle land, where the femtosecond is a unit that can be felt. If you multiply the pluses and factor in the minuses, you'd have to say that I was living somewhere between ten and ten thousand times as fast as I was used to.

Of course, there are objective measures of real time—by which I mean *True Love* time. Essie marked the minutes very carefully. To prepare a corpse for the queasy semistorage of her Here After chain took many hours. To prepare that particular stiff which happened to be me for the somewhat better storage she was able to arrange in the datafan, exactly like Albert's own datafan, took a great deal longer. When her part in it was done she sat and waited, with a drink in her hand that she didn't drink and attempts at conversation from Audee and Janie and Dolly that she didn't hear, although sometimes she answered something that they didn't hear either. It was not a jolly party on the *True Love* while they waited to see if anything at all remained to access of the late Robinette Broadhead, and it took all in all more than three days and a half.

For me, in that world of spin and charm and color and forbidden orbits where I was now transported to exist, it was—well, call it forever. It seemed that way.

"What you must do," Albert commanded, "is learn how to use your inputs and outputs."

"Oh, swell," I cried gratefully, "is that all? Gosh! Sounds like nothing at all!"

Sigh. "I am glad you retain your sense of humor," he said, and what I heard was, *because you'll damn well need it.* "You've got to work now, I'm afraid. It is not easy for me to go on encapsulating you this way—"

"Enwhat?"

"Protecting you, Robin," he said impatiently. "Limiting your access so that you won't suffer from too much confusion and disorientation."

"Albert," I said, "are you out of your *mind?* I've seen the whole *universe!*"

"You've only seen what I was accessing myself, Robin. That's not good enough. I can't control access for you forever. You have to learn to do it for yourself. So I'm going to lower my guard a little for you, when you're ready."

I braced myself. "I'm ready."

But I hadn't braced myself enough.

You would not believe how much it hurt. The chirping, chittering, bitching, demanding voices of all the inputs assaulted my—well, assaulted those loci in a nonspatial geometry that I still persisted in thinking of as my ears. It was torture. Was it as bad as that first naked exposure to everything at once? No. It was worse. In that terrible first blast of sensation I had had one thing going for me. I had not then learned to identify noise as sound, or pain as pain. Now I knew. I knew pain when I felt it. "Please, Albert," I screamed. "What is it?"

"These are only the datastores accessible to you, Robin," he said soothingly. "Only the fans on board the *True Love,* plus telemetry, plus some inputs from the sensors to the ship and crew itself."

"Make them stop."

"I can't." There was real compassion in his voice, though really no voice existed. "You have to do it, Robin. You have to select what stores you wish to access. Pick out just one of them and block out the others."

"Do what?" I begged, more confused than ever.

"Select just one, Robin," he said patiently. "Some are our own datastores, some are Heechee fans, some are other things. You have to learn how to interface with them."

"Interface?"

"To consult them, Robin. As though they were reference volumes in a library. As though they were books on shelves."

"Books don't yell at you! And these are all yelling!"

"Surely. It is how they make themselves evident—just as books on shelves are evident to your eyes. But you need only to look at the one you want. There is one in particular that, I think, will ease this for you. See if you can find that one."

"Find it? How do I *look* for it?"

There was a sound like a sigh. "Well," he said, "there's a stratagem that might be tried, Robin. I can't tell you up, down, or sideways, because I don't suppose there's any frame of reference for you yet—"

"Damn right!"

"No. But there's an old animal trainer's trick, used to cause an animal to perform complicated maneuvers it does not understand. There was a stage magician who used it to get a dog to go into an audience, select a particular person, take from it a particular object—"

"Albert," I begged, "this is not the time for you to tell me those long, rambling anecdotes!"

"No, this is not an anecdote. It's a psychological experiment. It works well on dogs—I do not know that it has ever been tried on an adult human, but let's see. This is what you do. Begin to move in any direction. If it is a good direction I will tell you to go on. When I stop telling you that, you stop doing that particular thing. Cast about. Try different things. When the new thing you do, or the new direction, is a useful one I will tell you to keep going. Can you do that?"

I said, "Will you give me a piece of bread when it's over, Albert?"

Faint chuckle. "At least the electronic analog of one, Robin. Now, start casting about."

Start casting about! *How?* But there was no use asking that question, because if Albert had been able to give me a "how" in words we wouldn't have had to try a dog handler's trick. So I began—doing things.

I can't tell you what things I was doing, exactly. I can give you an analogy, maybe. When I was in school in science class they showed us an electroencephalogram scanner, and showed how all our brains generated alpha waves. It was possible, they said, to make the waves go faster or get larger—to increase the frequency or the amplitude—but there was no way to tell us how to do it. We all took turns, all of us kids, and every one of us did in fact manage to speed up the sine trace on the screen, and no two of us described what we did in the same way. One said he held his breath, another that he sort of tensed his muscles; one thought of eating, and another sort of tried to yawn without opening his mouth. None of them were real. All of them worked; and what I did now was not real, either, because I had nothing real to do it with.

But I moved. Somehow, I moved. And all the time Albert's voice was saying, "No. No. No. No, that's not it. No. No—"

And then: "Yes! Yes, Robin, keep on doing that!"

"I *am* keeping on!"

"Don't talk, Robin. Just keep going. Keep going. Keepgoingkeepgo-ingkeepgoingkeep—no. Stop.

"No.

"No.

"No.

"No—yes! Keepgoingkeepgoingkeepgoingkeepgoing—no—yes! Keep going—stop! There it is, Robin. The volume you must open."

"Here? This thing here? This voice that sounds like—"

I stopped. I couldn't go on. See, I had accepted the fact that I was dead, nothing but stored electrons in a datafan, able to talk just then only to mechanical storage or other nonalive persons like Albert.

"Open the volume!" he commanded. "Let her speak to you!"

She did not need permission. "Hello, Robin love," said the nonliving voice of my dear wife, Essie—strange, strained, but no doubt at all who it was. "Is a fine place are in now, is it not?"

I do not think that anything, not even the recognition of my own death, was as terrible a shock as finding Essie among the dead ones. "Essie," I screamed, "what happened to you?"

And at once Albert was there, solicitous, quick: "She's all right, Robin. She's not dead."

"But she must be! She's here!"

"No, my dear boy, not really here," said Albert. "Her book is there because she partially stored herself, as part of the experiments for the Here After project. And also as part of the experiments that led to me, as I am at present constituted."

"You bastard, you let me think she was dead!"

He said gently, "Robin, you must get over this flesh-and-blood obsession with biology. Does it really matter if her metabolism still operates on the organic level, in addition to the version of her which is stored here?"

And that strange Essie-voice chimed in:

"Be patient, dear Robin. Be calm. Is going to be all right."

"I doubt that very much," I said bitterly.

"Trust me, Robin," she whispered. "Listen to Albert. He will tell you what to do."

"The hardest part is over," Albert reassured me. "I apologize for the traumas you have suffered, but they were necessary—I think."

"You *think*."

"Yes, only think, Robin, for this has never been done before and we are operating largely in the dark. I know it has been a shock to you to meet the stored analog of Mrs. Broadhead in this way, but it will help to prepare you to meet her in the flesh."

If I had had a body to do it with, I would have been tempted to punch him—if Albert had had anything to punch. "You're crazier than I am," I cried.

Ghost of a chuckle. "Not crazier, Robin. Only as crazy. You will be

able to speak to her and see her, just as I did with you while you were still
—alive. I promise this, Robin. It will succeed—I think."

"I can't!"

Pause. "It is not easy," he conceded. "But consider this. I can do it. So
do you not think you can do as well as a mere computer program like
myself?"

"Don't taunt me, Albert! I understand what you're saying. You think I
can display myself as a hologram and communicate in real time with
living persons; but I don't know how!"

"No, not yet, Robin, for those subroutines do not yet exist in your
program. But I can teach you. You will be displayed. Perhaps not with all
the natural grace and agility of my own displays," he boasted, "but at
least you will be recognizable. Are you prepared to begin to learn?"

And Essie's voice, or that voice which was a degraded copy of Essie's,
whispered, "Please do, dear Robin, for am waiting for you without patience."

How tiresome it is to be born! Tiresome for the neonate, and more
tiresome still for the auditor who is not experiencing it but only listening
to interminable woes.

Interminable they were, and spurred by constant nagging from my
midwives. "You can do it," promised the copy of Essie from one side of
me (pretending for the moment that I had a "side"), and, "It is easier
than it seems," confirmed the voice of Albert from the other. There were
no two persons in the universe whose word I would take more readily
than either of them. But I had used up all my trust; there was none left,
and I was scared. Easy? It was *preposterous*.

For I was seeing the cabin as Albert had always seen it. I didn't have
the perspective of two focusing eyes and a pair of ears located at particular points in space. I was seeing and hearing all of it at once. Long ago
that old painter, Picasso, painted pictures like that, with the parts spread
out in random order. They were all there, but so exploded and random-
ized that there was no overriding form to recognize but only a helter-
skelter mosaic of bits. I had wandered the Tate and the Met with Essie to
look at such paintings, and even found some pleasure in them. They were
even amusing. But to see the real world spread out that way, like parts on
an assembly bench—that was not amusing at all.

"Let me help you," whispered the analog of Essie. "Do you see me
there, Robin? Asleep in the big bed? Have been up for many days, Robin,

pouring old organic you into fine new fan bottle and am now worn out but, see, I have just moved hand to scratch my nose. Do you see hand? Do you see nose? Do you recognize?" Then the ghost of a chuckle. "Of course you do, Robin, for that is me all over."

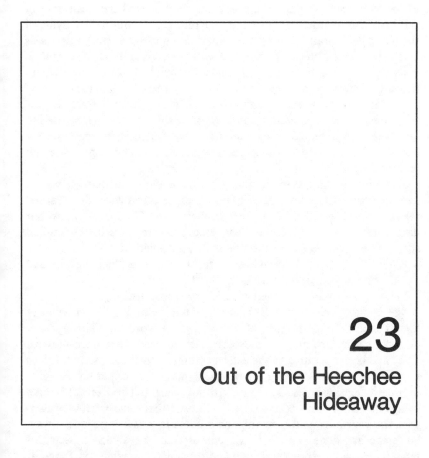

23
Out of the Heechee Hideaway

There still was Klara to be thought about, if I had known enough just then to think about her—not just Klara but Wan (hardly worth a thought, really) and also Captain and his Heechee, who were worth all the thoughts anyone could give them. But I did not then know that, either. I was vaster, all right, but not as yet a whole lot smarter.

And certainly I was distracted by problems of my own, although, if Captain and I had known each other and been able to compare, it would have been interesting to see whose problems were worse. Actually it would have been a standoff. Both sets of problems were simply off the scale, too much to be handled.

The physical closeness of his two human captives was one of Captain's problems. In his bony nostrils they *stank*. They were physically repellent.

Loose, bouncing, jiggling fat and sagging flesh marred the clean lines of their structures—the only Heechee ever that gross were the few dying of the worst degenerative disease they knew. Even then the stink was not as bad. The human breath was rancid with putrefying food. The human voices grated like buzz-saws. It made Captain's throat sore to try to frame the buzzy, grumbly syllables of their nasty little language.

In Captain's view, the captives were nasty all over, not least because they simply refused to understand most of what he said. When he tried to tell them how perilously they had endangered themselves—not to mention the Heechee in their hiding place—their first question was: "Are you Heechee?"

In all his troubles, Captain had room for irritation at that. (It was in fact the same irritation the sailship people experienced when they learned that the Heechee called them slush dwellers. That Captain did know but didn't think about.) "Heechee!" he groaned, then gave his abdominal shrug. "Yes. It does not matter. Be still. Stay quietly."

"Phew," muttered White-Noise, referring to more than the physical stink. Captain glared and turned to Burst.

"Have you disposed of their vessel?" he demanded.

"Of course," said Burst. "It is en route to a holding port, but what of the kugelblitz?" (He did not, of course, use the word kugelblitz.)

Captain shrugged his belly morosely. He was tired. They were all tired. They had been operating at the extreme limits of their capability for days now, and they were showing the effects. Captain tried to put his thoughts in order. The sailship had been tucked out of sight. These errant human beings had been removed from the vicinity of that most terrible of dangers, the kugelblitz, and their ship, on automatic, was being hidden away. So far he had done, he knew, as much as could have been expected of him. It had not been without cost, he thought, sorrowing for Twice; it was hard to believe that in the normal course of events he would still be enjoying her once-a-year love.

But it was not enough.

It was entirely possible, Captain reflected, that by this point there was no longer such a thing as "enough"; it might well be too late for anything he, or the entire Heechee race, could do. But he could not admit that. As long as there was a chance, he had to act. "Display the charts from their ship," he ordered, and turned again to the rude, crude mounds of blubber he had captured. Speaking as simply as to a child he said: "Look at this chart."

It was one of the minor annoyances of Captain's situation that the leaner, and therefore less physically appalling, of his captives was also the nastier. "You be still," he ordered, pointing a lean fist at Wan; his ravings had been even more nearly sense-free than the female's. "You! Do you know what this is?"

At least the female had the sense to speak slowly. It took only a few repetitions before he understood Klara's answer: "It is the black hole we were going to visit."

Captain shuddered. "Yes," he said, trying to match the unfamiliar consonants. "Exactly." Burst was translating for the others, and he could see the tendons writhing on their limbs in shock. Captain chose his words carefully, pausing to check with the ancestral minds to make sure he had the right words:

"Listen carefully," he said. "This is very dangerous. Long, long ago we discovered that a race of Assassins had killed off every technologically advanced civilization in the universe—at least in our own Galaxy, and in some nearby ones . . ."

Well, it did not go that swiftly. Captain had to repeat and repeat, a dozen times for a single word sometimes, before the blubbery creatures could seem to grasp what he was saying. Long before he was finished his throat was raw, and the rest of his crew, though they knew as well as he what perils were involved, were frankly dozing. But he didn't stop. That chart on the screen, with its clustered energy-sinks and its quintuple warning legend, did not let him relax.

The Assassins had done their work of slaughter millennia before the Heechee appeared on the scene. At first the Heechee had thought they were simple monsters from the primeval past, no more to be feared in their time than the Heechee equivalent of a tyrannosaur.

Then they had discovered the kugelblitz.

Captain hesitated there, looking around at his crew. The next part was hard to say, for it led to an obvious conclusion. His tendons writhing, he plunged ahead:

"It was the Assassins," he said. "They have retreated into a black hole —but the particular kind of black hole that is composed of energy, not matter, for they themselves were not made of matter. They were pure energy. Inside their black hole they exist only as a sort of standing wave in an energy sea."

By the time he had repeated it several times, in several ways, he could see that questions were forming; but the logical deduction he feared wasn't among them. The question was from the female, and it was only:

"How can a being composed only of energy survive?"

That was easy enough to answer. The answer was "I don't know."

Because Robin was, quite naturally, preoccupied with other concerns, I was not then able to discuss the kugelblitz with him in as much detail as I would have wished. Its statistics were interesting. Its temperature I calculated at about three million Kelvin, but that was not worrying. It was the energy density that disturbed me. The energy density of black-body radiation goes up as the cube of the temperature—that's the old Stefan-Bolzmann law—but the number of photons goes up linearly with the temperature, too, so effectively it's a fourth-power increase inside the kugelblitz. At one Kelvin it's 4.72 electron-volts per liter. At three million it's three million to the fourth power times that—oh, say, about 382,320,000,000,000,000,000,000,000 ev/liter. And there was a bunch of liters in that thing. What's the importance of that? That all that energy represented organized intelligences. Assassins. A universe of them, all stored in the one kugelblitz, waiting for their plans to mature and the universe to be remade to suit them.

There were, Captain knew, theories—theories that said the Assassins had once been creatures of physical bodies but had somehow cast them off—but whether the theories had any relation to fact even the oldest of the massed minds could not say.

But it was the very difficulty of survival for beings of pure energy, Captain explained, that led to the last and worst thing about the Assassins. The universe was not hospitable to them. So they decided to change the universe. Did something to create a good deal of additional mass in the universe. Caused the expansion of the universe to reverse itself. Holed up in their kugelblitz . . . and waited.

"I have heard of this missing mass often," said the male captive eagerly. "The Dead Men when I was a child spoke of it—but they were crazy, you know."

The female stopped him. *"Why?"* she demanded. "Why would they do this?"

Captain paused, bone-tired from the ordeal of trying to communicate with these dangerous primitives. Again the best answer was "I don't know," but there were speculations. "It is thought by the massed minds," he said slowly, "that the physical laws of the universe were determined by random fluctuations in the distribution of matter and energy at the first moment after the Big Bang. It is possible that the Assassins intend to interfere with that process. Once they have collapsed the universe and it rebounds, they may change those basic laws—the ratio of the masses of the electron and proton, the number that relates the gravitational force to the electromagnetic—all of them—and so bring about a universe in which they could live more comfortably . . . but you and I could not."

The male had been less and less able to contain himself. Now he burst out in squawking sounds, only gradually turning into intelligible words. "Ho-ho!" cried Wan, wiping away a tear. "What cowards you are! Afraid of some creatures that hide themselves in a black hole, to do something that won't happen for billions of years! What does that matter to us?"

But the female had grasped Captain's meaning. "Shut up, Wan," she said, her facial muscles tightening in an almost Heechee expression. "What you're saying is that these Assassins aren't taking any chances. They came out once before to wipe out everybody who looked like he might be going to get civilized enough to interfere with their plan. They might do it again!"

"Exactly so!" cried Captain with pleasure. "You have said it precisely! And the danger is that you barbarians—you people," he corrected himself, "are likely to bring them back. Using radio! Penetrating black holes! Flying all around the universe, even up to the kugelblitzes themselves!

Surely they have left monitoring systems to warn them if new technological civilizations emerge—you must very soon alert them, if you haven't
already!"

And when the prisoners had finally understood; Wan whimpering in
fear, Klara white-faced and shaken; when they had been given food packets and told to rest; when the crew clustered around Captain to know
what made his jaw tendons writhe like snakes, he could only say, "It is
beyond belief." To make the blubbery ones understand him had been
difficult enough; for him to understand them, impossible. He said, "They
say they cannot make all their fellows stop."

"But they must," cried White-Noise, aghast. "They are intelligent, are
they not?"

"They are intelligent," agreed Captain, "for otherwise they would not
use our ships so easily. But I think they are also mad. They have no rule
of law."

"They must have law," said Burst, unbelieving. "No society can live
without law!"

"Their law is compulsion," said Captain gloomily. "If one of them is
where the agencies of enforcement cannot touch him, he may do as he
pleases."

"Then let them enforce! Let them track down every ship and make it
stop!"

"You foolish White-Noise," said Captain, shaking his head, "think
about what you have said. Chase them down. Fight them. Battle them in
space. Can you imagine any louder commotion than that—and can you
imagine the Assassins will not hear?"

"Then what?" whispered Burst.

"Then," said Captain, "we must reveal ourselves." He raised his hand
to still debate, and gave orders.

They were orders the crew had never thought they would hear, but
they perceived Captain was right. Messages flew. In a dozen places in the
Galaxy long-silent ships received their remote-controlled commands and
came to life. A long dispatch was sent to the monitors near that central
black hole where the Heechee lived; by now the first word of warning
should have got through the Schwarzschild barrier and reinforcements
should be coming out. It was a herculean task for the short-handed crew,
and Twice's absence was regretted more sorely than ever. But at last it
was done, and Captain's own ship turned on a new course for a rendezvous.

As he curled into a sleeping ball, Captain found himself smiling. It was not a joyous smile. It was the rictus of a paradox too wounding to respond to in any other way. He had feared, all through the talk with the captives, that they would come to an unwelcome conclusion: Once they knew that the Assassins had hidden themselves inside a black hole, they might easily suspect the Heechee had done the same, and so the central secret of the Heechee race would be compromised.

Compromised! He had done much more than compromise it! All on his own authority, with no higher powers to approve or forbid, Captain had awakened the sleeping fleets and summoned reinforcements from inside the event horizon. The secret was no secret anymore. After half a million years, the Heechee were coming out.

24
The Geography of Heaven

Where was I, really? It took me a long time to answer that question for myself, not least because my mentor, Albert, dismissed it as silly. "The question of 'where' is a foolish human preoccupation, Robin," he grumped. "Concentrate! Learn how to do and how to feel! Reserve the philosophy and the metaphysics for those long evenings of leisure with a pipe and a stein of good beer."

"Beer, Albert?"

He sighed. "The electronic analog of beer," he said testily, "is quite 'real' enough for the electronic analog of a person. Now pay attention, please, to the inputs I am now offering you, which are video scans of the interior of the control cabin of the *True Love*."

I did as he said, of course. I was at least as eager as Albert to complete my training course so that I could go on to do—whatever it was possible for me to do in this new and scary state. But in my odd femtoseconds I could not help turning over that question in my mind, and I finally found an answer. Where was I, really?

I was in heaven.

Think about it. It meets most of the specifications, you know. My belly didn't hurt anymore—I didn't have a belly. My enslavement to mortality was over, for if I had owed a death I had paid it, and was quit for the morrow. If it was not quite eternity that waited for me, it was something pretty close. Data storage in the Heechee fans we already knew was good for at least half a million years without significant degradation—because we had the original Heechee fans still working—and that's a lot of femtoseconds. No more earthly cares; no cares at all, except those I chose to take on for myself.

Yes. Heaven.

You probably don't believe that, because you won't accept that an existence as a disembodied clutter of databits in fan storage can have anything really "heavenly" about it. I know that because I had trouble accepting it myself. Yet "reality" is—is "really"—a subjective matter. We flesh-and-blood creatures "really" perceived reality only at second or third hand, as an analog painted by our sensory systems on the synapses of our brains. So Albert had always said. It was true—or almost true— no, it was *more* than true, in some ways, because we disembodied clutters have a wider choice of realities than you.

But if you still don't believe me I can't complain. However many times I told myself it was so, I didn't find it very heavenly either. It had never occurred to me before how terribly *inconvenient* it was—financially, legally, and in many otherlies, not least maritally—to be dead.

So, coming back to the question, where was I really? Why, really I was at home. As soon as I had—well—died, Albert in remorse had turned the ship around. It took quite a while to get there, but I wasn't doing anything special. Just learning how to pretend to be alive when in fact I wasn't. It took the whole flight back just to make a start on that, for it was a lot harder to be born into fan storage than into the world in the old biological way—I had to actively *do* it, you see. Everything about me was a great deal vaster. In one sense I was limited to a Heechee-model datafan with a cubic content of not much more than a thousand cc, and in that sense I was detached from my plug in and carried through ous toms and brought back to the old place on the Tappan Sea with no more trouble than you'd carry an extra pair of shoes. In another sense I was vaster than galaxies, for I had all the accumulated datafans in the world to play in. Faster than a silver bullet, quick as quicksilver, swift as the shining lightning—I could go anywhere that any of the stored Heechee and human datastores had ever gone, and that was everywhere I had ever heard of. I heard the eddas of the slush dwellers from the sailship and hunted with the first exploring Heechee party that captured the australopithecines; I chatted with the Dead Men from Heechee Heaven (poor inarticulate wrecks, so badly stored in such haste by such inexpert help, but still remembering what it was to be alive). Well. Never mind where all I went; you don't have time to hear. And that was all easy.

Human affairs were harder . . .

By the time we were back on the Tappan Sea Essie had had a chance to rest up and I had had the time and practice to recognize what I saw, and both of us had got over some of the trauma of my death. I don't say we'd got over it all, but at least we could talk.

At first it was only talk, for I was shy of trying to display myself to my dear wife as a hologram. Then said Essie commandingly, "You, Robin! Is no longer tolerable, this talking to you on voice-only phone. Come where I can see!"

"Yes, do!" ordered the other Essie, stored with me, and Albert chimed in:

"Simply relax and let it happen, Robin. The subroutines are well in place." In spite of them all, it took all my courage to show myself, and when I did my dear wife looked me up and down and said:

"Oh, Robin. How lousy you look!"

Now, that might sound less than loving, but I knew what Essie meant. She wasn't criticizing; she was sympathizing, and trying to keep from tears. "I'll do better later, darling," I said, wishing I could touch her.

"Indeed he will, Mrs. Broadhead," said Albert earnestly, which made me realize that he was sitting by my side. "At present I am helping him, and the attempt to project two images at once is difficult. I am afraid they are both degraded."

"Then you disappear!" she suggested, but he shook his head.

"There is also the need for Robin to practice—and, I think, you yourself may wish to make some programing amendments. For example, surround. I cannot give Robin a background unless I share it with him. Improvements are also needed in full animation, real-time reaction, consistency between frames—"

"Yes, yes," groaned Essie, and set about doing things in her workshop. So did we all. There was much to do, especially for me.

I have worried about many things in my time, and almost always about the wrong ones. Worrying about dying hovered in the edges of my concerns for most of my physical life—just as it does in yours. What I feared was extinction. I didn't get extinction. I got a whole new set of problems.

A dead man, you see, no longer has any rights. He can't own property. He can't dispose of property. He can't vote—not only can't he vote in an election to a government office; he cannot even vote the large majority of shares he owns in the hundred corporations he himself has set up. When he is only a minority interest—even a very powerful one, as I was in, for example, the transport system that sent new colonists to Peggys Planet—he won't even be heard. As you could say, he might as well be dead.

I was unwilling to be *that* dead.

It wasn't avarice. As a stored intelligence I had very few needs; there was no risk of my being turned off because I couldn't pay the utility bills. It was an urgency more pressing than that. The terrorists had not disappeared because the Pentagon captured their spaceship. Every day there were bombings and kidnappings and shootings. Two other launch loops were attacked and one of them damaged; a tanker of pesticide was deliberately scuttled off the coast of Queensland and so a hundred kilometers of the Great Barrier Reef was dying. There were actual battles being fought in Africa and Central America and the Near East; the lid was barely being kept on the pressure cooker. What we needed was a thousand more transports like the *S. Ya.*, and who was going to build them if I were silent?

So we lied.

The story went out that Robin Broadhead had suffered a cerebrovascular accident, all right, but the lie that was tacked on said I was showing steady improvement. Well, I was. Not in the exact sense implied, of course. But almost as soon as we were back home I was able to talk, voice-only, with General Manzbergen and some of the people in Rotterdam; in a week I was showing myself, from time to time—swathed in lap robes supplied courtesy of Albert's fertile imagination; after a month I allowed a PV crew to film me, tanned and fit, if thin, sailing our little catboat on the sea. Of course, the PV crew was my very own and the clips that appeared on the newscasts were more art than reportage, but it was very good art. I could not handle face-to-face confrontations. But I didn't need to.

So all in all, you see, I wasn't too badly off. I conducted my business. I planned, and carried out plans, to ease the ferment that fed the terrorists —not enough to cure the problem, but to sit on the lid for a while longer. I had time to listen to Albert's worries about the curious objects he called kugelblitz, and if we didn't then know what they meant it was probably just as well. All I lacked was a body, and when I complained about that Essie said forcefully: "Dear God, Robin, is not end of world for you! How many others have had same problem!"

"To be reduced to a datastore? Not many, I should think."

"But same problem anyhow," she insisted. "Consider! Healthy young male goes ski-jumping, falls and cracks spine. Paraplegic, eh? No body that amounts to anything except liability, needs to be fed, needs to be diapered, needs to be bathed—you are spared that, Robin. But the important part of you, that is still here!"

"Sure," I said. I did not add, what Essie of all people did not need to have me add, that my own definition of "important" parts included some accessories to which I had always attached particular value. Even there there were pluses to set against the losses. If I no longer had, e.g., sexual organs, there was surely no further problem about my suddenly complicated sexual relationships.

None of that had to be said. What Essie said instead was: "Buck up, old Robin. Keep in mind you are so far only first approximation of final product."

"What does that mean?" I demanded.

"Were great problem, Robin! Here After storage was, I admit, quite imperfect. Learned much in development of new Albert for you. Had never before attempted complete storage of entire, and very valued, person unfortunately dead. The technical problems—"

"I understand there were technical problems," I interrupted; I didn't really want to hear, just yet, the details of the risky, untried, exquisitely complex job of pouring "me" out of the decaying bucket of my head into the waiting basin of a storage matrix.

"To be sure. Well. Now have more leisure. Now can make fine tuning. Trust me, old Robin, improvements can yet be made."

"In me?"

"In you, certainly! Also," she said, twinkling, "in very inadequate stored copy of self. Have good reason to believe same can be made much more interesting to you."

"Oh," I said. "Wow." And wished more than ever for at least the temporary loan of some parts of a body, for what I wanted more than anything else just then was to put my arms around my very dear wife.

And meanwhile and meanwhile the worlds went on. Even the very small worlds of my friend Audee Walthers and his own complicated loving.

When you look at them from inside, all worlds are the same size. Audee's didn't seem small to him. I took care of one of their problems very quickly; I gave each of them ten thousand shares of stock in the Peggys Planet ferry, the *S. Ya.* and its pendant enterprises. Janie Yee-xing didn't have to worry about being fired anymore; she could rehire herself as a pilot if she chose, or ride the *S. Ya.* as passenger if she liked. So could Audee; or he could go back to Peggys and boss his former bosses on the oilfield; or none of the above, but lounge around in luxury for all his life; and so could Dolly. And, of course, that didn't solve their problems at all. The three of them mooned around the guest suites for a while until finally Essie suggested we lend them the *True Love* for a cruise to nowhere until they got their heads straightened out, and we did.

None of them were foolish at all—like the rest of us, they acted that way now and then, maybe. They recognized a bribe when they saw one. They knew that what I really wanted was for them to keep their mouths shut about my present unpleasantly noncorporeal state. But they also knew what a friendly gift was, and there was that component in the stock transfer, too.

And what did they do, the three of them on the *True Love?*

I think I don't want to say. Most of it is no one's business but theirs. Consider. There are times in everyone's life—certainly including yours, most definitely including my own—when what you are doing and saying is not either important or pretty. You strain at a bowel movement, you have a fugitive and shocking thought, you break wind, you tell a lie. None of it matters very much, but you do not want advertised those parts of everyone's life in which he looks ludicrous or contemptible or mean. Usually they don't get advertised, because there is no one to see—but now that I am vastened there is always one to see, and that is me. Maybe not right away. But sooner or later, as everyone's memories are added to the database, there are no personal mysteries left at all.

I will say this much of Audee Walthers's private concerns. What motivated his actions and fueled his worries was that admirable and desirable thing, love. What frustrated his loving was also love. He loved his wife, Dolly, because he had schooled himself to love her all the while they were married—that was his view of how married people should be. On the other hand, Dolly had left him for another man (I use the term loosely in Wan's case), and Janie Yee-xing had turned up to console him. They were both very attractive persons. But there were too many of them. Audee was as monogamous as I was. If he thought to make up with Dolly, there was Janie in the way—she had been kind; he owed her some sort of consideration—call it love. But between him and Janie there was Dolly: They had planned a life together and he had had no intention ever of changing it, so you could call that love, too. Complicated by some feeling that he owed Dolly some kind of punishment for abandoning him, and Janie some sort of resentment for being in the way—remember, I told you there were contemptible and ludicrous parts. Complicated much more by the equally complex feelings of Dolly and Janie . . .

It must almost have been a relief to them when—orbiting idly in a great cometary ellipse that was pushing them out toward the asteroids and at angle to the ecliptic—whatever discussion they were having at the moment was interrupted by a gasp from Dolly and a stifled scream from Janie, and Audee Walthers turned to see on the screen a great cluster of vessels huger and more numerous and far, far bigger than any human being had seen in Earth's solar system before.

They were scared out of their minds, no doubt.

But no more than the rest of us. All over the Earth, and everywhere in space where there were human beings and communications facilities to carry the word, there was shock and terror. It was the worst nightmare of every human being for the past century or so.

The Heechee were coming back.

They didn't hide. They were there—and so many of them! Optical sensors in the orbital stations spotted more than fifty ships—and what ships! Twelve or fourteen as big as the *S. Ya.* Another dozen bigger still, great globular structures like the one that had swallowed the sailship. There were Threes and Fives and some intermediate ones that the High Pentagon thought looked suspiciously like cruisers, and all of them coming straight down at us from the general direction of Vega. I could say Earth's defenses were caught unprepared, but that would be a flattering lie. The truth was that Earth had no defenses worth mentioning. There were patrol ships, to be sure; but they had been built by Earthmen to fight other Earthmen. No one had dreamed of pitting them against the semimythical Heechee.

And then they spoke to us.

The message was in English, and it was short. It said: "The Heechee can't allow interstellar travel or communication anymore except under certain conditions that they will decide and supervise. Everything else has to stop right away. They've come to stop it." That was all before the speaker, with a helpless shake of the head, faded away.

It sounded a lot like a declaration of war.

It was interpreted that way, too. In the High Pentagon, in the orbiting forts of other nations, in the councils of power all over the world, there were abrupt meetings and conferences and planning sessions; ships were called in for rearming, and others were redirected toward the Heechee fleet; the orbital weapons that had been quiet for decades were checked and aligned—useless as arbalests, they might be, but if they were all we had to fight with, we would fight them. The confusion and shock and reaction swept the world.

And there was nowhere that suffered more astonishment and bewilderment than the people who made up my own happy household; for the person who gave the Heechee ultimatum Albert had recognized at once, and Essie only a moment later, and I before I even saw her face. It was Gelle-Klara Moynlin.

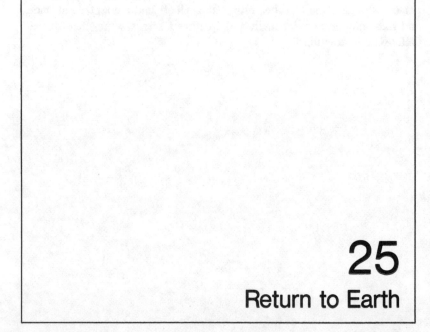

25
Return to Earth

Gelle-Klara Moynlin, my love. My lost love. There she was, staring at me out of the frame of the PV and looking no older than the last time I'd seen her, years and decades before—and looking no better, either, because both times she was about as badly shaken up as it was possible for a person to be. Not to mention beaten up, once by me.

But if she'd been through a lot and showed it, my Klara, she had plenty in reserve. She turned from the screen when she had delivered her message to the human race and nodded to Captain. "You zaid it?" he demanded anxiously. "You gave the mezzage prezisely as I inzdructed?"

"Precisely," said Klara, and added, "Your English is getting much better now. You could talk directly if you wanted to."

"Is too important to take chanzes," said Captain fretfully, and turned away. Half the tendons on his body were rippling and twitching now, and he was not alone. His loyal crew were as harried as himself, and in the communications screens that linked his ship to the others in the grand fleet he could see the faces of the other captains. It was a grand fleet, Captain reflected, studying the displays that showed them in proud array, but why was it *his* fleet? He didn't need to ask. He knew the answer. The reinforcements from inside the core amounted to more than a hundred Heechee, and at least a dozen of them were entitled to call themselves senior to him if they chose. They could easily have asserted command of the fleet. They didn't. They let it be his fleet because that made it also be his responsibility . . . and his own sweet essence that would go to join the massed minds if it went wrong. "How foolish they are," he muttered, and his communicator twitched agreement.

"I will instruct them to maintain better order," he said. "Is that what you mean?"

"Of course, Shoe." Captain sighed and watched gloomily as the communicator rattled instructions to the other captains and controllers. The shape of the armada reformed itself slowly as the great cargo vessels, capable of biting a thousand-meter spherical chunk out of anything and carrying it anywhere, dropped back behind the transports and the smaller ships. "Human woman Klara," he called. "Why do they not answer?"

She shrugged rebelliously. "They're probably talking it over," she said. "Talking it over!"

"I've tried to tell you," she said resentfully. "There are a dozen different major powers that have to get together, not counting a hundred little countries."

"A hundred countries." Captain groaned, trying to imagine such a thing. He failed . . .

Well. That was long and long ago, especially if you measure time in femtoseconds. So very much has happened since! So much that, vastened as I am, it is hard for me to take it all in. It is even harder to remember (whether with my own memory or some borrowed other) every detail of every event of that time, although, as you have seen, I can recall quite a lot when I want to. But that picture stays with me. There was Klara, her black brows scowling as she watched the Heechee jitter and mope; there was Wan, all but comatose and forgotten in a corner of the cabin. There were the Heechee crew, twitching and hissing to one another; and there was Captain, gazing with pride and fear at the resurrected armada on the mission he had ordered. He was gambling for the highest of stakes. He did not know what would happen next—expected anything—feared almost everything—could not be surprised, he thought, by whatever occurred . . . until something did occur that surprised him very much.

"Captain!" cried Mongrel, the integrator. "There are other ships!"

And Captain brightened. "Ah!" he applauded. "At last they respond!" It was curious of the humans to do so physically rather than by means of radio, but then they were strange to begin with. "Are the ships speaking to us, Shoe?" he asked, and the communicator twitched his cheek muscles no. Captain sighed. "We must be patient, then," he said, studying the display. The human vessels were certainly not approaching in any sensible order. It seemed, in fact, as though they had been detached from whatever errands they were on and thrown in to meet the Heechee fleet hurriedly, carelessly—almost frantically. One was in easy range of ship communication; two others farther away, and one of those battling an existing velocity that went the wrong way.

Then Captain hissed in surprise. "Human female!" he commanded. "Come here and inzdruct them to be careful! Zee what is happening!" From the nearest ship a smaller object had launched, a primitive thing that was chemically propelled, much too tiny to contain even a single person. It was accelerating directly toward the heart of the Heechee fleet, and Captain nodded to White-Noise, who instantly ordered a nudge into FTL velocity that removed the nearest cargo vessels from danger. "They muzt not be zo zlipzhod!" he cried sternly. "A collizion could occur!"

"Not by accident," said Klara grimly.

"What? I do not underzdand!"

"Those are missiles," she said, "and they've got nuclear warheads. That's your answer. They're not waiting for you to attack. They're shooting first!"

Do you have the picture now? Can you see Captain standing there with his tendons shocked still and his jaw dropping, staring at Klara? He chews at his tough, thin lower lip and glances at the screen. There's his fleet, the huge caravan of cargo transports resurrected from half a million years of hiding so that he can—with grave doubt; at great risk to himself —offer the human race, a couple of million at a time, free transportation and safe refuge from the Assassins, in the core where the Heechee themselves hid. *"Shooting?"* he repeated numbly. "To *hurt* us? Pozzibly to *kill?"*

"Exactly," flared Klara. "What did you expect? If it's war you want, you'll get it."

And Captain closed his eyes, hardly hearing the horrified hiss and buzz that went around his crew as White-Noise translated. "War," he muttered, unbelieving, and for the first time ever he thought of joining the massed minds not with fear but almost with longing; however bad it might be, how could it be worse than this?

And meanwhile . . .

Meanwhile, it almost went too far—but, fortunately for everyone, not quite. The Brazilian scoutship's missile was far too slow to catch the Heechee as they dodged. By the time they were in position to fire again—long before any other human ship could come close—Captain had managed to explain to Klara, and Klara was on the communication circuits again, and the word was out. Not an invasion fleet. Not even a commando raid. A rescue mission—and a warning of what made the Heechee run and hide, and was now for us to worry about.

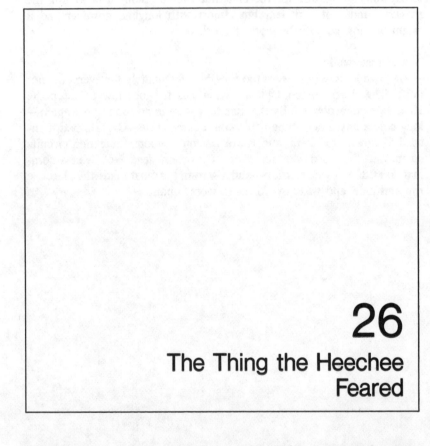

26
The Thing the Heechee Feared

Vastened as I am I can smile at those pitiful old fears and apprehensions. Not at the time, maybe. But now, ah, yes. The scales are all bigger, and a lot more exciting. There are ten thousand stored Heechee dead ones outside the core alone, and I can read them all. Have read them, nearly all. Go on reading them as I choose, whenever there is something I want to study more closely. Books on a library shelf?

They are more than that. I don't exactly "read" them, either. It is much more like remembering them. When I "open" one of them, I open it all the way; I read it from the inside out, as though it were part of me. It was not easy to do that, and for that matter hardly anything I have learned to do since I was vastened has come easily. But with Albert to help me and simple texts to practice on, I learned. The first datastores I accessed were only that—just data; no worse than consulting a table of logarithms. Then I had old Heechee-stored Dead Men and some of Essie's first cases for her Here After franchises, and they were really not very well done. I was never in doubt about which part of what I was thinking was me.

But after we had straightened out the misunderstanding with Captain and I got to consult their own records, then it got hairy. There was Captain's late love, the female Heechee named Twice. To "access" her was like waking up in the dark and putting on a whole suit of clothes that you couldn't see—and that didn't fit you anyway. It was not just that she was female, although that was an immense incongruity. It was not even that she was Heechee and I was human. It was what she knew, and always had known, that neither I nor any other human had guessed. Perhaps Albert had—perhaps that was what had driven him mad. But even Albert's conjectures had not shown him a race of starfaring Assassins who stored themselves in a kugelblitz to wait for the birth of a new—and for them better—universe.

But once the shock was over, Twice became a friend. She's really a nice person, once you get past the weirdness, and we have a lot of interests in common. The Heechee library of stored intelligences is not merely Heechee, or even human. There are musty old querulous voices that once belonged to winged creatures from an Antares planet, and slugs from a globular cluster. And, of course, there are the slush dwellers. Twice and I spent a lot of time studying them and their eddas. Time, you see, is what I have plenty of, with my femtosecond synapses.

I have enough time, almost, to want to visit the core itself, and perhaps someday I will. Not for some long time, though. Meanwhile and meanwhile, Audee and Janie Yee-xing have gone there, helping to pilot a mission that will be there for six or seven months—or, as we measure time out here, a few centuries; by the time they come back, Dolly's presence should no longer be a problem, while Dolly herself is happy enough with her PV career. And Essie has the grace not to be *too* happy, lacking the sweet physical presence of myself, but seems all the same to have made a good adjustment. What she likes best (next to me) is her work, and she's got plenty of it—improving the Here After; using the same processes that make CHON-food to make more important organic items . . . such as, she hopes before very long, spare parts for people who need them, so that nobody need ever steal another person's organs again . . . And, when you come right down to it, most people are happy. Now that we've borrowed the Heechee fleet and can lift a million people a month with all their effects to any of fifty fine planets waiting to be used. It's the pioneers and the covered wagons all over again, and a bright career for anyone . . .

Especially for me.

And then there was Klara.

We met at last, of course. I would have insisted, and anyway in the long run she couldn't have been kept away. Essie took a launch loop to meet her in orbit and escort her personally, in our own aircraft, down to the Tappan Sea. It made for a little problem in etiquette, I'm sure. But otherwise Klara would have been swamped in media people trying to find out what it was like to be a "captive of the Heechee" or "kidnapped by the wolf-child Wan" or whatever other phrases they chose to bandy . . . and, actually, I guess she and Essie got along pretty well. It wasn't as though they had to fight over me. I didn't exist to fight over, in that sense.

So I practiced my best holographic smiles and designed my best holographic surroundings and waited for her to get there. She came in by herself to the big atrium room where I was waiting—Essie must have had the tact to show her the way and disappear. And when Klara came through the door I could tell by the way she stopped, and gasped, that she had expected me to look a lot more dead.

"Hello, Klara," I said. It wasn't much of a speech, but what's the right thing to say in those circumstances? And she said:

"Hello, Robin." She didn't seem to be able to think of anything to add to it, either. She stood looking at me until I thought to ask her to sit down. And I, of course, did a lot of looking at her, in all the multiphased ways we electronically stored intelligences have; but in all those ways she looked pretty damned good. Tired, yes. She'd had some hard times. And dear Klara was not a classic beauty, not with those dark and thick eyebrows and that strong, muscular body—but, yes, she looked *fine*. I guess the staring session made her nervous, because she cleared her throat and said, "I understand you're going to make me rich."

"Not me, Klara. Just giving back to you your share of what we earned together."

"Seems to have multiplied a lot." She grinned. "Your, uh—Your wife says I can have fifty million dollars in cash."

"You can have more than that."

"No, no. Anyway, there is more—it seems I get shares in a lot of companies, too. Thanks, Robin."

"You're welcome."

And then there was another silence, and then—would you believe it?—

the next words out of my mouth were: "Klara, I've got to know! Have you been hating me all this time?"

It was the question, after all, that had been on my mind for thirty years.

Even then, the question struck me as incongruous. How it struck Klara I can't say, but she sat there with her mouth open for a moment, and then she swallowed and shook her head.

And then she began to laugh. She laughed loud and full-bodied, and when she had finished laughing she knuckled the corner of her eye, still chuckling as she said, "Thank God, Robin! At least *something* hasn't changed. You've died. You've got a mourning widow. The world's on the brink of the biggest changes ever. Some scary creatures are likely out to screw up just everything, and . . . and . . . and you're *dead*. And what you're worried about is your own damn feelings of guilt!"

And I laughed, too.

For the first time in, my God, half my life, the last little vestige of guilt was gone. It was hard to identify what it felt like; it had been a long time since I'd known that liberation. I said, still laughing myself, "I know I sound stupid, Klara. But it's been a long time for me, and I knew you were out there in that black hole with time slowed down—and I didn't know what you were thinking. I thought maybe you were, I don't know —blaming me for deserting you—"

"But how could I, Robin? I didn't know what happened to you. Do you want to know what I was really feeling? I was feeling terrified and numb, because I knew you were gone, and I thought you were dead."

"And"—I grinned—"you finally get back here and I am!" I could see that she was more sensitive about jokes in that area than I was. "It's all right," I said. "Really all right. I'm just fine, and so's the whole world!"

I really was. I wished I could touch her, of course, but that was beginning to seem part of a remote childhood past; what was present was that she was here, and safe, and the universe was open before us. And when I said so her jaw dropped again. "You're so damned optimistic!" she blazed.

I was honestly surprised. "Why shouldn't I be?"

"The Assassins! They're going to come out sometime, and what are we going to do? If they can scare the Heechee, they scare the *hell* out of me."

"Ah, Klara," I said, understanding at last. "I see what you mean. You mean it's like it used to be for us when we knew the Heechee had been somewhere and might come back, and knew they'd been able to do things we couldn't hope to do—"

"Exactly! We're no match for the Assassins!"

"No," I said, grinning, "we're not. And we weren't any match for the Heechee, either—then. But by the time they did come out—we were. With any luck at all we'll have time before we have to face the Assassins."

"So what? They'll still be an enemy!"

I shook my head. "Not an enemy, Klara," I said. "Just another resource."

About the Author

Frederik Pohl has been everything one man can be in the world of science fiction: fan (a founder of the fabled Futurians), book and magazine editor, agent, and, above all, writer. As editor of *Galaxy* in the 1950s, he helped set the tone for a decade of SF—including his own memorable stories such as *The Space Merchants* (in collaboration with Cyril Kornbluth). His latest novel is *The Cool War*. He has also written *The Way the Future Was*, a memoir of his forty-five years in science fiction. Frederik Pohl was born in Brooklyn, New York, in 1919, and now lives in New York City.